FATALLY BOUND

ROGER STELLJES

FATALLY BOUND By Roger Stelljes

Copyright © 2014 Roger Stelljes

All rights reserved, including the right to reproduce this book, or portions thereof in any form. No part of this text may be reproduced, transmitted, downloaded, decompiled, reverse engineered, or stored in or introduced into any information storage retrieval system, in any form or by any means, whether electronic or mechanical without the express written permission of the author. The scanning, uploading, and distribution of this book via the Internet or any other means without permission of the publisher is illegal and punishable by law. This book is a work of the author's experience and opinion. Names, characters, places, and incidents are the product of the author's imagination or are used fictitiously. Any resemblance to actual persons, living or dead, or to actual events or locales is entirely coincidental.

Published by Roger Stelljes

ISBN E-book: 9780983575856

ISBN Paperback: 9798653711961

E-book version 6.1.2014

Enjoying the McRyan Mystery Series?
SILENCED GIRLS (FBI Agent Tori Hunter) *is a new series with all characters.*

Never miss a new release again, join the new release list at www.RogerStelljes.com

ACKNOWLEDGMENTS

I'm consistently amazed by how many people are willing to help me as I go through the process of writing a book.

As always I have to thank my reading crew, particularly my two stalwarts Mike and Scott. They've been there for all five books. They keep me on track with their insight, thoughts and incredibly incisive rips. At times the tweaks sting a little, and deservedly so, but the end product is always the better for it.

I would be remiss if I didn't also extend my appreciation to Mary Pat and my parents for giving the book a read and letting me know their thoughts and telling me when I was and was not on the right track.

I wish to especially thank my wife for making this whole process go. It is a massive undertaking. If it weren't for her, there wouldn't be a fifth novel titled *Fatally Bound,* or any of the other books, for that matter. To my kids, once again I extend my thanks for letting me be a writer, a dad and a hockey coach.

Finally, I thank you the readers. Your constant support,

encouragement and feedback make the whole process of writing a story a wholly worthwhile endeavor. I hope you enjoy *Fatally Bound*.

DEDICATION

Someday.

That's what I used to tell myself, someday I'll write that novel.

For years I'd thought about, dreamed about and even tried to start writing a novel. I just could never get over the hump for any number of reasons, my job, raising a family and those eighteen holes of golf on Saturday and Sunday. Plus, I had no idea how to write a book or of the process to get one published. It seemed like such a huge mountain to climb. Nevertheless, the thought of writing a novel floated in and out of my mind often. It was one of those things I would do someday, yet life cruised along and someday never seemed to be coming.

Then one day on my drive home from work in the late 1990s, I was listening to a local Twin Cities radio personality named Dan Barreiro interview this new author Vince Flynn. Vince talked about how he'd quit his sales job and took up his dream of writing espionage thrillers while also coping with dyslexia. He was so committed that he self-published his first book and was going around to area bookstores to sell it out of the trunk of his car. That night I went out and bought *Term Limits*, Vince's first book, and loved it. I, along with millions of others, bought, read and enjoyed every one of his books ever since. Over the years, Vince's story became even more poignant to me because my son copes and yet is flourishing with dyslexia.

From that interview, I realized that if a guy could do all of this on his own, and with dyslexia no less, I had no more excuses if this was something I truly wanted to do.

Someday finally came.

It took me a little time and a few false starts, but I finally had a story I believed in. I started writing in 2002, finished the first draft in 2004 and published *The St. Paul Conspiracy* on my own in 2006, going around to Minnesota bookstores with boxes of books in the back of my car. I was following the Vince Flynn playbook. Through an acquaintance, I was able to get Vince a signed copy of my book which he so graciously talked up during a radio interview a few weeks later. You can only imagine how thrilled I was in 2009 when Vince provided a promotional blurb for the cover of my second book, *Deadly Stillwater*.

I never got to know Vince personally. I only met him a few times. However, I did have the privilege of getting to know his parents fairly well through one of my law partners. In meeting and getting to know them, it wasn't hard to see where Vince got his larger than life personality from.

Sadly, on June 19, 2013, Vince lost his long battle to prostate cancer. Vince was only forty-seven years old, which really hit me as he was only one year older than me. He was far too young and had so many more wonderful years to spend with his family and great stories to write. His passing at such a young age was a harsh reminder to all of us that every day we have is a gift. That we should approach each day with love, passion and the enthusiastic pursuit of our dreams, whatever they may be.

With *Fatally Bound*, I'm now publishing my fifth novel and I hope there are going to be many more to come. Writing these books has been a dream come true. However, I'm not sure I'd ever have gotten to someday were it not for hearing Vince during that long ago interview. Something about it motivated me into action. One true regret I have is that I never got to tell Vince personally how his story inspired me and I'm sure many others.

As a fan, I miss not having a new Mitch Rapp thriller each fall.

As a writer, Vince Flynn was and will continue to be a huge inspiration to me.

Because of him someday came.

Fatally Bound is dedicated to his memory.

PREAMBLE

He sat on the black metal folding chair in the dark, almost invisible to her, just a large, dark, hulking shadow with a deep guttural voice. The man leaned forward with his elbows on his thighs, his gloved hands clasped and his eyes behind his wool face mask boring in on her. The video camera, recording, sat high on the tripod to his left.

Over her head hung a solitary light bulb with a chain pull underneath a silver, coned shade to focus the light downward.

She was slumped in the chair, exhausted, hands cuffed behind her back while her legs were securely fastened to the chair with duct tape. Hours of tears and the resulting running mascara caked her exhausted face.

He was angry, angrier than he'd even been. The rage was unlike anything he had ever felt, it was overwhelming, it was becoming controlling. "So that's it?" he asked again.

"Yes!" she pleaded weakly, little energy left.

"You're sure," the deep voice asked darkly. "You've told me everything? You've left nothing out?"

She nodded.

"You've told me about everyone?"

"Yes," she whimpered.

"You've left no one out?"

"No."

Coming into it, he only wanted to get the truth and she knew what it was. The story was so much worse and coldhearted than he could have ever imagined. It wasn't an accident; it was a killing, it was a murder. It wasn't just one person either. Many had a role and none of them, NONE of them paid for it.

They all just walked away.

It filled him with a rage, a rage even worse than anything he'd felt as his life had spun downward these past five years, leaving him a broken man.

It all started with the woman in front of him.

The system wouldn't help him, and now, he decided it would *help* her, because even within the system, she could never *ever* pay a high enough price. She would never be punished the way she should.

He couldn't let it stand.

He wouldn't let it stand.

He reached up to his left and turned off the video recorder.

"What are you going to do to me now?" she asked weakly.

He stood up and pulled out the knife.

"No! Please No! No! No! *NOOOO!*"

Nobody could hear the screams.

1

"EVEN AS I HAVE SEEN, THEY THAT PLOW INIQUITY, AND SOW WICKEDNESS, REAP THE SAME."

TWO YEARS LATER - DOVER, DELAWARE

Hannah sang passionately along with Adele's *Rumour Has It*, the three Bud Lights providing her a little happy buzz, that and giving her phone number to Tyler. Tall and handsome, Tyler was a good-looking sales guy and he'd made a nice casual and smooth sales pitch at the bar. No cheesy lines, no tired moves, just some good solid verbal, physical and expressive flirty foreplay. Her friends said he was a player. She didn't necessarily disagree with that assessment, but she played it pretty cool herself. When Tyler asked for her number, she didn't hesitate, she offered it right up, although that was all she offered up, and he didn't push for more either. She would make him work for that, and from what she could tell, he seemed interested in putting in some work. He was going to call, for sure. She could tell from the look in his eyes. A text, a call, something would come tomorrow and it excited her, gave her heart a little flutter, the first she'd had in a long while, maybe even years. Lately she'd been thinking it was time to start living again.

She pulled her Audi A6 into her garage and let the song

run out. She loved the chorus and sang along with it: "*Rumour has it … Rumour has it … Rumour has it he's the one I'm leaving you for.*"

"God, I love that song," she exclaimed happily as she pushed herself up out of the car and grabbed her large purse from the passenger seat. She walked out the side door of the garage, hitting the opener button on the wall and watched to make sure the door went all the way down. The sensors had a history of being finicky, although not this time. With the door down, she locked the dead bolt for the side door of the garage and walked the fifty-foot sidewalk to the back door of her little two-story white house. The exterior light was off and she admonished herself for it, not remembering that she was going out for the night.

She fumbled with her keys, feeling for the house key for the back dead bolt. "Ah, there it is." She opened the back door and walked inside, closing the door behind her and locking it. She moved to the right into the kitchen and tossed her keys onto the counter and plugged her cell phone into its charger. From the refrigerator she poured herself a small glass of milk that she quickly downed, turned off the kitchen light and walked though the doorway into the living room.

The right hand and rag was clamped over her mouth.

The left powerful arm quickly wrapped around her chest like a vice.

She was lifted off the floor.

Hannah gasped for air and breathed in. The rag was soaked in something and she could feel the immediate effect of the fumes.

She fought with everything she had, squirming, kicking, writhing, struggling, trying to break free, but she couldn't get loose as the massive arms immobilized her and held her tight against his large body.

She screamed, but the sound went into the rag, covering her mouth like a mask.

Hannah looked around, searching for anything that could help, and saw a sturdy bronze candlestick. It could do some damage, but with her arms and body wrapped, she couldn't reach for it.

She was breathing frantically and thrashing her body, the fumes filling her lungs.

The man's vice grip tightened more, swallowing her into his body.

Then he dropped down to a knee and threw her down onto the floor and lay on top of her, pinning her to the floor, the hand never leaving her mouth.

She fought harder, gasping, trying to yell once again, but the sound went nowhere and caused her to inhale another large breath of the toxic fumes.

She convulsed, thrashed and tried to use her legs to push up, but the intruder was massive, heavy and couldn't be moved.

There was another deep breath and she sucked in more fumes.

She felt her strength leave and her arms would no longer respond to her commands.

Everything blurred.

Everything went black.

"Hannah, wake up," he stated flatly, leaning in close to her, lightly cupping and patting her face. Hannah mumbled a little but didn't come to, her head still drooping.

He slapped her hard, "Wake up!"

Hannah snapped awake. She blinked and became alert and immediately pulled at her restraints, her arms and legs duct taped to the metal armchair.

She looked around quickly, recognizing the thick cinder blocks of the cellar to her house. It might not have been soundproofed, but it was a close as could be without being so. When she was down here, she could never hear a thing from upstairs or outside.

A large, wide, menacing man hovered in front of her, dressed in black including a black wool face mask over his head and white gloves on his hands. On his right hip, looped through his belt, she saw a long sheath for a knife with the black hilt sticking out. To his right was a video recorder mounted on a tripod.

"Wh ... wh ... who are you? What do you want with me?" she asked frantically while fighting her restraints.

"That will be answered soon enough. As for what I want with you?" He sat down in the chair. "Hannah, I want, and you will give me, the truth."

"Truth? What truth?"

He held up a picture of a woman. "The truth I got from Melissa, you remember her, don't you?" He held up another picture. "And Janelle? You remember her, don't you?" He let those words sink in for a moment.

Hannah's eyes closed. Tears welled in her eyes and began to stream down her face. She sniffled, shook her head and sighed in resignation, "I ... I ... I always knew this day would come."

∼

11:03 A.M. Dover, Delaware.

The FBI Suburban pulled up to the crime scene tape. The driver flashed his credentials and another uniform lifted the yellow crime scene tape. The Suburban pulled forward one hundred feet and parked behind a Dover police patrol car.

FBI Senior Supervisory Agent Aubry Gesch sighed as he jumped out of the passenger seat. His partner, Supervisory Agent Grace Delmonico, slipped out of the backseat. If this in fact was their man, then they'd seen this movie two times before, but like always, it was a little different. This time the victim was killed in her home, a small two-story white house set in an idyllic tree-lined neighborhood of 1930s-styled homes. Probably the first time a murder occurred on this sleepy little well-kept street.

A police sergeant approached, "Are you the FBI agents from Quantico?"

Gesch and Delmonico nodded and showed their FBI badges and identification.

"Please follow me," the sergeant directed gravely, waving them to follow him up the front walk.

They fell in behind the officer and walked up the paver stone sidewalk, climbed two red-bricked front steps and inside the front door of the small, white clapboard, two-story home. Once inside, they were led to the left of the staircase dividing the house and back into the kitchen, then back down a steep set of steps into the house's cellar where the grisly scene, for the third time, unfolded.

Like the other two, she was staged in the fetal position with her arms wrapped around her upper chest, her lower abdomen sliced open in the shape of the Holy Cross, the blood from which created a large pool of deep red around the body. To the left of the body were the two chairs, one a metal folding chair, a metal office chair with arms, the chair he bound her to while he interrogated, tortured and ultimately gutted her.

"Just like the other two," Delmonico said as she crouched down to inspect the victim with her flashlight, looking for the note. Red flags had been raised with victims one and two, the notes and the staging of the bodies pointing to a potential serial. Three bodies made it official.

"Not quite the same," Gesch uttered ominously.

Delmonico looked up to her left to see Gesch pointing his flashlight to his right. She glanced back to her right to see a message written crudely on the cinder block wall in blood: "Even as I have seen, they that plow iniquity, and sow wickedness, reap the same," she quietly read out loud. Delmonico scanned farther down the wall with her flashlight, "Oh Lord."

There was a signature.

The message was signed this time.

The Reaper.

2
"RICH PEOPLE PROBLEMS."
ST. PAUL, MINNESOTA

The television played quietly in the corner of the second-story den. CNN was reporting on a serial killer operating on the East Coast. He'd given himself a name.

"The Reaper?" Richard Lich said. "Seriously?"

"I read earlier that the guy leaves biblical verses behind about reaping what you sow," answered Michael McKenzie "Mac" McRyan as he peered through the horizontal blinds with binoculars out the rear window of the house at the large Victorian mansion to the north across the alley. Inside the mansion, his cousin, St. Paul Detective Paddy McRyan, dressed as a member of the weekly cleaning crew, placed small cameras in strategic places in the house. One camera overlooked the alarm code panel and also provided a view down the center hallway and the stairs to the basement which led to the garage tucked under the mansion. The second camera was zeroed in on the wall safe located behind a picture on the wall in a lower-level office. Currently, he was working on the camera in the master bedroom, giving his cousin a small wave when he entered the room.

Mac felt his right hip and the Sig Sauer in his holster and his St. Paul Police shield on his belt and smiled inwardly. It felt good to be a cop again, even if it was temporary. The action, the weight of the gun, the shield on his belt and the fact that they were operating and on the hunt all felt good.

James Thomson, the former Minnesota governor, was elected president the previous November, largely as a result of a magnificently run campaign, but also partly as a result of Mac's investigation of a series of murders that started in St. Paul and tied into the campaign of the Republican candidate for president. The murder conspiracy, exposed a few days before the election, propelled Governor Thomson to a convincing victory. Sally Kennedy, Mac's girlfriend of two years, had taken a leave from her job as a Ramsey County prosecutor to work for the Thomson Campaign. In her brief tenure with the campaign, Sally impressed the governor and the governor's campaign manager and closest confidant, a political legend named Judge Dixon. Ten minutes after the networks declared Thomson the winner, she was offered a key political position in the White House political operation. Mac, not seeing how he could possibly deny Sally her dream shot, knew he was going with her. So, the day after New Year's, Mac packed a large U-Haul and moved to Washington, DC.

The decision to move was made easier by his newfound wealth resulting from the sale of a chain of coffeehouses he'd owned a minority interest in. He never needed to work again if he didn't want to, and in Washington that was exactly what he was doing, not working, not getting shot at and leading a relatively quiet and sedate life for a change.

Instead of the grind of police work, he was doing two things to keep himself busy. His first project was rehabilitating their dated Georgetown brownstone he bought as a place for them to live and as an investment. He liked working on it and seeing the progress as he restored the home to its original traditional Georgetown glory. When he eventually sold it, he was confident it would net six figures in profit.

His second project was working on a book about the election investigation with Dara Wire, the ex-FBI agent who worked the high-stakes case with him. Rather than succumb to media interviews that neither of them wanted to give, they instead agreed to split a large advance from a publisher to write the definitive inside story of the investigation. A ghost writer was working with them. A draft of the book for Mac and Dara to tweak and edit was a month away.

However, as busy as those two projects kept him, Sally worked extremely long hours, leaving him with a lot of downtime to fill. He'd been through all the Smithsonians, checked out all the monuments, and now was starting to play the DC area golf courses and even had played Congressional Country Club, but he was getting a little restless. His life was quiet and sedate, but it was a little too quiet and far too sedate. Mac didn't think he wanted to be a cop again full time, but he definitely missed a little action in his life. Finding the DC cop bar, meeting and befriending some local officers and detectives and even brainstorming on some of their cases only served to further feed his desire for something to do.

When he informed St. Paul Police Chief Charlie Flanagan, a father figure for him, he was leaving St. Paul for Washington, the chief refused to let him resign his position. "Mac, just put in for a long leave of absence. You never know, we might need you. You never know, *you* might want to come back."

That was seven months ago.

"Where's the fourth camera going?" Lich asked as he looked up from the laptop, now with three camera feeds on his screen.

"Third floor, remember?"

"*Riiiight,* the room that serves as the '*ahhhrt gallery,*'" Mac's partner mocked. "The room the *missus* complained was on the third floor, so hard for people to get to so they could see their *collection.*"

Mac chuckled, "Rich people problems."

"You know all about those," Lich needled.

"Not quite. The Sloane family is in an *entirely* different fiscal league, Dicky Boy."

Edward and Margaret Sloane were exceedingly wealthy, members of the Sloane family that the *StarTribune* had recently reported was worth north of $500 million dollars in their annual listing of the Twin Cities' wealthiest families. An article that was also no doubt noticed by the break-in crew they were now hunting.

For eight months there had been a slew of unsolved robberies throughout the entire Twin Cities' metro area, although mostly concentrated in the moneyed areas of Minneapolis and St. Paul. At first, the robberies were not connected, but eventually the various law enforcement agencies of the Twin Cities got together and realized a highly skilled crew was operating around town and an investigative task force was formed. The chief put his best boys, Detectives Pat Riley, Bobby Rockford and Mac's long-time partner, Richard Lich, better known as "Dick Lick," on it.

In conjunction with the Minneapolis PD and the State

Bureau of Criminal Apprehension (BCA), the best investigative minds in town were working the case, but the robberies continued unabated.

The crew was good and showed no signs of stopping. "A shark is not going to leave the waters if the feeding is good," the chief counseled.

There was a level of sophistication to the crew as security systems were easily defeated, forensic evidence was nonexistent and nobody ever seemed to notice them going in or coming out of the homes. No hairs, prints, saliva or any forensic evidence of any kind was ever left behind. It was like they were ghosts. In fact, the task force had taken to calling them "The Ghost Crew." The jobs were well planned and the crew clearly engaged in a great deal of research and preparation, as there were usually anywhere from two weeks to a month between robberies. Money, jewels, electronics, precious metals, furniture and art were gone without a trace. The estimated take from all of the jobs was over $10 million, assuming the merchandise was being moved. However, if the merchandise was being fenced, it wasn't being done so locally. The police hit all the known fences in town and applied all the pressure possible.

There was either an extremely high level of fear of the crew or nobody around town knew a thing.

"Town's too small to fence this stuff here," Riles suggested. The Twin Cities was an area of over three million people but still was small enough that if something high-end was moving, word would filter out somehow. "You fence the high-end stuff around here, we'd hear about it."

Three weeks ago, Sally left on a week-long trip to Asia with the president. The last time she'd left on a lengthy trip, Mac stayed back in Washington and ended up completely bored out of his mind. So with her gone for a week and no job to keep him tied down, Mac went home to see friends and family. While at the Flanagan's for dinner, the call came regarding the latest robbery, a mere three blocks from the chief's home in the Highland Park neighborhood on St. Paul's affluent far western end. "Mac, we have nothing on these guys. We could use some fresh eyes; go with the boys and take a look."

At first, Mac didn't see anything that struck him or led him to anything that the other detectives hadn't noticed. Other than the missing pieces of art work from the walls, you'd have never known the house was robbed it was done so cleanly and professionally. A smash and grab job it was not. Two days after the robbery, while sitting around the detectives' bullpen at the St. Paul Department of Public Safety, Mac was reading through the inventory of items stolen and something that had not been mentioned by the family when they were first interviewed caught Mac's eye.

"Riles, when we were interviewing the family, did they say anything about baseball cards?"

"Baseball cards?"

"Yeah, baseball cards. You know, like you bought at the drugstore as a kid. They have the tasteless piece of pink gum in them."

"Yeah, I know what they are asshole, but no, Mac, they didn't. All they were concerned about that night was the jewels, cash and bearer bonds that were stolen from their safe. It wasn't until the next day that the old man thought about his baseball card collection that he kept in a lockbox in his office over the garage. The box and cards were gone as well."

Mac read through the inventory of missing baseball cards and smiled. "This guy was a serious collector. His collection would have given Ken Burns a documentary hard-on. He had rookie cards for Joe DiMaggio, Mickey Mantle, Henry Aaron, Eddie Mathews, Bob Feller, Jackie Robinson, Whitey Ford, Duke Snider, Roy Campanella, Willie Mays, Stan Musial, Ted Williams, I mean all the greats from the 1940s and '50s. He had their rookie cards and several others. He claims they were in 'mint' or perfect condition. If so, that collection is worth some serious money, I bet well over a hundred thousand dollars."

"How do you know?" Lich asked.

"While it's nothing like this, I have a collection of my own," Mac answered. "I collected baseball, hockey and football cards when I was kid, plus I ended up with lots of cards that other older kids in the neighborhood were just going to throw out. And my dad, he collected when he was a kid and left me some really good baseball cards from the 1950s, '60's and '70's, not the rookie cards necessarily, but I have really good cards for Mickey Mantle, Willie Mays, Harmon Killebrew, Hank Aaron, Roberto Clemente, Sandy Koufax, Pete Rose, Johnny Bench, Tom Seaver, Robin Yount, Rod Carew and Reggie Jackson, among others. I had my collection appraised two years ago and the best card collector in town said I could probably get somewhere around $25,000 for my entire collection."

"Did you sell it?" Rock asked.

"No."

"Why the heck not?" Lich asked, surprised, salivating at the thought of twenty-five Gs. Money was seemingly always in short supply for Dick.

"A lot of those cards were from my dad. I still like to sit and look at them every once in a while. Helps me remember when he and I did that." He looked at the list more. "Assuming this crew wants to move these cards and get top dollar for them, there is a limited pool of buyers and sellers.

The people that move those kinds of high-end cards are a fairly small group of people and they all kind of know and network with each other."

"What are you thinking?" Riles asked, seeing the wheels turn in McRyan's head.

"The card collector I talked to who looked at my collection, he's pretty plugged in, or at least he seemed like it. He knows a lot of people in the card business, legit and, in some cases, illegitimate. If these cards start showing up, even somewhere else besides the Twin Cities, he's likely to hear about it."

A week ago, rookie cards for Mickey Mantle, Willie Mays and Jackie Robinson were walked into a small out of the way memorabilia store in south Chicago. Mac's card contact had called the store directly a week earlier to have him keep his eyes open. The store owner, well regarded in the card collecting industry, called Mac's contact while the man looking to sell the cards was standing right across the counter. "Didn't you tell me a few months ago you were looking for a Mantle rookie card?" he said to Mac's contact. "I might have a line on one for you."

The card collector contact relayed the call to Mac who had Chicago police in the store in less than ten minutes. The man looking to sell the cards was a high-end fence that CPD had been paying attention to for other reasons. It wasn't his first bust. He was looking at a long prison stretch and was ready to make a deal.

Washington, DC.

President Thomson grimaced as the telephone call continued. Two hours ago his press secretary's afternoon briefing went off the rails when she started getting pressed about the death of Hannah Donahue at the hands of what now appeared to be a serial killer. Hannah was the daughter of William Donahue, a big party contributor, a man who delivered a lot of campaign money to the president, among other politicians. That the White House didn't know about her death until asked only furthered the mess the briefing turned into. Then Donahue was caught on camera, emotional, blasting the FBI-led investigation and talking about how he would make people in Washington very uncomfortable until the case was solved. Not long after, pictures from inside the house with "The Reaper" and the biblical verse from Job 4:8 written in blood on a wall leaked online. Within two hours, a mini-media feeding frenzy engulfed Washington. The political nature of the victim meant the case was sure to be a talker for twenty-four to forty-eight hours. Were the victim a minority woman, it would have been buried inside the local news section of the paper. Since it was an upper-class white woman with a politically connected father, it was national news.

Following the debacle, the White House political operation sprung into action to minimize the damage and put the president on the phone with Donahue. A call to express his condolences to a key political contributor whose daughter had been brutally murdered in Dover, Delaware, had now stretched to fifteen minutes, was grinding along difficultly and had the president, rather than offering heartfelt condolences, on the defensive and dancing.

"Bill, I assure you and Barbara that the FBI is doing everything they can. I know that Director Mitchell has some of his best investigative and behavioral science people on this. He was in my office just before I called you to brief me personally. I have told Director Mitchell that I will work to get him any assistance he could possibly need. Everything that can be done is being done and will be done."

"Damnit, Mr. President," William Donahue replied bitterly, "if they were doing everything, this psychopath wouldn't have been operating for the past month, cutting these women up, including my Hannah. That's my Hannah they're talking about on the news, Jim, my little girl. *My Hannah, Jim, my Hannah!* My little girl was gutted by this monster, just like two other poor girls. Whatever they're doing is not enough. You need to get involved, Mr. President. You need to get *personally* involved."

"Bill, I can't tell you how sorry I am about this. I will now be getting constant updates on the case and if I learn anything, you will be the first to know."

"I appreciate that, Mr. President," but Donahue's tone said he didn't, not fully, "but you have to do more than that. Don't let another family go through this. Don't let this animal do this to another family, to another woman. Getting constant updates is not sufficient. I can get constant updates, *I will* get constant updates. But from you I expect more. I expect you to use that fancy office of yours, the one I helped put you in, by the way, to apply the resources and personnel to get this done."

The president pinched the bridge of his nose and sighed, "Bill, I sympathize, you know I do, I mean, I can't begin to imagine what you're going through, but you have to know that I can't dictate this investigation."

"Perhaps not, Jim, but you can apply plenty of pressure. More must be done and I will make sure to use whatever resources I have available to me to make sure that happens," Donahue answered in a threatening tone. "I have a lot of friends." That meant in Congress and the press. "This is on you now, Mr. President, this is *your* responsibility. You have to do whatever you can to stop this man. You owe me that and I will be watching closely, *very closely,* to make sure that this is indeed one of your top priorities." *Click.* Donahue hung up on him.

The president stared quizzically at the phone. It wasn't often he was hung up on when he was governor, let alone president of the United States. He exhaled lightly and gently put the phone back in its cradle and pushed himself up out of his desk chair. He took his suit coat from the back of his chair and slipped it on. He strolled out of the Oval Office and strode to the office he went to when he had a problem.

Judge Dixon was visiting with FBI Director Mitchell and White House Deputy Communications Director Sally Kennedy. "How did it go?" the Judge asked warily, seeing the president's pained expression.

"Not well, not well at all," the president replied and looked down to the FBI Director. "Thomas, are we *really* doing everything we can on this?"

"Mr. President, I have very good people on this and that was before Mr. Donahue's daughter was murdered. I am now directly in the loop on the investigation with Aubry Gesch, the lead senior agent. He is very good, someone I trust. He has extensive experience on cases like this. I will be pushing Gesch and this investigation hard on this until we nail this guy; you have my word on that, Mr. President."

"Fine, you have excellent people on it, but is there anything else you need? Is there anything more that can be done? Because let me tell you, William Donahue is about to make my life, and by extension, Thomas, your life, very difficult if we don't find this killer, and find him yesterday. Donahue is upset and feeding the media, Lord help us all."

"Mr. President," Sally interjected, "you can't get yourself involved in this. You made the call, which was the right thing to do. The investigation will have to play out and we'll manage it to the extent we have to."

"Ms. Kennedy is right, sir," Mitchell added agreeably.

"I get that, but my question still stands to you, Thomas, is there anything else you need? More manpower, resources, money, assistance from another agency, is there anything else you need? Anything? Tell me, and we'll make it happen."

The Judge sat back and listened to the whole conversation, his hands steepled under his chin, deep in thought. The former prosecutor, federal judge and attorney general knew a thing or two about investigations and he had a thought. "If I might, I have a slightly off-the-wall suggestion that will help you, Thomas, and at the same time I think will appease Bill Donahue."

8:03 P.M.

Dara Wire breezily walked out to the curb at Reagan National and waved for a cab which pulled up immediately. She felt good, really good actually; light on her feet and she suspected if anyone was paying particular attention, she would have been glowing.

Her phone buzzed in her purse. She pulled it out and looked at the message and smiled.

Martin.

Her trip to Miami had turned into the perfect mix of business and pleasure. Her name became known in political circles since the election and her phone had not stopped ringing ever since. Her private security consulting business was booming. The Judge, and a grateful president, sent nonstop business her way. It was their way of thanking her for the investigative work during the election. Along with the book she was working on with McRyan, she literally hadn't had a day off in six months. It had been even longer since she had a date. She loved the fact she was piling up a ton of money, but a personal life would be nice too.

This latest trip involved evaluating and implementing a security system for a wealthy Miami family heavily involved in Florida politics. The family's lawyer, the tall and handsome Martin Gonzalez, spent three days assisting her in the process of developing and implementing the security plan for the property. There were long days followed by late night dinners and then drinks. Martin had a lot of game to him, no doubt, but he was attractive and he didn't hide his attraction for her, nor, after a few days, did she to him.

When the job was finished, Martin invited her to his ocean-front condo in Key West. She'd spent the last three days there and she wasn't sure she ever saw the water. The last text was from Martin, inviting her back down as soon as her schedule permitted. She was pretty sure she would make sure her schedule would permit that soon.

A taxi cab pulled up. She slipped down inside and gave the driver the address to her new Arlington townhouse, one that she'd barely moved into. She settled into the backseat and began sending a reply text to Martin when the familiar face of the Judge appeared on her phone.

"Hi, Judge, by the way, thanks again for the referral to the Buchanans in Miami. ... Yes, they were great, just great. ... What? And the lawyer? How in the hell? Do you know everything about everyone?" she asked, leaning back and smiling, slouching in the seat. She'd told nobody about Martin and yet the Judge knew. He knew everything. "You're unbelievable. I think it would have sucked to have been your daughter. So what can I do for you?"

~

St. Paul. 10:42 P.M.

Mac and Lich were hunched over the laptop, watching the Ghost Crew work their way efficiently through the Sloane house. The crew defeated the security system within fifteen seconds. Another man had the safe open, lifting its contents which consisted of jewelry and cash. Additional jewelry had already been taken from the master bedroom and now most of the crew was in the third-floor art gallery, removing paintings and moving them down to the garage.

There were police teams east and west of the house. The St. Paul contingent of Riley, Rock, Paddy and Double Frank were in the neighbor's garage to the east. Minneapolis detectives and old friends Ed Gerdtz and Bud Subject had a team in the garage of the house to the west. Mac picked up the radio and spoke softly.

"Riles and Bud, move your teams into place."

"Copy."

"Copy."

Mac looked to his right and saw Riles's group slither out of the garage and along the fence of the alley. To the left, the veterans Gerdtz and Subject led the team out the side door of the garage and crept along the fence line. Both groups stopped just short of the driveway, held position and signaled one another with thumbs-up.

"We're set, Mac," Riles reported.

"So when the surveillance team said the crew had a black Town & Country minivan at their rendezvous point, you knew their plan, didn't you?" Lich asked.

"I suspected. Getting into the house and cracking the safe, all that is the easy part. Getting everything *out* of the house?" Mac smiled. "Now *that's* the hard part. That's what's been bugging me for the past three days since we knew this house was the target. How the hell were they going to get everything out without being seen? Black Town & Country just like the Sloane's? The pieces fell into place."

When the Chicago police pressed the fence looking to sell the stolen baseball cards, he pointed them in the direction of Xavier Foote. Foote was known to Chicago and had put together teams in the past. He was heavy on arrests but light on convictions, there being only one which led to a nickel stretch in Illinois's Statesville Prison for robbery. That was nine years ago.

After his incarceration, Foote moved back to Chicago and seemingly kept a low profile, working for his brother-in-law's plumbing supply company as a sales rep. The job required significant travel around the upper Midwest. In reality, he may well have simply been operating for years, putting together a new team, as there were strings of unsolved robberies in Des Moines, the Quad Cities, Omaha, Madison, Sioux Falls and Fargo. The MO was always the same, high-end homes, in and out clean, stolen items never turned up in the cities of their origin and the crew disappeared without a trace.

The Twin Cities task force, working with Chicago, tracked Foote back to the Twin Cities five days ago. That's when Mac got the call to come back home. "You got us on to him, don't you want to be around for the takedown?" the chief asked.

Charlie Flanagan didn't have to ask twice.

Mac watched the laptop closely with a satisfied smile. The camera focused on the security pad also provided a view of the back stairway down to the garage. He watched the last of the crew heading down the back steps to the garage.

"Riles, Bud, you guys set?"

"We're good, Mac."

"Thirty seconds, maybe a minute."

Mac moved back to the rear window to take it all in, his right hand resting on his Sig Sauer, just in case. The garage door started to open. Riley and his crew came around the fence from the right and Subject and his crew from the left. Eight cops in total were standing in position at the end of the driveway, thirty feet from the garage door. When the garage door opened, the good guys were waiting.

"POLICE!" Riles yelled in his booming voice. "Put your hands where I can see them!"

The driver and man in the passenger seat quickly complied. A team of four cops moved to the van's left side and opened the sliding door. Three men exited, hands in the air, and walked out to the driveway and laid face down on the ground. Patrol units pulled into the alley and more police invaded the scene. Mac took it all in quietly, a satisfied smirk on his face.

"Let's go down," Lich said, and led Mac downstairs and out the back door. By the time they reached the alley, everyone was in cuffs and lying face down on the driveway. Riles approached Mac, a huge smile on his face as he shook his head. "Unbelievable. Baseball cards," he just shook his head. "We nailed these guys because of flippin' baseball cards."

Mac just smiled as Riles walked away, calling the chief. Mac's own phone started buzzing in his pocket. He pulled the phone out and looked at the display.

"Who is it?" Lich asked.

Mac showed the phone's display to Lich.

"She's so hot," Dicky Boy panted.

Mac chuckled and rolled his eyes, "Dara Wire, as I live

and breathe, how the hell are ya?" Mac asked enthusiastically. "You won't believe what I'm doing right now. I'm standing here with Lich and we just took down this ... Wait, what? ... Say that again? You're serious? ... I know, I know, I know, you're always serious, but really, he wants to see us in the morning? ... Yeah, I saw that on the news. ... Boy, I don't know about getting involved in that. ... No, I suppose you're right, I can't really say no to at least meeting. ... No I don't suppose I can. I'll see you then." Mac hung up.

"What was that all about?" Dick asked.

"I have to get on a plane and go back to DC."

"What for?"

"I have a meeting at the White House," Mac replied, a confused look on his face.

"The White House, really?"

"Yeah."

"With who?"

"Wire, Judge Dixon and FBI Director Mitchell."

"What about?"

"The Reaper."

3

"A UNIQUE PERSPECTIVE."

WASHINGTON, D.C.

Dara Wire was waiting in the arrival lane with her Range Rover when Mac walked out of the Delta Airlines arrivals door at 10:45 A.M., sharply dressed in a dark blue suit with a navy blue dress shirt and dark burgundy tie. Mac deposited his garment bag in the backseat and jumped in the front seat to find a large Dunkin Donuts coffee awaiting his arrival.

"You know me so well," he exclaimed happily as he took a long drink of the dark roast as Wire pulled away from the curb. He put the coffee back in the cup holder and glanced over to Wire and immediately noticed a difference in her. She had a relaxed, light happiness about her, a kind of glow.

"Dara Wire," Mac observed with a big cheese-eating grin, "you got laid."

She blushed, but gave him a very satisfied smile, "Repeatedly."

"It's about damn time," he replied approvingly.

Wire maneuvered her Range Rover quickly through the midmorning traffic, the capital's rush hour over for a good hour. They had met and become fast friends and temporary partners less than a week before the presidential election. Mac was working a murder of a Washington-based political blogger in St. Paul. Wire, a former FBI special agent, was working for the Thomson Campaign, watching the campaign manager for the vice president's campaign, when their paths and investigations crossed. Judge Dixon, knowing both of their abilities, arranged for the two of them to work together. Their investigation saved the election. After the election, they were both offered and both quickly declined regular positions with the FBI. Wire had no interest in returning, having been cast out of the bureau four years earlier and now having a successful business that was making her serious money. Mac declined because he thought he might be done being a cop, and had even less desire to be a little fish in the big bureau pond. He simply didn't need a job and was sitting on plenty of money.

"You know anything more about this case?" Mac asked.

"No more than I knew last night. The president, the Judge and the director want us to help. How exactly? I'm not sure."

"Does it have anything to do with the White House press briefing yesterday?"

Wire nodded, "It does, but there's more to it than that. The father of the latest victim ..."

"Let me guess? He's politically connected."

"Extremely."

"That means money."

"It's always about the money."

"You want in on it?" Mac asked.

"Do you?"

Since he'd arrived from St. Paul six months ago, Mac had

been in the White House a half dozen times, although only one time outside of the West Wing and into the White House proper. That time was for a State Dinner, which, even for someone who detested politics and most politicians, was a bucket list kind of experience. Most of the time when he came to the center of world power, he was picking Sally up on a Friday or Saturday night on their way out to dinner. Today, for the first time, it was about business, or at least potential business. Mac wasn't sure he wanted in.

They checked in at the desk and made their way through the lobby of the West Wing. As they walked down the hall towards the Judge's office near the Oval Office, Mac was grabbed by his right arm and dragged into an office. Sally quickly closed the door and pressed him up against the wall, wrapped her arms around his neck and gave him a deep, soft, wet kiss.

"Hi."

"H ...h... hi. Wow," Mac replied, trying to catch his breath. He hadn't seen her in six days. "Deputy Communications Director Kennedy, does this mean you're happy to see me?"

She whispered seductively in his ear, "You have no idea," then pecked him twice quickly on the lips again. "And later, I will show you. But for now let's go to your meeting."

"You're in on this too?" Mac asked surprised.

"Yes, but I wanted to say hello *privately* first," Sally replied as she led him out of her office and walked him down the hall to the Judge's spacious office.

Judge Dixon, or the Judge, was a large man in size and political stature and he had an office befitting his importance, sitting just thirty feet from the Oval Office. The Judge was a political operator without peer, having elected his second man president, this time his good friend former Minnesota Governor James Thomson. Now, he operated in the White House with an amorphous senior advisor title, yet everyone seemingly answered to him. Few understood Washington like him, how it worked, its nooks and crannies, where and from whom to get information and how to get things done. In the uber-polarized political environment of current Washington, DC, every politician, regardless of party, would take calls from, listen to and accept counsel from Judge Dixon. While most new administrations flail away in their first few years, getting their bearings, not the Thomson administration. James Thomson was a skillful politician to be sure; you don't get elected president without being one. However, it was the Judge and his wise counsel that made the place hum and there had been far fewer of the usual missteps that befall most new administrations, the William Donahue situation notwithstanding.

"You two say hello to each other?" the Judge asked with a wry smile as they walked in holding hands. Mac's body language and perhaps the residue of Sally's lipstick on his lips gave them away.

"We did," Sally answered, a satisfied smile on her face.

"Thanks for coming, Mac," the Judge said, extending his hand. "You and Dara," then he pointed to his couch, "and of course, you both know Thomas," Dixon added, pointing to FBI Director Mitchell.

"Good to see you both again," the director added, standing up and shaking hands with both of them.

After ten minutes of pleasantries and Mac summarizing the bust of the robbery crew in St. Paul, the Judge got down to business. "Mac and Dara, we need your help."

"With the Reaper," Mac finished, grabbing a chair in

front of the Judge's desk. "What can Dara and I bring to the investigation that the FBI can't already provide?" he asked the Judge skeptically.

"A unique perspective."

"Oh bullshit," Mac retorted. "Political cover is what we bring."

"That too," the Judge answered, unbothered. "Everything decided in this office, in this building, in this town, is political, *why* would this be anything different."

"The difference is, I don't do politics," Mac replied.

"Oh bullshit."

"I don't ..."

The Judge dismissed him with a wave, "There isn't anything you wouldn't do for Charlie Flanagan, is there?"

"No, but he's ..."

"... a politician, son. Oh sure he gives off this I'm just a cop swimming in these shark infested political waters story, but give me a damn break. A police chief is a politician and Charlie's a damn good one. You don't stay police chief for twelve years without being a *really good* politician," the Judge counseled. "The director of the FBI is a politician. Cops work for politicians and you two are two of the best I've seen bar none. And I've been around, you know?" The Judge reached inside his suit coat pocket and pulled out a cigar and started twirling it in his fingers, something he did when he got going, thinking and operating. "Now, am I asking you and Wire here to get involved for political reasons? I won't lie to you, Mac. It's absolutely part of it. But there's another part of this which is even more important."

"Which is what?"

The Judge went for where Mac would be weak, where he would give in, where in reality, he would be any easy mark. "Women are dying, Mac," he looked Mac directly in the eye.

"There's a sociopath out there killing young women, three of them now. And as Thomas will tell you, they have some ideas of what makes him tick, but they are nowhere in catching him. Regardless of what you might have heard in the media, they have zilch."

"One of the reasons I offered both of you jobs after the election is because you're both really talented, gifted cops. Dara, you're a great reader of people, and Mac, you're an elite investigator," Director Mitchell added. "I'm not blowing smoke up your asses. You both know I'm right. Right now, I need all the help I can get, the kind of help you two can offer."

"So what does this make us, your 'in case of emergency break glass' people?" Wire asked skeptically.

"Something like that," the Judge replied seriously. "Listen, this case became political once Donahue's daughter was murdered. It will only get worse if we don't find this guy. Donahue will only get worse. And the other two murders are in Pennsylvania and Maryland, so right in our neighborhood here. The media is all over this thing already and the attention, pressure and even hysteria will only increase if this guy keeps killing and leaving notes. You two have a history of ... bringing difficult cases home."

"I just bet your people will love us sticking our noses in this," Wire remarked to the director. "That is, if we agree to do it."

"No, they probably won't, but I don't care," Mitchell replied sternly. "I will take care of that issue and it will not be an issue."

"And I don't think you just join the main investigation ..." the Judge started.

"No," Mac finished. "If we did this, we would run a separate investigation, adjacent to the case, taking our own look at it in our own way."

"Right," the Judge answered. "And out of the spotlight. We don't want it looking like we're sticking our nose into the investigation. So, to get started, the director has something for you."

Mitchell pulled two large red-rope files out of his large, black briefcase. "Entire case file, all three murders, forensics, profile, interviews, pictures, everything you need to get started and up to speed. I will get you linked to the electronic case file so you get every up to date piece of information we're getting."

"Do your people know about this? About us?" Wire asked, thumbing through one of the red-rope files.

"Not yet," Mitchell answered.

Wire and Mac both raised their eyebrows in annoyance.

"I didn't know for sure you were coming in," the director answered. "Are you?"

"Are we?" Wire asked, turning to Mac, "I mean, I will if you will?"

Mac didn't answer, thinking, sitting back in his chair, arms folded.

"Come on, Mac," Sally teased, walking to Mac's chair, sitting on the arm and putting her right arm around his shoulder, "you've been bored out of your mind."

"I thought you liked I wasn't detecting?" he replied, looking up at her.

"One part of me does," she answered. "I like that you're home safe at night." She reached for his hand. "However, the other part of me knows you could stop this guy. You went back to St. Paul to be a cop for a few weeks for something they really didn't need you on. This is something you're *really* needed on."

Mac looked to the Judge, smiling, "Ohhhh ... you've taught her well."

The Judge sat back in his chair, a smile spreading across his wide face. "She's a quick study. So what's it gonna be?"

"I'm in."

4
"WHEN YOU'RE THE LEAD DOG."

Wire, given her exhaustive schedule, hadn't been by Mac and Sally's Georgetown brownstone for a couple of months, so before they started, Mac showed her the recently finished kitchen. He installed all new white cabinetry, bringing the kitchen back to its original look, while also adding a center island, black granite countertops and wine refrigerator underneath the far end of the island. An eating nook in the form of a booth in the bay window overlooking the small backyard and patio was also added.

"I love the all white cabinetry," Wire remarked. "It makes the room look bigger," she walked around a little more. "Maybe taller is the word I'm looking for."

"Visually you're right. I'm not usually a huge fan of white, it shows fingerprints and can be hard to keep clean, but I wanted to restore it to its original look, with some modern conveniences, of course. It turned out quite well, I think."

"So what have you finished so far?"

"I've finished the master bedroom and bath, living room and now the kitchen."

"The rooms you two spend all your time in then."

"Yeah, the place is really livable now."

"What's next?"

"I want to do a little work on the second-floor bathroom, make it a little better for guests. I'll install a new sink, lighting, put on a new coat of paint and retile the shower. My mom is coming out to visit in October and I want to have it done by the time she gets here."

"So where do you want to work on the case?"

"Let's go up to the attic."

The brownstone had a spacious attic that Mac and Sally were using as an office. It had everything they needed: a large writing table desk, a wheeled whiteboard Mac bought at a surplus sale, a large blank white wall and a mini-fridge that had soda, water and a few beers. Mac removed some items from the desk, set a chair on the front side for Wire and put the files on the desk. "Let's start digging through this thing."

Mac was, in one sense, impressed by the volume of information that the FBI collected, collated and summarized. In another sense, it was amazing that given all of the information collected over the three murders, the FBI was not any closer to catching the killer. In fact, the FBI was nowhere in catching the killer.

There were now three victims. All of the women were killed in essentially the same way. The killer, which Mac refused to call "The Reaper," at least for now, used a rag soaked in chloroform to subdue the women and knock them out. Once they were subdued, he then injected the women with sodium pentothal, an anesthetic.

"Why the anesthetic?" Wire asked.

"It gives him time, for one. The chloroform acts for a

short time, but the sodium pentothal puts them out and lets him set up," Mac answered.

The setup was once the women were under anesthetic they were then bound to a chair. Once bound to the chair, and once the victims were awake, it appeared they were being interrogated and maybe even tortured. "What do you suppose the chair thing is all about?" Mac asked.

"Maybe the verses tell us that."

"Reaping what you sow?"

"Yeah, that he's interrogating them about something and ..."

"Then, when he's done, they reap what they sowed?" Mac finished. "So that begs the question, what did they sow?"

"Who knows?" Wire answered. "The way he kills the girls, gutting them with the knife, leaving the biblical verses, it's pretty ..."

"Demented? Sadistic? Cruel?"

"Yes. You almost wonder if he's more torturing them before he kills them, you know?"

Mac looked at the photos, "Or he wants us to think that."

"What do you mean?"

"I don't know," Mac answered. "I'm just not willing to draw any conclusions on it just yet. I'm keeping an open mind."

Once he moved in for the kill, the victims' abdomens were cut open in the shape of the Holy Cross, a long, deep, vertical cut was the killing wound. The killer would start below the woman's navel and would twist the knife inside. Given the depth of the wound and the ripping nature of the wound, it suggested the knife was seven inches long with both a smooth and serrated edge leading into the hilt. The knife was thought to possibly be a Ka-Bar KB1214, a combat knife.

"Nasty knife," Mac noted, examining a picture of a Ka-Bar. "This knife has only one purpose: killing."

"Military type," Wire added. "There was some thought the guy could be military by the way he hunts them."

"Possible," Mac answered. "I've seen it before."

After the killing wound was complete, it was then extended from just above the pubic area up to the victim's rib cage. After that, the killer made a horizontal wound that wasn't as deep, more superficial, again, part of the symbolism of the murder. The slicing of the cross then led to the final physical act which was staging the woman in what appeared to be the fetal position, knees up to their stomach and arms wrapped around their upper torso. With all three victims, biblical messages of reaping what you sow had been left, causing the bureau to call the killer the Reaper. Apparently the killer was now aware of this, signing his last biblical message in blood on the wall with the name the Reaper.

"Bureau moved pretty quickly to call this a serial," Wire noted.

"The staging of the body, the note with the biblical verse, all of that I think got the attention of the Harrisburg police and they called the bureau right away. It looks like the lead agent on the case, a guy named Gesch, was up there and the file indicates it was his view that this had all the hallmarks of a serial getting started. He was obviously right."

The women were all found in the basements of their homes or of buildings. "Places where there's privacy," Wire observed. In two cases, the victims were in the basements of buildings, one an abandoned building, the other a basement of a bar.

The first victim, Melissa Goynes, maiden name Melissa Ross, was killed six weeks ago in mid-May. A petite twenty-seven-year-old brunette, she was a waitress and manager at the Nittany Lion Sports Bar in Harrisburg, Pennsylvania. She was married with a three-year-old daughter.

"She was found in the basement of the bar," Mac mumbled, flipping through the pages of the police report, frowning. "She closed the bar with one of the bartenders, they talk for a few minutes in the parking lot at 2:20 A.M. or so. His car is parked closer to the building. After talking, he gets in his car and she walks the thirty feet to her car. Bartender says he saw her get into her car, start it and saw the headlights turn on. He then says he pulled away and drove home. His wife says he was home at 2:35 because she recalls him turning off the house's alarm and coming up to bed. She looked at the clock before rolling over and going back to sleep, so the bartender was cleared. Goynes's husband was home with their daughter, which the police confirmed. Their apartment building has cameras over the front and back door and he never left. No other suspects." He scratched his head. "So our killer is waiting inside of the car?"

"That's what the Harrisburg police and FBI seem to think," Dara answered. "Like you said, the bartender said he saw her get into her car, so the police's theory makes sense."

Mac flipped to another page. "She had an older car, a 2002 basic Honda Accord that didn't have a car alarm system, I guess, or if it did, the alarm didn't work."

"Or he defeats it. So he gets in the car and hides in the backseat. He waits for the bartender to pull away and chloroforms her from behind. Then what, carries her back into the bar, down to the basement and goes to work on her?"

"He would have had hours with her if that's what he did," Mac speculated, as he thumbed through the crime scene photos, laying them out on the writing table. "The photos aren't bad, but without actually walking the crime scene around the bar, they don't tell me as much. I think maybe we'll need to go up to Harrisburg."

"See how our guy's mind works?"

"Exactly, try to get into his mind, anyway," Mac replied. "I like to walk the crime scene and see the obstacles he had to overcome."

The second victim, Janelle Wyland, was killed two weeks later in Salisbury, Maryland. Salisbury was in the part of eastern Maryland across the Chesapeake and just below the southern border for Delaware. She was a twenty-seven-year-old redheaded insurance broker.

"Janelle was busted in an old-fashioned way," Wire smirked. "She was having an affair with her married boss. They went to a local hotel for a little rendezvous. According to the boss, he left the hotel at 9:30 P.M. and was home by 9:50 P.M., all of which was confirmed by his rather unhappy wife."

"Bet that was awkward," Mac chuckled morbidly, and then added while admiring her photo, "I can, however, understand her boss's attraction. Janelle was rather fetching."

"Have a thing for redheads, do you?"

"I might have a type," Mac answered. Sally was a fiery Irish redhead with a body that curved in all the right ways, just like Janelle. "Janelle's fate was similar to Melissa's," Mac stated, showing a photo of Janelle Wyland, lying naked in a pool of blood.

Wire grimaced. "Gruesome."

The final victim from two days ago, Hannah Donahue, was from Dover, Delaware. She was a twenty-seven-year-old, blond elementary school teacher.

Mac placed the photos of each victim on the whiteboard with the vital information. To the right of the whiteboard, he put a large map of the five state area surrounding Washington, DC, and put pins up to mark the cities where the victims were killed, numbering the victims. He stood back from the wall and soaked in the information.

"What are you thinking?" Wire asked, sitting at the desk, leaning back in her chair. She saw the look on his face as well.

Mac looked at his watch, 5:22 P.M. "I'm thinking I need a beer," he answered and walked over to the small brown fridge in the corner, "I've got Surly and Grain Belt Premium, fine Minnesota beers, or a Coors Light; what will it be?"

"Coors Light," Wire answered. She grabbed the beer from Mac, popped it open and took a long sip, "Ahhhh, the mountains are blue and the beer is ice cold." She took another sip, "So what do you think?" she asked, gesturing with her beer towards their handiwork.

"You ever work a serial killer case?" Mac asked, standing and turning back to look at the whiteboard, sipping from his Grain Belt.

"Once. I was a young special agent. It was before I got into undercover work going after the mob. I was stationed down in the New Orleans Field Office and we had a serial. I was more or less a grunt on that one. We had a guy going around killing prostitutes. Once it was determined it was a serial and the bureau came in full throttle, we got the guy within ten days."

"Let me guess, turned out the killer's mom was a prostitute, there was some sort of childhood trauma and he acted out on that."

"Something like that," Wire nodded. "How about you?"

"A couple," Mac answered. "We had a guy going around killing working-class girls along University Avenue in St. Paul a few years ago who left 'Have a Nice Day' smiley face balloons at his murder scenes. His trigger was an ex-girlfriend who caused him to snap and get a medical discharge from the Marines. You know what's common between your case and mine?"

"The killer had a type?"

"Exactly. In our case here," Mac gestured to the board, "the killer doesn't have a type, at least not that I can see—yet. Serial killers have a type of woman that they go after, whether it's based on hair color, body type or profession, something that ties the victims together. There is usually something that serves as a trigger for the killer."

"We certainly don't have that here," Wire agreed, leaning back on her chair, putting her feet on the desk. "We have a blond, a brunette and a redhead."

"Goynes was short, whereas Wyland and Donahue were more medium height and weight. One is from Pennsylvania, one from Maryland and one from Delaware. I don't see a type, I don't see a commonality. That bugs me."

"So what do we know?" Wire asked.

"He leaves messages, biblical verses that all relate to reaping what you sow. We have the following verses: Galatians 6:7—Be not deceived; God is not mocked: for whatsoever a man soweth, that shall he also reap.

"Matthew 26:52—Then said Jesus unto him, Put up again thy sword into his place: for all they that take the sword shall perish with the sword.

"And then two days ago: Job 4:8—Even as I have seen, they that plow iniquity, and sow wickedness, reap the same."

"You're the good Irish Catholic who regularly goes to church," Wire asked. "Stringed together, do they mean anything to you?"

Mac chuckled, "I go to church, but I'm no Biblical scholar. They all are a message of reaping what you sow, so I interpret that to mean he's punishing these women for *some* reason. I suppose if we could figure out what that is, that gives you a better idea of maybe how he's picking these women."

"The FBIs interpretation," Wire remarked, "is that the verses suggest he's a Mission-Oriented Killer."

"I know the type," Mac answered. "They justify their acts as 'ridding the world' of people they deem undesirable, such as homosexuals, prostitutes or people of different ethnicity or religion."

"Yeah, they see themselves as attempting to change society or curing some societal ill," Wire added. "I remember this from our behavioral science classes at Quantico. However, typically the mission-oriented killers have ..."

"A type," Mac answered, sticking to the theme. "The Zebra killers in San Francisco, you remember them?"

Wire nodded.

"They targeted Caucasians. The Green Valley Killer in Seattle targeted prostitutes. Your guy in Louisiana targeted prostitutes, my guy in St. Paul targeting working-class girls that reminded him of his old girlfriend. These guys are not psychotics," Mac sat on the corner of the desk, "these guys are cold and calculating. They hunt these unworthy people and forge ahead on their mission, fully aware of the risks of doing so."

"A predator, stalking his prey," Dara added. "However,

this still brings us back to the question, what is it about these women that made them unworthy? What did they reap and sow?"

"Damned if I know," Mac replied, setting his beer down and grabbing a memorandum summarizing the victims. "Donahue and Wyland are college graduates. Goynes, on the other hand, dropped out of college. She was going to school at Robert Morris and then bagged it after two years."

"I've seen that before," Wire suggested. "I had a couple of roomies at the University of Virginia who got sidetracked that way. They got into that bartending and waiting tables routine, all the cash and instant money with it, and they figure, I'll finish school later."

"And later never comes," Mac finished. "They weren't criminals, it doesn't look like. Goynes had a little issue nine years ago when she was ticketed for underage drinking. She was driving at the time she got herself into a little trouble."

"And our insurance broker," Wire noted, looking through the same summary, "Janelle, was busted with some weed eight years ago when she was in college at Virginia Commonwealth. You scan her background and it looks like she was something of a party girl."

"BFD," Mac remarked.

"So what is this guy's mission then?"

"To punish women like these for their sins," Mac answered. "So what is their sin? What is it that ties these women together? What did they do? What binds them together?" He took a sip of his beer, and tacked a different direction. "Is there anything in the autopsy reports?"

Wire shook her head, "Not that I've seen. They all read pretty much the same. Traces of chloroform and fabric from a dark blue rag he uses to put over the women's mouths plus the sodium pentothal in their system. They're all cut, really gutted. No sexual assault of any kind."

Mac was looking over her shoulder now, "And no trace evidence either. The way he's attacking them, from behind, even with the chloroform, you'd think we'd get some DNA from under fingernails or something, scratching at him, but nada."

"At least not yet," Wire answered. "But there must be something about these women, something they have in common."

"Whatever it is, the FBI hasn't found it yet. From what I can tell, they've gone pretty deep into these women's backgrounds." Mac stood up and stretched his arms up over his head and looked at his watch, 7:30 P.M. It had been a long day and they'd worked for nearly seven hours straight. "I should order us a pizza or something," Mac said.

He looked back and Wire was smiling at her phone, "I don't think that will be necessary," she replied with a grin. "Sally just gave me the signal. She'll be home by 8:30. She's bringing dinner and I am to make myself scarce by then. She wants you all to herself."

Senior Special Agent Aubrey Gesch pulled the door closed from the FBI director's office and nodded for Special Agent Grace Delmonico to follow him.

"What happened with the director?" Delmonico asked as they reached the elevator.

"Not in here," was Gesch's clipped reply.

The two special agents silently rode the elevator down and made their way to Gesch's Suburban in the parking garage. Once clear of the Hoover Building, Gesch opened up on the short drive back to the Washington Field Office.

"We have to go back to Dover in the morning."

"Dover? Why?"

"The FBI director is assigning us some *help* on the Reaper," grumbled Gesch in reply.

"What kind of help?" she asked warily.

"Open my briefcase and pull out the two manila file folders," Gesch answered.

Delmonico did as instructed and started reading through them. "Dara Wire and Michael McKenzie 'Mac' McRyan. Why do those names ring a bell?" It took her a second and then the names registered. "Wait a minute, aren't they the ones who ..."

"Did that investigation as part of the election," Gesch finished for her as he drove onto E Street.

"Great, but what do they know about serial killers?" Delmonico asked.

"The director says not much, but that the two of them have a talent for figuring things out."

"And we don't!" she replied bitterly. "How many of these psychos have we brought home over the years, Aubry? This is bullshit."

"Look, Grace, I tend to agree," Gesch replied as he approached Seventh Street. The two of them had a long day and were under a lot of pressure, and now this. "You know what, let's get a beer, relax and talk about this."

Gesch turned left onto Seventh Street, drove past the Iron Horse, did a U-turn and pulled into a spot along the southbound side of the street. The two special agents walked inside. It was a quiet night, perhaps only fifteen to twenty people in the bar. They grabbed a booth in the back, away from the rest of the patrons. A waitress quickly took their beer order. While they waited for the beer to come, they each read through the folders. Once the pitcher of beer arrived, Gesch poured them each a glass. He took a long sip and slumped back into the vinyl of the booth and exhaled.

"Let me guess, the White House, after the disaster of the press conference yesterday, put pressure on the director," Delmonico started, still bitter.

Gesch, the veteran senior special agent, nodded. "Yes they did."

"So the White House maneuvers these two into the case for cover."

"Something like that."

"Political bullshit, that's all we need."

"No we don't." Gesch took a sip of his beer. He'd been around the block more than once and the higher you got in the bureau, the more politics entered your world. "Look, I'm not happy about this either, Gracie, but it is what it is. They're coming in. And, while I'm loath to admit it, they might help us."

Delmonico snorted her disagreement while she started reading through the folder more, sipping at her beer. "This McRyan guy, he's a St. Paul cop. No offense to the Twin Cities, but this is a little different game here, a bigger game. This is no time for amateur hour."

Gesch nodded, "Perhaps, although that election investigation was a pretty big game and he did all right."

"And this Wire," Delmonico griped, "she was tossed out of the bureau?"

"Yes and no," Gesch answered. "She was a rising star years ago, doing undercover work against the mob up in New Jersey and New York. The last case she worked went bad, her man inside the Giordano crime family ended up floating in the Hudson. Then something happened and she was out of the bureau."

The way Gesch said *something happened* said he knew more.

"Spill it, Aubrey."

"Rumor was that her man was somehow compromised by Donald Wellesley Jr."

"You mean the former vice president's son who is now in federal prison?"

Gesch nodded. "Apparently Special Agent Wire was incensed that Wellesley Jr. blew her guy's cover. She tracked him down to a bar here in Washington and proceeded to beat the living hell out of him until the Secret Service peeled her off of him. I guess she turned Wellesley's face to hamburger."

"I think maybe I like her now," Delmonico said with a smile.

Gesch chuckled. "It took multiple surgeries to get things right for Wellesley. The whole thing could have all been ugly for the vice president and Wire if it all got out."

"So what happened?"

"Judge Dixon," Gesch replied, taking a pull from his beer.

"Color me shocked."

"Apparently Wire came to the attention of the great man while he was the attorney general. He intervened and negotiated a soft landing for Wire in return for keeping her mouth shut. That was almost five years ago. Wire ended up getting involved in that election case because she was working for Dixon and the Thomson Campaign and her little investigation crossed paths with McRyan's murder investigation in St. Paul. The rest, as they say, is history."

"Is she good?"

Gesch nodded. "I don't know her, Grace, only of her. All I've ever heard is she's smart, tough and clearly loyal."

Delmonico took a look at her picture and then another tucked behind it, a full-body shot dated last November. "She's tall," the special agent noted, "And quite pretty."

"I've also heard that."

"So Wire's smart. What about McRyan?"

"The director says he's even smarter."

Delmonico snorted her disagreement as she opened up the manila folder on McRyan. It took her a few minutes. McRyan had an undergraduate degree, summa cum laude, from the University of Minnesota and a law degree, again summa, from William Mitchell College of Law. "William Mitchell is in St. Paul, right?"

Gesch nodded.

McRyan passed the bar, had an attorney job lined up at a big Twin Cities law firm when two of his cousins were killed in the line of duty. "Looks like he comes from a family of cops," Delmonico reported, taking another sip of her beer.

"That's what the director told me," Gesch answered. "Director Mitchell knew McRyan's father, said he was one of the best local cops he ever ran into. Says Michael Mackenzie, or Mac, is better."

Delmonico kept reading. "He's had some pretty good cases besides the election case last fall. I remember this double kidnapping case. That was him?"

Gesch nodded.

"And it says here that he is dating ..."

"Lives with."

"... White House Deputy Communications Director Sally Kennedy. I've seen her on TV, the super attractive ginger, right?"

"That's the one."

"How did he land ... her ..." Delmonico had flipped to a picture of McRyan. "Okay, I see how he did that. Tall, blond hair, blue eyes, athletic looking with a big dimple in his chin, I guess I can see how she might go for all that." Delmonico exhaled, took another sip of her beer and slumped in her booth. "Okay, so I'll admit these two have pretty good backgrounds. What's their role with us?"

"The director said that these two would take a fresh look at the case in their own way. Like I said, the director said the two of them are just good at figuring stuff out. He says McRyan is what you call 'Natural Police,' a natural investigator. He's just good at it, sees things that others don't and thinks outside the box. The director offered him a job after the election, he offered them both jobs, in fact, and they both turned him down."

"Why?"

"McRyan has money, *lots* of money," Gesch answered.

"Another reason Kennedy probably went for him."

"It probably didn't hurt. It's not in the file, but he made a pile selling out a minority interest in some coffee chain based in the Twin Cities. Wire has her own business which is thriving, so I think she's been working and that's why, I think, they turned down the offers. Also, it's not generally well known, at least yet, but those two also got a sizable advance from a publisher to write a book about the election investigation, so neither of them needs the work or the paycheck."

"So why come into the case?"

"Because the Judge, and by extension, the president, asked them to. Those are two people you simply can't say no to."

"And I suppose neither can we."

It was almost eleven. Mac had to get up early to pick up Wire and drive to Dover, and he wasn't in the least bit of a hurry to go to sleep. Going to bed, yes, going to sleep, no. Of course, an hour ago, a bed hadn't been required. They christened the new kitchen instead.

"You know, we have a perfectly good king-size bed upstairs," Mac suggested while they dined on the mostaccioli and spaghetti Sally brought home.

"I came through the door and saw you and suddenly believed in the Fierce Urgency of Now," she answered with a big seductive grin.

Mac cackled, "Wow, now you're quoting MLK to explain our sex life."

"Like you objected," she cooed.

"I certainly didn't," he answered, leaning over and kissing her lightly. "I had no objections at all. In fact, there were a couple of your little maneuvers that were new. You'll have to do those again."

"I was reading the sex tips section of Cosmo while you were gone."

"Remind me to buy you a full year's subscription."

"The center island withstood our assault," she added with a mischievous smile. "I believe I can now fully trust in your craftsmanship."

Sally was always glib and flirty after sex. It was one of those little things he loved about her. The recap after they made love. It was never roll over and go to sleep. No, there was the postgame show and a breakdown of the highlights and the key moments in the encounter. Without fail, she always had something funny and seductive to say. It oftentimes led to another round, or overtime, as he'd taken to calling it. Sally had a way of always making him want her more.

Now, he was sitting on his kitchen floor and leaning against the center island in his boxers and Sally was sitting across from him cross-legged in nothing but his white University of Minnesota T-shirt with some of the best red hair porn he'd ever seen her have. Easy rock was playing lightly from the speaker on the counter. They were drinking red wine and eating right out of the take-out boxes. The only illumination was three candles, two on the counter and one on the center island. It was totally romantic.

For two hours they talked, touched, kissed and caught up with one another. It was two hours of conversations about anything but work. As serious people as they both were, they both loved their intake of pop culture. Both had tablets that were full of magazines that made for mindless entertainment reading. Mac always made time for his St. Paul boy Vince Flynn and would occasionally dive into a legal novel, although he preferred nonfiction, biographies and historical books. Sally was more of the fiction reader, with a thing for Gillian Flynn and Lisa Gardner mysteries. Where they agreed was an eclectic mix of television shows and they spent a half hour recapping their recent viewings of their favorites, *Diners, Drive-Ins and Dives, Rehab Addict, Homeland, Breaking Bad, Mad Men, Suits, Castle* and *Game of Thrones*. They talked about their families, from how Sally's brother was going to have his third child to Mac describing how his seventeen-year-old niece, Maura, was busted for minor consumption.

"It sounds like Tess was rather upset with Maura," Sally said, twisting spaghetti around her fork.

"Over the top, really," Mac chuckled as he shoveled in

more mostaccioli. "Minor consumption isn't the greatest thing to have on your record."

"We could probably fix that."

Mac nodded. "I made a couple of calls over to Minneapolis and we'll get it taken care of for her. She'll have her do a little community service. But Tess," he smiled ruefully, "was all over her like white on rice."

"Was Maura upset?"

"Natch. But I really think she was just more embarrassed that her mom and dad had to come and pick her up. Of course, I was able to cheer Maura up a little bit."

"How?"

"I told her about the time my dad and I went to pick up Tess from the jail up in St. Cloud. She was arrested for public intoxication and ended up with a minor consumption when she was a sophomore up at St. Ben's. Oh man, did Dad have fun with her on that hour-ride home. I told Maura all about it."

Sally laughed. "Tess will love you for that."

"I told her I told Maura about it."

"Oh God. You did not?"

"Hell yeah."

"When you have kids she will get you back."

"Kids? Did you say something about kids?" Mac asked with raised eyebrows.

"A conversation for another time," Sally demurred. "Let's get back to Tess. She had to be hot with you."

"Oh yeah, she went off on me something fierce. I said pot meet kettle. It was hilarious." He reached for the bottle. "More wine?"

"Please," Sally replied happily and Mac filled her glass with more of the pinot noir. He emptied the rest of the bottle into his glass.

"I could get another," he offered. The wine fridge was five feet away.

She waved him off, "I've had plenty and I do, after all, have to work tomorrow."

"You work every day," Mac replied.

"Such is life at the White House," she replied with enthusiasm, raising her glass in a mock toast. Mac figured at some point the euphoria of working in that building would wear off and it would become more of a job, with the usual grumbling and the like, but seven months in, she was still like a kid in the candy store.

"Man, did you and the Judge work me today," Mac said.

"A little," Sally replied, taking a sip of her wine, "but I didn't have to work you *that* hard, Mac. You wanted in on this."

Mac shrugged. It was the truth; he did.

"And that's okay," she added. "It's what you do, Mac. You're gifted at it. I figured something like this would happen eventually and I think the Judge did too, and you just needed a little *teeny tiny* push."

"I was just a little surprised you were so gung-ho for me to do it."

Sally shook her head, "I'm not necessarily. I was happy when you turned down the FBI job and I'm happy you're safe and I don't have to worry so much. But I didn't want you chained to the radiator with nothing to do either."

"You know I didn't turn down the FBI job for safety reasons." They'd never discussed his reasons. Sally always assumed he did it for her. She got after him pretty good after the election case, the danger of the case, the risks he took. There were some long conversations about it and she expressed her fears and worries that she was scared she would lose him. The fierceness of her worries put him back on his heels, she could tell. She'd always felt a little guilty about it.

"Then why did you turn it down?"

"There were a couple of reasons. I wasn't sure I'd have the same edge for the job after the election case. It's pretty hard to ever imagine having a bigger case than that, Sal. That was like the Mount Everest of investigations. I mean, think about it. What could top it? Would I bring the kind of effort and motivation to the run of the mill case anymore? I wasn't ... I just wasn't sure I could or would."

"What's the second reason?"

"I like being the lead dog, being the one at the head of the pack, not one of the dogs in the middle. In the job the director offered, as attractive and generous as it was, I wouldn't be the lead dog. I would just be one of the dogs. So I passed. Now, if I wasn't sitting on this pile of money, my decision might have been entirely different, but I didn't have to take the job. I don't have to take any job."

"The money helps," she suggested, looking down, digging for more spaghetti.

"You know what the money *really* does, babe?"

"What?" she asked, looking up.

"It lets me live life on *my* terms. It let me move here with you without even having to think about it. It gives me the freedom to do what I want. Whether that's rehabilitating this townhouse, writing this book or taking on a case if it interests me. Like the robbery case in St. Paul? That interested me. I made a difference there. I cracked that thing open. This case definitely interests me. Maybe I can make a difference here. And I get to be the lead dog the way this thing is set up. I get to work with Wire, someone I, *and you* by the way, can absolutely trust to have my back, so that's why I said yes."

She leaned forward and kissed him softly, "Good, I was feeling just a little guilty about working you."

"No you weren't."

Sally shook her head and got quiet, "No, I am, I was, but for very selfish reasons. I want you to find this guy, Mac, I really do. He's so evil. But ..."

"But what?"

"Please, just don't get hurt. Please don't get hurt." She realized she'd have to go back to living with that fear, a fear that had been gone for seven months. She'd gotten comfortable living without that fear. Now it was back.

"Part of the gig, babe," he answered, reaching for her left hand. "There's always some risk."

She nodded, looking down, "I know," she whispered. "You thrive on it."

Mac started to object. She put her fingers up to his lips. "It's okay. I don't think you'd be as good as you are if you didn't. *When you're the lead dog,*" she said, turning his phrase against him just a little. She crawled over to and straddled him, wrapping her legs around his back and her arms around his neck. "You live on the adrenaline that a case like this gives off. On cases like this you run into the fire without regard to the consequences," she pecked him softly on the lips and leaned her forehead against his. "Please, just don't get burned."

"I'll try not to," Mac answered quietly, leaning back, moving his hands gently under her T-shirt and lifting it over her head, admiring her wonderful figure in the flickering candlelight. "You are so gorgeous."

"You're not so bad yourself, McRyan," Sally purred back as she reached down and slid off his boxers. "So, what's the next surface we should test in here?"

As he watched the CNN report on the investigation and took a sip of his bourbon, the faces came back to him, particularly the two he made certain understood their circumstances and what he could do to them. Of course, as he watched he realized there was yet another; one that had disappeared inexplicably two years ago that, at the time, struck him as a conveniently fortunate elimination of the weakest link. Now, perhaps that disappearance had an explanation, and a troubling one.

Someone knew.

The situation was no longer under his or his client's control.

He picked up his cell phone and dialed.

"Wallace, I knew you would call."

"Then you have been watching the reports on the Reaper?"

"I have."

"I think we have a problem. You're going to need some protection."

5
"DO THEY PASS?"

Just before sunup, Mac pulled up in front of Wire's new townhouse in Arlington, a tall Starbucks in the cup holder for her. The tall, athletic brunette sauntered down her front walk dressed casually in blue jeans, a black sleeveless top with a light green blazer draped over her arm with her hair pulled back in a long ponytail. She had a black backpack, much like Mac's, hanging on her left shoulder. She matched Mac's casual look of blue jeans and thin, cream, button-down collar Polo dress shirt. A blue sport coat was lying in the backseat just in case he needed to class it up a little more. They both had bureau credentials but neither of them was wearing the bureau uniform.

"Nice Beamer," she said as she hopped in. "This is new."

"Had it about a month," Mac answered easily, dropping the fully loaded black BMW X5 into drive. "I didn't like driving the Yukon around Washington, it was too big, so I stored that in the garage back in St. Paul and bought this for here."

"Rich people problems," Wire teased.

"*Whatever*. With the book advance and the way your

business is booming, you're not exactly living check to check at this point, so you can stow the rich guy cracks. I'll take them from Lich, but not from you, honey."

Mac plugged the address for Hannah Donahue into the GPS, pulled away and began the two-hour trek east to Dover, Delaware. A little before 7:00 they hit the long stretch of the Chesapeake Bay Bridge and enjoyed the bright morning sun as it rose rapidly in the east over the deep blue, cloudless sky of the bay. The temperature would rise into the high eighties with plenty of summer stifling heat.

"In Minnesota in the summer, it gets really warm and there's humidity, but nothing like this. The humidity here is at another level."

"It does get thick in the summer," Wire answered. "I'm used to it, lived around here my entire life."

At 8:00 A.M. sharp, he pulled up in front of Hannah Donahue's house, the crime scene tape still floating with the breeze, keeping people away. In addition to an unmarked police car, there was a mid-forties man dressed in a brown suit and a red tie with graying hair at the temples and a petite woman, mid-thirties, dressed in a navy blue pant suit and white blouse with short black hair swept behind her ears, leaning against a black Suburban, drinking convenience store coffees.

Mac and Wire slipped out of the SUV, each grabbed their backpacks and walked over to the two FBI agents and introduced themselves. The weather was heating up but the reception was decidedly cool.

"So what do you two think you can accomplish here?" Delmonico asked with an edge. She might have resolved herself that they were coming in, but she still wasn't happy about it. She had some questions.

Mac was going to make this short, "Look, we didn't go

looking for this. We were asked to come in and see if we could help."

"How exactly? Neither of you have much experience with serials," Gesch stated.

"No, we don't," Mac answered reasonably. "I'm not a profiler, that's your specialty. Me?" he held his arms out, "I'm a homicide detective. I'm a hunter, a pretty decent one."

"And you're what?" Gesch asked of Wire.

"I read people and I'm former bureau," Wire answered. "Look, you guys don't want us here, we get that …"

"It's not necessarily that," Gesch started, putting his hands up. "It's just that this feels like a political maneuver. I've got enough on my plate and then to have to deal with that? I don't have time for it."

"Oh it is political," Wire answered. "The White House is worried about Donahue's dad making their life miserable."

"And you see, I don't see how that helps us," Gesch said.

"Neither of us really gives a rip about politics," Mac offered.

"Seriously?" Delmonico replied skeptically. "That's what you're going to go with? You're both here at the behest of the president and his political guru. And you," pointing at Mac, "you live with the White House deputy director of communications. So don't give me this 'we don't do politics' shit. You two reek of it right now."

Mac could understand where she was coming from and her view of things wasn't illogical. It was just that he didn't really give a shit. "Look, are you here to fight me or find this guy?"

"Find this guy," Delmonico answered, standing her ground.

"Really? Because, Special Agent Delmonico, I could swear you'd rather chew my ass. Me? I want to find this jackhole. So we can sit here and debate the finer points of why we're here, or how we got here, or who put us here; or, since we are here, we could start working to see if Wire and I can help you guys find this killer."

"So what's it gonna be?" Wire added, hands on hips.

Gesch looked at Delmonico, "Do they pass?"

Delmonico shrugged her agreement, "Yeah, I think so."

Mac and Wire both snorted their disgust. "Do we pass?" Wire bitched. Now their backs were up.

"Look," Gesch looked back to Wire and McRyan, hands raised, "the director gave us the lowdown on you two. I think you *can* help. I really do. We just wanted to make sure this wasn't some political or media play. Two suits showing up to look good and get some press for their book."

Wire laughed and Mac grunted.

"What?"

"Media play? You don't know us very well," Wire answered. "I don't talk to reporters."

"You know about the investigation we were involved in around the election, right?" Mac asked.

Gesch and Delmonico nodded.

"Neither of us granted an interview to anyone. So if I wouldn't grant an interview then, I'm certainly not going start seeking them out now, my girlfriend notwithstanding," Mac added. "When we nail this bastard, you can do the interviews, you can handle the press conference and I will be nowhere to be found. I'll go back to fixing the brownstone I bought."

"*Riiiight*," Delmonico replied.

"Watch me," Mac retorted.

"Okay, okay, okay, that's enough dog sniffing," Gesch stated, stepping between Delmonico and McRyan. "Everyone's marked their territory. So let's go to work." The senior

FBI agent led them up the sidewalk to the front door of the white-sided, two-story house. At the front door, a plainclothes cop awaited their arrival.

"Agents Wire and McRyan," Gesch stopped. "Is that what I should call you guys?"

"Dara or Wire works for me," Wire answered.

"Call me Mac," Mac stated. "Everyone does. This FBI agent business is temporary."

"Okay, well Dara and Mac, please meet Detective Dane Wente of the Dover PD. He's our Reaper Task Force man here in Dover."

Everyone shook hands and Wente cut the seal on the front door of the house and dug in his pocket for the key.

"The director told me he gave you copies of the case files, right?" Gesch asked.

Mac and Wire nodded.

"So, fresh eyes, anything jump out at you?" the senior agent asked.

"Only the question I'm sure you're asking; what is it that connects these women?" Mac answered. "Now you're the experts, but don't serials almost always have a type?"

Gesch nodded as he opened the door, "They usually do."

"We've seen nothing in the case files thus far that connects the women; that explains his type. Until we figure out how he's picking these women, we're not going to get far."

"I would agree," Delmonico answered as she led them through the living room, to the kitchen and the back stairway down to the basement.

The pool of blood was still on cement floor of the basement, sitting to the left of two chairs. The message from the Reaper was on the cinder block wall, and seeing it written in blood was chilling.

Wire opened up her backpack and pulled out the case file for Hannah Donahue. She handed Mac the photos and kept the case file. Mac laid the pictures on the floor around the area where Donahue's body was found.

Delmonico, Gesch and Wente stood back and let them work.

First, Mac and Wire worked the basement. Mac went to the chairs, noting the duct tape still on the chair to the right. He took the chair to the left, which was set back seven to eight feet from the other chair. Wire sat down in the other chair. They both looked up to the ceiling and Wire's chair was right under the single hanging light bulb. The shade focused the light such that, were the basement otherwise completely dark, Mac's chair would have been sitting outside the circle of light. "So he chloroforms her upstairs and then injects the sodium pentothal. Knocked out, he carries her down here, puts her in the chair and binds her to it. Then he sits here, and what? Interrogates her?"

"Something like that," Gesch answered.

"Why?"

"We don't know," Delmonico replied. "But her time of death was somewhere around 4:00 A.M. and she left a bar a little after 11:00 P.M. and we presume came right home."

"So he had her down here for a while, working her over," Wire surmised, shaking her head at the brutality of it.

"The biblical verses probably provide a clue on that," Mac suggested. "I've read the files. Is there anything not in the files we saw that provides insight on what these women did?"

"How do you know they did something?" Delmonico asked.

"I'm assuming based on the biblical verses. Reaping

what you sow. Taken literally, that suggests to me that they're being punished for something. What?"

"We've been through their lives," Gesch responded. "Nothing hits on them, at least yet."

"Is there any connection between the three of them?" Wire asked.

"We're probing that as we speak," Delmonico answered, "but nothing as of yet. They're all from different places, never went to any level of school together. As far as we know, they never crossed paths with each other."

For another hour, McRyan and Wire walked the house, looking in every room of the main level, checking every window and looking in all the closets. They next inspected the basement, which was simply a storage area.

"Thick cinder block," Wire noted. "You could scream down here and might not be heard upstairs, let alone outside."

Next was the second story. Wire searched Donahue's bedroom while Mac worked through her office. Wire searched her dresser and spent some time looking through her personal drawers, sifting through pictures and keepsakes but not finding anything probative.

At her desk, Mac looked through the file drawers, finding the typical items, bills, banking information, her mortgage and other papers about her house. There was a computer monitor on top of the desk but no computer tower, although there was a stand for one underneath. The FBI probably had it. In the center desk drawer were pens, paper clips, random photos and a series of business cards, one for an auto dealership, another for a roofing contractor, a series of business cards for various people and other random business cards and phone numbers written on sticky notes. To the left of her desk was a small bulletin board with flyers for events posted, a couple of pictures drawn by kids from her elementary school class and a hanging calendar with notes of events listed on various dates. Her father was a key political figure and Hannah was clearly interested in politics. Her office walls were adorned with campaign posters of candidates. She also had her college diploma from Cornell on a bookshelf, along with her high school diploma and a certificate for the American Honor Society for scholastic achievement in high school. Mac recognized it as he had one himself. All in all, standard stuff, nothing unusual or eye popping. Maybe when he looked at the other victims' lives in this fashion, something would emerge.

Wire stuck her head in the office, "Anything?"

"No, you?"

She shook her head as he followed her down the stairs and back into the living room where Gesch, Delmonico and Wente were sitting, reading through the case file and waiting.

It was time for first impressions.

"What are you thinking?" Mac asked Dara, as they both stood in the middle of the living room.

"Say I'm the killer. How do I get in the house?"

"No sign of forced entry," Mac said, looking at the forensic report. "The dead bolts were pretty new, no damage indicating they were jimmied in any way. No signs any of the windows were compromised. So how does he get in the house?"

"We had the same question," Gesch intoned. "We were thinking he perhaps grabbed her outside and forced her to bring him in."

Mac and Wire walked outside and into the backyard. There was a two-car garage detached from the house with a fifty-foot mostly exposed walk from the garage to the house. The backyard had one fairly large tree on its south side but there were no low-hanging branches, the tree having been well trimmed. There was a cement slab patio with four chairs and a small table leading to the two steps up to the back door. The landscaping around the house consisted of some small perennials, hostas and other small short plants and bushes. There was little if any cover, certainly not enough if you were to have to wait a significant amount of time for Donahue to come home. "If he took her out here, he's pretty exposed," Mac stated. "There are houses on both sides. Were the neighbors on both sides home that night?"

"They were. Nobody heard or saw anything, but it was dark when she arrived home; she'd been at a bar fairly late with friends," Delmonico reported. "That doesn't mean he didn't or couldn't have taken her out here."

"No, but I think it is unlikely," Wire replied.

"How about taking her in the garage?" Gesch inquired.

"That's an even worse problem, if you ask me," Mac answered, looking between the garage and house. "He'd have had to take her in the garage and then get her into the house. That would be more likely to be noticed than if, for example, he either took her in the garage or came up behind her when she was unlocking the back door. However, to do that he would have had to have been lying in wait out here and I don't see a good spot to do that."

"So you're thinking he was inside waiting for her?" Wire asked McRyan.

"It's an educated guess," Mac answered. "It makes the most sense. There is no security system for him to defeat. He just needed to get in the house and wait."

"So how did he get inside ahead of her?" Gesch asked.

"Maybe he had a key," Mac answered.

"We thought about that," Delmonico stated. "We didn't find one anywhere around the house."

"You wouldn't if he kept it," Wire stated. "Did you find a key holder perhaps? People stash one outside their house sometimes."

"That occurred to us as well but we never found one. We asked her family and friends and they weren't aware of one."

Mac crossed his arms and thought about it a little more. "Your profile on this guy says he's mission oriented, right?"

The FBI agents nodded.

"And we don't know what the mission is yet, because we don't know what ties these women together."

"Right," Gesch said.

"But as a mission-oriented killer, if that's what he is, he's a planner, right? On a mission you prepare. This killer is a schemer."

"Meaning?" Gesch asked.

"He hunted Hannah Donahue, stalked her and knew exactly when to strike, when she would be most vulnerable and he would be least vulnerable. He followed her for, I bet, at least two weeks before he took her. In those two weeks he watched her every move and somewhere along the line he found some way into the house."

"So what are you thinking, McRyan?" Delmonico asked.

"We need to go back through the last two weeks of her life, we need to reinterview all of her coworkers, friends, family, anyone she intersected with and see if anything pops."

"We've done all that already," Gesch answered skeptically. "We've had agents meet with these people. We used Wente's local detectives here in Dover. Nothing hit and we," he pointed to Delmonico, "I don't know that we can spend the time on that; we have to run this thing."

"I know you don't, and I don't think you should. Wire and I should," Mac answered.

"We'll run a parallel investigation," Dara added. "We'll go back through the case and work it backwards, while you're continuing to go forward."

"Exactly," Mac jumped back in. "Look, Agent Gesch, this is what we excel at. I think he had a key to get in. He got it somewhere in the last couple of weeks, I'd even bet in the last few days before she was killed. Somebody knows something, they may not even know they know it, but they do. Maybe the right person hasn't been talked to yet. Maybe they haven't been asked the right question yet. Maybe we don't even know the right question to ask—yet."

Gesch, Delmonico and Wente were about to object. Mac held his hands up, "I don't mean to suggest people weren't doing their jobs. They were. Everyone is trying to find this guy. And maybe we'll fail too. However, I think Dara and I are looking at asking some different questions. Maybe we'll get lucky. Sometimes when you go back a second time you stumble onto something that was missed the first time around."

Gesch looked to Delmonico, who nodded and then looked over to Detective Wente, who asked: "So what do you need?"

∼

It was time to start again.

Hannah Donahue was punished for her sins, just like the others. Having done it, he got away, laid low for a few days and now he felt it was safe for him to come out again and start scouting. With three down, he could actually see the finish line now. Once the final blow was delivered and his mission was complete, he would once again disappear.

His next target was prospering greatly, making a name for herself, a rising star and someone that people recognized. That made her both a more intriguing, and in many ways, a more dangerous target for him.

She pulled out from her parking garage in her little sports car and raced down the street, clearly happy in the success she was experiencing, a star on the rise.

He dropped the gear shift for the pickup truck, fell in three vehicles behind and followed, his wrist draped casually over the steering wheel.

The hunt always started this way, just loosely following his target around from a safe distance, looking to get a feel for the rhythm of her life. What time did she get up in the morning, what was her daily schedule, who did she see, did she have a significant other to complicate matters, were there any regular places she went at specifically scheduled times and, most importantly, was she on guard.

In doing all this he'd find the ideal time and place.

He would plan it down to every last detail.

6
"THERE ARE SOME ISSUES MEN ARE NOT EQUIPPED TO HANDLE."

So far, they were getting nowhere.

Mac eighty-sixed another Styrofoam coffee cup into the wastebasket and just stared at it, on top of three others he put in the garbage. There had been two days of Styrofoam coffee cups, stale donuts and fast food to go along with countless interviews and stacks of documents. So far, there was nothing to show for their efforts.

The plan was to go back through, as best they could, every stop of Hannah Donahue's life for the last two weeks. In fact, after they started they went back as far as eighteen days as Donahue had been out of town for five days over a school break and the second victim was killed in the middle of her time away. So from the day Hannah Donahue returned to Dover, they'd started piecing together every component of her life.

On three whiteboards in a conference room at the Dover Police Department, every minute detail of her life that could be accounted for was logged and noted. For two days Mac and Wire, with the occasional assistance of Detective Wente, methodically worked their way through Hannah Donahue's life.

The first step had been to go to the family home outside of Wilmington, an hour to the north of Dover, to meet with her family. Delaware, and the city of Wilmington in particular, was a financial center for the world because of the state's finance and banking laws. It was an oddity that Mac first learned of in law school when he took business organizations and learned of the whole line of Delaware law that applied to business transactions. It was why so many corporations were incorporated in Delaware, to take advantage of the Delaware law.

William Donahue made his fortune in the banking industry that was the life blood of Wilmington. Over the years his banking work necessitated spending many hours in Washington, working to massage the nation's finance and tax laws. It gave him access to the nation's power brokers which craved his dollars and robust connections to more of it. That access, that money, that power was why Mac and Wire were here.

"I see my threat got through to the president," Donahue said non-boastfully. He'd lost his daughter. He was devastated and simply wanted some closure now and would push any lever available to get it.

"The president and Judge Dixon thought we might be able to help, sir," Mac answered neutrally. "We're very sorry for your loss."

"Question is, Mr. Donahue," Wire asked, "can you help us?"

As bombastic and demanding as he was on television, he was as docile when interviewed. He simply didn't know anything helpful.

"I loved my daughter. I talked to her all the time, texted

with her, e-mailed her, and there was nothing in any of those conversations that led me to believe she was worried about her safety in any way. She said nothing," he muttered, rubbing his hands over his face. "What I should have done is kept her closer to home."

"How is it she ended up in Dover?" Wire asked.

Barbara Donahue answered, "Hannah was fiercely independent. She wanted her own life. Her brothers went into Bill's business and at first she was going to as well. Then halfway through college, she changed her mind and decided she wanted to give back. She thought she should pay forward for the fortunate and privileged life she had growing up. It was as if one summer she grew up and got serious about life. She loved children, so she went into teaching."

"She decided she wanted to blaze her own trail," Mr. Donahue added. "She wanted her own life. In all honesty, I admired her for it. It would have been easy to just tag along with the family business, but she decided on something else. The only thing she let me help with was a contribution to the down payment on that house and some money for her car."

The Donahues were devastated but simply couldn't provide any more help, nor could her brothers, who'd had little contact with her in recent weeks. "It wasn't that we weren't close," Adam Donahue stated, "it's just that we were busy with our lives, with our families, with our work, that we didn't talk to Hannah a lot, other than an occasional e-mail, text or phone call. I hadn't been down to Dover in three months. You know how it is."

Mac did. He was close with his three sisters, yet he didn't see them that often. Everyone was busy with their lives and with cell phones and computers it was easy to stay in touch without actually physically getting in touch.

"So are you making any progress?" Mrs. Donahue asked Mac, as she poured him a cup of coffee to go from the kitchen.

"We're trying, ma'am, but we've really just started," Mac answered. "The two of us have just gotten into the case. I'll let you know if anything pops and I'll call in two days just to let you know how it is going." As he was leaving the kitchen, he stopped to ask one last question. "Mrs. Donahue, I have three sisters. I know for a fact that they always talked to my mom about things that they'd never, in a million years, talk to my dad about."

Mrs. Donahue smiled, a wan yet knowing smile, "There are some issues men are not equipped to handle."

"So you know the killer left a message on the wall, right?"

"Yes, a biblical verse about reaping what you sow."

"That's right. This killer looks to be something we call a mission-oriented killer. He's viewing killing these women as fulfilling some mission and in his case to kill these women, including Hannah, for their sins, or at least that's what the messages he leaves seem to convey." Mac took a sip of his coffee and softened his voice. "This is a really hard question to ask, but did she have any problems that she told just you about? A secret that she wouldn't want to get out and have others know about?"

Mrs. Donahue shook her head, "Nothing I can think of, Mr. McRyan. She was a big party girl back in college, especially her first two or three years, like every kid did and does when they go away to college. But she never had any trouble with the police at school or got into any accidents, at least that I'm aware of. She was just a really *really* good kid," she answered and started to weep.

"I'm sorry, ma'am, I had to ask that question."

"I know," she answered quietly, sniffling. "I know."

Mac and Wire next went back down to Dover and to the elementary school where Hannah taught. Despite talking to every teacher, administrator and worker in the building, they learned little beyond what was already in the investigation's files. She was universally liked by teachers, administrators, students and parents. "She was a lovely young girl," the principal stated. "She never had a problem with anyone, just a stellar, wonderful teacher who adored her students."

"As you know," Wire stated, "the killer left a biblical message about reaping what you sow. We think he's punishing these women for some reason. Can you think of any reason someone would want to punish Hannah?"

The principal shook his head vigorously, "I can't for the life of me think of why anyone would want to kill Hannah. Not one reason."

"I noticed you have pretty robust security around the school?" Mac asked.

The principal nodded, "After Sandy Hook, we increased our security school district wide. Dover is a nice safe town and you wouldn't think we could ever have a school shooting, but I bet they thought the same up in Connecticut."

Wire spoke to the school's head of security, his assistant as well as the local police officer assigned to the school. None of them noticed anything unusual around the school in the days leading up to Donahue's murder. "The teacher's have their own parking lot that we have a camera on and we walk it all the time during the day. You're free to watch the tapes, but I don't think you'll find anything." Dover detectives and the bureau had been through the tapes. Other than the occasional kid chasing down a stray red gym ball, nobody had approached the vehicles other than school personnel.

At the end of the school day, Mac and Wire sat in small chairs at a table in a classroom and talked to Hannah's two closest teaching friends, Lana Meister and Nicole Moore.

"She never seemed worried about a thing," Meister said. "She was over to my house and had dinner with my husband and me just a week ago. She was fine, normal, nothing seemed unusual. As to your question, Ms. Wire, if there was something in her past, she never confided in me about it."

Wire went through the task of walking Meister through the last eighteen days and her interactions with Donahue. Nothing popped.

"We were close here at school and maybe occasionally went out for a drink, but I didn't do anything with her in the last couple of weeks outside of school."

"How about you, Ms. Moore," Mac asked. "Was there anything unusual that you recall happening in the last couple of weeks?"

"I can't think of anything."

Mac walked through the last eighteen days with Moore.

"The last time she and I really talked was when we went out for drinks a week ago, last Friday."

Mac looked at his notes, "She went out for drinks?"

"Yeah, she and I went after school. Then she had another friend join us, her name was Wendy, I think. An old friend of hers who'd just happened to come into town for a few hours. I think she worked for some international bank up in Wilmington or was in Wilmington for some meetings and lives somewhere else, something like that."

"Her name was Wendy?" Mac asked. There'd been no record of her. "Do you recall her last name?"

"Jones, Jonas, something like that. They were good friends and from what I could tell, they hadn't seen each other in a really long time. I had my drink and left them to catch up with each other. I figured I ... could ..." Moore's eyes started to tear up and she put her hand to her mouth. "I figured I'd just get a drink with Hannah another time, you know? And now ... there won't ever be another time." She broke down, hugging Meister.

Mac looked to Wire, "We should track down this Wendy. I don't think anyone has spoken with her."

Wire shrugged, "We should, although if she was just in town for a few hours, what would she know?"

On Saturday, they worked her neighborhood, talking to her neighbors. Donahue was young for her neighborhood, in her mid-twenties whereas most the neighbors were older, with families. Originally, some said there was concern when Hannah first moved in that, given her age, her house would be a party house. But as with her friends and everyone at her school, people loved Donahue. She was a great neighbor. There were never any problems and nobody recalled seeing any unusual vehicles or people around the neighborhood.

The last people they talked to were Donahue's immediate neighbors. To the north was an older couple of empty nesters who talked with Donahue frequently.

"I helped her from time to time," Mr. Empty Nester said. "She would have a problem that needed fixing in the house and she'd come and ask questions. She was funny."

"Funny how?" Wire asked.

"She always liked to try to fix something herself first. She'd get in way over her head and get stuck and then come and find me. My favorite was two months ago when she decided to put a toilet in herself."

Mrs. Empty Nester nodded and laughed, a sad laugh, "I told Earl he needed to stay around that day because Hannah was going to get herself in trouble again."

"And she did," Earl answered with a wistful smile. "Sure nuff, about 3:30 in the afternoon that little girl came over and knocked on the door, all frazzled and tearing up. She had her water off, the toilet out and it was a disaster."

"I've been there, Earl," Mac replied knowingly. "I'm rehabbing a townhouse right now. Plumbing's the worst thing I have to work on, especially in an older home. You can do everything right and it still won't work."

"Exactly right, young man," Earl Empty Nester replied. "Hannah? She did okay pulling everything apart but, of course, that's the easy part. The poor thing couldn't figure out how to re-hook everything back up. She had water dripping, she was looking at water damage, and if she had to call a plumber, she was probably out some big bucks."

"Earl's good with plumbing," Mrs. Empty Nester added.

"So I went over and took a look," Earl shook his head. "That little lady had a mess on her hands for sure, but I figured out the problem pretty quick. We made a run to the hardware store and within a couple of hours we had her all set to go." Mr. Empty Nester got quiet. "I'm sure going to miss doing those kinds of things for her."

The neighbors to the south were a young family named the Burroughs. There were four sons, all under the age of nine.

"My goodness, you have your hands full," Wire said to Mrs. Burroughs in her living room, standing amongst four laundry baskets of folded clothes.

"I'm used to it, Agent Wire," the mother of four replied.

"It is what it is. But you asked about the night that Hannah was ... killed ... and we just didn't notice anything. It was chaos around here until 9:30 P.M. or so, trying to get this crew through their baths, into bed, stories read and then finally to sleep. I can tell you that about fifteen minutes after these guys were asleep, my husband and I were in bed, watching television and would have been asleep by 10:00, 10:30 at the latest. Trust me; it was a very normal night around here."

"Do you recall seeing Hannah get home that night at all?" Mac asked.

"No I don't, but other than talking to her out in the yard on occasion, maybe borrowing from each other the occasional egg or cup of milk, we didn't talk a lot. I mean, our life was different from hers so there wasn't a ton in common. But she was a really nice girl, a very nice neighbor."

Mr. Burroughs came in the house and was of no more help. "I wish I could help you, I really do, but the night she was killed I was literally asleep five minutes after I finished the story for the boys."

Neither of the Burroughs noticed anything unusual in the days leading up to Hannah Donahue's murder.

Mac and Wire sat dejectedly on the steps for Donahue's house, the yellow crime scene tape flapping in the light breeze, the sun beginning its decline in the west. Three marathon days of working the case and they had nothing to show for it.

"Does it seem odd to you," Wire mused, "that nobody in this neighborhood recalls seeing anything unusual in the last two weeks? I mean, nothing at all? Not an unusual vehicle? No suspicious people? How is that possible?"

"Neighborhood full of busy people," Mac replied with a

yawn. "People with families who are so wrapped up in their own lives they don't notice anyone else's."

"I thought we'd have found something," Wire moaned. "We got nothin' and I have a message from the Judge, who apparently got a call from Donahue. I'm sure he was hoping for progress."

"I am starting to see why the FBI has nothing on this guy. He leaves nothing. We've talked to a lot of people and have zip. We've gone through her financials, e-mails, phone records, everything, and there's nothing that pops out or gives me even a tiny thread to pull."

Mac was not accustomed to failure. He closed cases. That was his history. He'd never gone three days on an investigation without *any* breaks, without making *some* progress, without some *new* development or lead to follow. Wire yawned and he could tell she was getting worn down.

"Tell you what," Mac suggested. "Two nights in the hotel is enough. Let's head back to DC, let the case percolate for a day in our minds and go from there."

"Do you have a plan from here?" Wire asked.

"Not right now," Mac answered as he pushed himself up off the steps. "In twenty-four hours, I will."

He pulled into the garage a little past sun down and found Sally relaxing in a deck chair on the back patio of the townhouse, a bottle of red open and two citronella candles burning to keep the bugs away. Mac walked up, kissed her and poured himself a glass of wine. He plopped himself down into the chair next to her, took a long sip of the Cabernet and shook his head in disgust.

"That bad, huh?"

"Don't ask," Mac grumbled, his frustration evident. "Please don't ask. I'll talk about anything *but* the case."

Talk they did, for an hour. She could always ease his

mind and sometimes he liked to just listen to her talk and it didn't really matter about what, something about her voice would soothe him. An hour later she walked inside and left him sitting on the patio to finish the last of the Cabernet. He closed his eyes, relaxed in his chair and listened to the hum of the neighborhood, the crickets, the light breeze through the leaves of the trees, the murmur of traffic in the distance. Fifteen minutes later he heard a window open above his head. He opened his eyes, looked up and saw Sally looking down from the master bathroom. "Come on up. Bring another bottle of wine."

Mac did as ordered, selecting another Cabernet from the wine fridge and making his way upstairs to find Sally waiting in the bathroom. She was in their large whirlpool tub, with candles arranged around the room. "Join me and relax. The warm water feels good."

They spent a lazy Sunday morning lounging around the townhouse. Sally had to watch the morning political shows and make a variety of phone calls. While she did, Mac took a long run to get a good lather going and to clear his mind. He ran from his home in Georgetown down to the Capitol and back, running along both sides of the Mall, past the reflecting pool and the Lincoln Memorial on his way back. After his run, he made waffles and they read the Sunday newspapers while sipping coffee and relaxing in the living room.

In the afternoon, they took a long walk down to the Georgetown Waterfront Park and relaxed in the sun and watched the boat traffic along the river. Mac had his boat garaged back in Minnesota. He was giving some thought to driving it out and finding a boat slip. *The Simon Says*, a thirty-foot boat that had once been his dad's, could easily handle the waters of the Potomac and Chesapeake Bay.

On their way back, they stopped in two pubs for a beer and finished by dining at a small Italian place they'd discovered four blocks from their townhouse.

At 7:30 P.M., Mac trudged up to the attic and started looking at the case again, hoping that twenty-four hours away would help clear his mind. He sat in the swivel chair, leaned back, put his hands behind his head and soaked in the whiteboard, focusing on Hannah Donahue because they'd worked her murder so hard. Sometimes when he sat before the case like this it would speak to him in some way. He would see a fact, a piece of evidence, a pattern that made all the pieces fit. After a while of looking at the board, he came to the conclusion that he needed more information on all of the victims. He needed to look at all of their cases with the same intensity they'd looked into Donahue's. If they did that, perhaps a clearer picture would emerge.

A little after 9:00 P.M., Wire called, "Any thoughts?"

"I'm looking at the whiteboard right now. It's not talking to me—yet."

"Any thoughts on a next step?"

"Yeah, pack a bag. We're going to Harrisburg."

"The first victim?"

"Yes," Mac answered. "Our killer is obviously very good at covering his tracks. I'm thinking we take another look at victim number one. He wasn't as experienced then. Maybe he left a bread crumb or two behind just waiting to be found."

"And if that doesn't work?"

"Then we go to Salisbury and look into Janelle Wyland."

"So we're going over all of the crime scenes then."

"Right. The quick find isn't there so we need good old-fashioned police work."

They agreed Wire would drive over for breakfast in the morning and then they'd head out for Harrisburg.

A little after ten, he turned off the lights in the attic and went down to the bedroom. As was often the case, Sally was sitting in bed with reading glasses on, engrossed in work papers and highlighting various passages, starting her work week already. After engaging in his nightly mechanics, Mac crawled into bed and turned on the television to watch SportsCenter.

At 10:30, Sally leaned over and kissed him, "I love you."

"I love you too."

"That was a really good day," she said, holding his left hand. "We need more of those."

"I agree, something for us to work on," he answered, leaning over and kissing her back lightly. "Now get some sleep." She worked long hours at the White House and she could never get enough rest.

Mac, more of a night owl and not someone who needed lots of sleep, lay back against the pillow and watched the scores roll across the screen with the sound down low. At some point, he faded off.

At first, he thought he was dreaming with the buzzing he was hearing. Then by cop instinct he reached for the nightstand and his phone.

It was 3:20 A.M.

Nothing ever good happens at 3:20 A.M., he thought. "Hello."

"Is this Agent McRyan?" a woman's voice asked.

"Yes."

"This is Wendy Jonas."

7
"IT'S LIKE YOU'RE TOO COOL FOR SCHOOL."

Ding-dong ... ding-dong ...
Dara heard the distant sound of the door bell ringing as she shifted her body under the comforter but she did not awaken and fell back to sleep.

Ding-dong ...

Her eyes fluttered. It wasn't a dream.

Ding Dong, Ding Dong, Ding Dong. Three straight pushes in succession, there was definitely urgency to the ringing.

She opened her eyes and looked at the clock on the side of her bed, 4:45 A.M. Only emergencies lead to someone ringing your door at 4:45 A.M.

Thump! Thump! Thump!

It must be an emergency if they'd transitioned to pounding on the door.

"Coming!" she grumbled as she threw her legs over the side of the bed and pulled on a pair of sweatpants and double-timed it down the steps and to the front door.

Thump! ... Thump! ...

She looked through the eyehole and quickly pulled the

door open, stopping McRyan in mid-pound. "Mac, what the hell?"

"First off, how is it that a security specialist doesn't have a security system?"

"Brand new place, I haven't gotten around to it yet. Why are *you* here?"

"Get ready, we have to get back up to Dover," Mac exclaimed excitedly as he walked inside carrying two tall gas station coffees. "Here, this one has the hazelnut," he said, extending one of the coffees.

"Ah, thanks, I think," she replied, taking the coffee and downing a long sip as she closed the front door. "Dover? Why Dover?" she asked, rubbing her eyes, still not completely awake. "I thought you had us going to Harrisburg next."

"We might have a break," he answered and then stared at her impatiently.

"What?"

"Don't just stand there, get dressed! *Chop! Chop!*"

"Okay, okay, but Jesus, what's the break?" she asked as she hustled up the steps to her bedroom. Mac waited downstairs, loitering in the entryway. She looked back down, "Hey, dumbass, come up here and stand outside my bedroom door at least and tell me what you got."

Mac started walking up the steps and bellowed, "Remember the name Wendy Jonas?"

"Jonas, Jonas ... Yeah, friend of Donahue's who showed up when Hannah and that teacher friend of hers were having drinks, right?" Wire answered from the bedroom.

"Exactly. Turns out she lives in Hong Kong and works for Asia Pacific Banking Worldwide, you know APBW?"

"I've seen the commercials, so?"

"Anyway, she was in Wilmington for a day for some

meetings and managed to sneak away to come down to Dover to see Donahue. After Nicole Moore left them, Jonas said they had a couple of more drinks, got caught up and when they were saying good-bye in the parking lot, Hannah Donahue realized she'd locked her keys in her car."

"So?"

"*Soooo*," Mac answered, taking a sip of his coffee. "Jonas says Hannah reached way under the driver's side door to the car and pulled out ..."

"A key holder," Wire said, sticking her head out of her bedroom door. "Are you serious?"

"I wouldn't joke about this. Jonas drove Hannah back to her house where she got her backup set of car keys, and then drove Hannah back to the bar so she could fetch her car."

"That's how he got in, Mac," Dara stated. "It has to be. He was watching and then found a time to get that house key. So did he make a copy or just take it?"

"Well, we need to get up there and see if the key is still there."

"And if it is?"

"Well that creates all kinds of potential new investigative avenues, now, doesn't it?" Mac said with hope. "So finish getting ready, will ya?"

"Okay, okay, okay. Five minutes," Dara answered, rushing back into her bedroom.

Just before 7:00 A.M., Mac turned into the alley behind Hannah Donahue's house and pulled up next to the detached garage. Dover Detective Wente and two techs from the county crime scene unit were awaiting their arrival. Everyone slid on blue rubber gloves. Inside the garage was Donahue's bright yellow Audi A6. The detective opened the garage and a crime scene tech took her camera and slid under the driver's side of the car. "I see the key holder," she said, snapping two photos in the cramped space. She started reaching for it.

"Wait!" Mac exclaimed, holding his arms out.

"What?" the tech asked.

"Let's get the car down to the county crime lab. If he left a print on the key, the holder or the car, we need to get it. It's too risky here. Let's play it safe and get it down to your lab."

An hour later, they were in the Kent County Crime Lab garage with the car safely up on a lift. A tech took pictures and then carefully removed the key holder, which was tucked under the fiberglass molding of the car and attached to an exposed piece of metal on the frame. More pictures were taken and a tech began dusting for prints. Another tech opened the key holder and there was a key inside. The tech held the key under a swing-arm magnifying glass.

"We're thinking a duplicate was made," Dara speculated. "What do you think?" she asked the tech.

The tech looked closely. "I think you're right, Agent Wire. This key was duplicated and recently. There are still some small minute shavings in the grooves."

"How about prints?" Mac asked, looking back to the forensic tech dusting for prints on the under carriage of the car. "I've got prints," he answered, inspecting them closely. "However, it looks like only one set."

"Which are probably Donahue's," Wire sighed.

"Maybe we'll do better on the key or key holder." The tech dusted the key and key holder. "Shoot. Nothing."

"Nothing?" Mac asked with his arms folded.

"Wiped clean, I'd say," the tech answered. "You can tell it was duplicated, the marks are there with some small shavings, but there are no prints on the key or case, so if your guy touched this thing, he wore gloves or wiped it down before he put it back."

Wire looked to Mac dejected, the elation of the last four hours draining quickly from her face. "I got excited there for a minute."

"Don't give up so easy," Mac answered evenly. "I'm not surprised. Our guy is *real* careful. There's a reason we don't have *any* forensic evidence on him. Leaving prints behind was a long shot. You know what I'm interested in figuring out, though?"

"What?"

"From the time Hannah Donahue used the key to get back into her house until her death creates a four-day window of time in which our killer grabbed it and duplicated it. So when and *where* did he do that?"

At the Dover Police Department and over a lunch of sandwiches and chips, Mac and Wire quickly set about once again reviewing the last four days of Donahue's life. On the whiteboard, from the Friday night of drinks until the Monday night she was murdered, Mac and Wire went through every detail of her life.

"Assuming Friday night, after Jonas takes her back to the bar and Hannah drives home, that probably is it for the day, don't you think?" Wire asked.

"I think so. That's when he discovers the existence of the key, that's where we start from," Mac answered. "He could have, I suppose, gotten into her garage and stole the key that night, but that's kind of risky. I'm banking that's not when he did it, and if he did? Well, then we're screwed."

Saturday was not a work day. Hannah had gone to hot yoga for an hour session early Saturday afternoon. Her credit card records showed that after yoga she stopped at a coffee shop for a large iced coffee and then stopped at a local clothing store where she purchased a blouse and a pair of designer jeans. There was no further financial activity on the credit card. Her cell phone records showed four calls on Saturday, none after 6:30 P.M. It appeared that she low-keyed it and stayed home on Saturday night, as she rented the movie *Safe Haven* on her home pay-per-view.

On Sunday, she went to yoga again and once again grabbed a post-session iced coffee. "He could have grabbed the key then," Wire speculated.

The yoga studio was located in a new strip mall which had video surveillance of the parking lot. On both Saturday and Sunday, Donahue arrived a few minutes before her noon class, parking in the second row in front of the studio both days. Probably part of a pattern as people tended to park in the same places, go to the same places, it was human nature, all routine.

"The bright yellow makes it easy to see her car," Wire noted.

On neither Saturday nor early Sunday did anyone approach the driver's side of Donahue's car. Her credit card records revealed that the better chance came later on Sunday. "Her credit card shows the purchase of a single ticket for *Iron Man 3* for the matinee on Sunday," Mac stated.

Wire flipped through her notes. "Yeah, she went with a friend of hers we talked to last week. A movie and then they went for an early dinner and drinks."

Mac searched the movie times at the theatre. "She bought the ticket at 2:44 P.M. and the movie started at 3:00. With previews running twenty minutes, plus the movie running over two hours, she doesn't get out of the theatre until ..."

"Close to six," Wire finished.

The movie theatre was part of a large shopping mall

near the Dover International Speedway. The mall itself had a large sprawling parking lot, needed, at least in part, to service the fourteen movie screens. The Dover detective took them to the mall's security office. The mall had surveillance cameras pointed out to the surrounding parking lots although the coverage was less than stellar. The surveillance system recorded in grainy black and white. A member of the security team pulled up the surveillance video for eight days ago, "Sunday, right?" he asked.

"That's right," Mac answered. "Let's start around 2:15 P.M. I know it's black and white, but we'll be looking for a bright yellow Audi A6."

The security technician started bringing up video for that day. "Sundays are busy days here at the mall, particularly at the movie theatre. That parking area is likely to be full." The tech had three monitors and he ran a replay for the cameras aimed at the common parking areas for the movie theatre. It took them an hour of scrolling through the video replay and a couple of false alarms before they found her. "I think that's her," Wire said, pointing to the left monitor. "Mac, what do you think?"

The tech rolled the tape back and then forward again. A light-colored Audi A6 pulled into the parking lot, about twenty parking slots out from the building. The car looked right and the woman looked like Hannah Donahue. "That's her," Mac answered. Then to the tech he said, "Let it roll."

It took eleven minutes of video time. A man came walking from the left, in a dark hooded sweatshirt and what looked like the bill of a baseball cap sticking out from the hood. "Was it warm eight days ago?"

"It wasn't sweatshirt and hood weather, if that's what you're asking," the tech replied. "Everyone else we see on the video is in shorts and short shirt sleeves."

The hooded man walked across the aisle and to the driver side of Donahue's car. The man took a quick look around and then disappeared down below the car. A few seconds later, the man was back up and walked back the direction he came from.

"That's our guy," Mac said, a small air of satisfaction in his voice. Perhaps they had finally caught a break. "We've got a look at you now."

"Not a great one though. Can we follow him?" Wire asked, her voice sounding calm, but she was a little amped.

The tech followed the man to the next camera. It was difficult to follow him as he walked farther out in the distance of the parking lot. It looked as if the man jumped into a white sedan and pulled away.

"Are there any cameras farther out?" Mac asked.

The tech shook his head. "No. I know they've talked about mounting cameras on the light poles but it's never happened." The man who took the key was so far in the distance at the far edge of the parking lot they couldn't make out the model of car, let alone a license plate. Mac started jotting down notes, which led to more questions. To Detective Wente, Mac asked, "Do you know if there are any traffic cameras in the immediate area?"

"I don't know that there are, but I'll try to find out."

The tech grimaced, "There are lots of ways out of this area. If he was smart, he'd avoid the monitored areas."

Mac nodded, "He is smart."

"So what is our time window here?" Wire asked. "He takes the key from the car at 2:56 P.M."

"To know our window, we need to know if our guy comes back. Run the tape."

The tech fast forwarded through the tape. "Stop it there," Wire ordered. It had been fifty minutes.

A man, not in a hooded sweatshirt, approached the Audi. He walked around the car, but then a woman appeared with him and it appeared they were simply looking at and discussing the car.

"It is a car that will draw some attention," Wire remarked.

"More importantly, the color also makes it very easy to tail from a long way back," Mac observed.

The tech started the video again. There was little activity for another forty-five minutes until the hooded sweatshirt man returned, this time coming from the right. He quickly ducked down behind the driver's side of the car. A few seconds later, he popped up and walked back to the right. The time in the upper right corner of the surveillance video said 5:03 P.M. The tech checked the next camera to the right. Again, they were able to track the man back to the white sedan, again parked far away from the mall, towards the far outer reaches of the parking lot. Other than a white sedan that looked like it may have been a Toyota, Honda or Hyundai, they could get no more.

"He takes the key at 2:56 and he's back at 5:03. So he left, got a key made, and was back basically within two hours," Mac noted as he took out his phone.

"What are you doing?" Wire asked.

"Web search for hardware stores in the area. I doubt he had the tools to make a key in that car. If he did, he would have been back sooner."

"He went and got a key made."

"Yes, and where else do you get keys made quickly but hardware stores? My search comes up with seven possible, with three very nearby." To Wente, Mac said, "We need pictures made of this guy. You can't tell much about him but it might be enough to spark a memory, and we need some men to help us go around to these stores."

"I'm on it," Wente said, cell phone out.

In the late afternoon, Mac and Wire started their canvas of the three hardware stores closest to the mall. They struck out at the first two. Detective Wente corralled another detective to take the other four stores and they struck out at the first two as well. The third was J.J. Atlantic Hardware out on Forest Avenue. Mac and Wire walked up to the front desk to a woman holding a clipboard, "Can you point me to the store manager?" Mac asked.

"That's me, honey, Ginny White, what can I do for you?"

Mac and Wire identified themselves.

"Feds, huh? You sure don't look like Feds."

"What do Feds look like usually?" Dara asked.

"You know, dark suits, ties, sunglasses, self-important yet boring. You two have the sunglasses, sure, but you're wearing jeans and dressed all casual. It's like you're too cool for school."

"Well, that's because we are, plus, we're special and helping on a specific investigation," Mac answered, smiling. "So we don't have to wear the federal uniform."

"Is it about that Donahue girl and that Reaper killer?"

Mac nodded and then got down to business. "Ginny, tell me, do you know if you cut any keys between 3:00 P.M. and 5:00 P.M. a week ago Sunday?"

"Well let's go take a look," the manager answered, waving them back to her cramped office in the back. She sat down at her computer and maneuvered her mouse around. "Take a seat," she offered, which they both did. "You said between 3:00 and 5:00 P.M.?"

"That's right," Mac answered.

"As I look through our sales, we cut nine keys that day

and … we cut two between 3:00 and 5:00 P.M."

"What were the times?" Mac asked.

"One was rung up at 3:42 P.M. and the other was at 4:48 P.M."

Mac looked to Wire, "Has to be the 3:42 one, right?"

Dara nodded, looking to the security monitor in the back corner that was split with four cameras. "Two questions, Ginny. Do any of the cameras focus on the area where keys are cut?"

Ginny pointed to the upper right corner of the screen, "That one is focused on the back hallway for the store where we have the counter where people get keys cut. What's the second?"

"How far back do you keep your surveillance footage?"

Ginny smiled, "One month," she answered as she made some more mouse clicks on her computer. She pulled up the surveillance footage of the back hallway of the store for eight days ago. She forwarded to 3:10 P.M. and let it run. Mac and Wire walked around behind her desk and looked over White's shoulder. At 3:18, a man with a hooded sweatshirt approached the back counter.

"There he is," Mac exclaimed. "That's our guy."

"He's a big guy," Ginny noted. "Given the height of that counter, I'd say he's 6'3", at least."

"And big, thick and muscular," Wire noted, looking at the man in a light-color hooded sweatshirt, baseball cap and wearing sunglasses with a beard. He was well disguised.

"You can see it in his shoulders, he's wired," Mac observed, which drew a look from Dara. "No pun intended, partner. He's just kind of twitchy and fidgety."

"Because he's on a clock," Dara remarked. "He has to get back in time. He probably doesn't know which movie she went to."

"God damnit though, he's keeping his head down or looking straight ahead or turning his back to the camera," Mac complained. "He knows the camera is there and he's being careful."

"It's no secret it's there," Ginny pointed out. "The black ball is hanging from the ceiling and is easy to see and intentionally so. We want people to think twice."

It took ten minutes to cut the key. The hooded man paid with cash. He turned toward the camera but with his head tilted down so that you could only make out the bottom of his bearded face beneath his baseball cap and sunglasses. He walked out of view.

"Just past the camera, there's a back door," Ginny reported. She pulled up the other store cameras for that same time period but they were unable to get another look at the man. They had Ginny save the video footage and e-mail it to Detective Wente. Wire was on the phone with him, saying they'd meet him back at the police station. Ginny also took a screen shot of their best look at the man. She e-mailed it to Mac's and Wire's phones. As they walked out of the store, they were both looking at their phones.

"It isn't much," Wire noted.

"No, but it's a start," Mac answered enthusiastically, now with some momentum for the first time on the case. "Now we got an idea of this guy. Somebody has seen this guy," Mac said optimistically as he started typing on his phone, sending the screen shot to Gesch and Delmonico via an e-mail. Then he dialed Special Agent Gesch, who picked up right away. "Gesch. I'm sending you and Delmonico a picture."

"Of what?"

"The Reaper."

8
"IT'S JUST A PIECE BUT ALL THE PIECES MATTER."

The first stop after identifying the Reaper was William Donahue's office in Wilmington. While he could generally care less about politics, Mac did care about Sally and making her life easier. A placated, even if only temporarily, William Donahue was one less thing she, and the White House, would have to worry about. Donahue expressed appreciation for the personal update.

"Find him, find that man," he said to them.

"We're working on it, sir," Wire answered.

"We'll find him," Mac added, sounding confident, not sure if it was the adrenaline from their discovery or actual confidence talking.

Now they were on a *The Fast and the Furious* like beeline on Interstate 95 back to Washington, DC, and the FBI Washington Field Office, getting constant phone and text updates from Delmonico while they made the frantic drive back. Delaware and Maryland State Police were in the loop that a black BMW X5 would be flying south on the interstate sporting a flashing gumball on its dashboard and to let it go.

That allowed a typical two-hour drive to be reduced to seventy-five minutes.

While Wente and the rest of the Dover police were out in the field with the Reaper photograph, Gesch distributed the picture to the other two cities and their Reaper Task Force leaders. As Mac and Wire entered a conference room, Gesch and Delmonico were preparing a conference call with FBI Director Mitchell.

"Mac and Wire, great work," Gesch said, greeting them with handshakes.

"We haven't found him yet," Mac cautioned.

"I know, I know," Gesch answered excitedly. "But damn if our first break on this thing doesn't have me at least just a little hopeful."

The call started, "Director Mitchell, we have these photos out in the field already to the three jurisdictions in our task force. I am recommending we get this photo to the media, along with a press conference, either tonight or first thing in the morning."

"Mac," Director Mitchell asked, "Agent Gesch has given me some background on how you found this man, but can you recap how exactly you found this man and this picture of him?"

McRyan and Wire took five minutes and walked the director through their identification.

"Mac, are you confident that this man is the killer we are looking for?"

"Yes sir," Mac answered. "We have him taking the key from Donahue's car and returning it and we have him making the copy. He's our killer."

"The problem is," Wire added, "that we don't have the greatest look at him."

"But it's a start," Mac rejoined. "It's enough that someone *could* possibly recognize him. At least that's the hope. We need to get this picture everywhere we can and see if anything pops."

"When?" the director asked the group. "Do we do it now or first thing in the morning?"

"Sir, if I might," Mac answered. "As anxious as I am to act right now, right this very minute, I think the morning would be better."

"Why?"

"This part of the country is going to sleep or is asleep right now. We won't get the maximum exposure and viewing of the photo for at least another ten to twelve hours, once everyone is up. In those hours, if our killer is watching …"

"He'll get a head start on going into hiding."

"That's what I'm thinking."

Director Mitchell made the call. "Gesch and I will run the press conference in the morning. Let's go at 9:00 A.M."

The conference call ended.

It had been a long day and Mac yawned, as did Wire. "Dara, you have a bag of extra clothes with you, right?"

"Yeah."

"Why don't you sleep at my place tonight," Mac suggested. Gesch and Delmonico's eyebrows rose in unison at the suggestion, which Mac quickly squashed. "*Relax*. Sally is there. Dara can have the guest room."

Mac called ahead and when he and Dara burst through the back door of the townhouse, Sally had a large oven-baked pepperoni and sausage pizza and two ice cold beers waiting for them. The three of them sat around the island, Mac and

Dara devouring the pizza and giving Sally a rundown on the case.

"And Donahue was good?" Sally asked, always looking for or trying to prevent the next political fire.

"Well, as good as he could be having lost his daughter," Mac answered, devouring a slice of the pizza. "The great man is pretty wrecked."

"I think he appreciated the personal touch though. Mac was good when he sat down with him, just the right tone," Wire added, wiping away some pizza sauce from her cheek with a napkin. "That was good work, partner."

"Yes it was, honey," Sally added with a smile, giving him a little kiss. "I'm going to bed. Dara, the guest room is all ready for you. There are towels and toiletries in the bathroom down the hall. Use whatever you need."

Wire and Mac had another beer, talked and unwound for another half hour and then, finally and fully exhausted, went to bed around 12:30.

As always, Sally was up and out of the house early, aiming to be at the White House by 7:00 A.M. every day.

Mac was someone who generally operated fine on four to five hours of sleep, some sort of genetic quirk. That made him both a night owl and a morning person. Sally worked long hours, so he liked being up when she left in the morning and often made her breakfast. As a result, he was up, drinking coffee and reading the *Washington Post* when Sally left at 6:30 A.M. After that he took a quick four-mile run to get his blood pumping, some sweat on his body and some quiet contemplative time to think. Once back he took a shower and engaged in the normal morning mechanics. By the time he exited the master bedroom fresh and dressed, Wire was opening the guest room door. Dara was going to need some work.

"Hey, sleepy head, are you hungry?" he asked cheerily.

"What do you think?" Dara replied crabbily, her hair askew, shuffling her feet towards the guest bathroom.

"Morning person, are we?"

"Not until I have my coffee. Speaking of which, where the hell is it?"

Mac laughed and saluted, "Yes, ma'am, I'll get right on it."

He quickly descended the stairs and fetched a cup of coffee, dropping in some hazelnut creamer, which Wire liked. He cracked the bathroom door and slid the cup onto the counter. "Coffee is served, my lady. You can stop your royal bitching now."

"Thank you ... and uh, sorry," he heard from the shower as he pulled the door closed.

Breakfast was his favorite meal to eat and cook. Back down in the kitchen, he whipped up a quick feast of eggs, bacon, toast and strawberries, watching *SportsCenter* while he did so.

"I see your Twins lost *again* to my Red Sox last night."

"Rub it in, why don't you," Mac answered as he poured her another cup of coffee. "Press conference is in fifteen."

They sat on stools around the center island watching the large flat screen Mac had mounted along the far wall. All of the cable news channels carried the press conference live and the Reaper's picture was repeatedly put on the screen.

"Do you think we'll get anything out of this?" Wire asked Mac as she sipped coffee.

"Oh, we'll get plenty of information and tips," Mac answered, loading dishes in the dishwasher. "Whether any of it proves useful?" Mac shrugged. "Well, that's another story."

It was a stunning thing to see your image appear on television.

The Reaper pulled at his beard just under his chin as CNN displayed his image on the right-hand side of the screen while FBI Director Thomas Mitchell and Special Agent Aubry Gesch conducted their press conference. He flipped around to the other news channels, FOX and MSNBC; they were all carrying the press conference, all carrying the same images and video clips of him.

The images were from the surveillance camera at the hardware store. He saw the camera globe the minute he walked in nine days ago, the little black ball hanging from the ceiling. Preparation was everything. He had on the hooded sweatshirt, a baseball cap and his sunglasses. The sweatshirt was generic, dark blue with no specific markings on it. The baseball cap was a University of Delaware hat, the Blue Hens, hardly uncommon in Dover. The beard helped as well, a good month's growth to its full thick status, although he'd started with just a small thin beard around his mouth. The sunglasses fully covered his eyes and really the upper third of his face. The additional details being reported about him, while not evident on the images and video, were nonetheless fairly accurate. He was in fact a Caucasian male, approximately 6'3" and was muscular, and while taller and bigger than the average white male, he was hardly out of the ordinary.

It was him, but there was no way anyone could *really* identify him from those images.

Nevertheless, his heart was racing just a little from this first bit of discovery of him. Enough so that he pushed himself out of his desk chair and as a precaution went to the windows. For ten minutes, he fingered open the curtains just enough so that he could scan the surrounding area. There was nothing of concern, no vans, no unmarked cars, no police patrol cars, no sirens, nothing unusual.

Would they be coming?

He seriously doubted it.

Not off of that image.

A loner would not be caught off that image.

He had no family, at least not anymore. Friends? Coworkers? Not for at least the last two years, and intentionally so. Before that people could have some recognition. Out of sight, out of mind, he figured. As a result, there were few people in the world that really knew him or were likely to recognize him. He was a physically large non-entity to people.

Wire and Mac arrived at the FBI Washington Field Office just after 10:00 A.M. Along with Gesch and Delmonico, the four of them spent the day reviewing the case, hoping for a break, having gone public with what images they had of the Reaper. There was a noon conference call with all of the jurisdictions in the Reaper Task Force. Everyone was out in the field, talking to families, friends and coworkers of all of the victims, going back near the murder scenes to see if the picture rang any bells.

In the late afternoon, while there were some calls and a few people quickly checked, there had been no truly promising leads reported. Gesch and Delmonico were discouraged, having to update Director Mitchell several times. Wire shared their discouragement. Mac was more even keeled about it.

"I thought we'd get something," Gesch said with an exhale as he plopped down in his leather desk chair and kicked his feet up onto his desk.

"I'm not surprised," Mac said flatly, leaning against the wall, opening a piece of Dentyne. "There isn't much on that image, Aubry. You can't tell much about the guy. We have the bottom of his face and it's a beard and his nose looks pretty normal, the top of his face is covered in sunglasses along with a baseball cap and a hooded sweatshirt. There is nothing distinguishing. Nothing to latch onto that is unique, at least that I see. It's the definition of a good disguise. The evening news, local news and cable shows will cover it tonight. Maybe we'll get a little lucky. Maybe our guy will get spooked, make a mistake and somebody will notice. People are calling in, so that's a good sign."

"Is that what you typically rely on?" Gesch inquired skeptically. "Luck? Your perp making a mistake? Is *that* how you solved all of these cases I've heard about?"

Mac shrugged, nonplussed by the little jibe. "Sometimes yes and sometimes no. What frustrates me is this investigation is so spread out. Typically, I'd be in the middle of what they're doing in Harrisburg, Salisbury and Dover, going around to every family member, friend, coworker and potential witness to see if the picture rang a bell with anyone. I'd be out hunting, trying to make my own luck. Waiting on others is, for me, a little weird."

"Mac, if we don't get anything out of this today, what would be your next move?" Gesch asked.

Mac had actually given that some thought. "Serials often, not always, but often start with someone they see, maybe not daily, but someone that triggers something. So, if we don't get anything today, I want to go to …"

"Harrisburg."

"Right. Old-fashioned police work. Pound the pavement. That's how we found our image here. It's how we'll eventually solve this thing. One little piece at a time. This image is unlikely to get us home. It's just a piece, but all the pieces matter."

In the early evening, Mac and Wire walked out of the field office to stretch their legs, taking a stroll towards the Verizon Center arena in search of a good cup of coffee. After four blocks, they found a coffee shop, where they ordered large iced coffees and continued their walk, stopping at the Navy Memorial Plaza and grabbing a bench to drink their coffees and enjoy the warm early evening air.

"How much do you see Sally?" Wire asked.

"Not as much as I'd like."

"But enough?"

"No," Mac shook his head. "No, it's never really enough, but it is what it is with her job, you know. Why do you ask?"

"I don't know," Wire replied wistfully. "I work so much these days, my business, the six months of the election investigation, doing this case with you, the book. It doesn't leave a lot of time for a personal life. It makes me wonder if I could ever find someone who would, you know …"

"Be there."

"Yeah."

"There's someone for everyone, Dara, I truly believe that." Mac turned to face her, "Wait a minute. You can't actually be worried that there wouldn't be someone for you, do you. Dara?"

She shrugged her shoulders. "I've never had *that* relationship, the one where you dive into it with both feet and really commit with someone. I'm thirty-three years old and I've never had it."

Mac scoffed, "Dara, you are far too normal, smart, not to

mention *ridiculously hot*, to go without someone if you *want* to find someone. If you truly want to find someone, there is someone for you. I mean, what about this guy you got laid with repeatedly?"

Dara shook her head and smiled, "He's the type for getting laid with repeatedly. He's not the type for the other part."

"Don't undersell the value of great sex."

"Is that what you and Sally have?" Dara asked mischievously, a smiley smirk on her face.

"Yeah, we do, actually," Mac answered seriously. "It's born of a great relationship. It gets better all the time and I think it is part of what makes us closer. I mean, look, I was married once and Meredith and I were never as close as Sally and I."

"Is Sally that *someone* for you, Mac?" Dara asked more seriously. "I mean, is she really *the one*?"

Mac looked at her with raised eyebrows, "Do you and I really know each other well enough to have this conversation? I mean, you're sounding a little like my mom here."

"We've gone this far, why stop now." Dara turned serious and she wasn't prying. This discussion was as much about her life as it was about his. "We're friends, we've bonded. You and I know each other pretty well, been through a few intense situations together. I trust you with my life if we get in a situation, and you can trust me with yours." She took a sip of her iced coffee, "I envy you and Sally, is all. It just seems you two are awfully happy together."

"We are. We're committed to each other, I know that."

"How do you know that?" she asked curiously. "How do you know you're committed? I mean, don't get angry at me for saying this, and I'm not channeling your mom here, but I don't see a big rock on her finger."

Mac thought for a minute. It was a fair question. "For one thing, every decision she or I make is made with the impact to *us* in mind. We make decisions together."

"Such as?"

"Coming to Washington. She wanted to come when she got the offer from the Judge. However, she didn't say yes until she talked through it with me. There was no way I was going to say no and I think she knew that, but still, we had to talk it through. What did that move mean for us? It was a 'we' decision, not a 'me' decision."

"Is it enough? Is what you have now enough?"

"In the long run, no. But it's enough for right now," Mac answered.

"Do you two have a plan?"

"A plan?"

"Yeah, you know, like marriage?" Wire asked. "I mean, what comes next?"

"A *specific*, laid out, step-by-step plan," Mac shook his head. "No. I ... I think, no, I know we both want to be married again someday, or at least I think so, but we haven't really felt the need to do it. Frankly, the 'm' word doesn't come up very often."

"Scared?"

"Oh. I think we both are," Mac answered, sipping his iced coffee through the straw. "This may shock you, but we don't really talk about it."

Wire looked at him skeptically.

"I swear to you, we really don't talk about marriage. Commitment—yes, but marriage?" He shook his head, "No."

"Why not?"

"Honestly, I don't think either of us really thinks being married would change our relationship right now. I really don't think I could love her more than I already do. I don't know that putting the ring on her finger would change my commitment to her or hers to me."

"What would? What would change the relationship? What would push you two over the precipice?"

Mac looked at a family of four walking fifty feet away and gestured, "Kids, I suppose. I want kids someday. I love kids. I want a family."

"Does Sally?"

Now she'd asked a question to which he admittedly didn't for sure know the answer and three years into a relationship he should. Like marriage, kids were not something that they often talked about, perhaps afraid what the other's answer might be. She certainly seemed to like kids and absolutely doted over her nieces and nephews with gifts and love. Sally was on the computer all the time with her brothers and sisters, checking out kid and baby pictures and was always excited to see the newest addition to the extended Kennedy or McRyan family. She loved to buy clothes and ship them off, to hold and play with the babies. When they were back in St. Paul, they did a lot of babysitting. But did Sally want kids of her own? He assumed so, but then again, they never really specifically talked about it. "I don't ..." his phone rang before he could finish his answer. "McRyan."

"It's Gesch. We need to go to Harrisburg. We might have gotten lucky."

9

"WE'RE BLOWN."

"I could get used to this," Mac remarked lightly to Wire through his headset.

One thing about working on a priority federal investigation, you get access to all the tools *and toys* of the eight-hundred-pound US Government gorilla. In this case, the FBI chopper screamed through the night carrying Gesch, Delmonico, Mac and Wire and making a beeline for Harrisburg, Pennsylvania.

The Reaper's first victim, Melissa Goynes, was a bar manager and waitress at the Nittany Lion Sports Bar in Harrisburg. Gesch explained that two Harrisburg detectives attached to the Reaper Task Force had set up camp at the Nittany Lion all day with the photos and video from Dover, talking to every customer, salesman, distributor and employee who came in the door. Throughout the day they'd struck out, the images not registering with anyone. However, there was a big pay-per-view for Mixed Martial Arts (MMA) tonight and the bar was packed to capacity with lots of regulars hanging out looking to watch the matches.

"Mac, your instinct to think that the killer may have

focused on someone he saw frequently for his first victim may have been right. The picture and video started resonating with some patrons a few hours ago," Gesch stated. "The people at the bar named this guy," Gesch reported, handing a DMV photo to Wire.

"Cedric Lewis," Wire stated, reading from the DMV photo. Lewis was 6'1 ¾", two hundred twenty pounds and broad shouldered. He had a beard and the mouth looked kind of like the man's in the images from the hardware store. She handed the photo to Mac, "Your thoughts?"

"What triggered it for them?" Mac asked Gesch as he took in the photo.

"The image from the surveillance camera reminded them of a guy who comes into the bar from time to time, especially when they have the MMA fights on. He works out at a local gym, Wrex Gym, which has a rather bold and colorful logo so that's part of how they remember him. He usually wears clothes with the logo on it. In any event, Harrisburg tells me that staffers started looking at the photo, recognized the beard, hoodie and sunglasses look, and they think it's this guy."

Mac took the photo from the hardware store and held it next to the picture of Lewis. After a minute, he shrugged. "It's possible."

"There's more," Gesch added. "Our guy has a criminal record with a history of smacking ladies around. Two domestic charges in his past and a restraining order from an ex-girlfriend. Apparently, he's been in a fight or two at the Lion and at another bar down the street where apparently he drew a big knife. He likes violence, or at least is violent."

Mac gestured for the file. Gesch handed it to him and Mac began thumbing through it. "He's an MMA fighter himself. Looks like on the local circuit, does some sparring with bigger names." He took another look at the DMV photo and his measurements. Mac thought back to his University of Minnesota days, working out on campus for hockey and interacting with other athletes, including wrestlers. Minnesota has one of the best wrestling programs in the nation. This guy cut that look. "He has the look of a wrestler. Maybe even a heavyweight back in the day, his neck muscles are massive and you can just tell he has a broad chest, thick through the shoulders." As he studied the photo more, he zeroed in on the eyes, which were dark, set back under a large brow and troubling. In Mac's view, the picture said, "Don't Fuck With Me." In reading the profile on Lewis, something bothered Mac, something about him perhaps not being right for it. However, he had the right look and his background of violence, use of a knife even, suggested he could be right. "So where is he now?"

"We don't know," Delmonico answered. "Harrisburg has two units sitting on his apartment complex, but he hasn't shown. The gym he works at is closed for the night. His cell phone must be turned off as we can't track him that way. He's in the wind right now, which suggests he might have bolted town, but we've got an all points out. But there is one other possibility, which is where we're headed."

"What's that?" Wire asked.

"It's 8:40 right now," Delmonico replied. "The people at the bar say he usually shows up for the pay-per-view MMA events, so, if he hasn't gone to ground, we're hoping he'll show tonight. The main fights start a little after 10:00 P.M. eastern time."

The chopper landed in the Harrisburg Police Bureau parking lot. The Harrisburg task force detective was named Angelo Dorsett, a short, stout, barrel-chested man with a high and tight military haircut for his jet black hair and a thick black beard around his mouth. He greeted them off the chopper. Introductions were quickly made and Dorsett hustled everyone into two unmarked cars, one black and one car silver. "The bar is less than ten minutes away, up on Forster Street."

The unmarked units stopped two blocks short of the bar on a side street sitting a half block back from Forster, which was a busy main thoroughfare. Mac and Wire climbed out of their unit and walked up to Dorsett's, which was leading the group and carrying Gesch and Delmonico. Wire leaned down to the passenger side front window to speak with Dorsett. "How many men do you have inside?"

"Just two inside, but I have a unit watching the front," Dorsett answered. "I didn't go in because my face has been on the news with this case. I didn't want to spook him if he saw me."

"Then Delmonico and I shouldn't go in either," Gesch replied. "We were on the news here a few weeks ago and certainly we were on the news plenty today."

"We'll go in," Mac suggested. "We have no profile on this. Our only problem is we don't know who your men are, Detective Dorsett."

Dorsett took out his handheld radio. "My two people inside are detectives Stiglitch and Lee." Then into the radio, "Stig, I have two people coming in, Feds, one guy probably six-one, short blond hair, blue eyes, casually dressed in jeans, black sport coat with a blue and white button down, open at the collar named McRyan. He'll have a tall brunette with him, skinny blue jeans, white T-shirt, black jean jacket, coming in the front door, her name is Wire." Dorsett looked up to them and pointed with his radio. "Walk up to Forster, cross the street and then turn right and the Nittany Lion is two blocks up on the left."

Mac and Wire took their guns, checked them quickly and stuffed them behind their backs and began walking the rest of the half block on Susquehanna Street to Forster Street. At Forster, Wire said, "Wait a second." She pulled her hair out of her ponytail and played with it until it fell nicely just below her shoulders. Then out of the inside pocket of her jean jacket she pulled out some lipstick and applied it.

Mac took it all in, admiring. He rarely saw her with her hair down looking like this. It was always business.

"What?" she asked. He was staring.

"Nothing." Were he not a man madly in love, he'd be awfully tempted.

Forster was a busy boulevard, two lanes in either direction with a tree-lined median down the middle. They made their way across the street, turned right and walked along the sidewalk, seeing the neon marquis for the Nittany Lion two blocks ahead. Wire slipped her left hand under Mac's right arm.

"Fulfilling a fantasy," Mac quipped as they walked.

"You are so full of yourself," Wire retorted. "We're undercover. We should look like something besides cops. You're just good looking enough that people would think it's possible, just possible, you could be with me."

"Ouch."

The Nittany Lion had large windows along the front and as they approached the entrance, Mac looked to his left inside and saw what must have been at least forty large flat screens mounted high up in the middle over the bar and on the walls. Just inside the front door was a sign that said capacity of three hundred, and it looked like all of that and probably more were packed inside the bar. Mac took in the layout of the place, which was really a large open floor plan. There was a large rectangular bar occupying the middle. Another circuit of tall tables and stools surrounded the bar all the way around. Then there was a step up and a third ring with tables to the left and back and deeper booths with tall dividing walls for privacy along the right side under a lower hanging ceiling. The rear entrance was visible, offset to the left of the bar and near the hallway to the restrooms in the back left corner. It was a large and open space.

Wire grabbed Mac's hand and led him towards the bar. He stood behind her as she ordered Diet Cokes with limes when a voice whispered in his ear, "Name is Stiglich."

"McRyan. Wire is ordering," Mac answered, glancing just briefly right to see the Harrisburg detective, a man with light brown hair, dressed in blue jeans with a bulky V-neck nylon navy blue Penn State pullover.

"I'm parked on a bar stool by the front door. Lee is wearing a Phillies sweatshirt and khakis, sitting on a stool on the right corner at the far end of the bar. I talked to the owner and he's got a booth for you two over to the right, about halfway down the walkway. We should have it covered then."

"Any sign of our boy?" Mac asked quietly out the side of his mouth.

"Not yet."

Wire turned around with two drinks, made eye contact with the Harrisburg cop, who then moved past her to the bar. To cover talking to Mac, he ordered. Mac tilted his head to the right and then he and Wire pushed their way through the crowd, climbed two steps and then walked left down a walkway, finding the empty booth with a reserved sign on their right. They each took a side of the booth, Wire with eyes to the front of the bar and Mac watching the back.

It was 9:34 P.M. They each casually sipped at their sodas

while scanning the bar, the DMV picture of Lewis pulled up on their cell phones.

The pay-per-view fights started at 10:00 P.M.

"Do you ever watch these MMA fights?" Wire asked.

"I did one time. A friend bought the pay-per-view for an event like tonight. It struck me as human cockfighting."

"It should be illegal."

Mac shrugged. "Since the time of Rome, we've had gladiators. This is just the latest incarnation of it."

"We who are about to die, salute you," Wire quipped, quoting from *Gladiator*.

"At my signal, unleash hell," Mac retorted, quoting General Maxiumus and they both shared a chuckle.

The anticipation in the bar grew as 10:00 P.M. approached. The volume on the pay-per-view was turned up so that the crowd could hear the announcers analyze the night's fight card. There were three undercard matches before the main event between two heavyweights. A last minute surge of people filled the bar.

"I take it the fire marshal is not in attendance," Wire quipped.

The first fight started, two mid-sized white guys stood in the octagon. "What are those guys?" Mac asked. "Maybe one hundred fifty pounds?"

"'bout that, I'd say. They both look ripped."

"It's a little hard to tell with all the tattoos."

Mac and Wire kept scanning the crowd for Lewis but he wasn't in the bar. The Nittany Lion crowd started roaring in the second round, when the more tattooed of the two fighters was sitting on top of the other, on his knees, leaning in and furiously pounding on his opponent with lefts and rights, the ground and pound. His opponent was squirming, moving his head side to side, shielding with his arms.

"The guy is defenseless. Geez," Wire yelped and grimaced as the man on the mat took a wicked right hand to the face.

"That's the nature of the fight," Mac answered as the man on the mat gave in and tapped out. The referee frantically waved his arms to end the fight and the winner ran and jumped up to the top of the ring's fencing, holding his arms up in victory. "Like I said earlier, it's nothing more than human cockfighting." Mac looked away from the television towards the back of the bar and to a man who walked in wearing a black hooded sweatshirt over his head. He had a beard, was over six feet with broad shoulders. A man, even in an extremely crowded bar, people gave space to.

"Casually turn to your right, Dara, ten feet inside the back door. See the guy in the black hoodie? Is that our guy?"

Wire did as instructed, peering over her right shoulder, looking to the back of the bar. She turned back and looked down to her phone and then slowly back again. "Maybe."

Mac dialed Stiglitch, who answered on the second ring. "From your position, look 10:00 to 11:00, maybe ten to fifteen feet inside the back door and the guy wearing the dark hoodie. What do you think? Is that Lewis?"

"I'd say it's worth a look." Mac casually slid out of the booth and led Wire down the walkway, casually glancing to his left in the direction of the hooded man. Detective Lee, dressed in the red Phillies pullover, pushed himself up off his barstool and slowly maneuvered his way through the mass of bodies toward the hooded man while Stiglitch was approaching from the front, coming down the opposite side of the bar dividing the Nittany Lion.

Wire watched the hooded man's eyes. Instinctually, the man sensed someone or something boring in on him. He looked straight ahead, the direction from which Stiglitch was approaching. The two locked eyes and Stiglitch halted and hesitated for just a split second. The hooded man took a step back. Mac and Wire saw it.

"Mac?"

"We're blown."

It was Lewis, who bolted out the back door.

Stiglitch and Lee gave pursuit, losing distance, getting caught in the wash of the crowd. Mac barreled his way through the crowd, yelling "Move! Police! Move! Police!" Dara was right on his six, hand on his back, pushing.

Out the back door, Mac could see Stiglitch and Lee running twenty yards ahead, across the street and into a block of old two-story houses slotted tightly together. He and Wire sprinted to the edge of the block and the houses. Behind them Dorsett pulled by, yelling they were driving around to the north side of the block. The other unmarked car, the silver Dodge Charger, was driving down the street on the south side, aiming the spotlight in between the houses. Sirens were approaching from the distance.

"Come on." Mac led Wire into the grouping of houses, quickly picking their way along, listening and looking. Then there they heard a loud grimace of someone in pain and a crash up to the left. Mac pushed ahead and found Lee lying on the ground, moaning. "Stay with him," he whispered and Wire leaned down to the detective who was holding his right arm.

Mac looked up and took two steps forward and heard another crash up to the left. The spotlights, filtering through the gaps between the houses, illuminated them, a quick flash of a silhouette on the side of a white house of two men battling. One man was on top of and pounding on the other. McRyan sprinted towards the silhouette. As he came around the corner of the house, he was tackled violently off his feet and down onto his back by Lewis, who began pounding on him with his fists one after the other, Mac trying to block them with his arms, unsuccessfully.

Wire charged from the left, lowering her shoulder. Lewis sensed her coming and at the last second ducked and Wire flew over him. As she did, her right knee caught the top of Lewis' head, dazing and pushing him enough to give Mac room to free himself, roll to his left, get on his feet, reach back and draw his gun.

Lewis was up "cat" quick and charged Mac, who sidestepped just to his right as the man wrapped him in his arms and pushed him back into the side of the house.

Mac, his right arm free slammed down on the back of Lewis's head with the butt of his gun, dazing him, eliciting a groan, loosening the bear hug and freeing Mac's legs. With both feet on the ground now, Mac up kicked the man in the chin with his right knee, which caused his head to snap back. With a round-house right, Mac pistol whipped him again on the side of the head, sending him crashing to the ground. He jumped on top of Lewis, rolled him over onto his stomach and pulled the man's right arm high up against his back, causing him to groan again in excruciating pain, immobilizing him. Wire, still a bit dazed, was up, stumbled over and quickly slapped her handcuffs on his left hand and pulled the left arm up to meet the right and finished cuffing him.

Mac rolled off the man and onto the ground, lying on his back, breathing heavily. "Jesus," he exclaimed as he lay on the ground, trying to catch his breath.

Wire kneeled down, her right hand on his chest, "Mac, your face, you're all bloody."

He sat up and wiped at his face. His hand was smeared

with blood and he could feel the wetness in his scalp. "I'm just cut, I think. Are you okay?"

Wire nodded.

The commotion on the block had porch and floodlights turned on and people coming out onto their back steps to see what all the commotion was. To their left, Mac and Wire saw two people leaning over and tending to Lee. Gesch, Delmonico, Dorsett and another plainclothes officer came running between the houses from the north side of the block and found everyone lying around. "Are we all right here?" Dorsett asked, holstering his gun and turning off his flashlight.

Stiglitch was up, walking slowly and woozily towards them. "He looks relatively okay," Wire said. "But Lee?" She pointed twenty feet back to the east and the two neighbors. "He's in tough shape. I think he has a broken arm and maybe more."

Gesch leaned down and pulled the hood back on the man's head. "So you're the Reaper."

"Reaper?" Lewis replied, confused. "What the fuck are you talking about?"

10

"MIGHT BE AN UNTAPPED GENIUS."

It was after 1:00 A.M. by the time McRyan and Wire made it back to the Harrisburg Police Bureau, returning from the emergency room. Mac was now the proud owner of eleven stitches covering two gashes in his upper forehead, one in his scalp, the other just below with a butterfly bandage over it. The doctor said he was likely to end up with a shiner in a few days as well and he had bruising around his right eye already. He looked like he'd been in a bar fight, which to a certain degree he had been.

"Mr. McRyan, I'd suggest a lot of Ibuprofen, ice and rest to keep the swelling down." Mac had no doubt there would be plenty of Ibuprofen, perhaps some ice, but little if any rest in the coming days.

The ice pack was applied on the ride back in the car, but Mac dumped it in the garbage can once they went inside. The arrest was already on the news with headlines that the Reaper may have been caught.

Sally and the Judge called upon seeing the reports and video footage on the cable channels, "Is it true? Did you get him? That's what all the cable news channels are reporting."

Wire looked to Mac, who shook his head and stated, "Don't believe everything you hear."

The Judge heard the tone, "Mac, you don't think he's the guy, do you?"

"Just don't get out ahead of this yet." Something about Lewis didn't compute to him. He couldn't put his finger on it yet.

Mac was then cross-examined by Sally for five minutes about his medical status. Sally had seen the footage of him with his bloody face, in fact it was plastered all over the cable channels. "Just a little wrestling while trying to subdue the suspect is all," he answered. "I have some stitches, no big deal."

"*Riiiight*," Sally replied. "I guess that's why the media is reporting two Harrisburg cops are in the hospital for observation after a little wrestling to subdue the suspect." He thought about trying to deflect some more but decided not to. It would only inflame her. Instead, he tried a different tact, with a lighter tone, "Hey, you volunteered me for this duty."

That didn't work either.

"Yeah, and I can un-volunteer you in case you've forgotten who I work for," she retorted, a sternness in her voice.

"I'm fine," and with a little extra growl in return, added, "And I ain't leaving," His tone said the conversation was now closed and Sally backed off. Sometimes he thought she cross-examined him just so she was on the record and later could say, "I told you so," which he swore were four of her favorite words.

They both liked to be right.

They both rarely admitted defeat.

They both were usually smart enough to know when to walk away from the fight before they said things that were really hard to take back.

Instead, they let it go and made nice to each other for a few minutes and by the time he hung up he felt like smiling.

"Is everything all right?" Wire asked. "I wasn't listening but watching suggested it got a little heated."

"Nothing you haven't seen or heard before. She just worries."

"And she's feeling guilty," Wire added. "She pushed you into this case. If something happened, she'd have to live with that for the rest of her life."

"She pushed, sure, but I decided. It was *my* call."

"Trust me," Wire answered, stopping, looking Mac dead in eye so he understood. "I led men and women into going undercover against the mob, Mac. It can be your decision all you want it to be, but if something happens to you, if this thing does go all sideways somehow, she'll blame herself. *I know. I did.*"

Mac took the measure of Wire and asked, looking her right in the eye: "Do you ever get over it?"

"No. You learn to live with it but you never get over it."

"Good to know, I guess," he said as they started walking back down the hall.

Dara talked as they walked, "Look, the point is, at the end of the day you're right, it was your decision, Mac. You're a cop. She knows that when you walk out the door every day that there are big risks with that job. In the past, that was your call and she had nothing to do with it. But this time, she played a role in you walking out the door and into the line of fire. That isn't something she usually would do. So if something happened, she'll spend the rest of her life asking herself 'what if?' So just cut her a little slack on this one, is all I'm saying. She's going to be edgy."

Mac thought about it as they kept walking and then said quietly, "You're right."

It wasn't a bad thing to get some perspective on where Sally was coming from. As much as he missed Lich, Riles and Rock, Wire gave him insight and advice he wouldn't otherwise get from *that* crew.

Cedric Lewis, given his history, was quite familiar with the mechanics of the legal system and immediately invoked his right to an attorney. His criminal lawyer, accustomed to late night phone calls, was now meeting with his client. While they waited to deal with Lewis, Mac and Wire found Gesch and Delmonico waiting in another interview room.

"According to Dorsett, Lewis's attorney is an old pro who knows what he's doing and is walking through things with Lewis," Gesch reported.

Mac and Wire, sipping coffee, were tag team reading through the file on Lewis, each pointing at various pieces of information as they read through his background.

Cedric Lewis was twenty-six years old. His current employment was twofold, as a roofer and he was a mixed martial arts fighter, although his record suggested it wasn't a long-term career path. "He's six and six in his professional matches," Wire noted.

"He's six and seven now, I took him tonight," Mac replied.

"Typical," Wire snorted, shaking her head at Mac.

"What?"

"I think you had *some* help."

Mac mockingly rolled his eyes, "Okay, correction, *we* took him tonight."

"Thank you."

Dorsett stuck his head in the room, "They're ready for us."

Gesch and Dorsett took the interrogation. Mac, Wire and Delmonico watched from the observation room. As the ground rules were laid, Mac continued to read through Lewis's file, and what bothered him about their suspect finally crystallized in his mind. As Gesch was about to begin questioning, Mac blurted: "Twenty bucks he's not our guy. No, make that a hundred. In fact, make it a grand."

Wire knew Mac and the look. She said: "No bet."

"How can you be so sure?" Delmonico asked, skeptical. "He's got a history of violence against women. You said it yourself that serials often start with someone they know. Lewis is a regular or at least semi-regular at the Nittany Lion where he came across Melissa Goynes. He's the right size, has the beard, the hoodie look tonight and he did his best Running Man routine tonight to get away."

"He's probably guilty of something. but not this."

"Why not?"

"Our killer is organized, methodical, a planner, gets away from each crime scene without leaving any evidence, knows to keep his head down around surveillance cameras, attacks and kills these women in the perfect places so as to not be discovered and administers an anesthetic before carving them up. I mean, three for three and the best we've got on him is a grainy surveillance image of the lower half of his face and he has a beard."

"So?"

"Would you agree that takes a certain amount of intelligence?" Mac asked Delmonico.

"Yes."

"Well, our boy Lewis here never graduated high school. He has a menial job as a roofer and a mixed martial arts fighter, although, from his record, you might as well stamp Everlast across his forehead because he's nothing more than a punching bag. Sure, he has a police record for violence and as Gesch said, he likes violence, is drawn to it. So he's a bad guy, a thug who smacks women around when he's not getting smacked around in the octagon. He's a hammer in search of a nail. But is he the Reaper?" Mac shook his head. "He just doesn't have the brain power for it."

"Might be an untapped genius," Delmonico speculated, more hopeful than convinced.

"No," Mac replied, shaking his head. "He's not our guy. Are you going to take my bet Grace?"

"I'm thinking," she answered.

She wanted nothing to do with the bet.

It took about twenty minutes of the interview to see Lewis wasn't their guy. He ran because he and his girlfriend got in a fight, he hit her and he thought she'd called the police. When he saw the detective at the bar, he ran. He had an alibi for Donahue's death. He was sparring with a top heavyweight fighter out at a farm where he trains in Altoona, two hours west of Harrisburg. Lewis claimed to be doing the same for the date of the murder of the second victim, Janelle Wyland, in Salisbury, Maryland. He wasn't sure about the night Goynes was killed but vehemently denied killing her.

"We'll need to run the alibis," Delmonico said dejectedly.

A Harrisburg detective came into the observation room and handed a piece of paper to Delmonico. "We have the search warrant for Lewis's place. Let's go take a look."

Lewis lived in a rundown three-story 1970s-style apartment building. His one-bedroom unit was on the third floor. The man did not keep a neat house, with dilapidated furniture, little in the refrigerator and clothes strewn about the apartment. His television was an old box kind that sat on a fabricated entertainment center well into its third decade. There was no organization, cleanliness or frankly, signs of intelligent life.

"We'll get the crime scene people through here," Delmonico suggested. "Just in case," she was warming to Mac's theory.

Four hours later, the alibis were confirmed. Lewis was not their guy. In the observation room, Mac, Wire, Delmonico, Gesch and Dorsett talked about next steps. Lewis would technically remain a person of interest for a while, but he wasn't the Reaper. Mac looked at the surveillance photo of the Reaper and said to Gesch, "I want to ask Lewis a question, is it okay if I go in?"

"To do what?"

"Take a long shot."

Mac stepped into the interrogation room. "My name is Detect ..." he had a hard time of thinking of himself as a federal agent, "make that Agent McRyan, I'm working with the FBI on the task force looking for the Reaper."

Lewis recognized him from their earlier fight, "How's your head?" he asked mockingly, pointing to the butterfly on Mac's forehead.

"How's yours?"

"They don't allow pistol whipping in MMA."

"Yeah, but that vicious upkick I put into your chin with my knee is allowed, right? I mean, as I analyze our encounter, that was the critical momentum turning blow, was it not?"

Lewis shrugged and nodded, massaging his jaw.

Mac looked to the lawyer, "I want to ask your client a question about this picture." He put the surveillance photo in front of Lewis.

"That's not my client," the lawyer stated.

"That's not me," Lewis exclaimed, thinking the questioning was beginning again.

"Can you tell me who it is then?" Mac asked. "Does the guy look familiar to you? You've been in the Nittany Lion enough that people thought this was you. So if they're wrong, do you know who this is? Do you recognize him?"

"So you're not asking if I did anything this ... Reaper guy did?" Lewis asked, still uncertain.

Mac shook his head, "I'm asking if you know who this is?"

Lewis took a look at the picture, at first cursory but then lingered over it for a bit. "Are there any other pictures?"

Mac looked back through the two-way window. Seconds later, Wire was in with a laptop and showed the footage of the Reaper to Lewis. He studied the images more. Mac and Wire shared a look. Lewis was seeing something. "There was a guy I remember seeing at the Nittany Lion. He walked like this. You see how the guy in the images here, see how he kind of bounces when he walks."

Mac and Wire rewound the footage and watched for themselves. "Yeah, I see what you're getting at. It's ... what is the word I'm looking for?" Mac struggled for the word.

"Distinctive?" Wire asked.

"That works," Mac answered.

Lewis nodded, "I just remember there was this one guy a couple of times in there, you know. You share a look, size each other up a little bit, see how he carries himself because he had the look of someone who could throw down. He was big, thick, but light on his feet. It was the way he walked that sticks with me, you know. I don't notice much in this world besides women and guys who can fight. This guy looked like he could fight, he could carry himself. Like when you two walked in here," he pointed to Mac and Wire. "I can tell you both can handle yourself."

"Right, so?" Mac asked, leading him on.

"In the pictures here," Lewis pointed to the photo, "this guy has a full beard. The guy I'm thinking of only had the half beard, you know, around the mouth kind, trimmed pretty thin."

"Do you remember anything else?"

"He wore glasses, thick dark rims that are in style. You know what I'm talking about?"

Mac and Wire nodded.

"His lenses were tinted though. I also thought that was weird. People usually don't have tinted glasses, at least not ones they wear inside."

"Anything else?"

"He wore a baseball hat."

"How about tattoos? Marking on his face or arms? Moles? Scars? Anything like that?" Wire asked.

Lewis shook his head, "Not that I recall."

"How about a name?" Mac asked.

Lewis shook his head. "No."

Mac assessed Lewis and the degree in which he was studying the images. Lewis wasn't jacking him around. There was recognition there. He was seeing something. They just needed to extract it. "Listen, Cedric, if we got a sketch artist in here, could you describe him?"

"I can try."

Two hours later they had a sketch. It was still general,

but they had a full face now, a bit round and jowly framed by short light-colored hair, small beard around the mouth, nose thin at the top but wider on the bottom and tinted glasses with a baseball cap.

Mac held it up for everyone, "Now maybe we're starting to get somewhere."

11
"THAT'S ME."

The cabin was a good location. It was relatively isolated. The yard area around the cabin and detached garage was surrounded by dense woods with neighbors hundreds, if not thousands, of yards away, neighbors he'd made no effort to get to know. The garage was a double, a long unused fishing boat in the right stall surrounded by mounds of junk and his truck now snuggly parked in the left side, the garage door down.

The cabin was rustic but decently sized and usable year-round with running water, electricity, a functional fireplace and cable for his television and Internet access needs. The best part of it all was that the cabin wasn't in his name and that was a good thing.

A new picture of him was on the airwaves now.

They were a little closer.

The cabin would be his home now. In his estimation, the apartment wasn't safe anymore even though he'd made no effort to get to know anyone in his time there either. Now that the drawing of his face was out there, he simply couldn't take the chance.

He saw the stories from two nights ago about the police taking Cedric Lewis into custody in Harrisburg. When the picture of Lewis was displayed, he instantly remembered him from the Nittany Lion. The mixed martial arts fighter, the guy who walked around the bar on a hair trigger, the kind of guy you avoided, and he'd made a point of trying to avoid Lewis. He didn't want the attention. He thought nothing of it really at the time other than he was relieved nothing came of it. In fact, he was trying to do everything he could to not draw attention to himself. That was really the key all along, avoiding being noticed and just blending in.

Avoidance was the strategy at the busy and crowded Nittany Lion when he was prowling around after Goynes. He quietly sat in the shadows at the Nittany Lion for a few nights getting a feel for Melissa Goynes and her movements, whom she ran with, the hours she worked and the patterns she'd followed. A confrontation with someone like Lewis would have drawn too much attention and required him to move on and skip Goynes. That would have screwed up his plan before he'd ever really gotten started.

Initially, he was amused watching the footage of the police arresting Lewis and the cable networks going wall to wall that the Reaper was caught. Knowing the answer was wrong made it all the more pleasing to watch, knowing all the talking heads would have to walk the story back and that whoever was feeding the information to the networks would have significant egg on their face. It took all of twelve hours for that tune to change and the news channels and networks were forced to report that in fact the Reaper had not been caught and remained at large.

But now, it was clear that Lewis remembered him and was talking to the police, undoubtedly in the hopes of getting out of whatever trouble he was actually in.

The image was closer, a full face now. The beard was right for that particular time, although the mouth wasn't quite right; he had larger lips and his jaw line was a little more square than in the picture, but this was much closer. He knew it was his face in the images. Now, he was actually looking at himself. Lewis had done an admirable job with the sketch artist.

"That's me."

CNN was continuing to display the image while recapping the story, playing the footage from the arrest and focusing on Lewis being put into the squad car, but that's not what drew his interest.

What drew his interest was when the camera panned away from Lewis and instead focused on his pursuers, whom he recognized as Special Agents Aubry Gesch and Grace Delmonico. He researched them both. They were good agents with solid track records of closing cases, particularly with serials, although both had high-profile failures as well, cases still open, killers that were not found and victim's families without final answers.

As he watched the video, Gesch and Delmonico were talking to two other people in plain clothes. One was a sturdy man with an athletic look about him, short blond hair and blood all around his face. The other was a woman, tall and athletic.

These two were new to the scene.

As of yet, he'd seen neither of them identified in the media.

They weren't locals from Harrisburg.

An attractive woman like that would absolutely not be a cop in Harrisburg, maybe in Philadelphia or New York, but not in Harrisburg, Pennsylvania. The blond-haired guy with the bloody forehead never appeared when the investigation started nearly two months ago. But he was a cop. He acted like a cop, carried himself like a cop and had a gun on his hip. No doubt about it, he was a cop, but he was new on the scene.

As he watched and re-watched the footage, what he could tell was that Delmonico and Gesch spoke to the guy and the brunette as equals, which meant they were probably bureau people.

He was pulling out tomorrow to continue his scouting, having taken a break. With a face out there now, he needed to be careful about having too much exposure. Besides, a plan was forming in his mind on how to take her, one with a twist, but he needed to work out the approach and exit. There would be downtime while he did that. Time while she was working, sleeping, visiting with friends. That would leave him with some time to ascertain if there were some new people hunting him.

He knew what he was up against with Gesch and Delmonico. But if those two had help now, he wanted to know who the new players in the game were.

12

"MAC, YOU LOOK LIKE SHIT."

5:55 P.M.

Mac drove his X5 through the eastern Maryland countryside north on State Highway 50, having left Salisbury an hour earlier. It was four days since taking down Lewis in Harrisburg and ten days since Hannah Donahue was murdered in Dover, Delaware. Based on the Reaper's history with his three victims, they were getting into the zone when he would strike again.

In the last four days, Mac and Wire methodically went back over the two crime scenes in the hope of finding something that was missed, something that would give them a foothold on the case. There was the extra day spent in Harrisburg after the sketch based on Cedric Lewis's description was released. Mac and Wire reinterviewed her husband and family, went through the autopsy reports, searched her apartment, walked the crime scene in the daylight and even made the bartender who walked her to her car the night she was killed go through it again with them, at two in the morning. Mac and Wire both concluded that the Reaper was waiting for Goynes in her car, put the chloroform over her mouth and shot her up with sodium pentothal from the backseat and then carried her back into the bar and down to the cellar. It was the only thing that made sense to them.

Next, sticking with the order of the killings, they trekked south through Baltimore, then east over the Chesapeake Bay Bridge and into southeastern Maryland to Salisbury for the second victim, Janelle Wyland.

Janelle was an insurance broker and was doing quite well for herself at the age of twenty-seven. She made over $100,000 in the year before her death. Janelle was single, never married and did not have children. She was last seen leaving a prime two-story motel on the outskirts of Salisbury, following a tryst with her boss, something the two were apparently doing for several months.

"Might explain the $100,000 plus in income in the previous year," Mac speculated.

"Figures," Wire replied tartly. "You think the only way a woman could make a hundred grand is by spreading her legs."

"Hey, now, wait just a minute ..."

Janelle was next found just before noon in the basement of an abandoned office building four blocks from the motel, her BMW the lone car parked in the cracked and weed-infested parking lot.

Mac and Wire went through her home, reviewed her financial and cell phone records, interviewed her coworkers and friends and even her boss. His alibi for the murder was he arrived home from their little gathering and was in bed with his wife at the time of death, which the coroner pegged at sometime around 3:00 A.M. The police and bureau sweated Janelle's boss, but his wife eventually backed his story. Of course, she then justifiably served him with divorce papers.

"Janelle's boss had a very bad week," Mac remarked when they left the apartment he was now living in.

"Janelle's was worse."

As with the others, they walked the crime scene, evaluating how it is the Reaper could get so close without being seen. In the case of Wyland, she parked behind the motel so as to not be detected. There was little lighting and no surveillance cameras. The motel, lightly populated on a midweek night, provided for no witnesses and Wyland wasn't discovered until the following morning.

After dark, Mac stood in the back parking area behind the aging motel, which was a combination of gravel and cracked blacktop backed up to a wetland interspersed with trees. There was one solitary dim light to illuminate the back area, a good two hundred feet away. It was a dangerous place for an unaccompanied woman. "I've seen this location in a hundred movies," he muttered. "It's the cliché place where someone *always* gets killed."

"Man, he finds these women at their weakest point," Wire moaned. "They're vulnerable, their guard is down and boom, he hits them."

"What I can't figure out," Mac said, "is what did Janelle Wyland do to deserve this? What did Melissa Goynes or Hannah Donahue do to deserve this? I don't get it."

"Nothing," Wire said.

Mac vehemently shook his head, "That's where we're wrong, Dara, they did *something*. I'm not saying they did something wrong, or evil, but they did something, whether they even knew it or not, they did something to set this guy off on them. They did something that this guy says they must reap what they sowed. I mean, I keep coming around to the verse he left on Janelle, Galatians 6:7—Be not deceived; God is not mocked: for whatsoever a man soweth, that shall he also reap. I mean. did they witness someone get killed?"

"Or did the three of them together kill someone?"

"No connection between the three of them," Mac answered. "If there were, then I'd start thinking something like that was the connection, given the verses. But these women did something, Dara. They did *something*. They have something in common that set this guy off."

"There's nothing in their backgrounds that ties them together," Wire responded. "I mean, you're looking at the same stuff I am. There's nothing."

"That's where we're wrong," Mac answered as they approached Annapolis. "There is *something*, Dara. We just haven't connected it or found it yet. I'll bet you a thousand dollars it's there. We just need that one little piece of information that somehow ties it all together. All the pieces we've found matter, we just don't know why or how yet."

"Problem is, Mac, will we figure it out in time?" Wire asked with a dire tone. They'd both been obsessing over the passing days on the calendar. "It won't be long now."

The media knew that as well.

A serial killer known as "The Reaper" was terrorizing the states around the nation's capital. One of his victims was the daughter of a prominent political player. That and a twenty-four-hour news cycle led to the case garnering a certain amount of media coverage every day now. It wasn't over the top coverage, and in many ways was tailing off, but it was nevertheless a story that was receiving follow-up inquiries and coverage.

As Mac and Wire operated out of the media spotlight, working away on the case, Gesch, Delmonico and FBI Director Mitchell found themselves on the front line of the media attention. Gesch and the director had suggested leaking the fact that Mac and Wire were working the case as a way to provide something new to report, instead of repeating the mantra of little progress. Mac and Wire successfully pleaded with them not to do that, at least yet. "Listen, give us a couple of weeks on this," Mac begged. "Give us the time to work this thing without some reporter sticking a microphone in my face. I don't do well with reporters. My typical reactions to their questions will bring attention you don't want."

The pictures and images generated from the sketch created from Cedric Lewis's description were a constant presence, however, both because the media needed something to show and because the task force hoped that if enough people saw the images, something would pop. The images, as much as anything, kept the media's attention.

The pressure from the media, not to mention the director and people like Bill Donahue, led Gesch and Delmonico to call Mac and Wire several times a day looking for updates. "God, Mac," Gesch said, "I'd give my left nut for a break."

"I'd give your left nut too," Mac answered wryly.

The bright glow of Washington was appearing in the distance. Mac and Wire, going flat out for eight straight days, sixteen to eighteen hours a day, nothing but hotels, motels, coffee and bad food, desperately needed a break. He dropped Wire off at her place in Arlington and Mac knew she would be asleep before he reached the interstate. It was a little after eight P.M. when he called Sally, who was, naturally, still at the White House.

"I walked today," she said. "Why don't you stop in? The Judge would like to see you."

"Do you mean to tell me that the Judge is still working at 8:00 P.M.?" the man was in his mid-sixties. "Cripes."

Mac dropped the X5 in guest parking. He took a look at himself in the rearview mirror. His hair was disheveled and his stubble was three days old now, almost stylish. His attire left something to be desired, a green and white checkered Polo button-down collar, a navy blue sport coat and dark blue jeans with dark brown slip-on loafers. It was not the attire to appear at the White House, but it was what it was. After the perfunctory chat and check through security, he found Sally working in her office.

She pushed up from her desk and came around and gave him a kiss and a long hug which he soaked in. After a minute, she stood back and took in his appearance.

"What?"

"Well, a few things," she replied with concern, arms folded across her chest, analyzing him. "You look really weary," then she reached and rubbed the right side of his face, "and you really could use a shave."

He laughed. "Weary?"

"Yeah, your eyes look heavy, circles under them even though the bruising is gone or at least almost gone. You just look exhausted."

Mac shrugged, "Yeah, well, a maniac is probably days away from killing another woman and after four straight days on the road, we really got nothing."

"Nothing?" They both turned to see the Judge standing in the doorway along with another visitor. Well, in this building he wasn't a visitor.

"Good evening, Mr. President," Mac greeted, standing up a little straighter, trying to look a little fresher and now really *really* regretting his appearance.

The president shook his head, "Mac, you look like shit."

"Thank you, sir," Mac answered crisply and everyone chortled.

"Let's go over to the residence and have a drink and relax," President Thomson replied, waving everyone to follow. "Mac, I want you to tell me about the case. I'm getting the official line from Tom Mitchell. I want to actually know what is what."

For the next hour, Mac, with Sally at his side, reviewed the case with the Judge and President Thomson while sipping smooth Kentucky bourbon. Mac couldn't help but be amused at the oddity of the president of the United States getting up out of his chair and refilling his and Sally's glasses. President Thomson had the common touch, a man who came from humble beginnings, built a business from the ground up, worked his way up the political ladder step-by-step and through hard work, a little luck and a fair amount of political instincts, won the ultimate job. But tonight, it was obvious he wanted nothing more than to sit around with three friends, have a couple of drinks and relax, just that it was in the White House residence. Mac was sitting where Thomas Jefferson, Abraham Lincoln, Franklin Delano Roosevelt and John F. Kennedy sat and dealt with the world's issues. It was another bucket list experience for him. He needed to start writing these down.

"So, Mr. President," Mac asked, having answered questions for an hour, "how different is my version than the one you've been getting?"

"It's a blunter, more direct and less sanitized assessment of the case for sure, which I appreciate, my boy. The director tells me the case is being worked hard, which clearly from what you're telling me, it is. They tell me they have leads and they're following them."

"It isn't a lack of effort, Mr. President, but in reality it's actually a lack of *real* leads. We have an idea of what the guy looks like but as of yet, no clue as to where to look for him and we haven't figured out what ties the women together," Mac answered, taking a sip of his fourth drink and starting to feel the alcohol. Sally would surely be driving. "It is maybe the single most frustrating case I've ever worked."

"Is there anything you need? Are there any more resources we can apply? Is there any more that we could be doing to help?" President Thomson asked.

Mac shook his head, "We just need that one break, Mr. President. We need luck, a mistake, a connection, something, and the case will start breaking, I think."

"I thought the picture you got would have led to more," the Judge suggested.

"Wire and I talked about that earlier, Judge. Fact of the matter is that this guy is very good at hiding. If people got a look at him, it was for a brief second and he didn't register in any way with them. He was just a face in the crowd, a guy walking down the street, that you pass in a hallway or you see driving by in a parking lot. He's blending, keeping his distance but he's an ever present shadow in the lives of his victims, they just don't sense or realize it."

"You will catch him though?" the president asked.

Mac nodded. "We'll get him, sir."

"You just won't guarantee me when?"

"Nor how many will die before we get there."

"Wallace, I got a voice mail from Helen."

"And?"

"She thinks this killer, the Reaper, might be following her now. She's seen a man meeting the general description a couple of days here now."

"Is she sure?"

"No. She said it could be that she's getting paranoid given what happened to Melissa, Janelle and Hannah. But she's freaked. She can't run and hiding completely is difficult with her job."

"What does she want from you?"

"Protection."

"Protection?"

"Yes."

"Do you want to provide it?" Wallace asked from behind his desk, pouring himself another glass of whiskey. "I can make that happen if you want."

She thought for a minute, taking a sip from Wallace's fine whiskey. "We could do that. Or," she said as she took a long drink to finish the glass, "I have another thought."

"Which is?"

"How close is the FBI to finding the Reaper?"

"From what I understand, not very close at all. Beyond the pictures, which are pretty rough, they have no idea who he is, how he's identifying his victims or why he's choosing his victims. The president got the FBI to put a couple of his people on the case and what progress has occurred has developed because of them, but even with all of their work, they're not close."

She considered that for a moment as Wallace filled her glass. "Logically, I'm the last target. He wants me the most so he'll be coming for me last."

"Agreed."

"So, my thought is we can let this guy take care of the loose ends for us and when he gets to me, we let him get close and we take care of him then. We've got people who can do that, don't we? People willing to do that? People willing to do more than just protect?"

"We do."

"Okay then. We let him take everyone out, then we kill him and this thing will be put to rest once and for all."

∼

He waited in his truck, an hour until showtime, and reached for his laptop. He wanted to watch the video again, to get in the proper mood, to remind him of why he was doing this. The Reaper fast forwarded to the part he needed to watch.

He pushed play.

There she was again, her arms bound behind her back, her legs fastened to the chair with duct tape, her mascara running down her face with the tears. The sniffling, the exhaustion apparent on her face and in the way her body drooped in the chair.

"So what was her role in all of this?" he asked in a monotone voice.

"No more, please no more," the woman whimpered.

"Answer the question," the Reaper replied sternly. He thought back to the night he made the video and he'd slapped her three times already by this point to make her compliant. "What was Helen's role in all of this?"

"She said 'we have to get out of here.' She really pushed that."

Those last words, "we have to get out of here," ran through his mind as he watched her approach her little sports car, a member of her crew following her to the car. It was clear she was wary, trying to be a little safer. It was a different guy each of the last few nights. Tonight, it would be her friend's unlucky night.

She'd backed the car into the parking space. Helen reached the car and fiddled in her purse with her keys. She found them and pushed the key fob. It was three steps from behind the tree. He moved when the car alarm beeped. The man, a gentleman, opened the door for her when the Reaper hit him from behind with the tire iron, putting him down.

"No!" she screamed but the "o" was barely out of her mouth before the rag was over her mouth and he was dragging her back into the woods behind the long, untrimmed branches hanging down just off the ground.

The chloroform did its job as he pressed it to her mouth and up against her nostrils. She had no choice as she struggled but to breathe it in.

"We have to get out of here. We have to get out of here," he repeatedly and angrily grunted quietly into her right ear as he pressed the rag ever harder to her mouth. "That's what you said, Helen, we have to get out of here."

Those would be the last words she would hear.

In less than a minute she succumbed to the fumes and went limp in his powerful arms. He pivoted his left foot back and violently threw her down to the ground with his right arm.

Quickly, he moved back to the parking lot and dragged the man back between the cars to the edge of the parking lot, out of the immediate eyesight of anyone who would come out to the lot.

He ducked under the tree and looked down at her lying unconscious on the ground.

This time there would be no interrogation.

He ripped the knife out of the sheath, dropped to his knees and plunged the blade into her and grunted in exhilaration as he ripped violently upward from her pubic bone.

A little after midnight, Sally lay with her head on his chest, her naked right leg comfortably draped over him, the sweat cooling on their bodies, their breathing regular and easy now. They didn't talk, they just let themselves be. The only ambient noise was the air conditioner fighting to cool the house from the muggy June air.

Mac didn't want to move. He just wanted to soak Sally in, feel her skin on his and lightly run his fingers over her back. He was totally relaxed. His mind, for the first time in a few weeks, was totally free and at ease.

Eventually she drifted off and he fell into a deep exhausted sleep. He could go days on end without more than four or five hours a night, but tonight and into tomorrow, he was going to catch up and recharge. He was too tired to even dream.

But the nightmare came.

The *Dragnet* ringtone woke him; it was Gesch.

He picked up his phone, 4:47 A.M.

He answered: "Where?"

"Baltimore."

13

"DO YOU HAVE SOMETHING YOU WANT TO SHARE WITH THE CLASS?"

BALTIMORE, MARYLAND - 6:03 A.M.

"I think this investigation will have the media's full and undivided attention today," Wire said in an understatement, as Mac pulled up to the crime scene behind Baltimore television station KBLT Channel 6. Sandy Faye, the 10:00 P.M. news anchor, was victim number four.

Mac and Wire flashed their FBI credentials to a uniform officer who gave it a quick glance and then raised the yellow tape and let them through. He pulled forward another one hundred feet and stopped directly behind Gesch's Suburban. They slipped out of the X5 and Mac looked to the south behind his truck and took in the scene and the media gathering. In one sense, it was a morbidly amusing scene. Channel 6 was fighting for space behind the police tape, *on their own property*, with all of the other local television stations. The amusement was short lived, however, as he realized Dara was right, "This is going to be a shit show now," he remarked. "The media lost one of their own tonight. They're going to be relentless."

"Gesch's problem," Wire remarked.

"It'll be ours as well," Mac warned. He saw a familiar

face in the crowd of media, a face that he unfortunately made eye contact with. And with that, he knew that he and Wire's time operating in the background would soon be coming to an end. He turned away and looked to the north towards the portable lights and small crowd standing at the edge of the tree line and made eye contact with Gesch who nodded for them to come forward. Wire handed Mac a pair of light blue rubber gloves as they walked towards the body.

This would be a first experience for them on the case, actually seeing the fresh crime scene and body. To date everything had been well after the fact. Gesch was about to fill him in when Mac said, "Let me go take a look first. I want to see it with a clear mind."

Another barrier of yellow tape had been strung well around the victim. Mac and Wire ducked underneath and approached the body. This time was different, the body was outside. Sandy Faye was lying in the woods thirty feet from the edge of the parking lot in a band of thick trees and bushes. The coroner was doing her examination, taking notes. A crime scene tech hovered around and was taking pictures.

Mac and Wire identified themselves, "Special Agent Gesch said you two were coming," the coroner answered.

Mac knelt down near Faye's body. The first thing he noticed was she was pretty, petite with black hair and olive-colored skin. She was lying in the fetal position, her arms wrapped around her upper torso, her knees pulled up to her chest. Her abdomen has been sliced wide open, internal organs visible from the vicious gash once again in the shape of the Holy Cross. The cutting was getting more vicious with each victim and Sandy Faye had been savagely gutted. The blood had drained from her body and formed a large pool in the dirt and mud around her. All of the victims were killed in the same manner but the wound this time was more vicious, almost ravenous, as if he'd plunged the knife in that much deeper. The horizontal cut, usually more superficial, this time made it look as if she'd been cut in half.

Wire pushed in for a little closer look and gasped, "Oh my God," she croaked, and let out a big exhale, "Oh my God. It's one thing to look at the pictures ..."

"And another to see it like this," Mac finished flatly. Seeing the body up close and personal was far more shocking than anything you would see in a crime scene photo. Mac was a homicide detective and would always think of himself that way. Over the years, he'd seen many forms of man's inhumanity to man. The Reaper's handiwork was simply another display, exceedingly horrific as it was. It was vicious, animalistic and inhumane. Yet, sadly, he thought to himself, he was unfazed by the blood and gore, desensitized and simply analytical.

Wire, on the other hand, was not a murder police in that sense. While she'd seen dead bodies before, this was something entirely different, being this up close and personal. He took a quick measure of her. She was struggling a little bit but she kept it together. She wasn't going to be sick. Not right now at least.

Mac turned back to the coroner. "Do you have an approximate time of death?"

"Body temperature says sometime between 11:00 P.M. and midnight," the coroner answered.

"Do we have a biblical verse?" Wire asked, having stepped back and away from the body.

The coroner nodded and handed a plastic bag to Wire: "A proud look, a lying tongue and hands that shed innocent blood." The note was typed onto a three-by-five note card.

"Proverbs 6:17," Mac replied. He'd looked up biblical verses about reaping what you sow and this was one he remembered. However, this particular choice of verse and its language struck him as having more of a message to it, or at least that was his initial gut reaction to it. From his crouched position he looked back to the parking lot and the crowd. "Is her car one of the ones on the edge of the parking lot?"

"Yes," the crime scene tech answered. "The sporty white Mercedes, the one backed into the parking spot. She was being careful yet she was killed anyway."

"Careful how?" Wire asked.

"She had a coworker escort her out here. They found him lying near the edge of the weeds here, unconscious. He was hit in the back of the head with a tire iron. He's at the hospital now in surgery."

"So the Reaper stood at the edge of the tree line in wait for her," Wire remarked, hands on hips with her back to the body, still getting her breathing right from the sight of the victim.

"And he doesn't care that she has someone escorting her," Mac continued, moving back to the parking lot and to the car door for the Mercedes. "He has the tire iron. When his back and Faye's back are to him, he jumps from the trees there, hits him from behind right here, puts him down and is on her instantly. He might even be dragging her out of the car." Mac slowly walked backwards, "He has the rag to her mouth and drags her back into the woods to here."

"He drops her where she's lying now, goes back and drags the guy who escorted her to the edge of the tree line."

"So nobody would see him, at least not for a little while. At least long enough until he could finish the job on Faye and ... get away."

Mac looked away from Wire and to the north into the woods. With the early morning sun shining, he peered straight ahead through another twenty yards of trees and could see a soccer field and farther in the distance a larger soccer stadium with a large seating pavilion and lights. Turning a little more to his left, with his back now to the body of Faye, looking more to the west, he could see a bare area with random gravel, sand and dirt piles. Wire saw where he was looking and walked around behind him and looked into the woods towards the piles. She kneeled down with her flashlight.

Mac came up behind her. "Pretty big print," he remarked.

"Size thirteen or fourteen, I'd say, and there's another one," she pointed five feet ahead. It led towards the direction of the piles. Mac led them out, their flashlights scanning ahead, seeing a general path towards the opening and the piles. Mac picked his way through the woods to the left of the path. He could see three more of the same sized prints in dirt patches, two going towards the piles, and one print towards Faye's body. They were large prints with a boot tread of some kind.

At the edge of the tree line they came to an opening of grass for ten yards to a dirt road. On the other side of the dirt road were additional grassy areas surrounding bare patches of the sand, gravel and black dirt piles. In addition to the soccer fields there were also baseball and softball diamonds available as part of a larger athletic complex. Also now visible to them, another hundred feet away to the northwest, was a maintenance shed which was likely for the athletic fields they could now fully see.

By now Gesch and Delmonico had noticed where the

two of them were going and were following. "What are you two seeing?" Delmonico asked.

Mac and Wire were crouching down, looking at indentations in a section of grass just off the dirt road. He looked at Wire, "Pickup truck or SUV?"

"Based on width of the tires and how far the tracks are apart, yeah."

"What?" Gesch asked.

"He parked here," Mac said, pointing to the indentation and then the fresh tracks on the dirt road. "A truck or SUV. He walked into the woods from here to the edge of the trees at the parking lot." Mac stood up and walked to one of the large footprints. "These prints are fresh and go back and forth into the trees. So he parked here, went into the trees and waited for her and for her friend."

"Her car is backed into her parking spot," Wire added, picking up on Mac's thread. "Those huge trees are practically hanging over the edge of the lot. All he had to do was stand behind the trunk of one of those large trees along the edge. In the dark, dressed in all black, he was invisible. I bet he stood here a few nights first, just to get a feel for things."

"Right," Mac agreed. "And he knew she had someone escorting her at night."

"So he knew that when she or her friend opened the door to the car, with their backs to him, he could attack."

"My guess is there aren't any traffic or security cameras right around here," Mac stated. "But we should pull traffic and surveillance cameras anywhere remotely around here and see if we see a truck or SUV leaving this area between 11:00 P.M. and midnight."

"We'll do that," Gesch answered. "However, I lived in this town for a while and know this area. There are lots of ways in and out of here, mostly through residential neighborhoods," which meant no cameras, "but we'll try."

Gesch was on his cell phone immediately.

"We know how he got to her, but why kill her outside?" Delmonico asked. "That's different."

"Maybe there was never a chance to get her somewhere inside," Wire answered.

"Or maybe leaving her body lying outside the television station, gutted unlike anything I've ever seen, has some symbolic meaning particular to Faye. She was a reporter, maybe there is something symbolic about that."

"Man, a reporter. This is going to be awful," Delmonico moaned.

"He's getting braver and more daring for sure," Mac suggested, "not to mention confident."

"And vicious," Wire added. "That wound ..."

"He's escalating." Mac agreed. "And ..."

"What?" Delmonico asked.

He shook his head, "He wouldn't dare, I don't think."

"What?" Wire and Delmonico asked in unison.

"He wouldn't be hanging around, would he?"

Delmonico stopped, stared at him and said, "Probably not, but we shouldn't ..."

"Take the chance," Mac finished the thought. "We need all footage being shot, we need pictures and we need to go right now and see who is hanging around that shouldn't be."

He wanted to stay around and watch. The itch to do it was there, especially with Sandy Faye.

"*A proud look, a lying tongue and hands that shed innocent blood.*"

Proverbs was perfect.

Hers was, so far, the most satisfying of the kills.

She was the one who pushed hard for them to keep going and not stop. She had her career, already off to a good start at the time, and nothing could get in the way of that.

Now, all her friends, colleagues and rivals would be coming to the scene. The media swarm would have been fascinating to watch. It was tempting, but ultimately, the smart play was to stay away. Where he took her, where he left the body, the location behind the television station, all made the location too difficult to get to and not look out of place. That and the fact that the FBI might think he would be hanging around made it too dangerous, at least this time.

The risk was simply too big.

The news coverage would have to do.

He wasn't doing this for himself. This mission was to avenge someone else. However, he'd expected more media attention when it started, the biblical verses, the brutal murders, the Holy Cross, all elements that made for a great media story. With Donahue, and her family's political and financial prominence, he thought more coverage would come, and there was an increase after her murder and plenty of attention was paid to the false alarm in Harrisburg. But overall, he expected more, he wanted more. To a certain degree, he was counting on it, to help with the misdirection.

He was pretty certain now he would get it.

Her prominence and his viciousness would assure it.

Since her body was discovered early in the day, the news channels were just getting up to speed on the discovery, mostly borrowing from the local Baltimore television feeds. The FBI and local authorities were keeping the media a good distance away from the crime scene. In time, though, the people he'd been looking for appeared. First he saw

Gesch and Delmonico. The agents chasing him for nearly three months now looked grim and tired. It took another while of flipping around from channel to channel on the coverage until he saw them, the tall blond man and attractive brunette. They were on the scene again.

He'd been pretty certain they weren't local cops in Harrisburg.

They were Feds.

Then around 8:30 A.M. as he was watching the coverage on Morning Joe on MSNBC, he finally was able to get names to go with the blond and brunette. Heather Foxx, an NBC correspondent, reported from the scene: "It appears that the FBI task force investigating the Reaper has added two investigators, Mac McRyan and Dara Wire."

"McRyan and Wire," the Reaper muttered. "Those names ring a bell."

Heather Foxx continued: "As you will recall, they are the two that broke open the investigation on the Wellesley Campaign and their attempts to manipulate the vote in the days before last November's presidential election."

"Heather, how is it we know Mr. McRyan and Ms. Wire are involved?" Joe Scarborough asked.

"They were seen arriving at the crime scene this morning, Joe, almost within the hour of the discovery of Sandy Faye's body."

"Heather, do we know how it is that these two have become involved in the investigation and how long perhaps they have been involved?"

"We don't as of yet, but that will be something we'll be following up on to learn what role they may be playing."

"Thank you, Heather," Scarborough then turned to Mika and the panel, which included Mike Barnacle and John Heilemann. "Well," Joe stated, "let's discuss this for a minute. Here's what I'm thinking, guys. As you will recall, the Reaper's last victim was Hannah Donahue, the daughter of William Donahue. We know Bill Donahue spoke with the president the day after his daughter's death. Is it possible that the president turned to two trusted hands to help with the investigation? Is it possible Mr. Donahue asked the president…"

"Bill Donahue doesn't ask for things," Heilemann said with a smile, "he demands things."

"Okay," Scarborough replied. "Is it possible that Bill Donahue *demanded* results and the president perhaps suggested to FBI Director Mitchell that he assign some of his trusted people to the investigation?"

"I think without question," Mike Barnacle stated. "That's what we'll find out. I mean, how better to mollify Bill Donahue than to put two people like that on his daughter's murder investigation. What more could the president possibly do?"

The Reaper turned off the television. Interesting, he thought. The president is watching developments of the case. He pulled his laptop over and typed Mac McRyan and Dara Wire into Google Search.

~

"Mac will be thrilled," Sally said, sitting on the couch in the Judge's office.

"It was inevitable," Judge Dixon stated, running a fresh cigar under his nose. "Their faces are too recognizable. I thought it would come out after their little incident in Harrisburg."

"How do you want to handle it?"

"Handle what?"

"The White House's role in putting Mac and Wire into the investigation. We, meaning the White House, are going to get asked about it. I mean now that Scarborough and his crew have figured this out, it won't take long for the other networks to get in on the act."

The Judge was nonplussed, "For now, Director Mitchell will have to handle that. It's his show."

Sally smirked, "We're going to get asked. The White House is going to get asked. The dots have just been connected."

"And if we do, we do. Look, if this were a political investigation of something we did wrong or the government did wrong, some law was violated and we maneuvered those two into the investigation, then we'd need to cover our tracks and be very careful about how we responded. This is a serial killer case and one of our good friend's daughter was killed. We offered all assistance, including asking two first-class investigators to help. If someone wants to make a political issue out of that …" the Judge looked to her skeptically.

"Bring it on," Sally finished, understanding the Judge's point.

"Exactly," the Judge answered. "Of course, perhaps you should mention that to Mac when you call him here in a minute."

"I'm calling him?"

"Yes you are, and when you do, tell him to avoid the media on this and let those in a higher pay grade handle it."

"I won't have to tell him *that* twice."

"Understood," Mac answered Sally as he followed Baltimore detectives to Faye's condo in downtown Baltimore on the

Inner Harbor. He had her on speaker so he could sip his Starbucks. He'd been planning on ten plus hours of sleep. He might have gotten four.

"So where are you going?" Sally asked.

"Gesch and Delmonico are going to the autopsy. Others are questioning the staff at the television station. Wire and I are going to check out Sandy Faye's condo."

"Hmpf," Sally snorted.

"What?"

"They're giving you two the B or even C duty?"

Mac smiled, "To the contrary, my lady, Wire and I wanted this. We have a theory."

"Do you now?" Sally asked, interested.

"Yes we do."

"Care to share?"

"Ahh, no."

"Why not?"

"I don't need to have my theory appearing in the media thirty minutes later, Ms. Deputy Director of White House Communications. Especially now that the media is aware of our involvement and quite rightly speculating the White House got us involved. Time to build a Chinese Wall."

"I'm hurt, Mac," Sally replied lightly and he could imagine her smiling. "I'm hurt, just so hurt, that you think I'd do that."

"Whatever," Mac answered, rolling his eyes. "Look, if our theory pans out we'll let you know." With that he hung up.

"And what exactly is our theory?" Wire asked curiously, sipping her coffee.

"I don't know that it's a theory as much as my gut, but we're only going to find what connects these women by knowing them inside and out. There is something that connects them, there has to be, we just haven't found it yet, or maybe we found it and we just don't realize it."

"What if there isn't, Mac? What if there isn't a connection between them? What if our killer is just a nut job gone wild?"

"I just don't think that's the case. He's not your standard serial killer. This is something different."

"Why?" Dara asked seriously. "I mean, why can't the guy just be crazy?"

"Something is clearly amiss with his brain chemistry, Dara," he answered. "That part's for sure, and what he's doing is bat shit crazy. But the way he's going about doing it is not. He's methodically selecting and hunting these women. There is nothing random about them. They're all in the same age range, generally attractive, good citizens and successful for the most part. And, with the exception of Sandy Faye this morning, he's interrogated them. Why? What's he after?"

Wire shrugged, "I don't know."

"Dara, it's because there is something they have in common or that our killer thinks they have in common and once we find that, then maybe we get a little insight into our killer and how to find him. That's my story, that's my theory anyway, and I'm sticking to it."

Working the anchor desk must have made Sandy Faye good money. You needed it to live where she was, in a condo right on the southeast side of Baltimore's Inner Harbor. For all the problems Baltimore had, and the city had many, one thing they got absolutely right was the development of the downtown Inner Harbor area. There were new condos, restaurants, office towers, not to mention Oriole Park at Camden Yards for the Orioles and M & T Bank Stadium for the Ravens. For an attractive successful twenty-eight-year-old professional, this was the place to be.

The Baltimore detective let them into the condo. Mac and Wire once again slid on rubber gloves. Faye's condo was a two-bedroom unit. As they walked in, the kitchen was to the left and then led into an eating area that looked out to the patio area that overlooked the blue waters of the harbor. Straight ahead was a family room area with a couch, two chairs arranged in a horseshoe to view her large flat screen and to the right was the hallway to the two bedrooms and bath. Faye had converted the spare bedroom into an office.

As had become their pattern, Mac took the office and Wire the bedroom.

In the bedroom, Wire started with Faye's closet which consisted of her large wardrobe of business suits and outfits for her anchor work, along with high-end casual attire for her nights out. While she undoubtedly wore comfortable shoes, probably flats at work when she wasn't on camera, she wasn't afraid of stiletto heels and had three rows of them on shoes racks in her closet. There were three boxes stacked in a corner. She pulled them out and opened them quickly. Inside one box were photo albums, framed photos and other assorted photos. One was from a high school track team, another of Faye and others outside a television station in Albany, an earlier television job, and another of a group of men and women at a summer camp in upstate New York. One thing she learned was Sandy Faye changed her name. Her given name was Helen Williams. Sandy Faye probably sounded like a better, and probably hotter, media name. The second box contained what looked to be papers from college. The last box contained knickknacks, a few old sports trophies and other miscellaneous items.

Next she moved to her bed and the nightstand. In the

drawer on the clock radio side were the usual items, notepad, pens, remote control for the television, old cell phone, hand lotions and some medications. In the nightstand on the other side, Faye exposed her kinkier side, with fuzzy handcuffs and other various toys to enhance the sexual experience. Wire smiled; she had some of these items stored away somewhere, and if Martin Gonzalez came up from Florida, she might have to find the moving box they were stored in.

In the master bathroom she found the usual items for a woman of Faye's age, makeup, lipsticks, curling iron, various medications, her birth control pills as well as a bottle with the morning after pill, which was interesting but didn't really tell her anything.

Wire completed her review and walked across the hall to find Mac looking through Faye's desk. He was staring off into space, a thick wad of papers in his hand. "Find something?"

Mac shook his head, "I'm going through some old papers and I've seen something that looks familiar but I can't put my finger on it."

"Which item?"

"Sandy was a smarty. She has a lot of scholastic awards. Something in them is familiar, that I've seen before."

"On the case?"

"Maybe. Can't put my finger on it," he answered as he put the papers into an evidence box.

Mac continued working through Faye's desk, pulling at the drawers while Wire worked another part of the desk, going through her old-fashioned Rolodex. She flipped through the names and business cards. "Typical reporter, she must have a couple hundred contacts in here."

"Reporter on the rise," Mac answered, working his way

through a filing drawer. "From what Gesch told me, Baltimore would not have been her final destination." He stopped, snorted and shook his head with a rueful laugh.

Wire saw it, "What?"

"Faye reminds of my first big case that I had back in St. Paul. This smokin' hot reporter back in the Twin Cities, I found her strangled in her own bedroom. Claire Daniels. She was on her way, beautiful, smart, really driven and the investigation revealed her to be, shall we say, rather sexually active and adventurous."

Wire laughed, "Well, maybe it's something about media work because Sandy Faye had a nice little sex toy collection in one of her nightstands and the Plan B pill in her bathroom. What happened with that case back in St. Paul?"

"We originally thought she was killed by Senator Mason Johnson."

"Oh, I remember this case. Turns out he didn't do it, right?"

"That's right. He was set up, killed to hide it, but we eventually figured it out as part of a larger case. That case," he smiled again, "that was when Sally and I met. She was the county attorney assigned to our investigation."

"Love at first sight?"

"Attraction for sure. The rest didn't take long." His phone rang, it was Gesch. The autopsy was in progress. "But you two should get down to the television station. One of her coworkers thinks she recognizes our guy."

Twenty minutes later Mac and Wire pulled up to the WBLT station building. The chaos of earlier in the morning had now dissipated somewhat, although all of the local television stations were retaining a presence just outside the crime scene barrier. Mac and Wire walked inside and were immediately greeted by a large, rotund Baltimore detective named Landsman. After quick introductions were made, Wire asked, "What do you have?"

Landsman waved them back into the building and walked them into the television studio. The Baltimore detective called to a tall, thin, redheaded woman in a headset. "Agents McRyan and Wire, this is Brenda Bell, a producer here at the station. She was a friend and coworker of Sandy Faye. Please tell Agents McRyan and Wire what you told me."

"The detective showed me a picture of this man," Bell pointed to the sketch of the Reaper in Landsman's hand.

"You recognize him?" Mac asked.

"Maybe. Sandy and I would go running Monday, Wednesday and Friday mornings down along the Inner Harbor, around the water, just a little three-to-four-mile run from her condo, around the Harbor to the end of the pier by the Marriott and then back. And a few days here recently, there was a guy who looked kind of like this man in this picture that was, I don't know, maybe watching us."

"Watching you?" Mac asked, quizzically. "Watching you how?"

"It's hard to describe other than, he seemed to be looking for us, you know?"

"Like he expected you? Was waiting for you?" Wire asked.

"Yeah."

Mac asked, "So what made *you* notice him?"

"He was a big guy, leaned with his elbows on the iron fence, hands clasped, in the same spot like three straight days when we were running, where we would turn at Pier 3 towards the National Aquarium. Then on Monday he was at the end of the bridge on Harbor Bridge Walk and Pier 6, just past the Pier 6 Concert Pavilion.

"Was he staring at you, watching you?"

"Staring? No. I don't think that but watching or maybe more like noticing, yes. I mean, to a certain degree when you were with Sandy you're used to that because of who she is and how she looks, she was gorgeous and men noticed her. But when we were running, she didn't look like Sandy the television personality. Instead she looked like just another stylish runner in running clothes, sunglasses, and a ball cap, not that recognizable, or at least as recognizable, but he seemed to know who she was."

"What did he look like, other than looking like this picture?" Wire inquired casually, but she and Mac were anxious.

"Different clothes, although usually a dark T-shirt, sunglasses and a baseball cap. He didn't have a beard though, clean shaven."

"So what makes you think it was the guy in these photos and the sketch?"

Bell shrugged, "He just looked like it. He was a big guy, maybe a little squarer in the jaw, but big broad shoulders and arms. He had on wraparound sunglasses and always a baseball cap."

"Did this alarm Sandy in any way?"

Bell shook her head and then stopped, "Alarmed isn't the right word."

"What is?" Mac asked.

"Now that I think of it, cautious is the better word. I know that for the last week or two she had a member of the crew walk her to her car at night in the parking lot."

"Just like last night?"

"Yes. It wasn't the same person every night, just someone from the crew who was available. It didn't seem like a big deal at the time, a woman asking for an escort at night. It's pretty common."

"So why do you mention it now?"

"Sandy always ended up parking at the back end of the lot. You know how it is, you tend to park in the same place all the time, and since when she typically arrived for work the lot was full, she parked in that last row. She's done it for a couple of years. But only in the last two weeks did she ..."

"Have someone escort her to the car," Wire finished the thought.

"Yeah."

"And the only time you ever remember seeing this man we're talking about is in the last week or so?"

"Yes."

"Okay," Mac asked Bell, "give me the days and times again. And can you show me on a map where you saw this man?"

After they were done talking to Bell, the three stepped into a small conference room Landsman was using to conduct interviews. "Detective, we need to get back down to the Inner Harbor and see if we've got any security cameras of these areas."

"Follow me," Landsman answered. "I'll be in the black Ford Fusion."

As they drove back down, Mac was noticeably quiet. "I know the faraway look. What's on your mind?" Wire asked.

"Faye noticed this guy. She's in the media, she's probably reported on the Reaper story and she sees this guy who maybe looks like the Reaper. However, instead of calling the police, she starts having people escort her to her car and watching her back. She was on guard, she took some precautions but she didn't call the people who could have really protected her."

"So?"

"Why not tell the police? Why not report it? I don't get it."

Wire agreed, "It is very odd behavior."

"So odd it's got me thinking a very terrible thought."

"Which is?"

"That whatever connects these victims, Dara, is so bad they can't go to the police. If they go to the police, they'll be exposed and that exposure is so bad, they'll risk their lives to avoid it."

With the locations given by Bell, Mac, Wire and Landsman made their way down to the Inner Harbor. It was midafternoon, the sun was bright in the sky and the temperatures approaching a sultry ninety degrees. Mac was down to his off-white casual dress shirt and jeans and Wire had shed her black nylon jacket and was down to her black sleeveless shirt and blue jeans. Following the map they found the first location at Pier 3. Mac stood right where Bell said the man was standing. He looked in every direction and didn't see a camera anywhere.

"We have uniforms that walk this area all day," Landsman said. "But it would not appear surveillance cameras."

"Let's try the other spot," Mac suggested and Landsman led them off on a ten-minute walk as they weaved their way through the various piers that jutted out into the harbor. Each pier contained a collection of shops, restaurants and seating areas. They passed the large concert pavilion and walked over a footbridge from Pier 6 to East Falls Avenue. Once again, Mac stood where Bell described the man as standing, elbows resting on the railing, underneath a series of small shade trees. Again, there were no visible surveillance cameras covering the area. Mac turned to look to the east, towards the Marriott Hotel and smiled, "Detective," Mac pointed to two cameras hanging down from the Marriott parking structure.

"Worth a try," Landsman answered and the three walked over to the Marriott.

Ten minutes later they were led by the hotel's head of security back to the security offices. A security technician pulled up the replay of footage from the day before.

"What time window?" the tech asked.

"Between 10:30 and 11:30 for this past Monday. We need the footage for the two cameras on the northwest corner of your parking structure," Mac answered.

The tech maneuvered the mouse on his computer, "Here we go, starting at 10:30 A.M."

It took a half an hour and then there he was, walking from the northeast towards the bridge to go to Pier 6.

"There he is, Mac," Wire said. "Just like Bell said, he's wearing jeans, dark T-shirt, baseball cap and sunglasses."

"I'd give anything, just once, *just once*, for this guy to not be wearing sunglasses," Mac answered and then thought. "If he's coming from the northeast, are there any other cameras that might have caught him?"

The tech maneuvered his mouse, opened another file and started the playback. It took a minute. "There's your man," the tech pointed. "He's walking northeast and as he crosses there, he's probably continuing east on Fleet Street. He could turn left and go more north on Presidential, but I would think he's just continuing east on Fleet."

Wire looked to Landsman, "Detective, looks like we need to check the businesses on Fleet Street and see if we can keep tracking our guy. Or maybe get an even better look at him."

Mac's cell phone rang. It was Gesch. Mac filled him in on

what they were finding. "I'm thinking maybe we can trail him back to his vehicle."

"Mac, that's great. Keep the Baltimore detective on it and I'll get him some help right away. I just got the autopsy report and we're going to do a conference call with the director here shortly. I need you two here for it."

"Aubry, I'd much rather stay on this ..."

"If it were my call, I'd let you, but it's not my call. The director wants you two on it. You and Wire are all the rage with your media debut this morning." After another minute of back and forth, Gesch hung up.

"Detective, keep on this and help is on the way. An even better picture of this guy would be great. Finding him getting into his vehicle, getting a make or plate would be even better," Mac stated and he and Wire left him to continue.

The conference call started at 5:30 P.M. in a conference room at the Baltimore Police Department. The call included Gesch, Delmonico as well as the Baltimore Police commissioner, a Colonel Wilson, the head of detectives, as well as two other detectives who'd been assigned to the ever growing Reaper Task Force.

Gesch handed Mac and Wire each a copy of the autopsy report and then began the conference call. "Good afternoon, Director Mitchell. I have a number of people in the room with me ..."

The autopsy report wasn't going to tell him anything, so Mac tossed it onto the table. Baltimore detectives brought in several boxes from Faye's apartment.

"Those were in her closet," Wire explained as Mac walked over and tossed the top off the first banker's box and started flipping through the photos in the box while listening to Gesch run the conference call.

"It appears," Gesch reported, "that McRyan and Wire did confirm that the Reaper was tracking Faye. They have him on surveillance footage."

"Is that right, Mac?" Director Mitchell asked.

"Yes sir," Mac answered looking up from a photo album. "It looks like our man was watching Faye while, among other things, she was taking a regular morning run along the Inner Harbor area here in Baltimore. He appears, however, to have shaved off his beard. Baltimore PD detectives are working right now to see if they can get an even better image than the one we have. Another thing that we've found is that Faye appears to have been cautious lately, having people escort her to her car at work, something she'd never done until recently. She's in the media, she has undoubtedly seen the photos of the Reaper and she saw him, or someone who sure looks like him, yet ..."

"She never called the police or the FBI," Director Mitchell said over the phone.

"That's correct, sir."

"Any idea why, Mac?"

"No sir," Mac answered, deciding now wasn't the time he wanted to get into his terrible thought. That was for later.

Gesch continued the report and Mac returned to the photo album and scanned a few more pictures. He put the album back in the box and started flipping through individual photos when he stopped on one, a group photo of college-aged men and women in front of Lake Seneca Lodge. The kids were stacked up on the steps as well as leaning over the porch and second-floor balcony railings. The date on the photo was seven years ago almost to the day in July. He found Faye standing on the steps. Even back then she was a looker, wearing short white shorts and a tight red tank top that accentuated her figure which caused Mac to linger over the photo for a moment, then he froze. The woman standing right behind her, "You look familiar," he muttered.

Mac scrambled back to the table and started thumbing through the files until he found the photo array he was looking for. He took out his cell phone and thumbed through his applications and found his magnifying app.

Wire noticed the frantic look on Mac's face and slid her chair over and whispered into his ear, "What are you doing?"

Mac pointed to the picture, "There's Sandy Faye," he said, pointing to the attractive Faye. "And who is that standing two steps up behind her?"

Dara peered at the picture through the magnifying glass app on Mac's cell phone and her jaw slowly dropped open, "Oh my gosh," she whispered, looking at the photo closely. "Look at the logo on her shirt, on a lot of the shirts."

"AAHC," Mac answered. "I knew I'd seen that somewhere before."

"You know, I wonder," she muttered, scanning the rest of the photos.

"Right, anyone else?" Mac added, scanning with his finger and a few seconds later their fingers landed on a face standing on the second-floor balcony and their voices shouted in unison, "There!"

Their excitement drew stares from everyone in the room.

"You two have something you'd like to share with the class?" Gesch asked, a perturbed look on his face.

"Aubry, there's no connection we're aware of between our victims, right?" Mac asked.

"That's right. No record of their paths ever crossing as far as we know."

"Well now there is," Mac answered, holding up the photo. "Seven years ago, Sandy Faye, back then named Helen Williams, Melissa Goynes and Hannah Donahue were in a picture together at Lake Seneca Lodge for the AAHC, American Academic Honor Society. That is not a coincidence."

"Mac, are you sure?" Gesch asked walking towards them.

"No doubt," Mac answered as Gesch leaned over the table. Mac held his cell phone over the picture, still using the magnifying glass app. "See?"

"I'll be damned," Gesch said in agreement. "Director, we've just found a connection between at least three of our victims. They were at the AAHC camp in Lake Seneca, New York."

"Aubry, get after it," Director Mitchell ordered.

Ten minutes later Mac, Wire, Gesch and Delmonico looked at a blowup of the picture on a large flat screen. There were seventy people in the picture, thirty-eight women in the picture along with thirty-two men.

"Janelle Wyland is not in the picture," Gesch stated, going over it again and again. There was not one redhead.

"Any chance she had a different hair color back then?" Wire asked.

They all scanned the picture again, each holding a picture of Wyland. She was not there.

"So we have three of the four victims in a picture. There is a connection of some kind," Mac answered. "And we have thirty-five potential other victims and …"

"Perhaps thirty-two potential suspects," Wire finished, scanning the men.

"And we don't have a serial killer just picking women at random. We have a killer with a very specific purpose."

14

"QUIT WORKING ME."

WILMINGTON, DELAWARE

In the late afternoon, Mac pulled up to the Donahues' family compound on the southern outskirts of Wilmington. Gesch and Delmonico were on their way to see the parents of Sandy Faye and Detective Dorsett in Harrisburg was on his way to see the family and friends of Melissa Goynes.

Seven years ago all three women served as counselors at the AAHC camp on Lake Seneca for eight weeks from mid-June through mid-August for junior high and high school students. A quick call up to the lodge revealed that the three of them had been students who attended the camp in prior years, although never together. However, for that summer, they spent eight weeks together. The three of them may not have stayed close or in contact in the years since, but for eight weeks, they were together at a lodge in upstate New York.

Now seven years later, within a matter of two months, the three of them were murdered by the same killer.

This wasn't a coincidence.

Mac was thinking something bad happened in upstate New York.

"So we have a serial killer interrogating, torturing and killing women and at least three of them served as counselors at this summer camp. So what happened up there and what's Wyland's connection to them?" Wire asked.

"My initial thought is maybe she was at the camp as a student," Mac answered, "but Wyland's actually a year older and the camp had no record of her, but she fits in here somehow, Dara. I think we're eventually going to have to head up to that camp and start poking around."

"Maybe the Donahues can shed some light on it."

"That's the plan."

The Donahues welcomed them into the home and walked them back to a sunroom that overlooked the Delaware River. Coffee, iced tea and cucumber sandwiches were waiting for them.

"So, do you have news?" William Donahue asked, sitting next to his wife on a small sofa with his elbows on his knees, leaning forward. "I saw on the news this morning that this man ... struck again in Baltimore, a television news anchor. Please tell me you have made some progress."

Mac nodded, sitting down in a chair across from the Donahues. Wire took a chair to his right. "We may have made a breakthrough this afternoon, but to know for sure we have to ask some questions about Hannah's time up at Lake Seneca Lodge."

"Lake Seneca Lodge?" Bill Donahue asked, confused.

"When she was a camp counselor?" Mrs. Donahue asked. "That was years ago."

"Seven to be exact," Mac answered and pulled out the picture from the camp. "Seven summers ago Hannah was a counselor at the camp. Now, I think when we were here last time we asked if you'd ever heard the names of our first two victims Melissa Goynes or Janelle Wyland and whether Hannah knew them, right?"

"And we don't think she did."

"Turns out she probably knew one of them and she knew Sandy Faye," Mac answered and showed the Donahues the picture. "Have you ever seen this picture?"

Both the Donahues shook their head.

"Well, here's Hannah," Mac pointed and then moved his finger, "Here's Melissa Goynes and there's Sandy Faye. Back then her name was Helen Williams. The three of them were at Lake Seneca Lodge for the summer together."

"That can't be a coincidence."

"No, we don't think it is," Mac answered.

"Do you remember anything about Hannah's time there?" Wire inquired. "Was there anyone she had problems with?"

Bill Donahue shook his head but Mrs. Donahue didn't right away. Mac picked up on it. Bill Donahue noticed the look on Mac's face and turned to his wife. "What is it?"

"I don't know, but now that I think of it, when Hannah came back home from that summer she was … different."

"Different?" Mac asked, "Different how?"

"Hannah was a very outgoing, energetic and happy person. Maybe I was the only one who noticed it, but when she came home that summer she was more, I don't know …"

"Serious," Bill Donahue added, remembering now. He looked to Mac and Wire and explained. "Up to that point, she'd been something of a party girl, not all that serious about school, a little bit like a rich girl who had Daddy's money. She didn't have to worry about how to pay her Cornell tuition or room and board. She had it pretty easy and was having a really good time."

"It wasn't long after that summer that she started talking about giving back, working with kids and becoming a teacher," Barbara Donahue noted. "She'd never ever talked of that before."

"Did you ask her what triggered it?" Wire asked.

"No," Barbara Donahue answered, shaking her head. "I always figured it was that she matured, maybe had something to do with serving as a counselor those summers up at Lake Seneca with those younger kids. Sooner or later most college age kids figure out they have to get their act together and plan for life. Whatever it was, when she left that summer, she was carefree. The change wasn't dramatic, but when she came home, she was a different and a more serious person."

"And she never said what might have triggered that?" Mac pressed.

The Donahues shook their head.

"And you never asked? You never asked Hannah what's changed? Where did all of this sudden maturity come from?"

They both shook their head.

"Seriously?" Mac pushed, going bad cop, needing to be sure. "I find it hard to believe you noticed this change in your daughter and you never asked her what triggered it."

"I don't like the tone," Bill Donahue barked.

"I don't care. I'm trying to find a killer."

"And we're trying to help."

"We're just trying to be thorough," Wire suggested quietly, putting her hand on Mac's knee to calm him while putting her hand out towards the Donahues. "There's a connection here. The Biblical verses the killer leaves behind suggests he's punishing the girls, they're reaping what they sowed. So we're just trying to find anything that gives us some insight into what that might have been. We have three of the four victims as counselors from that camp. We think something happened up there."

"Hannah and I were very close," Barbara Donahue answered, her eyes welling. "And she never said a word. To be honest, I just thought she started maturing and found some purpose in life. I was happy with what she decided to do and had no desire to question it."

"We were proud of her," Bill Donahue added. "I respected what she was doing and the direction she chose."

Mac still pressed forward. "And now seeing this picture, Melissa Goynes and Sandy Faye don't mean anything to you?"

"No," Bill Donahue answered emphatically. "I swear to you, McRyan, I never heard her mention those names."

"If she knew them, she never said a word to me about it," Barbara Donahue added, wiping the tears away from her face. "We've seen, and I'm sure, in fact I know, Hannah has seen Sandy Faye on television doing the news and not once did Hannah ever, *ever*, say she knew her. Not once."

"How about Janelle Wyland," Mac asked, still pressing. "Her name never came up?"

William and Barbara again shook their heads. "Other than these killings, we've never heard the name before. We don't recognize her. She was not a friend of Hannah's."

The Donahues' sons arrived at the house and Mac and Wire walked them through the same series of questions. Hannah's brothers recognized Sandy Faye from television but had never met her and never heard their sister talk about her. The same was true of all of Donahue's friends that Mac and Wire talked to, including Wendy Jonas, who they reached in Singapore.

From the front lawn of the Donahue's home, well away

from the house, the sun quickly descending in the west, Mac put his phone on speaker and called Gesch and reported in. Gesch basically received the same responses from Faye's family and friends as did Dorsett from that of Goynes's family. They even had the detectives in Salisbury questioning Wyland's family and friends even though she wasn't in the picture, the thought being if Donahue, Goynes and Faye were connected, Wyland fit in somehow.

None of the names rang a bell with anyone.

The picture triggered no recollections.

"I thought this was our break," Gesch moaned.

"It is Aubry, it is," Mac answered.

"But what is it? What happened, Mac?" Wire asked. "I keep running it around in my head and I ask: what happened up there?"

"Something bad," Mac answered. "Something very *very* bad. Something that these women experienced that they never talked about, never acknowledged and I'm betting never spoke of again. In fact, I'm betting they agreed not to see or talk to each other ever again."

"You don't know that's what it is," Delmonico stated.

"I'm guessing, sure," Mac answered, "but I've got four dead bodies, three of them with a direct connection yet no record of them being in contact with one another since that summer seven years ago. If something bad happened to make someone angry enough to start killing, then it's not a stretch to think these women vowed never to discuss it, never to see one another again."

"Get back to DC, Mac," Gesch ordered. "Tomorrow morning I'm flying you two up to Lake Seneca. If something bad happened up there, it's time for the two of you to find out what it was. And Mac, one other thing."

"What's that?"

"I don't want to read about our break in the *Post* tomorrow morning."

~

Just after midnight, Mac slithered into the bedroom and Sally popped awake. "Hey."

"Hey," he answered, coming over and kissing her lightly. "You should be sleeping."

"That always happens better when you're in bed with me," she answered sweetly. "Besides, I wanted to wait up for you. Why so late?"

"We were briefing the director and attorney general."

"You got a break, didn't you?"

"Why do you say that?"

"Seriously?" Sally answered and then did her best cavewoman, "Me prosecutor, me really good reader of witnesses, me know you and see look in your eyes, me know you caught break," she said smiling. "Besides, if you're briefing the attorney general and director late at night, you have something more than an update to provide. So what happened?"

"A small break, nothing big. I'm going on a day trip to upstate New York tomorrow to look into something," Mac said as he put his clothes in a hamper and then walked back into the bedroom in his boxers.

"That's it? That's all you've got."

"That's all I'm giving," he answered as he slid into his side of the bed.

"What? You don't trust me?"

Mac leaned over and kissed her, "Trust? You work in the White House. People are already talking about how you got us involved in the case. I think it might be time for me to talk less and you to ask less."

"Really? You think I'd compromise your case?" Sally asked, lying on her side, facing him.

Mac shook his head, "No. But I wouldn't put it past others in the West Wing."

"Didn't take you long to get cynical."

"What are you talking about? I came to this town cynical," he answered as he adjusted his pillows.

"But now you're cynical about me," Sally said, a tinge of hurt in her voice and on her face.

Mac turned to face Sally and saw the disappointed look on her face and felt terrible, for about three seconds. Then he recognized her expression for what it was, "Quit working me."

"Shit," Sally replied, laughing, rolling onto her back. "I almost had you."

"Listen," Mac answered, seriously, leaning on his side, facing her. "I'd like to tell you more but I think the less you know right now, maybe the better. If the director wants to give the White House more, he can give it. I'm keeping my mouth shut."

"I have just one question."

"Sally," Mac warned, rolling onto his back.

"Have you found something that could embarrass the White House?"

"I don't think so," Mac answered, hedging. He'd not worked that out in his mind yet.

"You'll tell me if we could be damaged, somehow, you'll tell me, you'll let me know, right?"

"Yes," he answered and then rolled and gave Sally one last kiss. "Now go to sleep."

15

"SMALL TOWN COP WITH BIG CITY BRAINS."

The FBI jet landed at the Penn Yan airport and two black Suburbans awaited their arrival along with two stereotypical agents in dark suits, sunglasses and their hands clasped in front of them. "They look like extras in a Michael Bay movie," Mac quipped.

One Suburban was for them, which Mac quickly drove to the north side of Lake Seneca, through a large stone arch with Lake Seneca Lodge engraved in the stone, underneath which hung a wood carved sign announcing it as the summer home of the American Academic Honor Society. Through the arch, Mac drove down a long tree-lined drive that emerged into a large open area with the road splitting the manicured lawn and eventually circling in front of the large lodge. As Mac hopped out of the SUV, he could see the small dorms set back into the woods as well as the deep blue waters of Lake Seneca.

A woman who looked to be in her mid to late forties, a white golf shirt with an AAHS logo and long tan cargo shorts came quickly down the steps, extending her hand.

"I'm Alice Walton, the executive director of the camp. Please come inside."

Mac and Wire followed Walton inside the main lodge entrance, straight through a large seating area of couches and chairs and past a large stone fireplace soaring high into the dark timbers of the rafters. Past the fireplace, they turned left down a long narrow hallway to a corner office with large windows that overlooked a grassy hill descending gently down to the sandy beach and the lake.

Walton's corner office was spacious with a U-shaped desk in the corner. To the right as they entered the office was a seating area arranged around a rustic two-toned colored wood carved table. Coffee and pastries were placed on a tray on the table between a couch and two soft chairs that awaited their arrival. Walton sat down on the couch and quickly served them and then stated, "I can't tell you how shocked we are to learn that three of our former counselors were murdered by this killer you call The Reaper. Have you learned anything further?"

"Only that the three of them were here at the same time," Mac answered, opening his leather folder to take notes.

"Well, from what I've been able to uncover from our records, it was just the one summer they were all here together," Walton answered taking three manila folders out of a brown red-rope file. "Melissa Ross was here as a counselor that summer, as was Sandy Faye, back then her name was Helen Williams. Hannah Donahue was the only name that rang a bell here initially because she was a counselor here for three summers and her father William was and remains such a generous contributor. They of course were all students here when they were in high school but not the same weeks."

"How is it they became counselors?"

"We like to have college kids as our counselors and we recruit the counselors from the students who were here when in high school."

"The summer they were all here together, was there some sort of conflict or incident that would have been cause for concern?"

"There is nothing in the files that point to that," Walton answered, shaking her head and then sipping her coffee. "I have a lot of turnover of staff, in addition to a new batch of counselors every summer. I've been contacting people who were here at the same time to see if they remembered anything and at least so far, nobody has."

"We'll need a list of those people," Wire stated.

"Of course," Walton answered, handing over a folder with the information. "That's what I have so far and we'll give you anything we have, just let me know."

"How about the relationship of the three women; what, if anything can you tell us about that?" Dara solicited.

"The only information I can glean from our records is that Hannah Donahue and Melissa Ross were counselors in the same dorm and in fact were on the same floor. Helen Williams worked in the next dormitory over."

"So Hannah and Melissa knew each other fairly well then," Mac suggested.

"I would say that's likely. You work as counselors together on the same floor, by the end of the summer you'll know each other well."

Mac shook his head, "Odd."

"Why?" Walton asked.

"There is no evidence whatsoever that Melissa and Hannah Donahue ever were in contact again after that summer in any way shape or form. No phone calls, no e-mails, Facebook, texts, nothing. In fact, that's true of all four of our victims. Other than the picture we found with Hannah, Melissa and Sandy Faye, there is no record of contact and we still don't know where Janelle Wyland fits in."

Mac and Wire spent the next half hour working through the files and questioning Walton, but nothing probative came to life.

"Let's turn to speculation then," Mac asked, pouring another cup of coffee. "If these three were to have gotten in trouble in that summer up here, how could that have possibly happened?"

"I've been thinking about that since last night. The only time I think something like that could have happened would be on a Saturday night."

"Why on Saturday night?" Wire asked.

"Sunday through Friday night, the kids are locked in here and the counselors are looking after them in the dorms. Nobody gets out of here then. But Saturdays are the transition day here. The students from the previous week leave by noon on Saturday and the next batch of kids doesn't arrive until Sunday afternoon. Saturday nights the counselors have free and we do let them leave the camp so if they go out and get involved in something on a Saturday night ..."

"You might not know about it," Mac finished, nodding his head.

"Right. That's all I can think of," Walton answered. "Otherwise, we'd have a record of it because if kids get out of line or the rules are violated, we deal with it. We've sent kids home for trying to sneak out at night or otherwise violating the rules of the camp, and that's true of both students and counselors. We don't have many problems, but every once in a while something happens."

"But there's nothing in any of these three girls' records to suggest anything like that happened?" Mac asked as he thumbed through the files, which contained general information, dates of birth, high school and college records and reviews of their performance, exemplary in all cases—three girls with incredibly bright futures.

"No," Walton answered, pouring herself more coffee.

"What would the counselors do when they left on a Saturday night?" Dara asked.

"Go into town, maybe find a party to go to and just do whatever young college age kids do. This is vacation land up here. Lots of college age kids are around in the summer so you can imagine what they might possibly get into. College kids are college kids. Sometimes, if they don't find trouble …"

"It finds them," Mac finished. "But from what you're telling me, you don't recall anything from that summer?"

"I'm sorry, I don't and I don't have anything in my files, no incident reports, anything for these three, or for really anyone that summer. Other summers have been a little more eventful but seven years ago we had a good quiet year."

Mac sat back in his chair and sipped from the coffee, which wasn't bad. He looked to his right to Wire who was looking out the window to the lake, thinking.

"One thing you might want to do is talk to the police chief in Geneva," Walton suggested. "Chief Whitlock was here back then. Perhaps the girls got into something we never found out about and maybe he'd have something for you."

"Does that happen?" Wire asked. "Where your students get into trouble offsite and you don't hear about it?"

Walton nodded. "Let's say the chief has informed me of some mischief he and his officers have come across over the years that he's not told us of until a much later date. These things are usually minor, sneaking out or sneaking back in midweek or some other issue when they happened. But then a year or two later, he'll get this big smile on his face down when I see him down in his booth at the Cozy Cousin Restaurant and he'll say: 'Did I ever tell you about the time …'"

After a stop at the Geneva Police Department, Mac and Wire were directed to find Geneva Police Chief Percy Whitlock at the Cozy Cousin Restaurant, a classic diner sitting on the corner of Exchange Street and Paradise Alley in downtown Geneva, two blocks from the lake.

Whitlock, a large, round, African American man with his aviator shades tucked in the breast pocket of his shirt opposite his badge, was occupying a significant percentage of a corner table with an elderly gentleman, both ordering lunch. They walked up in time to hear the chief order an open-faced turkey sandwich with gravy and mashed potatoes. After introducing themselves and displaying their identification, Mac and Wire took seats opposite of the chief and Milo Fissure, the former and now retired chief of police for Geneva. Whitlock and Fissure cordially invited them to join for lunch, and given the time of day, Mac and Wire agreed, ordering quickly from the menu themselves. "The food here is tremendous," Whitlock exclaimed happily pointing to his rotund stomach. "As you can see, body by Cozy Cousin."

"Where did you come from, Chief?" Mac asked as Whitlock looked to be in his mid-forties.

"Buffalo. I was a homicide detective but the hours were running me ragged and the wife, well, she wanted a slower life, so when the position opened up here, I came over and interviewed with ole Milo who was setting to retire. A week later he offered and I took it and I ain't never looked back." Whitlock guffawed, "In a life full of sometimes questionable decisions, this was a great one. So," he gestured to Mac and then Wire, "has the FBI dropped their dress code?"

Wire and Mac were both casually dressed. "No, we're more like consulting Feds than real ones."

"Ahh, you're the ones I heard about on the news the other day if I'm not now mistaken."

They both nodded.

"Refusing to wear the FBI uniform? A sort of, shall we say, form of fashion defiance?"

"I don't know about her, but I left all my dark suits back in Minnesota," Mac answered smiling and the conversation continued for a few minutes on various matters, everyone getting to know each other, Whitlock and Fissure were both bullshitters. As their food arrived, Mac finally got a chance to explain the purpose of their visit, even though Whitlock had undoubtedly been alerted to what this would be all about.

"Chief, you would have been on the job here a year or so seven years ago, and I suspect I'm really pushing the limits of your memory here, but do you recall anything in that summer that these three girls were involved in?"

Whitlock shook his head, "Sorry, I can't, at least off the top of my head. I can pull reports and the like, but none of those names, obviously outside of their recent roles as victim, rings a bell with me."

"How about an incident, perhaps unexplained that they could have been involved in?"

Whitlock shook his head, "Nothing that I can recall."

"What kind of trouble would you have had around here back then?"

"Probably the same as we have now. We're in something of vacation country here in the summer months, so there are parties of course, issues at the taverns, the occasional vehicular incident, but I'm scratching my head for that time period and nothing pops." Whitlock reached for his radio on his hip. "Let me call in to the department and see if they can pull reports from that time period, probably June through what, mid-August for seven years ago, right?"

"Correct," Wire answered, and then added, taking a bite of her Cobb salad, "This is delicious."

"And this pastrami is to die for," Mac added, taking another bite. "I need to get the recipe for this for Shamus," a comment which led to a lengthy discussion about McRyan's Pub back in St. Paul, the second McRyan family business, the first being policing.

"My old man was a bartender back in Buffalo," Whitlock stated with a wistful smile. "He's been gone a few years now, but I grew up in that place. It was a place for the brothers to hang out back in the day, both for the ones carrying a badge and for those defying the ones carrying the badges, if you know what I mean."

"Neutral territory?" Mac asked.

"That's right."

"I can relate," which led to ten minutes of Mac explaining McRyan's Pub's sordid history during the era of prohibition.

"John Dillinger drank in the basement of your family's bar?"

"There is a picture of Dillinger, my great-great-grandfather and the St. Paul mayor."

"That's terrific."

"Agent McRyan," Fissure asked, veering to different territory.

"Call me Mac, Chief."

"Mac, you said this was seven years ago?"

"Yes. Does that ring a bell with you, Milo?"

"Not right around here, son, but a number of years ago, which includes my time as police chief in this fine burg, we had issues with parties over by Auburn, which is a half hour to the east."

"What kind of issues?"

"With field parties at abandoned farms or businesses out in the sticks and a big part of the problem were the people coming down from Syracuse. I believe the kids called the parties raves. Kids from all the towns around here were going to those parties and we had issues with drugs, some overdosing and what not. Maybe something happened at one of those."

Mac looked over to Wire, "What do you think?"

"Long shot," Dara answered and then shrugged, "What do we have to lose?"

Mac turned back to Whitlock, "Would you be able to pull reports of any incidents, things of the like over that way, see if there is anything?"

A half hour later, lunch complete, they followed Whitlock back to his office. Sitting on his chair was a report which he quickly thumbed through and then handed it to Mac, "That's the report I asked for when we were at lunch. Nothing jumps at me, but you two should look. But this is just here in Geneva. Now let me see about broadening it out," he said as he walked out of the office.

Mac and Wire flipped through the report. There were party incidents, minor intoxications, vehicle stops, domestic complaints, a few robberies and three burglaries which were ultimately solved and one homicide for the summer that resulted from a domestic incident. "Nothing that seems to fit," Wire remarked.

Ten minutes later Whitlock strolled back in with a report. "Here's the same kind of report basically covering the ten counties around here. Again, I didn't really see much in the report of interest, but take a look."

Mac and Wire flipped through it and it was essentially the same report with more incidents covering a broader area. There were eight homicides, six of which were closed, two that remained unsolved. One unsolved involved the murder of a woman in her fifties in an alley behind a bar in Auburn and another involved a vehicular homicide on August 17, a Saturday night. The victim was named Rena Johnson. Wire was perusing the record as well.

"Chief, can you look up any more on this Rena Johnson case?" Mac gave him the case number.

Whitlock made a few mouse clicks. "Rena Johnson was killed on Saturday, August 17th." The Geneva chief pushed his reading glasses up to his eyes and began perusing the file and snorted.

"What?"

"Milo is like Andy Taylor from Mayberry. Small town cop with big city brains."

"Are you Barney Fife then?" Wire asked, smiling.

"No, dear," Whitlock answered with a wry smile. "It's just that Milo's instincts are pretty good. Rena Johnson was apparently at one of those rave type parties at an abandoned farm that Milo talked about. She wandered away from the party and was walking down Country Road 5 when she was hit by a large silver vehicle and killed."

"How do we know it was silver?" Wire asked.

"Forensics found silver metallic paint on her body. The paint was common to Chrysler and Dodge vehicles, but that in and of itself did not lead to anything. Nobody ever came forward or even called it in. She was found in the ditch around six the next morning by a passerby out for a morning run," Chief Whitlock noted, reading from the crime scene report on his computer. "She was found lying in the ditch in the fetal position ..."

"Did you say fetal position!" Mac and Wire exclaimed in unison.

"I did," Whitlock replied, nodding, suddenly upright in his chair, the casualness suddenly gone. He understood the meaning of that notation. "Let me pull up the crime scene photos." The chief made a few more mouse clicks and then bolted back in his chair and shook his head. He reached for the phone.

"Chief, who are you calling?" Wire asked.

"My opposite's number in Auburn, Chief Pat Dye. You all might want to roll over to Auburn and check this out." Whitlock turned his computer monitor so they could see. "Look familiar?"

On the screen was a crime scene photo from seven years ago, August 17. The victim, Rena Johnson, bloody and battered from the impact of the hit-and-run, was lying in the ditch in the fetal position holding rosary beads to her chest.

16

"IT'S A HAIL MARY, MAC."

Mac made the trek east to Auburn in just under thirty minutes. Auburn Police Chief Pat Dye greeted them in front of the police station. Dye, a stocky man with a military buzz cut to his gray hair, led them right to his office, and awaiting their arrival was another man dressed in plain clothes. Dye introduced them to Detective Flynn, balding and rotund, dressed in a blue suit that probably fit him a few years ago. Perhaps there was a Cozy Cousin expanding everyone's waistlines in Auburn as well.

"Agents, I asked Detective Flynn in here because he investigated the crime scene seven years ago."

Detective Flynn flipped open a folder and slowly shook his head and exhaled, "This is a sad one. We found the poor girl lying in the ditch, grasping her rosary beads, as if she was praying to the Almighty."

"She knew she was going to die in that ditch," Dye added, looking at his own set of crime scene photos. "You two think this girl's death somehow has something to do with this Reaper killer?"

"Maybe," Mac answered. "Certain components of it make us wonder."

"How she's lying in that ditch, I assume?" Dye asked.

"Yes," Wire answered. "From what we were able to glean, it doesn't look like you were ever able to find a suspect."

Detective Flynn shook his head, "That's correct, Agent Wire. Never came close."

"What do you think happened?" Mac asked.

"Rena Johnson was at a rave party at an abandoned farm. We tracked down a few people who were at the party and they remembered seeing her there. Apparently she somehow wandered away from the party and ended up walking along the county road." Flynn took out a map. "This road here is County Road 5, a winding road and in the area of the accident it weaves its way through deep woods. The gravel shoulder on the road is very narrow, so she was practically walking on the white line. You see this sharp bend in the road here. Well, whoever hit her came around this corner, hit her, knocked her flying back and down into the ditch. We have footsteps in the small dirt shoulder along the road that we think were Rena's coming from the south, so we think the vehicle came from the north, around the corner and struck her."

Mac was reading from the file, "Coroner didn't think her death was instantaneous."

"No. She would have been alive for some time, although very badly injured."

"Just with it enough to reach or hold her rosary," Mac suggested.

"That's right, Agent McRyan," Detective Flynn answered. "I doubt she landed in the fetal position holding her rosary."

"No," Mac answered. "There was no 911 call, nobody saw or found her until morning?"

Flynn shook his head, "Jogger saw her down in the ditch. He checked for a pulse, nothing. He had to run to the nearest house to call 911. Just for reference, the nearest house was over a mile away."

"So a silver SUV or truck or van hits her, doesn't stop, just keeps right on going. That makes it a ..."

"A homicide," Flynn finished. "She died of massive internal injuries."

"Is it your theory that the vehicle was at the rave party?"

"I think it's possible if not very likely, but the few witnesses we had that even remembered or recalled Rena at the party, didn't remember any silver vehicles or at least ones that stood out in any way."

"So let me ask," Mac inquired, continuing to look at the picture of Johnson lying in the ditch. "What's a girl who has rosary beads with her doing at a rave party?"

"We don't know," Flynn answered. "Her mom and dad were out of town. Her brother, a cop, was working down in Ithaca and had no idea what she was up to. Nobody knows what she was doing or how she got out there. Like we said, we did find some local people who were at the party who were surprised to see her there, as those types of parties were not her typical scene."

"But none of those locals saw who she came with?"

"No, and we leaned on them hard. We put them through the wringer and they all came out clean. They saw her there, saw her drinking there and saw her engaging in some of the other intoxicating options at the party."

"Such as?" Wire asked.

"She had Ecstasy, some weed and booze in her system according to the toxicology report. Her blood alcohol content was .23, which for someone who didn't have a history of doing much drinking, was a lot. She was an extremely impaired young lady."

"I assume she was going to college?"

"She was, at Canisius College in Buffalo."

"Anyone else in town go to Canisius?" Wire asked.

"A few kids in town did at that time but none of them were at the party."

"No luck on the vehicle?" Mac asked.

"Other than silver paint for a Chrysler vehicle, that's it. We called every repair shop in the state and nobody recalled doing body work on a Chrysler car, truck, SUV or van in the days following the accident and we ended up with nothing." Flynn looked to Mac and Wire, "What does this have to do with your case?"

"The Reaper's victims are posed in the fetal position with the Holy Cross carved in their abdomen. He's sending a message with that. There are certain … similarities to how Rena was found and how our victims have been staged. I'm starting to wonder if our three victims who were at the AAHS Academy at Lake Seneca played some role in her death."

"And someone, namely the Reaper, somehow figured that out and is now imposing his own sentence," Dara added. "At least that's the theory, extremely tenuous as it may be. So that begs the question, Detective Flynn and Chief Dye, who would have the desire to seek revenge on Rena's behalf?"

"Well, not her family," Chief Dye answered.

"Why not?"

"Because they can't. Tragically, her mom and dad died within six weeks of one another five years ago. Mom of breast cancer and then Dad had a heart attack."

"What about her brother Drake?" Mac asked. "File says he was a cop down in Ithaca. Did he look into her case?"

"Yes he did," Flynn answered, nodding his head. "We discussed the case a number of times in the years following his sister's death. They were not close in age, but I got the sense that she was pretty important to him. So for a long time he called every couple of months to see if we had anything. He did that right up until he died two years ago."

"How did he die?" Wire asked.

"Sadly, like his sister. Drake Johnson died in a car accident in the middle of a late winter snowstorm. His car slid off an icy road, down a steep embankment and hit a tree, exploded and burned. The body was charred so badly it was unidentifiable. They had to identify him with dental records."

"So the brother is a dead end," Mac stated.

"Nice, Mac," Wire needled, rolling her eyes at the tasteless pun.

"What?" Mac replied. "He's been dead over two years." Then he turned back to Dye and Flynn, "Is there anyone else who was digging into this? A boyfriend perhaps? Some other relative, is there anyone like that?"

"No. The only one was the brother," Flynn answered. "He peppered us for a while, but ultimately I think he understood the harsh reality of it."

"Which was what?" Dara asked.

"That she was a college kid who got in over her head at a party," Mac answered.

"That's right, Agent McRyan," Dye stated, gesturing with the file, "And she wandered off away from her friends and support, or they left her behind, but in either case, she paid the ultimate price."

"And nobody else ever came around looking into this,

other than her family which are now all deceased."

Detective Flynn shook his head, "I think there was a half-brother up in Rochester, much older than the girl, but he never came around. At least not that I see in the file or recall, Agent McRyan," The Auburn detective took his glasses off and disgustedly stuffed them into the breast pocket of his shirt. "I gotta tell ya, retired detectives tell me about that unsolved case that they take to their grave. That one case they couldn't close that just bugs the snot out of them for the rest of their lives. This has been *that* case for me. If the Reaper is seeking revenge on behalf of Rena Johnson, I don't know who I'd point you to for motive or revenge. I mean, do you really think that's what this Reaper character is doing?"

Mac looked over to Wire, who gave him a shrug, a way of saying: maybe. Certain parts fit, certain part didn't.

A half hour later, Mac and Wire were making their way back over to the Lake Seneca Lodge, having agreed to update Dye and Flynn if they developed further evidence that Rena Johnson's death seven years ago played into the Reaper killings.

They discussed the case on the drive back. "Do you really think this Johnson case has anything to do with ours?" Wire asked. "What does that gut of yours say?"

"My gut says yes," Mac answered. "There's a thread here. We should keep pulling it."

"Why?"

"There's just enough there that I think it's connected somehow. I think Donahue, Goynes, Faye and Janelle Wyland were involved in Johnson's death. They were either at that party or in the vehicle, maybe both, but they had something to do with it."

"How can you know that?"

"I don't know it, Dara. I can't prove it—yet," Mac answered, right arm extended, his hand casually draped over the steering wheel of the Suburban. "But with a little imagination, this all fits together. We have to talk to all of the people who were counselors with Donahue, Goynes and Faye at that camp. I bet somebody knows something."

"Maybe even if they don't know it?" Wire suggested.

"Exactly," Mac answered. "They don't have to be culpable, but they might point us further down the road to finding out if anyone else is."

"It's a Hail Mary, Mac."

"Hail Marys work sometimes. Besides, what else do we have?"

"At this point, nothing," Wire answered as she slumped in her seat and stared out the window, watching the countryside pass on a warm, gentle summer day. The kind of day you'd just as soon be out on a boat on the cool waters of Lake Seneca, or any lake for that matter. "You know, Mac, there are four women dead. That could easily be all there was in the vehicle or involved at that party. If your theory is correct, this could all be over."

Mac sighed and nodded, "That's a possibility," he said as he turned down the tree-lined drive to the lodge.

Director Walton had continued to work through the AAHS records. "Agent McRyan, I found the other two women who served in the dorm with Hannah Donahue and Melissa Ross, well, she is now Melissa Goynes. I also found the three girls who were counselors with Helen Williams, or excuse me, Sandy Faye. I was thinking they might be able to help you."

"Director Walton, does the name Rena Johnson mean anything to you?" Mac asked, showing a picture to Walton.

Walton gazed at the photo and thought for a second and

then shook her head. "No. Should it? Was she a student or counselor here?"

Mac shook his head, "No, just a victim of another crime."

Twenty minutes later, Mac and Wire were driving back to the Penn Yan airport. Gesch called and Mac put him on speaker. "Mac, there is no record of any of the girls either owning a silver Chrysler vehicle or, for that matter, any of their families owning or renting such a vehicle. We went back at least twenty years and nothing."

"That perhaps means then," Mac mused, "that there are others involved still out there he's yet to get. If this were an SUV or van, there would be room for more than four passengers."

"Or," Wire posited, "there are other victims we don't know about. Who knows, maybe he didn't stage another victim for us to find."

"That's not a bad thought," Mac started. "I've wondered that myself. Is Goynes really the first victim?"

"Well, until we figure either of those scenarios out, we keep pushing the investigation," Gesch answered. "What's your next step?"

Mac and Wire look to each other, "Aubry, for now, the Lake Seneca Lodge and the AAHC is ground zero for us. If in fact our victims were involved in the accident that killed Rena Johnson, and if that is in fact what is motivating this killer, then we need to keep talking to people who were working at the camp that summer. I want to start with the two roommates Hannah Donahue and Melissa Goynes had in their dorm that summer."

"Then the good news for you, Mac, is they both live in the DC area. Get on the plane, get back and go see them. The clock is ticking."

17

"SO THAT'S THE MAN WHO'S GUNNING FOR ME."

The sun was peeking through the shades of the cabin and he yawned. His coffee cup was empty but he couldn't really drink anymore. He'd spent the entire night hunched over his computer searching the Internet for background on McRyan and Wire.

Wire was not someone for whom a great deal of information could be found. Her name appeared as part of the election investigation and she was heavily involved in it along with McRyan. The stories alluded to her history as a former FBI agent who left the agency under mysterious circumstances. Surfing the Internet, he found she now owned and operated a security consulting business based out of Arlington, Virginia. The website showed a picture of Wire, a striking brunette, and listed as part of her background her years of service in the FBI working organized crime cases. Otherwise, there was little to be found about Ms. Wire, at least on the Internet.

That was not the case with Michael McKenzie McRyan. Despite the fact that he was in his early thirties, there was extensive information to be found in cyberspace on young Agent Mac McRyan. It made for interesting reading.

McRyan's name was most prominently tied to the investigation regarding the former vice president's campaign and several murders. McRyan and Wire appear to have been the parties responsible for exposing the plot. Much of the reporting was supposition and based upon interviews with other unnamed sources involved in or close to the investigation. As far as he could tell, neither McRyan nor Wire ever were interviewed regarding the investigation. In fact, there was one article in which a large component was the fact that neither McRyan nor Wire would sit down for an interview or otherwise discuss the case. It was hard to tell if it was humility, a desire to avoid media attention, questionable elements to what they did or that they were waiting to tell the story their way. From what the Reaper could tell, it appeared to be the last. A small blurb on the *Huffington Post* indicated that the two were working on a book about the investigation, both having received sizable advances from a publisher. If you were going to write a book, no sense in giving interviews for free. A savvy business move, which apparently wasn't McRyan's first.

He stumbled onto an article in the *Economic Times* about the sale of the Grand Brew Coffee Chain to a large grocery chain. McRyan was a minority owner of the business and appeared to have walked away with millions for his ownership interest. Therefore, he had financial freedom and could do what he wanted.

He found a note in the *Star Tribune* gossip section indicating that following the campaign investigation, McRyan was taking a leave from the St. Paul Police Department. McRyan was dating Sally Kennedy, now the White House deputy director of communications. Kennedy was a beautiful redhead who looked as if she could have been the twin sister of Amy Adams, in the Reaper's opinion. In reading between the lines, it appeared the two were living together, as "moving trucks were reported at the McRyan/Kennedy house in the Highland Park area of St. Paul." The article intimated McRyan would be following Kennedy to Washington, DC, but again, those were the words or thoughts of others, as neither McRyan nor Kennedy were quoted. The gossip columnist speculated that with the move, perhaps a wedding would be in the offing for the lovebirds. The two were undoubtedly living together, somewhere in and around Washington, DC. He was thinking it might be worth a look to see where McRyan lived.

The more he researched, the more he realized the campaign investigation was far from McRyan's only case, it was just one of many. His name appeared regularly over the last four years in the newspapers in the Twin Cities, the *Star Tribune* in Minneapolis and the *Pioneer Press* in St. Paul, although again, he rarely, if ever, was quoted or interviewed. It was clear, in St. Paul, if there was a high-profile case, McRyan was involved. He even ran across a recent case involving a home invasion crew from a month or so ago, and his name appeared. It was also clear that McRyan was not afraid to drop a body to close a case. There had been a number of shootings but never a whiff of impropriety in any of them.

The one time he was able to find McRyan going on the record was an on-camera interview that had been uploaded on YouTube. The interview was conducted by Heather Foxx, the NBC News reporter who noted McRyan's and Wire's presence at the crime scene this morning.

The Foxx interview was from two years ago when she was still a local television reporter in Minnesota. The interview took place after a kidnapping case that had captured national attention over the Fourth of July holiday. The on-camera interview revealed an exhausted yet very well-spoken and intelligent cop. After watching the interview for a second time, one word came to mind to describe McRyan.

Relentless.

The facts of the kidnapping case spoke for themselves. McRyan would not quit. He kept digging, pushing, working and angling, willing to do anything to close the investigation and find the girls. He simply wouldn't stop in his pursuit of the kidnappers.

As he dug further into McRyan, he found an exceedingly interesting background. Like any good detective, he was extremely street smart. However, he was also scary book smart, a summa cum laude graduate of the University of Minnesota as well as William Mitchell College of Law in St. Paul. He'd been a star high school athlete in three sports and received an athletic scholarship to play hockey at Minnesota. While there, he captained the team to a national championship. In a feature article in the *Pioneer Press* Sports Section, McRyan was described as a fearless grinder, an indispensible leader, a left wing willing to do the dirty work that allowed the scoring stars the freedom to roam the ice. As he searched further on YouTube, he found a long video with highlights of the national championship game. The sports section article indeed aptly described McRyan. As a player, he went into every corner, body checking everyone in sight and spending his entire night harassing the opposing goaltender, scoring a key third-period goal on a rebound with two defenders draped all over him. He was, in a word, relentless.

A star athlete, graduating from college and then law school with high honors, so why was he a cop?

He could not find an answer.

From what he could tell there were other McRyans in the St. Paul Police Department. He found an obituary for a Simon McRyan, who was survived by, among others, a son named Michael. Based upon the date of the obituary, Simon died when McRyan was in high school, an unfortunate victim of a hunting accident. Simon McRyan was a highly regarded police detective, so perhaps that was part of it, the son following in the father's footsteps. The name McRyan appeared in other old news articles as well and it appeared that being a cop was something of the family business in St. Paul. Still, if being a cop is the family business, why go to law school? It was a question that remained unanswered as the blazing sun pushed its way through the shades.

The Reaper sat back from his computer, rubbing his tired eyes and sore neck. "So that's the man who's gunning for me."

He'd done some research on Special Agent Aubry Gesch when he took Wyland. Gesch had a long and fairly distinguished FBI career, a worthy adversary who'd closed plenty of cases but had some misses over the years.

From what he could tell of McRyan, however, there were no misses. If he got into a case, he finished it.

This was the man now on the hunt for him.

Based on what he'd seen, Gesch was still running the investigation but McRyan was no caddie. He was heavily involved and undoubtedly responsible for the recent breaks in the case, including his picture now being displayed, one a surveillance image with his beard and two sketches, one with a half beard and the other now without. All of this progress occurred since McRyan became involved. The powers that be had put that unyielding force on the case and McRyan would be coming for him. If McRyan's other cases were any indication, there would be no hesitation about a finish to the case that involved the Reaper being dead.

Three more left to punish.

What was becoming apparent was that he would have to avoid McRyan to finish and time was not his friend.

Two weeks between kills was too long.

18

"ACTIONS HAVE CONSEQUENCES."

The flight back took less than an hour. They were back in the X5 with a late drive-thru lunch. At 3:30 P.M. just northeast of DC, Mac was maneuvering his way through the streets of Landover, Maryland, making his way to Fallway Medical Clinic.

While the name wouldn't necessarily suggest it, Fallway Medical Clinic provided family planning services. The clinic building was set back with a cluster of three buildings in a small treed enclave. The family planning clinic was set to the east on one side of the street, with the other two set to the west, one building hosting doctors' suites and the other a pediatric clinic. The Fallway Clinic was a nondescript rectangular cement building with few windows beyond those framing the front entrance. For all intents and purposes, it looked like a warehouse compared to the sleek stainless steel and glass of the other two buildings. The sign on the front of building to the right of the front main entrance simply read Fallway Medical Clinic and nothing more.

"Well, they're not advertising what they are," Wire observed. "That's a pretty bland-looking building."

"Not bland enough," Mac answered, pointing to the people holding picket signs. "The protesters know it exists." There were six protestors hanging around loosely on the sidewalk in front of the clinic. When Mac drove by, the protestors briefly came to life and raised their signs, but once Mac and the FBI sedan behind him pulled by, they relaxed again.

Mac pulled around to the back of the clinic to a small parking area for staff that separated the clinic from the thick woods behind the clinic. As they parked, a woman opened the back door to let them in. Her name was Sylvia Kostas, an administrator working at the clinic. She led them into her office and closed the door.

"I'd like to keep this as private as possible, I've seen the news reports about you two," Kostas stated.

"Then you know what we're investigating?"

"I assume Hannah Donahue's murder. How can I possibly help?"

"You served as a counselor at the AAHS camp at Lake Seneca Lodge in the same dorm with her seven years ago, correct?"

"Yes. I was on the floor above her, Leslie Felding and I."

"And we're going to go see her next," Mac answered. "Do you recall the other counselor in your dorm?"

Sylvia squinted, thinking back. "I think her name was Missy, or at least we called her that."

"Actually her name then was Melissa Ross," Wire noted.

Kostas snapped her fingers, "That's right."

"Her married name was Melissa Goynes," Mac added and put out a picture of Goynes. "She was the first victim of the Reaper. Hannah was the third."

Kostas sat back in her chair, shocked. "I never made the connection. Oh my God!" she exclaimed, looking at the picture, starting to shake. "You have my attention now. What's the connection?"

"We're hoping you can help us with that," Mac stated. "Let me ask, did you know Hannah well?"

Kostas shrugged, "I got to know her pretty well that summer. We had to work together quite a bit."

"Did you stay in contact since that summer?" Wire asked. "Were you friends after that?"

"Yes, although I wouldn't say we were super close," Kostas answered, nodding. "I suppose one of the reasons we stayed in some contact is that I'm from Delaware originally, Dover, so when I'd go home to visit, I'd go see Hannah. I actually helped her move into her house a few years ago when I was visiting home that weekend."

"So in those years since you worked together, how did she seem?" Wire asked, leaning forward, elbows on her knees.

"What do you mean?"

"Happy? Sad? Different?"

"I'm not sure what you're getting at, Agent Wire."

"Think about it this way, Sylvia," Mac suggested. "Was she somehow different from when you were with her that summer at camp?"

Kostas sat back and thought for a minute. "It was probably another year after that summer before I saw her again. When I did, now that you ask these questions, she was different, I guess. She'd committed to being a teacher and she was more serious and mature about ... everything."

"Which was different from what she had been like?"

Sylvia smiled and nodded, "Hannah was very popular at

camp for a reason. She was a fun rich Cornell party girl with a stash of weed and wine in her footlocker at camp."

"And she was never caught with that?" Wire asked.

"No, and she never worried about getting caught. Like I said, she was a rich Ivy League party girl. She never worried about the repercussions. She didn't have to with her family's money and influence, it's like there were no consequences."

"And a year later?"

"Not as much like that. The personality was still there, but you had to work a little to get it out."

"How so?"

"It's hard to describe it," Kostas replied, sorting through her vocabulary options in her head. "It was like … like she needed permission to smile, to laugh, to have a good time. She used to go from zero to sixty in five seconds when it came to laughing, joking and partying. Then a year later … it was just different. Sometimes I wondered if something had happened to her."

Mac and Wire shared a knowing look. "Did you ever ask what brought about this change?" Mac pushed.

Kostas shook her head.

"Did she ever say anything?"

"No. Why are you asking?"

"We think something happened or she was involved in something that summer that is coming back to haunt her and maybe the other victims. Does the name Rena Johnson mean anything to you?"

Kostas thought for a second and shook her head, "No, should it?"

Mac didn't answer, instead asking: "Did anything bad happen that summer at camp that Hannah was involved in? Something that would have been … I don't know … a life altering type of event?"

"Like what?"

"Like an event, an accident, an incident of some kind that could have gotten her into serious trouble?"

"What are you getting at?"

"We're particularly interested in an event that occurred on Saturday, August 17th of that summer. Do you recall anything about that date?"

"No I don't, why?"

"Nothing at all?"

"That would have been at the end of the summer camp, I would think. I'm not sure I'd have even been around."

"Why not?" Dara asked, her turn to be confused.

"I think, given that date, that Saturday would have been the end of the last week of the summer camps. I know for a fact that once all the kids left about two hours later, I packed and I left for a summer vacation with my family in Maine. I'm pretty sure I wouldn't have been around that night."

"How about Leslie Felding, would she have been there that night?"

"Maybe. I don't know for sure, you'd have to ask her. Why do you keep asking about that night? What happened that night? Who is Rena Johnson?"

Mac and Wire explained.

Kostas simply shook her head, "Honestly, if Hannah was involved in that, she never, *ever* said a word."

6:10 P.M.

Nervousness set it.

Her husband had left two hours ago in a cab with a rolling suitcase. He was going out of town. You don't take a rolling suitcase for a day trip.

She wouldn't be back until at least 9:00 P.M. if not later given her work hours. It gave him time to contemplate how he planned to work his way inside. The house was at the end of the street with the stream running to the south of the house and the alley in the back ended in that fashion as well.

He opened his backpack sitting in the front seat of his pickup.

Lock picks.

～

"Listen, we need to talk."

"Where are you calling me from?"

"My office."

"We shouldn't be talking."

"We have a problem. Somebody knows."

"I told you, I told all of you that night that we could never speak of this again. We could never see each other again."

"Have you been watching the news? Have you seen what is happening? *Somebody knows.*"

"Knows what?"

There was silence on the other end of the phone.

"There is nothing to know. There is no evidence."

"Then explain what has happened to Melissa, Janelle, Hannah and Helen. Explain that?"

There was a pause, "Okay, listen, you need to stay calm."

"How do you expect me to stay calm? Jesus Christ, someone is coming for us. They're picking us off one-by-one." The voice paused. "Look, maybe we ought to go in and tell the truth. Whatever trouble we'd be in would be a better price to pay than our lives."

"No, we can't do that. I'll handle this. If you're afraid, I'd suggest you figure out a way to make yourself scarce for a while. The FBI will find the killer soon enough."

She hung up the phone and looked at it. This was a problem. She scrolled her contacts for the number. There was an immediate answer.

"Yes."

"I think we need to have our people pay someone a visit. She may be cracking."

~

Sally nibbled on carrot sticks and sipped from her bottle of water as she took a break from her laptop and crafting language for the president's upcoming speech on immigration reform. CNN was on the television mounted from the ceiling in the corner. Politically, the news cycle was slow at the moment, so CNN was, as were the other networks, continually coming back to the murder of Sandy Faye in Baltimore and the ongoing Reaper investigation. The Grim Reaper graphics weren't helping nor were the constant recitations of the biblical verses, which were now coming out. In the last twenty-four hours, the media significantly intensified their coverage. The media lost one of their own as victim number four. This was on top of the previous victim, the daughter of William Donahue. There was blood in the water and a big story to be reported on.

It had been twenty-four hours since Faye's murder and very little new had come out beyond another new picture of the killer. The image was a grainy surveillance image from some distance but now the killer was without a beard. That led to a revised drawing of the killer with a clean shaven face. While the image was constantly being shown, there were no new breaks in the case being reported. That wasn't necessarily a surprise. Sally thought there was little distinctive about the face. You could walk by him on the street and think nothing of it.

Now retired FBI agents and big city homicide detectives with serial killer case experience were coming out of the woodwork to comment and speculate on the investigation. Someone had ducked their head into Sally's office earlier in the day to tell her that the Investigation Discovery Channel was now running a twenty-four-hour serial killer marathon. The first three stories on the front of the *Huffington Post* dealt with the investigation as well. The media was slowly but surely turning up the heat and the FBI task force was feeling it, Mac was feeling it. Drinking tequila shots before coming to bed told her he was feeling the heat.

The press briefing from later in the morning provided little new about the investigation other than to answer questions and state that the investigation was ongoing. Mac's and Wire's names came up and there was constant speculation from the various talking heads on CNN, MSNBC and FOX as to whether the White House had involved itself in the investigation. FBI Director Mitchell attempted to defuse that issue. He acknowledged their role in the investigation but stated that the bureau asked them in to assist. The press remained undeterred. And in Sally's mind, why would they be? The network correspondents who regularly covered the Justice Department as well as the litany of retired FBI agents commenting on the investigation all stated that in their experience, it was highly unlikely the FBI would bring in people from the outside unless specifically pressured to do so.

In the case of the Reaper investigation, that wasn't entirely true.

When the Judge strongly suggested bringing Mac and Wire into the case, Director Mitchell eagerly agreed, if they wanted in. He wanted the two of them to come back into the fold after the campaign investigation. Perhaps he viewed the Reaper case as another way to get them to come back.

With nothing new and the speculation becoming boringly repetitive, Sally muted the television and went back to the immigration speech. A few minutes later there was a knock on her door and she looked up to find Judge Dixon.

"What's up with your boy?" the Judge asked.

"I assume you mean Mac?"

"I do, what's he up to?"

"What do you mean?"

"How's the investigation going?"

Sally pointed to the muted television, "Haven't you been watching? All Reaper all of the time, or at least it feels that way."

"I've been watching but it doesn't tell me anything. What do *you* know?" The Judge was fishing for information.

Sally shrugged, "Nothing really. Mac got home very late last night and was out the door early this morning ahead of me. He was going somewhere on an FBI jet but thought he'd be back tonight. Judge, I don't get how he does it. He goes for days on end with little sleep when he gets his teeth into something like this. He won't let it go until it's done."

"He didn't say anything about the case though?"

Sally shrugged her shoulders, "He said there was a small break but he wouldn't share with me beyond that."

"What was the break?"

"I don't know, he wouldn't tell me."

"Why not?"

"He said something about keeping a wall between the

investigation and the White House. I got him to commit to tell me if anything came up that would be an issue for us."

"Did he say why he got home so late?"

"He said something about briefing the attorney general and FBI director."

The Judge sat down on the small couch that filled the left wall of her office. "I heard there was a late night briefing as well, which strikes me as odd, unless ..."

"There was some sort of break in the case."

"And not a small or minor break either," the Judge stated. "Small potatoes doesn't get the attorney general hanging around for late night meetings. I know. So what was it?"

"Like I said, Judge, whatever it was, Mac wasn't talking."

"Is that unusual?"

She thought about it for a minute, "There usually isn't any reason for him to not tell me. He's always shared his cases with me. From time to time I've helped and served as a sounding board."

"Except, look where you work now?" the Judge answered, pulling out a cigar and running it under his nose, inhaling the aroma.

"Did you call the attorney general or the FBI director?"

"Yes."

"And," Sally replied, rolling her palms open waiting for a response.

"They both said there was nothing new to report other than they obviously had the newspaper reporter as victim number four and I guess Mac and Wire tracked down another image of our killer from a surveillance camera, again with a hat and sunglasses, but this time without a beard. That's been on television and online all day."

"Maybe that's what they were briefing the attorney general and director about."

"At midnight?" The man shook his head.

Sally had known the Judge for just a little over a year now but she could read the signs. The Judge smelled something. "You don't buy it."

"No. I've called around to some of my other sources over at Justice and they knew little other than there was the late night meeting. It's very tight lipped over there."

"So ..."

"I came down here seeing as how you and that boyfriend of yours are so close."

"Well, we do live together so I'd say yeah we're close," Sally answered, not picking up on the Judge's drift.

"No," the Judge said, shaking his head. "You're *close*. You're as close as any married couple I've ever seen, Sally. You should see yourself watch him and vice versa. You should see your face light up when he calls. You turn into an entirely different person."

"I do not!"

"Hah," the Judge laughed. "Most of the time around here, you are as serious and driven a person as there is in this building. Just like your boy, tunnel vision. People are intimidated by you because you're strong, smart, a creative thinker and they know the president and I trust you implicitly. Yet when Mac calls, you turn into this girl who blushes and smiles and gets all giddy."

"I do not get giddy," Sally protested defensively.

"Bullshit, you absolutely do," the Judge answered, needling her now, having some fun. "And Mac? Same thing. He's as wired and focused a person as I've ever seen. Complete tunnel vision when he's on the hunt with a total edge. I mean, Mac can be an absolute prick sometimes. Yet when he sees you, this calm washes over him, he becomes totally at ease. The edge, that disappears."

"What's your point, Judge?"

"You've seen it all day. The media is going ape shit because one of their own was murdered here. In twenty-four hours, Sandy Faye will be a journalistic saint. The press secretary has been getting hammered all day with questions, people looking for updates, answers, information, it's been relentless. I've had press people calling me because they got wind of some conference call yesterday where the FBI had some sort of breakthrough on the case but nobody is saying anything. Something is going on, they've got some sort of break and nobody is talking and I mean nobody. Even he didn't tell you and there is only one reason he wouldn't, and that's to protect you."

"Or the White House."

The Judge shook his head, "No, no, no. Mac doesn't give a damn about the White House, but he gives a big one about you."

"And you want to know."

The Judge nodded, "I don't want to get blindsided. We put Mac and Wire on that investigation."

"According to Director Mitchell, the FBI asked them in," Sally demurred.

"He was fine with it, of course, eager for it, but you were at that meeting; hell, you pushed Mac that extra bit to get him in. *We*," the Judge pointed to himself and Sally, "put them on this damn thing, so we are now invested in it."

"I thought the other day you told me it was Thomas Mitchell's job to deal with Mac and Wire questions. That the White House did nothing more than get two exceptional investigators to help with the investigation. If people had a problem with that, bring it on and all that."

"I did."

"What's changed?"

"What if what they find becomes an issue for us?"

"Mac said he'd tell me if that happened."

"Maybe, but he's not going to compromise his investigation either and, no offense, but he's not the most politically adroit. He may not see the issues the way we see the issues."

Sally took the measure of the Judge. She could sense the Judge wasn't telling her everything either. "Maybe Mac hasn't told me everything, but what aren't *you* telling me?"

"I got a question from a reporter asking me some background on Bill Donahue and his daughter. I could tell by the way he was asking questions that he was fishing, but he had something as well, something he wouldn't disclose to me, but this guy is a pro and has worked the Justice Department beat for a long time."

"Your radar is up?"

"It is."

"What did the reporter tell you?"

"There's the BMW X5," the reporter noted. "That's the right plate. They are here. Yes!" she exclaimed happily. This tipster had paid off a few times before, but now this tip was leading to the White House and might have the chance to be salacious.

"How are you going to play it?" the cameraman asked.

"We jump him, camera in his face. No room to breathe."

"You sure?" the cameraman asked warily. "He's not someone to mess with."

"You keep that camera running. It's the ultimate protection." Local news was boring and she wanted out. This was a national story and she wanted to get to a national stage. There was no way she was leaving empty-handed.

∼

Having finished with Kostas, Mac and Wire were walking down the back hallway of the clinic. "Given how Kostas described the change in Donahue, I'm starting to believe it, Mac. These girls might have been involved in that accident."

"Donahue's parents made a similar observation about their daughter, how she changed after that summer, so there is something to it," Mac answered agreeably. "Whether it connects to this, who knows."

"But let's say they were involved," Dara posited. "She didn't call 911, she didn't do anything for the victim. But she goes back to school, realizes what she did wrong and what? Decides to get her life in order?"

Mac nodded. "Possibly. She thinks she's lived a careless life and now, as a result, someone is dead. I need to do something. I need to make a difference. I need to pay for what I've done. So she decides to become an elementary school teacher. A life that will not lead to the luxuries she's had her entire life but a life that could potentially help and impact others. Maybe Leslie Felding can shed more light on that."

"So is our new operating theory that these girls had a role in that accident and someone is punishing them for it?"

"Actions have consequences," Mac replied nodding.

"You approve of the Reaper?"

"No. No, no, no. But I believe in karma, and she can be one angry, vindictive bitch," Mac replied as he pushed out the back door and the camera and microphone was immediately in his face.

"Why are you investigating this clinic?" a short blond woman with a microphone asked. "Why are you here?"

"No comment," Mac answered, at first surprised by the microphone and camera in his face, but now with his bearings, he walked by the reporter, Wire in tow, heading for his SUV. The reporter and cameraman maintained pursuit.

"Is it true that the Reaper is targeting women because they had abortions? Were the victims patients at this clinic?" the reporter pressed.

"No comment," Mac answered flatly, looking over to Wire who had her head down as they split to get into the X5. He hit the key fob and the taillights flashed.

"You were going through medical records, right? Seeing what women had abortions, right? Is the Reaper targeting women on that basis?"

"No comment," Mac answered again as he reached for the door handle. Another television news van pulled around the back of the building.

"You have to be here for some reason, Agent McRyan. You're on the Reaper Task Force. There must be some investigative reason for you to be here at Fallway Medical Clinic?"

"No comment."

The reporter was unsatisfied with Mac's responses. She wasn't getting the scoop she hoped for, apparently. He wasn't saying a thing.

She needed to get him to talk.

Then the reporter crossed the line.

"Perhaps you're here on personal business, Agent McRyan. Perhaps you and Agent Wire have something to hide you don't want people to know about? You were inside for quite some time."

"Whoa," the cameraman muttered, but he didn't stop filming.

Mac stopped in his tracks and turned, "Excuse me?" He glanced over to Wire who was equally stunned by the question.

"It's a simple question. Are you here for personal reasons? Did you and Agent Wire have some 'personal' business to take care of? Something you wouldn't want the White House's deputy director of communications Sally Kennedy to know about?" the reporter persisted, a feisty young blond, looking for a big scoop.

Mac was stunned by the absolute brazenness of the question. It was completely out of bounds, "Are you for real?" His anger was starting to show. "I'd be very *very* careful if I were you."

"What business did you have inside then? In the absence of any comment, I can only assume it was for personal reasons, for both you and Agent Wire. Maybe you two are hiding something? Wouldn't be the first time someone wondered that. You two seem *awfully* close and you spend a lot of time together."

"*Mac, don't!*" Wire warned, seeing his face redden but it was too late.

Mac stormed towards the reporter, angry now. The cameraman stayed close, too close for Mac's comfort. He put his left hand up to the lens and forcefully shoved the camera out of way, which caused the cameraman to fall backwards and onto the ground. All of which was caught by the other television station, now out filming. Mac got into the reporter's face, an inch from her nose, "I'd suggest you stop right now."

"Why's that?"

"You *really* don't want me angry with you," Mac answered through clenched teeth. It was a threat, one he looked very ready to follow through on.

"Oh, really, what happens when you get angry?" the reporter goaded, an evil smile on her face, the cameras still rolling, the microphone picking up his threat. In that moment, no matter how out-of-bounds the reporter was, he knew he'd gone too far.

She'd gotten the best of him.

Wire grabbed at his arm, "Mac, let's go." She pulled him away from the reporter. Dr. Kostas stood at the back door in horror at what she'd just witnessed. "Get in the truck. *Get in the truck!*"

Mac backed away from the reporter, glaring at her. Once in the X5, he quickly backed out and pulled out of the lot before any more damage was done. His phone was ringing. It was Sally. How would he explain this?

"He won't pick up for some reason," Sally reported to the Judge.

"Let me know when he does," he answered, picking up the phone, continuing to work his sources.

Sally walked back to her office and started working on the speech again and contemplated the fact that it was getting late in the day and she was getting hungry, the carrots simply not doing it for her. What she was really in need of, more than anything else, was a beer and a burger. Were Mac not so involved in the case, she would have called to have him pick her up to go to one of the dive bars they'd found. Maybe listen to some live music, even dance a little, although for an excellent athlete Mac had very little rhythm on the dance floor.

"Oh my God! Oh my God!" Sally's assistant screamed as

she came into the office and grabbed the remote off her desk. "You have to see this. It's Mac."

"What?"

"Just watch."

Sally watched the encounter outside the back of Fallway Medical Clinic with the small blond reporter. "Abortion? That's what's motivating the killer?" Sally questioned. "That doesn't seem right."

The confrontation continued with Mac issuing no comments. Then the tenor of things changed.

"She didn't just ask that!" Sally squawked in reaction.

"*Oh yes she did*," the Judge answered from the doorway.

Sally saw the change in her boyfriend's expression. The violence appeared in his eyes and the anger in his face as he stormed towards the reporter. "That's not good." Then Mac pushed the cameraman down and made the threat. "That's really not good." Then she heard the verbal exchange. "Oh Mac, that's really *really* not good."

The optics of the whole encounter were horrible. Sally grabbed the remote and started flipping around to the other news channels. On every one she caught some portion of the confrontation. She sat back in her office chair, exhaled and shook her head. "Nice job, Mac," she muttered and immediately grabbed for her cell phone.

"But that question, that would set anyone off," Sally's assistant suggested.

"He's not allowed to be just anyone in that situation," Sally answered. "Cripes. What a mess."

"Well, now we know why he's not taking your calls," the Judge offered, smiling, but wearily shaking his head.

19

"SHIT HAPPENS."

Mac was fuming with himself. He'd never lost it with a reporter. Of course, when rule number one is to never talk to reporters, you generally don't have any problems losing it with them. In this case, he'd been Pearl Harbored without any preparation or chance to see it coming and on top of that, he was accused of having an affair with Wire, having her get an abortion no less, and the whole confrontation would show up on national television in no time and would be run continuously.

It would require an explanation.

Mac wasn't sure what would be worse, explaining it to Sally or the rest of the country.

He'd lost it with others before, the mayor of St. Paul a few times, the now incarcerated president of a company another time, the occasional suspect or witness he was exasperated with. However, never like this. He completely lost his composure. There were times he thought it was helpful to lose it, if you lost it strategically and were in control of it. That was not the case with this reporter. In this case, he came momentarily unglued.

"Man, I so stepped in it there," he said as he sipped coffee with Wire trying to get things back under control. They were at a small out of the way diner that did not have a television anywhere on the premises.

"Did you ever!" Wire seemed only too happy to point out.

"Whose side are you on here?"

"Yours, but I had no idea we were an item."

"This isn't funny."

"No, it's not," Wire answered bitterly. "It's a shit show and you weren't the only one who drew fire in this fiasco. Apparently, you and I have been having an affair."

"Man," Mac groaned. "I'm so sorry about that."

"Yeah, for people to think I'd have actually slept with someone like you," Wire mocked. "I do have standards."

"I know, it must be *soooo* embarrassing for you," Mac answered, rolling his eyes and shaking his head. "Unbelievable."

"I'd like a half hour with that reporter in a cinder block room, no cameras, no nothing."

Mac looked at his cell buzzing for the fourth time in the last hour, "I know someone else that would like that same shot," he moaned, staring at the display, his elbows on the table, his face resting in his hands, rubbing his temples, trying to make the headache go away.

"As your friend," Wire suggested, "answer it. Guaranteed she's seen it. Answer the phone and get it over with."

He nodded, exhaled and answered: "Hey, Sal."

"Are you okay?"

Maybe this wouldn't be so bad, "Yeah."

"You're sure? You're absolutely sure?"

"Yeah, why?"

"Because I just saw you do the stupidest thing."

He was wrong. This would be bad.

"Look, that reporter ..."

"Was a raging fucking bitch, Mac," Sally barked. "But you can't let her or anyone get to you like that. This is fucking Washington, DC, not St. Paul. You can't do that!"

"Look, I'm sorry, babe."

"Don't you babe me. Don't you dare right now," she replied heatedly. "You've been avoiding me for hours."

"I haven't been avoiding you." He had been. "I've been working ..."

"Don't bullshit me like that, Mac. You can't pull it off."

He could rarely get anything by her. She was in complete prosecutor cross-examination mode and he was a hostile witness. The verbal beating continued, "Oh, by the way, you and Dara looked so lovely coming out the back door of a family planning clinic, by the way. Nice visual there, sneaking out the back door. You two *actually* looked like you had something to hide."

"Seriously, that's the card you're going to play here?" Mac asked in disbelief, his thermostat starting to rise again. "You know better than that."

Sally did and quickly changed gears, "How about taking a call then? You almost always take my calls and certainly don't make me call five or six times to get a hold of you and I needed to talk to you."

"About what?"

"About what? Seriously, that's what you're going with? *Hello.* I needed to talk to you about the case, the big break you wouldn't tell me about last night. You know, the break in your case that involves a really important person to my boss."

"Oh, jeez, for a minute there I thought you might be concerned about me."

"Excuse me?"

"Apparently this isn't about me, it's about you."

"Now you wait a minute ..."

"I don't think so, Sally," Mac answered, his irritation no longer suppressed. "You're pissed I didn't tell you, the White House, about our case. Well, the last time I checked I don't work for you and if you think that's the case, then one of us seriously has misunderstood this working relationship. Last time I checked, my credential reads Federal Bureau of Investigation, not West Wing or White House or Judge Dixon's Bitch. If that's what Wire and I are supposed to be, well then I'm done."

"Careful, Mac," Wire whispered, reaching for his hand and warned. "Don't say something you can't take back."

Mac exhaled and closed his eyes. His partner was right. He was stepping close to that line. "Look, Sally. You're right, I didn't tell you about the break because we were trying to keep it under wraps. We didn't tell anyone and I'm trying to protect you because if we are right where this is going, Hannah Donahue is going to look bad, which by extension will make her father look bad and maybe even the White House since you got us on the case to begin with. I think it would be better for you to know less."

"Actually that's even more of a reason for you to tell me about it."

"Why?"

"So if it is bad, we could be prepared. Mac, it is not your job to determine what I need to know politically. That's mine. I needed to know this might be an issue for us. So I could have ..."

"Leaked it, perhaps," Mac finished. "Because that's what you'd have done, right?" Mac retorted. "Leak it, control it, minimize the damage to the White House, maybe actually distance yourselves from Bill Donahue, at least until you need him for his money, yet still spin it that the White House appointees to the investigation have developed an important lead that may have broke the case. Hey, political points for us, woo hoo," he mocked.

"Yeah, well you pretty much screwed the pooch on that idea an hour ago," Sally retorted, sarcasm oozing from her voice.

He was tempted to say something else but heeding Wire's advice, he didn't. "That idea is exactly why I didn't tell you. This is a murder investigation, and if something leaks, that could set us back just when we might be making some headway. This is murder, not politics, Sally. There isn't a cloture vote on this damn thing."

"Well duh," was her snooty reply, "but here's a news-flash, superstar. You and Wire being on the case makes it political, Mac. We put you there. That means we've got serious skin in the game. So what do you do? You go ahead and find a way to wrap abortion into this. That's a brilliant maneuver, that's so helpful. I mean, couldn't you have at least addressed that? Couldn't you have said the investigation had nothing to do with that?"

"I'd rather have people thinking that, the Reaper thinking that's where we're going, as opposed to him and the public having an idea what this thing is really all about."

"Sweet, so now we can deal with the political fallout. You should see my in-box, all of our in-boxes and voice mails, thanks to your little brainstorm."

"Not my concern."

"Not your concern? You're supposed to be helping us. I mean, for someone as smart as you are, you are borderline brilliant, how could you meltdown like that? How? How is that possible? The way you left it the country thinks your investigation is either about abortion or that you had Wire get one. Had you given me a call earlier in the day, we could have discussed this. I would have suggested to you that if the media shows up when you're at the Fallway Clinic, here is what you should say. This is what I do, Mac, communications, messaging, anticipating trouble and preparing for it. So given all that, I would have thought that even a political Neanderthal such as you would have taken a couple of minutes and given me a call and a little heads-up."

"Well I didn't." He didn't really have anything more to say. At this point he just wanted to eject.

"That's all you got? I just didn't?"

"At this point Sally, the way my day is going, it's probably best that's all I say. And you know what? You might just want to consider pulling a punch or two as well." He'd pretty much had enough. They rarely fought, but when they did, there were usually fireworks. Neither of them had a lot of back down in them.

"I think we're done here," Sally said, fuming on the other end.

"Hey, for once we agree," and he hung up and tossed the cell phone onto the table.

"Well that went well," Wire said, rolling her eyes, shaking her head at Mac. "Is there anyone else left you want to piss off today?"

"Nope," Mac answered. "Pretty much filled out my Yahtzee Card."

"Good news for you is she loves you so damn much, she'll get over it and forgive you."

"Forgive me? And what about me? Don't I get to get over it? Don't I get to forgive her?"

"Nope. You just have to apologize."

"For what?"

"For being a pigheaded, prideful, dumbass arrogant male," Dara answered, looking at him like he was an idiot. "Listen, partner, *we do* represent the White House. Like it or not, they put us on this case. Sure we said yes, and the FBI director was totally on board with it, but the White House made this happen. They do have skin in the game. We can't and won't take orders from them, but at the same time we can't ..."

"Make them look bad." Mac shook his head. Then the realization really hit him where it hurt. "I made Sally look bad."

"No, it was *we*. I was there too."

"But I'm the one ..."

"Yeah, you're the one who stepped in it big time, but it's on me too. You're my partner. I'm in for a penny ..."

"In for a pound. Just know, if you step in it, I'll feel the same way."

Wire nodded and for the first time in a while, smiled. "Look, next time, tell Sally. She and the Judge understand an investigation like this. They would have known how to handle this."

Mac was about to object but she stopped him. "Mac, you'd have told Sally about our break, but Gesch gave you so much shit last night about your White House girlfriend that you got your back up about it. Your pride got in the way. You could have told her. You *should* have told her. Would they have done something with it? Maybe, but come on, she and the Judge would have known how to handle it, they wouldn't have screwed us."

"No, they probably wouldn't have."

"That's right. Face it, okay, you fucked up. I would suggest that when you apologize to Sally, *and you will apolo-*

gize, you just fall on the sword, it'll be the least painful option for you."

He took a long sip of his coffee, sat back in the booth and shook his head. "Okay, so we've established I'm a royal screw up and I have some amends to make. Can we *please* move on?"

"Sure, as long as you're cooled down now. You've been running pretty hot the last hour or two."

"Maybe I'm just exhausted."

"Me too," Wire answered. "Want to call it a day?"

"No. As you can imagine, I really don't want to go home at the moment."

"Remind me to never piss *you* off," the Judge said ruefully, sitting on Sally's couch. "Did you treat hostile witnesses this way when you were a prosecutor?"

"He can be such an arrogant ... ass sometimes," she said, still furious with him.

"Yeah, but it's that arrogance, that stubbornness, that edge, that 'I'm the smartest guy in the room' mentality, that makes him good."

"Any more days like this and Director Mitchell will have him working the FBI motor pool."

"I seriously doubt that," the Judge answered, chortling. "Sure, Mac screwed up today, but the only reason he was in a position to screw up in the first place was because he and Wire are the ones who keep making things happen on that investigation. That task force was nowhere before those two got involved. Now they're somewhere. They're going to find this guy and soon."

"Really?" Sally asked skeptically, perhaps because she was still so pissed at Mac.

"Yeah, Mac discovered some connection between three of the victims yesterday. It's tied to a summer camp they attended seven years ago in upstate New York. I suspect he was at the clinic to interview someone who was at the camp and knew Donahue or one of the other victims. He and Wire have created every break on that case, Sally, every single one. They're working their asses off and you said it yourself earlier, Mac's operating on fumes, he's exhausted. That's when shit like this happens. It's one of the differences between St. Paul and working here and he just learned that lesson the hard way."

Sally snorted and shook her head.

"Listen, it's up to you, but I'd cut your boy a *little* slack."

"That damn reporter," Sally wanted a piece of her, going after Mac that way. She would never admit it to him but she'd have shoved the microphone down the woman's throat.

"Oh, I think we'll figure out a way to deal with her. That was more than just a little out of bounds."

Sally grimaced, "Does the president know about this?"

The Judge nodded. "You know what he said?"

"What?"

"Shit happens."

"That's what he said?" Sally asked skeptically.

"Yup."

"Maybe, but Mac's shit left the FBI and us a hole to dig out of if my e-mail is any indication." Her in-box had exploded in the last hour, as had her voice mail box.

"Ahh, we'll be fine," the Judge replied with a dismissive wave and a rueful laugh. "I've seen worse, and if Mac brings this thing home eventually, nobody will give a rip about today or at least not much of a rip. Look, I've already talked to Thomas Mitchell, within the hour the FBI will be out with a statement indicating that the investigation has nothing to do with abortion. That will take care of the in-box and voice mails. That won't be an issue."

"You sure?"

The Judge nodded confidently, "I know you're worried, but don't be. Mac stepped in it, but the funny thing is, give it a few hours or a day and something else will come along to command people's attention. Like I said, it's up to you, but I think Mac deserves a break on this one. What happened at that clinic ..."

"Is not Mac's fault," she finished the thought for him.

"No, when you really think about it, it's not. And let me tell you something else. There's nobody I'd rather have going after that evil son of a bitch than Mac McRyan," the Judge stated, pushing himself up off the couch. "And let me tell you something else young lady. Given what happened today, Mac's going to be *extra* motivated and *that* my dear, is a very good thing. That's turning lemons into lemonade."

20

"THIS IS GONNA HURT."

GAITHERSBURG, MARYLAND

After Mac's cooling off period at the coffee shop, he and Wire made their next stop at the home of Leslie Felding, a twenty-eight-year-old financial analyst for Starling Industries. She lived in a brick two-story colonial-looking townhouse north of Interstate 270.

Felding opened the door and recognized them immediately, "You two were on television earlier," but then she went on guard and looked confused. "Why are you here?"

"We have some questions about the murders of Hannah Donahue, Sandy Faye and Melissa Goynes. You were a camp counselor with them seven years ago at Lake Seneca Lodge," Mac stated.

Felding let them into her townhouse and took them back to the kitchen where they could all sit around the table. "I remember Hannah," Felding stated as she sat down. "I don't remember a Melissa Goynes or Sandy Faye."

"Melissa Goynes is our victim's married name, her maiden name was Ross," Wire replied, taking out the AAHC picture from seven years ago and pointing to Melissa Ross. "Sandy Faye is a television reporter in Baltimore, but her real name back when you were at camp with her was Helen Williams."

Felding's eyes went wide, "I remember Melissa Ross. She worked in my dorm that summer. The Helen Williams name doesn't really ring a bell, nor does the picture, but then again, that was years ago." She shook her head, holding the picture in her right hand, looking it over, "My gosh, Melissa."

"Have you been following the news reports on this killer people are calling the Reaper?"

"A little," Felding answered. "I knew Hannah fairly well, at least that summer. I've hardly seen her since but obviously when I heard her name I paid some attention to the news reports but after the first day I didn't really follow it. It was a little gruesome and depressing."

"When you say you've hardly seen her since, define hardly?" Wire asked, taking the cap off her pen and flipping open her notebook.

"Hardly is once," Felding answered with a shrug. "I ran into her maybe three years ago, just randomly at a bar down in DC. I give her credit, she's the one who recognized me, came up and gave me a hug. Then after that she and I were Facebook friends, you know, you see an old friend, the next day I looked her up and friended her, but otherwise, I haven't stayed in contact with her."

Mac and Wire ran through the summer seven years ago, picking and probing at what Felding remembered of her time with Donahue, Goynes and Faye. It was clear that Donahue was the only one who really stuck with Felding, that she spent any real time with. "I liked Hannah, she was a real personality, fun, liked everyone, liked a good time and wanted everyone involved. I always wished I could have had that in me, you know, that open personality, but

I've just never been able to be that ..." Felding struggled for the right word, "open or free with myself, to others. Hannah was not so encumbered so people were drawn to her."

"Did you ever go to any parties when you were at the camp?"

"Parties?"

"For example, rave parties? Around the time you were at the camp, rave parties were popular not far from there."

"I know what a rave is, Agent McRyan. I remember going to one that summer, it was in July, I think, on a Saturday night. It was the middle of summer. I know that." Felding snapped her fingers. "I remember because I went with Hannah. She had a friend who had a lake place somewhere around there. She drove over and picked us up from the camp and took us to the party. It was the only time I went to one of those."

"Why only once?" Dara asked.

"They were too crazy for me. I went to college at Maryland so it's not like I never went to a party or drank. However, the rave was out of control, the drinking, all the drugs, the sex and people were just wacked out and crazy."

"Not your scene?" Mac asked.

"No, it wasn't. I don't judge and to each their own, but I was uncomfortable."

"And what about Hannah, was she uncomfortable?"

Felding smiled and shook her head, "Hannah was comfortable in *any* environment. She knew people who were there and it was clear she knew how the party worked and she partook in all of it."

"So you never went to another rave party that summer?"

"No."

"How about the last weekend of the summer, that

Saturday would have been August 17th, do you recall anything about that date?"

Felding sat back in her chair, folded her arms and thought. "Like what?"

"Did you go home that day, spend one more night, go home Sunday, go to a different kind of party, did others at the camp go to a party? Do you recall anything along those lines?"

Felding smiled, "I do know I was there that Saturday night and didn't leave until Sunday."

"Why do you recall that?"

"A boy named Austin Lane is why I remember that night."

"I see," Wire replied, smiling. "A night to remember?"

"I'll say," Felding answered, smiling, a memory of a good night. "I've never forgotten that night. The next day, I left the camp."

"Did you keep in contact with Austin?" Mac asked, jotting down notes.

Felding shook her head, "He went to college out in California. I never saw him again but after a summer of making eyes at each other, we did have that one night."

"On that last day, do you remember seeing Hannah Donahue or Melissa Ross or Helen Williams?"

"If they were there, I'm sure I did," Felding answered. "But I honestly don't remember anything about it."

"But you remember Austin," Wire stated, smiling.

"Oh yes, *him* I remember."

"Does the name Rena Johnson mean anything to you?"

Felding shook her head, "No, should it?"

Mac showed her a picture of Johnson. Felding shook her head, "I don't think I've ever seen her before."

"I know it's been seven years, but do you remember the name of Hannah's friend that drove you to that rave party?"

Leslie Felding shook her head. "I'm sorry, I don't. I can visualize her a little. I remember that she was brunette, average height, thin with an athletic kind of body, like she ran track or cross-country. I can't remember her name. I just remember that her parents had a place not far from the camp, a summer place so she came over and picked up Hannah and me and a few others and took us to the party."

"Do you remember what kind of vehicle she took you in?" Mac pressed.

Felding shook her head, "I don't."

A half hour later, after a call to the Donahues, Mac and Wire had a name. Kelly Drew. In another half hour, Gesch had a full dossier sent to their phones on Drew, who actually lived farther north a half hour up I-270 in Frederick and operated a coffee shop.

"No sense stopping at this point," Mac stated. "To Frederick we go."

It had taken him twenty minutes from when he parked his truck three blocks away. Taking sidewalks, his baseball cap pulled down low, as he zigzagged his way through the neighborhood to the dirt walking path in the thick woods running to the immediate south of his target. Once inside the woods, he stopped, pulled on his all black clothing and stocking cap, sweating in the thick summer heat, even in the total shade of the woods.

Now, prepared, he walked carefully ten feet deep inside the tree line on a narrow path weaving its way through the thick woods, the creek just down the steep embankment ten feet to his right. With the dense woods and thick ground cover, he was nearly invisible. He reached the alley, scanned the immediate area and then slipped out of the woods, down a slight incline to the south side of the garage. He quickly pulled on rubber gloves and then took out his set of lock picks and started working on the lock to the side door of the garage. Within thirty seconds he had it open. Once inside the garage, he closed the door and relocked it. Next, he went to work on the door leading into the house, also locked. In another minute it was open.

He pushed the door open and took three steps up to the junction landing. Straight ahead was the stairway down to the cellar. The cellar could wait. Instead he turned left into the small kitchen which he passed through into the front of the small one-story house, nearly tripping over a softball bat and glove lying on the floor. In the front of the house he surveyed the small dining room area leading into the family room, separated by an arch. On the right wall of the family room was a hallway to two bedrooms and a bathroom.

He looked at his watch and surveyed his surroundings.

"Cripes," Mac moaned. "This was inevitable."

"What?" Wire asked as they were walking towards Totally Caffeinated, a strip mall coffee shop owned by Hannah Donahue's friend, Kelly Drew.

"My phone, the boys back in St. Paul, they saw it too."

"Let me see! Let me see!" Dara answered excitedly.

"Wow, I thought you were a friend."

"I am, one that's allowed to find humor in your misery. So let me see, let me see," she pleaded excitedly.

He read them off.

"This one's from Rock: Hey dumbass, how's life in the big leagues? Are you missing little old St. Paul yet? Then there's a couple from Riley of course."

"A couple?"

"Yup. First text: What's Rule No. 1 Moron?"

"What is Rule No. 1?" Wire asked.

"Never talk to a reporter."

"What's the other one from Riles?"

"Rule No. 2, when you talk to a reporter, give them nothing. You answered a stupid question with an even stupider answer. #Simon Wouldn't Have Done It. P.S. You have no excuse. Simon created Rules 1 and 2."

"Ouch, bringing your dad into it."

"Riles always goes for the throat," Mac answered and kept scrolling through his messages, alternating between chuckling and groaning. "Here's a good one: 'Cue Sade: *Smooth Operator* – NOT,' that's from my cousin Paddy."

He scrolled farther down. "Oh you'll love this one. I'll give you three guesses who sent this one and the first two don't count. 'So you and Wire are an item? I bet she's a freak in the sack. I demand details!'"

"Lich," Dara answered, rolling her eyes. "He is such a pervert."

"It's his most endearing quality. He lusts for you, by the way."

"And what man doesn't."

It was Mac's turn to roll his eyes. "And you think my ego is big." He scrolled down farther through his texts. "Shamus has it right. He asks: 'How pissed is Sally?' I can respond to that one." Mac texted a quick reply and laughed, a wry, weary laugh.

"What did you say?" Dara asked warily as she opened the door.

"On the pissed-off scale of one to ten, Sally's at about thirty-seven and climbing."

"By the way, are there any texts from your girlfriend?"

Mac shook his head, "Radio silence."

"She's probably cooling off," Dara answered.

"Or all my clothes will be on the front lawn when I get home."

"It's your house, isn't it?"

"Like *that* matters."

Wire went to the barista at the counter and flashed her FBI credential, "I'm looking for Kelly Drew."

Kelly Drew looked back and watched the garage door close behind her. She arranged for her assistant manager to run the store for a few days and she was going to run off to upstate New York and her parents' place. She needed to pack quickly and get on the road to her parents' summer home. She needed some time to think things through, maybe talk things through with her mom and dad. She was giving serious thought to coming clean.

She moved quickly through the kitchen into the family room.

The rag was over her mouth.

The left arm wrapped around her chest and tightened like a boa constrictor.

She was lifted off the floor, her legs flailing.

Kelly gasped for air and breathed in. The rag was damp, sweet smelling, and she could feel the effect of the fumes.

It was the Reaper.

She knew it. She'd seen the news. He was targeting women just like her.

Kelly fought, kicking with her legs, knocking over two chairs from the dining room table.

The arm stayed tight.

She reached for the table with her legs, set her feet and pushed back. The man fell slightly backwards into the wall while she struggled.

The man tried to regain his balance, falling forward, the two of them crashing into the dining room table, which collapsed under their weight.

∽

Her body went immediately still underneath him. No fight and no push. He stayed on top of her for a few seconds to make sure she wasn't playing possum. She wasn't.

The Reaper rolled her over and immediately noticed the massive gash in her forehead from falling onto the table. Blood streamed rapidly down her face from the deep wound in the left side of her forehead, just below her scalp line. He felt for her pulse. It was there, but extremely weak.

He pushed himself up from her when he heard the car door slam.

∽

Mac and Wire walked up the front walk. "There's a light on inside," Dara noted as Mac hit the doorbell.

"Well, good she's home then. We can get this taken ... care ... of. " His hand went to his Sig Sauer on his right hip.

"What?" Wire whispered, stepping back.

"There's a body lying on the floor inside to the left," he answered quietly. "I can just see her legs from behind the sofa."

"Any movement?"

Mac shook his head and nodded to the screen door handle.

Wire took out her Sig Sauer, held it in her left hand and reached for the screen door handle with her right, opening the door slowly.

Mac checked the door, it was locked. He took a step back.

Mac led with his right foot and kicked the front door in and rushed inside, weapon drawn, sensing for movement. Dara moved past him to the right and into the kitchen in the back of the house.

He kneeled down to the body and checked for a pulse, noticing the gash on her forehead. It was fresh, still oozing.

Mac reached for his cell phone when he sensed sudden movement back to his left. He turned in time to see the blow coming, raising his left arm.

McRyan was down. The bat took care of that, one blow crashing down on his arm and the other on his upper back just below his neck.

"Mac?" a voice called from the kitchen.

The Reaper darted to the wall to the left of the opening into the kitchen. Wire came rushing out of the kitchen and past him. He swung fully, hitting her in the upper back, knocking her forward, stumbling past McRyan and down onto living room floor.

McRyan, dazed, started pushing himself up.

He side kicked McRyan in the head with his right leg, hit him with a round house in the head with his left leg and then jumped kicked him in the forehead with his right foot, laying him out flat on his back on the floor. McRyan wasn't moving.

Wire stirred, dazed, struggling to push herself up. He pounced on top of her, pinning her to the floor, pushing the rag to her mouth.

She came to full life, grunting and fighting with all the strength her long athletic body could muster. Wire pushed up with her left arm, trying to roll him off.

Her move worked to his advantage. He curled his free left arm around her left arm and pinned it to her body and tightened his hold around her, keeping her right side to the floor, shielding his own face behind her body.

She flailed and kicked her legs.

She frantically and repeatedly tried to head-butt him backwards but he ducked the attempts and she couldn't get a direct hit. His hand never left her mouth.

Dara Wire was strong, far stronger and more capable than any other woman he'd subdued. However, he had position, a significant weight advantage matched with the benefit of superior strength and she was weakened by the blow of the bat. She needed space and he wouldn't give her any, instead he slowly closed what little space there was with his left arm and left leg, wrapping it around hers, pinning it.

She battled him, but he stayed in control, keeping the vice around her and the rag pressed to her mouth.

He could tell she was holding her breath, trying to not suck the fumes into her mouth, knowing exactly what was on the rag. But she couldn't hold out. Nobody could hold out. The rag stayed and he pressed it harder, shoving it up to and over her nose.

After a minute, or maybe two, the flailing and kicking started losing their punch and slowed, the fight draining from her body, the resignation setting in to her muscles, to her strength, if not yet her mind.

Her fight was game, but like all the others, she eventually succumbed, it just took far longer.

Dara Wire's body finally went limp underneath him. He stayed on top of her for thirty seconds to be sure. She was out.

He released the grip and quickly pushed to his feet, getting his bearings.

Was anyone else coming?

There were no sirens.

He looked out the windows and nothing was stirring. He ran to the back of the house and looked out the kitchen window and there was nothing, no movement. Back in the front of the house, he pushed the front door closed and killed the porch light. He then went back and turned out the kitchen light.

The Reaper rushed back into the living room. McRyan was down and not moving. Drew and Wire were both out.

Lying on the floor he noticed a cell phone. It was Wire's. He stuffed it in his pocket.

He pulled out the syringe and vile of sodium pentothal.

It was as if fortune had shined upon him, two for the price of one.

It was the searing pain, his left side, his lower left arm, that first stirred him. Then it was the sounds that percolated into his head, the sound of a door closing, then the padding of footsteps that were quick and rushed, shaking the floor.

He could taste the heavy pool of blood in his mouth.

Mac slowly rolled his head to the right and tried

opening his eyes but it required effort and he realized the pain was not limited to his left side.

His head was pounding and his neck and back ached.

He sucked in a small breath and raised his eyelids.

It was hazy, blurry and dark.

There was a rectangular shape, lighter than the room, a window, a picture window, he was in a house. Then there was a body, a big body, moving about quickly.

The Reaper.

Mac froze. His mind snapped back on.

The Reaper was moving around the room to his right, ten feet away.

Where was his Sig Sauer?

He'd been hit with an aluminum softball bat which he saw lying on the floor. The gun must have gone flying. He did a quick scan of the floor but couldn't see it.

What about his backup piece?

Mac could feel the weight of his old Glock 9mm on the inside of his left ankle.

Keeping his head lying to the right, squinting, Mac could see the massive body of the Reaper, who had his back to him, standing over a body. As his vision focused, he could take in the presence of the killer. He was huge, the broad shoulders, the muscles and the heavy breathing as he stalked around Wire's body, reaching down to pick something up.

The man was a monster.

The sofa was between Mac and the Reaper, giving him some cover. Slowly Mac started to turn onto his right side and slowly raised his left leg up to his right hand.

What to do?

Drew's house was at the end of the block, secluded and nobody seemed to have noticed or heard anything. No sirens and no neighbors sticking their heads out of their houses.

Looking down, he saw Dara Wire, and looking back, he recognized McRyan lying on the floor. The agents were involving themselves in something that wasn't their business. In fact, the FBI was intruding on something that wasn't their business.

It was time to send a message.

He unsheathed the knife, the blade glinting in the light when he heard the grunt and rustling behind him.

He pivoted to his left.

The first shot whistled by his head.

The effort to pull the gun from his ankle holster made things blurry again.

Mac fired at the fuzzy large shape.

The Reaper jumped left towards the front door.

Mac moved his arm left with the movement and fired again.

The monster was out the front door.

Mac pushed himself up with his right arm. He scrambled towards the front door, nearly tripping over Wire. He looked outside and caught a glimpse of the Reaper running to the left two houses away.

He pushed the screen door open, stumbled out onto the front stoop and fired again, missing. The Reaper kept running, turning left after the second house.

A neighbor stepped out onto his front stoop, "What the

hell?"

"Federal agent," Mac grunted as he ran past, "call 911, this address," he ordered as he gave chase, running as fast as he could, the pain searing through his left wrist and hand as he pumped his arms.

∼

The Reaper sprinted across the street to the sidewalk, slowed briefly and looked back to his left.

McRyan came around the corner and caught sight of him. Seeing his prey, he stopped, set his feet and raised his right hand.

The Reaper turned away and ran full speed.

Pop! Pop! Pop!

One shot hit the fence to his right. Another hit a large tree to the left as he ran by and the third hit the pavement just in front of him as he ran.

He turned right down an alley and sprinted full out, not looking back.

His truck was a block and a half away.

∼

The jostling from running exponentially intensified the aching pain in his left wrist. Mac careened around the corner of the fence and peered down the alley. He could see the Reaper running, nearing the far end of the alley. The big man was way out in front now.

Mac set his left foot to the front, his right behind him. He needed both hands and gauntleted the Glock in his left palm. "This is gonna hurt."

Pop! Pop! Pop! Pop! Pop!

He fired until the man disappeared around the corner.

The pain overtook him and Mac collapsed and fell against the fence.

The last thing he heard before blacking out was the sirens.

∽

His job was to deliver a message.

He pulled up just short of the street leading to Kelly Drew's house. The area was swarming with squad cars for the Frederick Police Department. Wanting a closer look, he took his cell phone out of its holder and slipped it into his suit coat pocket and then hit the three number combination on the radio touch screen that opened the hidden compartment in the dashboard. He placed his Walther in its holder and closed the compartment and then exited the SUV.

The crime scene tape was up at the end of the street, holding back the gathering crowd of onlookers. He reached the crime scene tape and sidled up to an elderly woman. "What happened?"

"Not sure exactly," the woman replied from under her gardening cap. "There are two ambulances in front of that house and there's another one a block over to the west. One person said she talked to Drew's neighbor and he said as he came out on the front steps there was a man firing a gun at someone from the front steps of Drew's and then gave chase. He said he was a police officer and he was chasing some suspect." Then her hand went to her mouth, "Look," she said and pointed.

He saw the paramedics urgently exiting out of the house. On the stretcher was a woman, bloodied about the head, with an oxygen mask over her mouth and two tubes in her arms. The paramedics quickly got her into the ambulance and he heard someone yell, "Go, Go." The ambulance immediately pulled away and accelerated quickly with lights and sirens on full.

He looked back to the house and a minute later a second set of paramedics exited the house with a woman on a stretcher, no oxygen or tubes. The paramedics didn't move as urgently and from what he could tell, she may have been injured but was nowhere as critical. He recognized her.

Farther to the west he noticed another ambulance. He casually but quickly strolled in that direction, up to the police tape a half block short of the ambulance. He engaged in some idle chitchat with some of the people standing by the tape.

The paramedics pushed a stretcher out of the alley with a man on the stretcher with an oxygen mask on his face. There was no rush to the ambulance. The man on the stretcher's left arm was immobilized and he had a tube in his other arm. He recognized the man on the stretcher.

"So I've seen three ambulances," he stated to a man standing along the tape line. "Are there any more?"

The man shook his head, "Isn't three enough?"

"I'd say so. I was just curious is all, quite the night, especially for around here."

"Unlike anything I've ever seen. I thought I was hearing fireworks but turns out shots were fired. I've seen the cops marking shell casings on the ground."

A minute later he slowly backed away from the scene and walked to the Tahoe and jumped inside. He pulled his cell phone out, pulled up the directory for the letter W, found the name and pressed the screen. The man answered on the second ring.

"We were too late. It looks like he got to Drew before I was able to get here."

"Is she dead?"

"No, but from what I can tell, she's very badly injured, but he wasn't the only one here to see her. McRyan and Wire were here as well."

"Did they catch the Reaper?"

"No."

21
"WE CAN'T FIND THE ELEVENTH?"

He licked his lips and immediately felt the weight on his left arm. He'd felt weight like this once before on his arm, when he was in high school. A hard hockey stick slash between the top of his hockey glove and the bottom of his elbow pad broke his right wrist, putting him in a cast for six weeks. He was awake, wanted to open his eyes, but when he tried, the pain shot through him and he moaned.

"Mac?" a relieved voice asked. "Mac, are you awake? Are you there?" It was Sally, her hand on his left shoulder.

He exhaled and squinted, straining to see. "I can barely open my eyes."

"That's because you have two of the worst black eyes I've ever seen, son," replied the deep voice of Judge Dixon.

Mac's head pounded and he winced.

"And a concussion," Sally whispered, kissing him softly below his ear.

"And a broken left wrist, I assume," Mac replied, trying to push himself up, a searing pain shooting through his upper back which caused him to groan.

"No, no, no," Sally cautioned, stopping him and laying him softly back down. "I'll raise you up."

Sally slowly adjusted his hospital bed up.

"That's good," Mac said and Sally stopped the bed. He exhaled and struggled to push his lids open, at least enough to see. "Hey?" he said to Sally. She never looked so good.

"Hey," she said, smiling, but worriedly.

"Where am I?"

"Frederick Memorial Hospital," Sally replied. "Frederick, Maryland."

Mac looked towards the window to his hospital room and the sun was starting to come up. "How long have I been down?"

"Seven, maybe eight hours."

"Wire?" Mac suddenly asked, panicked. "Where is she?"

"Right here," a hoarse voice answered from the hallway. Dara walked into the room gingerly, followed by Delmonico. "How are you feeling?"

"Like I had a really *really* bad day," Mac answered, closing his eyes. His head, face, eyes, back and neck all ached. "This case is so kicking my ass."

"It could have been worse," the Judge answered.

"How?" Mac groaned, his eyes closed, "How could it have *possibly* been worse?"

"I wasn't killed, I lived," Wire added, grabbing his right hand. "Thanks, partner."

"Well there is that I suppose," Mac grumbled, a slight smile on his face.

Wire slapped his right foot lightly.

"What about Kelly Drew?"

The room went quiet. "Well, she's alive," Wire said quietly.

Mac recognized the tone and suddenly remembered the gash to her forehead. "How bad is she?"

"She's in a coma. Closed head injury."

"Brain activity?"

"None, at least not right now," Gesch stated, coming into the room. He took one look at Mac and then got down to business. "Can you tell me what happened? Dara told me what she remembered."

"Which isn't much after I blacked out," Wire answered.

"Chloroform?" Mac asked.

"And sodium pentothal, I'm a bit unbalanced chemically at the moment," Wire quipped.

"Have you been to the scene?" Mac asked Gesch.

"Yes."

Mac nodded, breathing deeply, and collected his thoughts with his eyes closed. "We go in the front door. Wire goes to my right into the kitchen while I remember leaning over Drew. I saw the gash in her forehead. I checked for a pulse and was reaching for my phone when there was this …" he struggled for the word, "flash … of movement to my left. It was literally like he came out of nowhere, super quick, super quiet, stealthy. I glanced up, put my arm up and I was knocked down hard, dazed."

"That's what I must have heard," Wire added. "He hit you with that softball bat. That's what made me come running."

"Mac, do you remember what happened next?"

"I remember trying to push myself up and then I was kicked in the head, twice, really fast, I think, and then things went black …" Mac exhaled. "I was out of it."

"For how long?" Gesch asked.

"I don't know," Mac answered and then closed his eyes for a minute, trying to remember. "I was out and then I remember hearing some noise and when I opened my eyes, he was hovering around near the front of the house, I think over Wire. Then I saw the knife in his hands and I reached down for my backup piece on my left ankle, pulled it and started firing."

"And you gave chase?" Gesch asked.

"Yeah," Mac answered, nodding. "It's a little foggy but I think I shot twice in the house. Then once from the front steps and then I ran after him, popped off a couple of more and then I couldn't keep running anymore. So I took my last crack in that alley and fired until I couldn't see him and then everything went ..."

"Blank?" Gesch finished.

"I must have blacked out or something."

"Frederick police found you unconscious lying against a fence," Gesch stated. "They found your identification and recognized the name, mostly because of what happened ..."

"... earlier in the day at the Fallway Clinic?" the Judge asked.

"Yup," Gesch answered and then looked back to McRyan. "Mac, was the clip in your backup Glock full? Were there fifteen rounds in it?"

Mac nodded lightly, lying back against his pillow, "Yeah. I checked it the other day. Why?"

"There were four left in the clip so it looks like you fired eleven times."

Mac closed his eyes and thought back, "If you say so, I honestly can't remember, Aubry," he answered. "I don't know ... I probably shouldn't have even been shooting in the first place, but ..."

Gesch nodded, "Risk was worth the reward. We've found ten slugs so far, so that's why I'm asking. We can't find the eleventh. Do you think you hit him?"

Mac lightly shook his head, "I don't know. If I did, it wasn't enough to get him to stop apparently."

Gesch's phone rang which he answered and walked out of the room.

"So can I get out of here?" Mac asked. He hated hospitals.

"I don't think you should go home," the Judge answered, "you or Wire."

"Why?"

"The incident here is all over the news. The media is all over the hospital and I just heard from a friend of mine checking on some things that the media has both of your homes staked out. I don't think you two want to go there right now. You need rest and to be left alone."

"So I assume you have something in mind?" Mac asked.

"In fact, I do."

The Reaper grimaced as he inspected the stitches, ten in all, in his upper right arm, on the outside of his massive bicep. The stitches were crude, with dental floss, and the scar he would end up with would likely be cruder, but going to the Emergency Room was not a viable option. His prior training and the Internet helped. A YouTube video on how to suture a wound was enough, as were the supplies from his First Aid kit.

The wound wasn't deep, more or less just a flesh wound. He would have full function of the arm in a day or two, once the throbbing pain relented. Unfortunately, the Ibuprofen was doing little to alleviate the constant pulse of pain but he didn't dare venture out for something stronger.

He cleaned up the mess, the blood, the bandage wrappers, his blood-soaked black jean jacket and other detritus and dropped it in a black garbage bag. With the sun peeking over the horizon, he went outside and pulled his pickup truck into the garage. Inside, he cleaned the interior of the truck. The blood was smeared on the upper right side of the leather driver's seat and then trickled down lower, pooling in the break between the seat and seat rest. Not a huge amount, but in the two-hour drive, he bled enough. Next, he cleaned the exterior of the truck and the light smear of blood on the frame outside the driver's side door and the vertical panel between the front and back side doors. He put the garbage bag in the rear bed of the truck and closed the topper and went back inside the cabin and turned on the television.

Kelly Drew was alive, albeit barely, on life support.

After the first frantic minutes and escaping the immediate vicinity of Drew's house, as he drove to the cabin, all he could wonder was, how did they find him? Was it luck or were they on to what he was doing? He was betting the latter. McRyan and Wire made some connection between the women.

He was sitting in front of the television now, twirling the SIM card for Dara Wire's phone in the fingers of his left hand, thinking about how he might use it. He put it down on the coffee table and sipped at his Coke. The television media coverage was fascinating to him, watching all of it unfold now for the first time, particularly McRyan's confrontation at the clinic from yesterday.

The local television reporter went after McRyan viciously. The offense McRyan took, the way the look on his face went dark, the way he charged the reporter and threatened her, lost his cool, was captivating to him. "Perhaps you have a temper," the Reaper mumbled, something that could be used down the road.

The task force, probably McRyan and his pretty partner Wire, must have made the connection on his targets. How he didn't yet know, although he suspected it probably had something to do with the camp. He'd wondered about leaving one of those three women to the end, making that connection harder. Of all of the women involved, they were the three who really had a clear identifiable connection, although he'd learned the three of them had not stayed in touch. He often wondered if they even all knew each other's names. Only victim number one was able to make all of those connections and he'd dealt with her long ago.

The FBI, Gesch, Delmonico, McRyan and Wire, they had an idea of what this was all about and an idea of what he looked like, but they didn't have all of the puzzle pieces yet, but they were on the hunt and looking in the right direction now. Add to that, Kelly Drew survived. She was severely injured, of that he was certain. The head wound and blood, coupled with how her body went immediately limp when they collapsed the table, told him she suffered a serious closed head injury. The kind people don't come out of; the kind that if they do, they don't have regular brain function. If that were the case, well she was as good as dead then, getting her deserved punishment. However, if she came out of it, and retained her memory, she could possibly alert the others, especially with McRyan and Company at her bedside knowing some of the puzzle pieces.

He couldn't take that chance.

He was almost to the end.

If he was going to get there he needed to heal and then move fast.

The results of last night's events were going to force him to significantly move up his timeline.

He would need to move quicker and he needed to get McRyan and Wire off his trail.

The Reaper pushed himself off the couch, picked up the SIM card and walked to the window and opened the curtains slightly with his right hand. He looked to the side of the garage and what would be his new home. He looked down in his left hand. In his fingers he again twirled the SIM card for Dara Wire's phone over and over.

22

"ARE YOU BUTT DIALING ME?"

Mac woke up, the bright sunlight pushing through the curtains of the bedroom. He looked to the clock on the nightstand, 10:44 A.M.

The Judge's idea was to sneak them out of the hospital and drive out to a private farm estate an hour outside of Washington, DC. The estate, named Pleasant Springs, was owned by a close political and extremely wealthy friend of the Judge, who provided free use for as long as was needed.

Pleasant Springs was an expansive two-story red brick with white pillar colonial set high upon a hill so as to overlook the sprawling river valley resting well below the estate grounds. There was a stable with horses set back a hundred yards behind the house. A large swimming pool area sat comfortably in between the stable and mansion. The entirety of the estate was surrounded and shaped by bright white horse fencing. After arriving, Mac was too sore and tired to tour or enjoy the plush accommodations. He went straight to bed, leaving Sally, the Judge and a less injured Wire to take in the luxury accommodations.

As he lay in bed contemplating whether to get up or try

to sleep more, he heard voices downstairs. After a minute staring at the slowly rotating ceiling fan cooling the room and listening to the voices, he realized there were more voices than just the Judge, Sally and Wire. And the voices were familiar, *and loud*. "You've got to be kidding me," Mac mumbled with his eyes closed but a small smile spreading across his face.

Mac rolled to his right side, put his feet on the floor and stood up and immediately had to steady himself. The concussion was better. The heavy pounding had subsided to more of a really bad headache. The bright light filtering through the curtains wasn't as bothersome as yesterday when he needed sunglasses and a blanket over his head to keep the light out while they drove to the estate. However, he still needed to move his battered body slowly as his entire torso ached.

From inside his duffel bag he took out a pair of tan cargo shorts and navy blue golf shirt and gingerly pulled them on. Dressed, he eased his way out of the bedroom and descended slowly down the winding staircase, keeping his right hand tightly on the banister. As he reached the bottom of the stairs, he noticed three small suitcases and a duffel bag resting by the front door in the foyer.

In the large kitchen and eating area to the right of the staircase, sitting around a long table, drinking coffee and dining on pastries with Sally, the Judge and Wire were Lich, Rockford, Riley and one other man. They all turned to see Mac standing in the archway of the kitchen. Mac was sporting a heavy cast on his left wrist, dark bruising on the left side of his neck, a swollen lip and two red, purple and yellowish puffy, bruised and barely open black eyes.

"Our boy is alive!" Riley cheered loudly with a big smile.

"Hey man," Rock said, standing up and walking over to

shake his hand, his big black paw swallowing Mac's good right hand. "How are you buddy?" the big man asked softly with concern as he carefully guided Mac over to an open chair at the head of the table.

Lich expressed his concern as well, "You look grotesque," he exclaimed with a big smile on his face, walking over to slap him on the back, which caused Mac to wince, "Oh man, sorry, Mac."

Mac grimaced a smile. "It's okay," he said as he slowly sat down into the chair and looked around the table. "Not that I'm not happy to see you guys, but *what in the hell* are you doing here?" he asked in a scratchy voice, almost a croak.

"I've learned over the years," the Judge explained with a knowing tone, "that when times get a little tough, it's good to have some Minnesota around."

"The doctor said you need some time to rest and heal. I can only stay out here for another day," Sally added, hugging him softly and kissing him on the cheek. "The Judge thought why not fly these guys out for a few days to keep you company."

"Mac," Wire said, pointing to a man sitting to her left, "this is my brother Dominic."

Mac gingerly stood up and extended his right hand, "I've heard a lot about you, Dominic."

"You might like me anyway," Dominic Wire answered with a smile and everyone laughed.

"I figured Dara could use a shoulder to lean on as well," the Judge answered. "You two need to rest for a day, maybe two, and get yourself together. That son of a bitch is still out there and I don't think he'll be caught without you two."

"So we're still part of the investigation?" Mac asked.

"Yes," the Judge replied. "But FBI Director Mitchell is wisely going to keep you guys out of the limelight. That little incident at the Fallway Clinic is causing a few political fires we've had to extinguish, which neither of you should concern yourselves with, *they weren't your fault.* Sally and I and our friends at the White House will take care of that. But, everyone in town is wondering where the heck you two are. I think we should keep it that way for a while."

"Let them wonder," Mac retorted and then looked to his friends. "But you guys didn't need to pay to fly out here for me. I'm okay. I'm fine."

"No offense, Mac," Rock noted, tapping Mac's cast and pointing to his head, "but you don't look fine, buddy. You look like you got run over by a Freightliner."

"Besides, we didn't pay to fly out here. I like you, but I don't like you *that* much," Lich quipped with a big smile, causing the entire room to laugh again and keep the mood light.

"I have a friend or two who owed me a favor and were more than happy to provide their corporate jet to get the boys in," the Judge explained.

"Mac, that plane was *waaaay* cool," Rock exclaimed like a little boy, a man not accustomed to experiencing how the other half lived. "I sat on a couch all the way here drinking not good, not great, but awesome, and I mean awesome, bourbon. You gotta get your ass kicked more often."

"Thanks. Rock, I'm touched, really," Mac replied ruefully. "But seriously, is it okay for you guys to be away?"

"Chief said no worries," Riles answered. "He sends his regards, by the way. Look, things are pretty quiet back home now that the home invasion crew has been taken care of."

"What about these gang fights and flash mobs I'm hearing about on the East Side?"

"That's under control. We have people on that and the one homicide is closed." Riley turned serious. "Mac, right now, all we're worried about is you there, my friend. I hate to agree with Dick Lick but, ah ... you've looked better. Are the eggs still scrambled?" Pat asked, pointing to his head.

"Not as. I just have a bad headache now, it isn't throbbing as much and it's getting easier to open my eyes." Mac looked around the kitchen, "I think I could eat."

"*That* we can handle," the Judge said, calling for the chef. For the next hour, everyone sat around the table talking and dining on pancakes, eggs and bacon.

The pain medication for his broken wrist made him loopy. That, plus the effects of the concussion and just general soreness, caused Mac to spend most of the day in bed, getting up for only an hour or two at a time. Sally checked on him frequently, taking a long rest with him during the afternoon, plus the two of them needed to make some amends.

"I'm glad I get to say I'm sorry," Mac said quietly, his eyes closed.

"Me too," Sally answered. "When I got the phone call ..." her voice trailed off.

"I know. But I'm alive and I'll be fine."

"Tell me about it?" she asked.

"About what?"

"Drew's house and the fight with that man, tell me about all of it."

"You heard my explanation at the hospital, didn't you?"

"Yes."

"Do you really want to hear it again?"

"Yes," she answered, sitting up on her left side, looking him in the eyes. "Tell me, and in this version, I want all the details."

"Look, Sally, I don't want you feeling like this is in any way your fault ..."

"I ... I ... I don't ... really."

"BS," Mac answered. "And it's BS if you are feeling that way. I'm a big boy and I knew what I was getting into and I said yes. I could have said no and I said yes."

"I know," Sally answered, her eyes watering, "It's just that I pushed you ..."

"This is not on you," Mac replied, sitting up, leaning on his right arm, facing her. "Don't do that to yourself. Don't beat yourself up about it; don't give it another thought. This is not on you, do you understand me?"

Sally nodded.

"Do you still want me to tell you about it?"

She nodded again.

Mac laid back down on his back and ran through what happened at Drew's house. He didn't hold back, he told her everything. Sally just listened, only occasionally asking what happened next.

"Be honest with me," she asked. "I want to know what was going through your mind. Did you think you were going to die?"

He didn't answer right away, thinking through the answer. He shook his head lightly. "I knew I was in trouble, babe. I knew I was hurt. I knew I was vulnerable, but when I came out of the fog and understood my situation, I didn't think about dying. I thought about acting and I knew I had to and fast."

"When did you start carrying a second gun?"

"When I went back home and worked the robbery case. After that election investigation, I figured I should start carrying something extra."

"Are you still carrying that switchblade?"

"I haven't been."

"What's Leroy Jethro Gibbs Rule No. 9?" Sally asked quoting from *NCIS*, one of their favorite shows.

"Don't go anywhere without a knife."

"So?"

"From now on I won't go anywhere without a knife."

They rested silently for a while longer and then Sally asked, "Tell me about him ... the Reaper."

"He kicked my ass."

"He got the jump on you."

"And he kicked my ass. I'm no easy mark. Wire's no easy mark. He handled us like it was nothing, like he was batting away mosquitoes."

"He's a big guy."

"He's more than big. He's a monster, Sally. The size, the viciousness, the strength and the way he just remorselessly pulled out the knife was scary. He was like the Hulk."

"He scares you." It wasn't a question.

"He should scare anybody."

"Are you going to keep after him?"

"I said he scares me and I now have a healthy respect for who I'm up against. But he should be scared too, because I'm not quitting. He gave me everything he's got and I'm still standing."

Sally carefully laid her head across his chest and he wrapped his right arm around her. They didn't say anything else for the rest of the afternoon, just resting. The pain medication was working on his wrist, the pain in that part of his body a mild irritant at this point, much less irritating than the cast itself. As for his head and neck, if he could just get them to settle down a little more he would feel a lot better. His friends were downstairs. They were here for him and he wanted to be with them.

For Wire, she couldn't get the fight with the Reaper out of her mind. It came to her in the hospital and again while trying to sleep at the estate. She didn't want to close her eyes. The feeling of helplessness as she fought him, the inability to break free and fight him off, it just kept swirling around and around in her mind. The nightmares made her bolt awake in a cold sweat, gasping for breath, and when she realized it was just a nightmare, she would break down. It was only two nights but she was thinking she might have to get some therapy if it continued.

Dominic kept watch over her, resting in a soft chair on the other side of the room, reading under a small lamp, a loaded Remington shotgun sitting at his feet. He wouldn't need it, but Dara said it somehow made her feel better because that might be the only thing that could stop the Reaper if he came.

"He's not coming for you, sis," Dominic said soothingly at 3:30 A.M. when she burst awake once again, the second time of the night. He walked over and sat down on the side of her bed.

"You don't know that," Dara answered, breathing hard, sweat running down the side of her face. "He could be."

"He's not, but if he does, I have that shotgun and before he got here he'd have to get through Mac's friends. And let me tell you something, they came loaded for bear. You didn't see the arsenal they arrived with, and I watched them go through and load that arsenal. I don't see him getting through those boys, particularly Riley or Rockford; those two are not to be messed with."

"Neither is the Reaper."

After she'd calmed and it was clear she wanted to stay

awake for a while, Dominic asked: "Do you wish you'd have said no when Dixon asked?"

Dara didn't respond immediately, looking away, out the dark window. "No. I owe the Judge."

"And he owes you, sis. He and the president are in the White House because of you and McRyan."

"Yeah, and I'm not in federal prison or the poor house thanks to him, so ..."

"So when the man calls ..."

"I answer. I have to. I always will."

"How about McRyan? Do you think he wishes he said no?"

Dara shook her head, a small smile creasing her face, "No. He's kind of funny, Dom. He puts up this front sometimes about how he doesn't need this or got talked into that, but ..." she shook her head. "Mac man thrives on the hunt. Once he's into the case he's like a dog with a bone, he ain't giving it up."

"He might want to now."

"No way. He's licking his wounds but he won't back down. He's just gonna be more pissed off."

"I suppose that means you won't back down either?" Dominic asked, resignation in his voice.

Dara shook her head, "I'm pissed off too."

The next morning Mac felt well enough to be up and about and joined everyone for a massive breakfast of scrambled eggs, bacon, sausage, hashed browns, fruit and toast. Breakfast spanned the lunch hour, everyone opening up and having a good time, glad Mac could finally join them. He passed on the Bloody Marys and stuck with water, although he did sneak a sip from Lich's drink when the fat man wasn't looking.

When the laughter and storytelling got particularly loud, Mac would wince a little in pain but for the most part he felt better and sat back and smiled as Rock, Riley and Lich swapped stories. Dominic Wire, a prosecutor in his own right, added a few of his own. Mac even joined in, adding some much needed context and self-defense when the punch line involved him. He must have said, "Now wait a minute, that's not *exactly* what happened," a half dozen times.

Everyone steered clear of the Reaper case. It wasn't hard to tell that Dominic and the boys were itching to talk about it, but not until Mac and Dara were ready, and they weren't —not yet. After breakfast, Sally began to pack and get ready to go back to the White House. When she finished, Mac decided to plant a seed with her, something he'd been thinking about for a while.

"Sally, there's something I think we need to talk about. I don't need you to answer right now, but I want you to think about it."

"Okay," Sally replied warily, picking up on his tone and demeanor. This was serious. "What?"

"What is our plan?"

"Our plan?" She didn't understand the question.

"Yeah, you and me, do we have one? You and me, our future, what is our plan? Where are we going?"

"Are you talking, you know, the 'm' word?" A word both of them rarely uttered. They more or less talked around it. Perhaps it was time for that to stop.

Mac shrugged, "I don't know. No ... yes ..., maybe, but not necessarily right now, but I mean, what is our plan? Is it

Washington for four years? Eight years? Then what? Go home? Go somewhere else?"

"What's bringing this on?" Sally asked, sitting down next to Mac on the end of the bed.

Mac looked to the floor, "I don't know, Sal, maybe my life passing before my eyes? Maybe our knock-down, drag-out argument just before that happened? Maybe it's that we're closer to thirty-five than thirty? Maybe it's you have something to get up and go to every day and I don't? Maybe it's that I don't like operating without a plan and I don't think we have a plan and it's starting to freak me out?"

"You did turn down a job from the FBI director, you know?"

"I know, and I don't regret it for a minute, but at the same time, other than this case, I feel a little adrift, which is okay, if I know eventually I'll hit some dry land." He looked Sally in the eye and could see her apprehension, "I don't want you to be freaked out here."

"I'm not," Sally answered, shaking her head, but he could tell she was at least a little nervous. "I'm not," she said again, quietly.

"Liar," Mac replied, with a small smile, reaching for her hand, reaching for her chin and tipping it up for her eyes to meet his. "You're scared of this and so am I, because what we have right now is so comfortable and so good and I'm not looking to change that. And I think ... no, wait, I know we both want our future to be with each other, right?"

Sally nodded, head still down.

"I guess I'm wondering what that future is and all I'm asking is for you to think about it. We've never really talked about this. We've just kind of happily floated along. We've talked about talking about it, but if we're really honest with each other, we've never had the real 'talk.' I think it's time. Don't you?"

Sally smiled, her eyes moist, but she smiled and kissed him. "I've known this was probably coming, I've been expecting it and you're right, we need to … talk about it. It's just that it's …"

Mac nodded, "A little scary."

"Yeah."

After Sally left, Mac took a nap. In the midafternoon, when the boys and Dominic decided to go horseback riding, Mac and Wire took a walk along a riding trail to stretch their legs.

"You sure you're up for this?" Wire asked. Mac still looked tired and was moving slowly.

"Yeah. I'm not as tired as I probably look, and I need some air and to move a little," he answered, taking a sip from his bottle of water. "I just took some more meds, I'll be good. Let's just take it slow and easy."

They walked in silence for several minutes down the path, both sides with a white horse fence barrier.

"How's Sally?"

"Fine."

"You two make up?"

He looked to her, "We're good. I took your advice, I said I was sorry."

"Good."

"I also told her this morning before she left that we needed to talk about what our plan is."

Wire stopped and stared him down, "And how did that go?"

"Okay, I guess. She was a little freaked about it. Heck, I'm a little freaked about it."

"It's a step, a big one … and a good one." Dara was a fan

of their relationship. She liked the two of them together and wanted it to stay that way.

They continued walking, enjoying the peace and quiet, the sound of birds singing in the trees and the sun warming them. In the distance they were able to watch the others carefully ride the horses, amused at the sight of Lich, a cowboy hat on his head and his rotund body bouncing along. "That poor horse's back may never be the same," Mac quipped.

"Will they be able to put Humpty Dumpty back together if he falls?" Wire wondered jokingly.

They both steered clear of the case; neither wanting or willing to talk about it yet, the shared experience of it enough for them at this point.

"Did I hear a phone call from Martin?" Mac asked with a smile.

"You did."

"You should go see him. Let him make you feel better."

"I will," she replied, "after we find this bastard. We are still going to try and find him, right?"

"Does a bear shit in the woods?"

"Yes he does."

"There are more rounds left in this fight."

They reached a fork in the path where they could go left or right. Looking back, they were a considerable distance from the house. "Should we turn around?" Wire asked when Mac's cell phone started ringing.

He looked at the display and frowned.

"What?"

"Are you butt dialing me?"

"Huh?"

He held up his phone. Dara Wire was calling him.

"Maybe you don't know how to use that new phone of yours."

She pulled out her new phone from her back pocket, "I'm not calling ... you... Mac," a panicked expression overtook her face. "Mac?"

"He took your cell phone," Mac answered, using the speaker function: "McRyan."

"Is this Mac McRyan?" a deep, eerie voice asked.

"Yeah. Who's this?"

"Oh I think you know who it is," the Reaper teased in a low ominous voice. "How does that arm feel?"

Mac paused for a moment, but the anger welled up inside him. Through gritted teeth he asked, "What do you want?" Wire had already peeled off, dialing Gesch.

"I wanted to know how you are feeling."

"Never better."

"Oh come now, Agent McRyan, or is it Mac? Do you mind if I call you Mac?"

"Sure, if you tell me your name, asshole."

"Oh I don't think so, Mac. But you know you talk awfully tough for someone who suffered such a severe beating. And your friends in the media are so concerned for you and Ms. Wire, and they have absolutely no idea where you are," he mocked.

"Like Dick Cheney, I'm at an undisclosed location."

"Mac, are you and Dara Wire hiding?" he asked in a light, whimsically evil teasing tone.

"I'll tell you what. I'll come out if you come out from under your rock. Name the place and time I'll be there, you and me and nobody else. One-on-one and we'll finish this thing."

The Reaper's voice turned cold, "That's not something

you want, McRyan. If I were you, I'd stay right where you are. Where you're safe and can't be harmed."

"Really? You don't know me very well then. I'm coming for you."

"I'd think twice about that. You're lucky to be alive," he said coldly. "I made a mistake. I could and should have finished you when I had the chance. It won't happen again."

"Is that right?"

"It is," the Reaper answered deeply. "I am nearly done. This will be over very soon. Let me finish what I've started and you and Wire will not be harmed. My battle is not with you."

"You know we can't do that."

"Final warning, Mac. If you and Wire get in my way again, I promise you, you both will die."

The line went dead.

He took the SIM card out of the burner phone and tossed the phone into the river and jogged back to the panel van and pulled away down the dirt road, a mile back to the state highway.

The right arm was feeling better although there was still pain and he didn't comfortably have full range of motion, but overall it was improving. Mostly it was the cut through the skin and the rudimentary stitches hidden under his light long-sleeve shirt that pained him, both of which would heal and eventually disappear.

As he turned left onto the highway, he rewound the conversation with McRyan in his head.

Was McRyan bruised and battered? Yes.

Was he putting on false bravado? Yes.

Was he down for the count? No.

McRyan and his pal Wire would still be coming for him.

Rarely in life do people live up to their press clippings. However, McRyan and his friend Dara Wire were doing just that. In many ways, he was lucky to get away from Kelly Drew's. McRyan had several shots at him. Had the man not been seeing double and giving chase with a severely damaged left arm, he may well have finished the job.

But McRyan didn't get it done.

Now, the job was there waiting to be finished.

He was ready to leave the country. The documents, the identity, the way out were all in place and he could just slide away now and never be heard from again. He told himself he might have to run at a moment's notice when it all started. In the two years that were spent planning his mission, identifying the people to be punished, of processing that night two years ago when the vengeance first rose up and took over in him, brought him to the place he was now. He knew the plan could fall apart, that he would have to run before he finished his mission and avenged Rena's death.

Had he just started, he could have walked away. Maybe let the investigation settle down and fade from memory and then come back later. But now, so close to the end, just days away, there would be no stopping now.

The threat he made to McRyan would be unlikely to shake the man, not if his past was any indication. McRyan may hesitate, he may take some time before he came after him, but keep coming he would. The phone call was confirmation of that.

The concern was the FBI, McRyan and Wire knew how he identified his victims, or at least four of the five. The question was did they know who was left to be punished?

What he needed was to throw off McRyan and Wire.

He drove along the highway with light rock music playing over the radio, thinking things through. Thinking about what would come next and how he could finish with McRyan and Company after him and beginning to understand him.

What he came to realize was that there was a flaw in his plan.

He'd become predictable.

If McRyan and Wire were going to keep coming, he had to change up and had to take the fight to them as well.

As he drove through the Maryland countryside, an idea began percolating in his mind. The idea was extremely risky in one sense, requiring him to go back to a place he left, but in another, the payoff could be big. It could give him another chance to hurt, if not finish off, McRyan and Wire.

23

"EVERY CONSPIRACY HAS A LEADER."

Gesch traced the call back to a burner phone and the call was bounced off a cell tower near Keymar, Maryland. "We have no traffic cameras and no real way of tracing the burner. Chances are, if he has half a brain, which we know the sadistic bastard does, he dumped the phone the minute he was done and the burner didn't have any sort of GPS tracking or anything like that. So other than the cell tower, we got nothing."

"It was worth a try," Wire replied.

"What I can't figure is why he took Wire's phone to begin with?" Gesch asked.

"To torment me," Mac answered, "or based on today's call, to warn me or us off. He could have killed Dara and Kelly Drew and then haunted me with it, calling me, taunting me, reminding me of how I'd failed. That's what the call was to a certain degree. It was a warning, telling me he's not done."

"But he'll be done soon," Wire added. "And he's saying that we should just leave him alone to finish and he'll let us live."

"Are you going to leave him alone?"

"Oh *hell* no. Question is, Aubry, what is our role here?"

"When you two are ready..."

"We're ready right now," Mac answered hotly, but winced. His headache was not gone.

"No you're not. You're better, you both are. I can hear it in your voices. But I can also hear in your voices that you're not healthy enough yet. Maybe tomorrow, maybe the day after, and then when you are ready, we're going to get back to how we originally had this structured. Remember, you were running a side or parallel investigation and that kind of merged into what we're doing."

"Now wait a minute, Aubry..."

"Easy, Mac. That's nobody's fault and it is not a criticism. It just kind of happened based on what was happening with the case and depending on how things go, it may well happen again. But for now, Director Mitchell is pushing the reset button and getting us back to the original structure. I'm running point, you and Dara parallel, playing your own angle. You just need to figure out what that angle is and I'll get you whatever you need."

"I feel like we're being shoved aside," Mac persisted.

"No," Gesch answered assuredly, "we're doing just the opposite. What we're trying to do is give you room to maneuver. You two are pretty hot right now and the minute you start showing up, it'll end up being news, you'll have a tail and your movements will be watched. That will hamper your effectiveness and we can't afford that."

"The media is *just* a bit riled up at the moment," Wire said in an understatement.

"Have you seen it today? Can you say feeding frenzy?" Gesch replied with a little chuckle. "For two people as supposedly media shy as you two, you're all the rage at the moment."

Mac understood what Gesch was saying and nodded, "I'm all for keeping a low profile."

"Good," Gesch answered. "So when you're ready, we want you to go back to working this thing from the outside. So think about how you want to do that, what your next move is. Mac, you had a bad concussion, a broken wrist and last I saw you, you looked like Floyd Mayweather did a tap dance on your face. Get yourself right and come back to work." Gesch hung up.

Mac was steaming, not at Gesch, not even at being relegated back to the parallel part of the investigation. Working in the shadows was fine by him and what he wanted really.

Wire suspected she knew where the white smoke was coming from, "The call?"

"I had eleven shots at him, Dara. Eleven fucking shots! How do I not hit the son of a bitch at least once?"

"Mac, you were all beat to hell. Your wrist was broken, your eyes were half shut, you had a concussion …"

"Bullshit. I had chance to finish it and I choked. You can't miss eleven times, you just can't. And now that motherfucker is calling me, taunting me, threatening me, threatening *you*."

Riley came into the room and immediately recognized the mood. "Oh, I've seen that look before," Riles noted, taking in the vibe of the room and Mac's demeanor. He and the others knew about the call from the Reaper.

"So here's what we're going to do." Pat, a master of the act of blowing off steam and clearing the mind, took control. "Mac, we're going to eat dinner, a big massive *huge* dinner, and once we're done, we're going to pretend this place is Patrick's Room. We're going to get the beer flowing and the bullshit roaring and you two are going to walk us through the Reaper case."

Mac was about to object but Riley wouldn't have it, holding up two fingers. "Two things. One, we're all curious as hell to learn about it, and second ..."

"And second?" Mac asked, perturbed.

"Yeah, you little shit," only the six-foot-three hulking Riles could get away with referring to Mac that way, "the second thing is maybe we can help. Need I remind you that you were brought into our little home invasion case as a second set of eyes. Turnabout is fair play."

"Point taken," Mac conceded.

"Come on, man, let's party," Riles exclaimed, throwing his arm carefully around Mac's neck and leading him to the kitchen.

After the dinner plates were cleared and the staff retired for the evening leaving a tub full of beer on ice, Mac brought his backpack containing the Reaper file into the kitchen and everyone got really quiet, which Mac noticed and quipped with a grin.

"Guys, it's not like I've got the Holy Grail or the Ark of the Covenant in here. Relax, breathe, talk."

The estate was occasionally used for corporate retreats and therefore had on hand the necessary supplies for meetings, including rolling dry erase whiteboards. Rock wheeled two such boards into the spacious dining area while Mac and Wire laid out the various folders, notepads and pictures from the case on the table. Mac pulled out his laptop and started it up and connected it to a projector so that he could project onto one of the whiteboards. He looked over to Wire. Two nights ago was still raw with both of them and Dominic quietly told him about her night terrors. So before he started he wanted to make sure she was okay: "Are you sure you're ready for this?"

"No, but let's do it anyway," she answered while holding out her fist which Mac bumped back. "That phone call means he's still out there and is going to kill some more. I disagree with Gesch. We don't have any more time to get better. It's go time."

"True that."

Everyone was taking a seat, opening beers and settling in. "Rock, beer me," Mac bellowed, still pounding away at the keys on his laptop.

"Are you sure?" Rock asked with his hand deep in the cooler. Mac was still on pain medication.

"If I'm talking about this shit, I'm having a beer."

Wire gave him a stern look.

"Not a word to Sally."

The beer tub was full of local Virginia microbrews. Rock tossed him a Starr Hills Jomo Lager. He opened it and took a long sip of the light amber ale. Why not start with a shocker, he thought, "What you guys don't know, what nobody knows yet, is that the Reaper is *not* a serial killer."

"Not a serial killer?" Riles asked.

"No. At least not a serial killer in the typical sense you would think of."

"What is he then?" Rock asked.

"We think," Mac gestured towards Wire, who nodded, "that he's a killer out to avenge the death of this woman."

Wire held up a photo of Rena Johnson and put it up on the left whiteboard.

"Dara and I think this is what this case is all about," Mac stated.

"I haven't seen any of this reported at all," Riles noted,

taking a pull from his beer. "Is this the FBI's operating theory?"

"I would say ... one of them," Wire answered haltingly, taking a sip of her own beer.

"Meaning?" Riles pushed.

"They haven't necessarily gone all in on it, they're investigating all possible theories," Mac answered, but then looked Riley right in the eye. "*Wire and I have gone all in.*"

"Then you better start from the beginning," Riles answered as he got up and fetched a beer from the tub. "I suspect this might take a while."

"Then let's start from the beginning. The first victim is Melissa Goynes ..." Mac and Wire tag teamed the explanation of the first four victims, Goynes, Janelle Wyland, Hannah Donahue, Sandy Faye and finishing with how they ended up at Kelly Drew's. Mac's buddies and Wire's brother were professionals. Riley was right, a second opinion was a good idea. A second opinion only worked if he and Wire gave them all the facts. As a result, it took a good hour to work through all the details. The boys popped in a few questions along the way but they mostly listened.

"We had no connection between the victims until we were going through Faye's personal effects, records, financials and photos, when I ran across this photo from the American Academic Honor Society Camp from seven years ago," Mac stated, projecting it onto the whiteboard. In the picture, the heads of Goynes, Donahue and Faye were circled. "I noted Goynes and Donahue first and then a minute later we found Faye."

"That doesn't just happen, not in nature," Lich said, studying the photos. "How is that picture of ..." he pointed towards the board.

"Rena Johnson?" Wire asked.

"Yeah, who is she and how does she fit?" Lich inquired, twirling one end of his bushy mustache while taking a look at the picture. "I don't see her in this picture."

"She's not," Mac answered. "She wasn't at that camp."

"Then what's her relationship to the victims?"

"We're not *exactly* sure yet, other than she's the catalyst for all this, I can feel it," Mac suggested, taking a sip from his beer. "Short story is she was killed in a hit-and-run car accident on August 17th seven years ago on a county road outside of Auburn, New York, after having apparently left a rave party that took place at an abandoned farm. Seven years ago there was a big problem with such parties in the area, particularly around Auburn."

"And your three murder victims, the ones in the picture, fit in how? Close the loop for me here?" Dominic Wire asked.

"They were involved in her death somehow," Mac replied. "We think they, and perhaps others, such as Kelly Drew, were at that party as well and were somehow involved in her death. Johnson's toxicology report showed Ecstasy in her system, among other drugs, and a blood alcohol of .23 when she was hit while walking along the side of that road."

"And the Reaper?" Riles asked.

"The Reaper, whoever he is," Mac answered, "is out avenging Johnson's death."

"How do you make that connection?" Rock asked, looking over Lich's shoulder. "I know you like your leaps in logic, but this seems like the Grand Canyon."

"Yeah, the FBI thought that too until the other night at Kelly Drew's," Mac answered. "It's connected."

"How?" Riles asked.

"I have a theory."

"We have a theory," Wire admonished with a smile.

"We have a theory," Mac replied with a smile. "But a little background first. Goynes, Donahue and Faye were counselors at the AAHC Camp up on Lake Seneca in New York."

"Is that the Finger Lakes region?" Dominic Wire asked.

"Yes, Lake Seneca is one of them," Dara answered. "Lake Seneca is a half hour from Auburn."

"Saturday nights for the counselors was their free time," Mac continued. "The kids from the previous week left by noon on Saturday and new kids didn't arrive until Sunday, so the director at the camp said that the counselors often go out on Saturday nights. As for August 17th, that was the last Saturday of the summer for the camp. All the counselors would be going home the next day so they were free to do whatever they wanted that night. The camp director told us the counselors often went out on the town or to parties. It is vacation land up there, plenty to do on a Saturday night."

"Great," Riles critiqued. "Again, what connects all of this?"

"What if Goynes, Donahue and Faye, along with Wyland and Drew, were at this party at an abandoned farm near Auburn and somehow were involved in the hit-and run death of Johnson? Maybe some of them were in the vehicle? Maybe others were involved in getting her drunk and high so that she wandered off from the party? Witness accounts in the Johnson file indicate that while some locals recognized her, they didn't really know who she came to the party with. Maybe she went to the party with a friend, maybe that friend was friends with our victims and then the tragedy ensued where Johnson ends up dead in a ditch a mile from the farm."

"How do you draw that conclusion?" Riles asked. "The dots still aren't connected for me."

Mac took out photos of Johnson lying in the ditch. He put the photo of Johnson lying in the ditch, her rosary beads clutched to her chest, lying in the fetal position up on the whiteboard, next to the murder scene photos for Goynes, Wyland, Donahue and Faye lying in the fetal position, the Holy Cross cut into their chests. "How about now?"

The room went quiet.

Mac didn't have to explain the relationship between the photos.

"The symbolism of it," Riles muttered, nodding, getting it sooner than everyone else. "The victims have been left staged in essentially the same way."

"Except instead of rosary beads ..." Mac started.

"He's cutting the Holy Cross in their chests instead," Riles finished, taking a sip of his beer. "Okay, Mac, I see how you're getting there."

"Why the biblical verses?" Rock asked. "What's that all about?"

"A message," Wire answered, standing up and putting each of the messages on the board, "maybe a couple of messages. These women are reaping what they sowed. They were involved in the death of Rena Johnson and didn't report it, didn't try to save her and didn't dial 911. Instead they fled the scene and now they're paying the price for it. 'Actions have consequences' as Mac said the other day. They're reaping what they sowed."

"The killer knows they were involved in Johnson's death," Mac added, pointing to the victims. "This is a message to them, to everyone, that he knows."

"You said something about a couple of messages?" Lich asked, looking to Dara.

"Johnson was religious, more of a bible camp attendee than a rave party attendee."

"And the killer knows this?"

"That's what we're thinking. He knows her and he knows what happened."

"How does he know?" Riley asked. "I get the knowing Johnson part, but how does he know *these* women were involved? What does he know that you don't? What does he know that the detectives investigating this seven years ago don't?"

Wire and Mac shared a look and shrugged. This was the answer they didn't have. "We don't know. But he knows, somehow … he knows."

"One thing we think he's doing," Wire mentioned, "is interrogating the women."

"Interrogating them?" Rock asked.

"Yes," Mac answered as he made some keystrokes on his laptop, pulling up some photos. "If you look closely in these photos of the crime scene for Goynes, as well as Donahue, you can see markings on the floor that look like they're from the four feet of a chair, one facing the other. Goynes and Donahue had ligature marks on their ankles and wrists. They were found in the basement of a building and a house where he would have the isolation and time to interrogate them thoroughly."

"And as part of those interrogations, he learns who was involved in the death of Johnson?" Lich asked.

"That's what we're thinking," Mac answered and waved to Rock for another beer.

"You sure?" Rock asked.

"Yes, damnit," Mac barked.

"Okay, but that's it," Wire ordered sternly, having talked with Sally earlier who asked her to make sure Mac didn't get into one of the usual drinking contests with his crew. "Dara, as much as I love those three oafs," Sally had said to her, "I know they'll get going into the beer and booze and will try to drag Mac along. They know how to push his buttons. Don't let them."

Dara promised and two would be Mac's limit. "You're still on heavy meds. You're now cutoff. Do you read me?"

"Yes, Mom," Mac moaned sheepishly. "Guess I'll have to put a nipple on this one." Everyone started laughing and the discussion of the case ceased for a bit, everyone grabbing more beer with small discussions breaking out.

Riley moved next to Lich and started flipping through the Reaper case materials while everyone was taking a break and chatting. After ten minutes, Mac started drifting away from a conversation with Rock and the two Wires and focused in on Riley.

For all of Pat Riley's gruffness, drinking and general horsing around, the big man was an exceptionally capable detective and learned at the hands of Mac's father Simon. Riles had successfully handled three serials over the years. A fourth he investigated with Mac's dad went unsolved, although the bodies stopped dropping. Pat had been around the block more than once and was a savvy detective.

Mac studied under Riles for years, learned from him, picked his brain and knew him like an older brother. Something didn't add up for Riles, and Mac could see it in his eyes, in his facial expressions and in his posture. There was something in the files and conversation that was gnawing at him. After another few minutes, Riles closed the file, stood up and grabbed another fresh beer, popped the top off and took a long sip and came and sat back down next to Mac.

"Mac, the first victim, something doesn't ring true about her. I can't put my finger on it, but ..."

Mac smiled because Riles brought up something that bothered Mac from the moment they made the connection at the camp. "Something has bothered me about it as well and it's that ..."

"He just starts with Melissa Goynes in Harrisburg."

"Yes, and you're asking ..."

"Why? Why Melissa Goynes?"

"I've wondered that as well, Riles," Mac answered.

"To me that's an important question," Riles mused. "How does he start with Goynes? How does he know to start with her? Mac, is there anything in her background, history, photos, messages, anything that suggests why she's victim number one? I don't know if we classify your guy as a serial or not, but whatever he is he is on a mission, killing specific people for a specific reason. How does the mission start with a mother who is a bar manager and then he graduates to an insurance broker, teacher and daughter of a political power broker, then to a news anchor on the rise, and then a coffee shop owner?"

"Doesn't make sense, does it," Mac answered. "Unless ..."

"Unless," Riles smiled. They were reading each other's minds. "Unless Goynes isn't ..."

"The first one," Mac finished.

"That's right," Riles answered. "I can't tell you why she isn't your first other than she doesn't make sense, she doesn't feel right." The veteran detective took a long sip of his beer. "Mac, as you say, your killer is not your typical run of the mill sociopathic serial killer. She's not compelling enough to be number one. There's nothing in her past that says she triggered something in this guy. Look, I know the McRyan family commitment to the legal distribution of mineral spirits. Believe me, I've experienced it. However, in the case of Melissa Goynes, I doubt seven years ago when she was a bright college student attending that camp that running a bar in Harrisburg was her end all career goal. There is nothing about her that says she needs to be killed as an act of vengeance, that she would be the trigger. Now, if there was a true typical sociopathic serial killer on the loose, I'd say sure why not, she could be number one. But this guy isn't the typical serial, if he's a serial at all. He's a killer out for vengeance and I just don't see her being the first target, the one that gets him going. There is nothing that says I have to get Melissa Goynes first, she's number one."

"If our theory holds that these women abandoned the scene, maybe it wasn't her idea," Mac suggested. "If we're talking a conspiracy, then ..."

"Every conspiracy has a leader. She's a follower, not a leader," Riles answered. "Nothing about her screams leader, the mastermind behind covering this up."

"So you're saying what, Pat?" Wire asked.

"You don't know who your first victim is, Dara. You started in the middle of the story. Melissa is the first you've identified or know about, but she's not your killer's first. You need to go back to the beginning and find your first victim, your *true* first victim. If you find the first victim, then you will find the pieces that bring this together."

"And," Lich suggested, "you'll probably find something to tie back to your killer. This Reaper fella might not be a serial killer, but how does he know that these women are involved in Johnson's death?"

"Because there is something about her that ties it all together," Mac finished the thought. "Our first victim very well knows ..."

"Our killer," Dara added. "I think they're right."

"No question in my mind, Dara, they *are* right," Mac finished.

"Thing is, Mac, do you have any idea who the killer is?" Lich asked.

Mac shook his head and went back to the file. "She has no immediate family. Her parents are dead, her brother, who was a cop and detective, died two years ago in a car accident. There's a half-brother who is twenty years older who lives up in Rochester, New York, but he wasn't close to her, is under six feet tall and is in his mid-fifties. The bureau has been through Johnson's life, interviewing people who knew her back then. There was no boyfriend in her life that we've been able to find, so we don't have a good lead on that yet. It's the one thing that makes me question our theory, that if Johnson is the trigger of this thing, there should be someone in her past that makes sense as the killer, and there isn't, at least not that we've yet identified."

"I'm amazed," Dara suggested, "that given all of the pictures we have out there, we haven't gotten a better lead on this guy. Someone has to have seen him. Someone has to have recognized him."

"Not necessarily," Lich suggested seriously. "People aren't seeing it in context."

"And they may not be seeing him depicted in the way they'd recognize him," Rock added. "I've seen these pictures too, Ms. Wire. We've been following this thing pretty closely because our boy here's been on the case. This guy you're after is pretty average looking, nothing special about him, nothing really striking. You can tell me he's a monster all you want and I don't doubt you for a second, but he looks like a chunky tubby guy you see every day. But what if he had longer hair before? Maybe he wore a different style of glasses, wore his beard thicker or maybe thinner, wore different clothing or had plastic surgery. I mean, it's not like you have a dead-on straight driver's license picture of this guy. Your pictures aren't in hi-def. They're grainy surveillance, from awkward angles, and sketch artist renderings."

"Exactly," Lich added. "My point exactly, the photos are out of context. Find the right context and you'll have a better chance of identifying him. At least, that's what my *mildly* trained veteran less than sober detective mind thinks."

Mac sat back, nodded and looked to Wire. "We have to find victim number one, Dara."

"Well, Gesch said we need to go back to working parallel. This would be parallel, extremely parallel, off the grid parallel. Where do we even start looking?"

"The thirst to kill comes from somewhere," Rock mused.

"It always does," Dominic Wire agreed. "If he's this proficient at it now, if he was that proficient when he killed Melissa Goynes in Harrisburg ..."

"He's done it before," Rock agreed and clanked beers with Dominic. "He's killed before, because he has it down to a science. I mean, think about it, he stages Goynes perfectly as a first victim. He'd given it some thought. He's done it before."

"So if this train of thought is right," Dominic suggested, "it seems you're looking for maybe a stabbing of a woman with a knife similar to the Ka-Bar our guy is using somewhere in the five- or six-state area here that occurred sometime in the months before Melissa Goynes was killed."

Mac looked to Wire, "And had some sort of relationship to one of our victims."

"I bet Gesch could put some resources on that," Dara answered with a smile and reached for her cell phone.

Mac snorted. He believed in his gut. It was usually right, and his gut told him the boys were on the right track and together they had all come up with some serious insight into the case. It was like being at home, like being in

Patrick's Room at the Pub. It felt good, felt right. He raised his nearly finished beer, *"Man it's good to see you guys."*

∽

Twelve-year-old Samuel Belanger lay on his back in his sleeping bag, scanning the ceiling of the tree house and the stars he and his nine-year-old brother Ethan had placed on the ceiling they'd painted black. The tree house was set upon thick stilts with a large branch from an oak tree weaving its way through a corner of the structure. The tree house was the envy of all the kids in the neighborhood. Sam, Ethan and two other neighbor boys were doing their first sleepover in the house since their dad, an engineer, constructed it in the spring. The boys had just returned from vacation where they slept out in tents overnight twice. Since they handled the tents on vacation, they figured they were ready for the tree house in the backyard.

"Sam and Ethan, did you guys hear about the police shootout a few nights ago?"

"Yeah," Sam answered excitedly. "Police were chasing someone through the neighborhood, right?"

"That's right," Johnny Franks answered. "We all heard them. The shots, they don't sound like they do on TV. The shots don't boom."

"What do they sound like?" Ethan asked apprehensively, the youngest of the group.

Johnny thought for a second, "More like a popping sound, almost like popcorn. I didn't really know what the sound was until my dad explained it the next day."

"And there were lots of cops?" Sam asked.

"Oh yeah," Ryan Snerk replied. "There were lots of lights and sirens and even TV trucks. It was waaaay cool."

There was a boom in the distance.

"What was that?" Ethan asked fearfully. "Was that someone shooting?"

"That was a boom, not a pop. That was thunder, bro," Sam answered, smiling at his little brother who wanted to hang with the big kids and be brave, but was just a little bit scared. "It sounds like it's a long ways away."

Five minutes later, as the boys still played with their flashlights and talked, a light rain started.

"Sam, it's raining, should we go inside?" Ethan asked.

"Nah. It's just a little rain, no big deal. I don't want to run inside and have Dad tease us we couldn't hack it. Because you know he will."

A few minutes later, Ethan felt drops on his face. "Sam, water is coming through the ceiling."

Sam put his flashlight up to the ceiling and water was coming through from the roof of the tree house. "Darn it. I guess we will have to go back inside."

"But now we can give Dad a hard time. The roof is leaking," Ethan said with a wry smile.

The next morning, Mark Belanger climbed up into his sons' tree house with Samuel and Ethan trailing close behind.

"So where was this hole in the roof, boys?"

Ethan pointed to the ceiling above where he'd been laying. "Right there, Dad. I can see a little light shining through."

Mark Belanger inspected the hole in the ceiling. "What the heck?"

He'd built the tree house and put the shingles properly on the roof. Such a hole wouldn't happen naturally, not within a month of completion.

"The hole is cylindrical," he said out loud. "Hmm."

He opened his toolbox and pulled out a long, thin, Phillips screwdriver and stuck the screw-end through the hole and looked the other direction. Embedded in the wall, just below where the roof met the wall, in a line of nail heads, was the larger nail, or was it? Belanger inspected it. A former Marine, he knew a bullet when he saw one.

He took out his cell phone and dialed 911.

24

"THERE'S BLOOD ON IT."

"Your insight serves you well, Mac," Gesch answered in his best Obi Wan voice. Mac and Wire were eating ham sandwiches in the kitchen of McRyan's Georgetown condo, having returned from the Virginia estate when Gesch called.

After the brain storming session of the night before, Gesch, Delmonico and the rest of their team went about going through the backgrounds and reinterviewing family members and friends when late in the morning something popped. "A little over two years ago, in April, a friend of Janelle Wyland's named Rebecca Randall went missing."

"Missing?" Wire asked, taking a bite of her sandwich.

"Yes," Gesch answered over the speakerphone. "She was last seen leaving a local shopping mall in Ithaca, New York."

"There's that area again," Wire remarked. Ithaca was forty miles south of Auburn, New York.

"It gets better," Gesch added, "Rebecca Randall is originally from Auburn, graduated high school with Rena Johnson, and from what we've been able to learn, the two of them were very good friends."

"Seriously?"

"Yup."

"There has to be a connection then," Wire added. "So what happened to Rebecca Randall?"

"She was reported missing by her husband the next morning after she was last seen. Her car was found four days later, forty miles south of Ithaca, pulled off into the woods. The body was found a day later lying in a ditch, barely visible due to all the high grass and cattails. A searcher practically stepped on the body when they found her. I'm e-mailing you the file now."

Mac and Wire made their way up to the attic office and Mac's laptop computer. McRyan opened the e-mail file and immediately started printing pages. At the time of her sad demise, Rebecca Randall was a recently married twenty-five-year-old manager at a local clothing store. Mac scanned the murder scene pictures of the shallow grave in the farm field and of her vehicle while Wire assembled the investigative file spewing out on the printer. The cause of death was stabbing. Her stomach brutally ripped open, although not in the shape of the Holy Cross, as with other victims, nor was she staged; she was simply dumped in the ditch. "She wasn't killed in that ditch."

"Why?" Aubry asked knowingly.

"Lack of blood, very little in the ditch or in the trunk of the car," Mac answered. "She was dumped there but she was killed somewhere else."

"That's what the Ithaca PD surmised as well," Gesch answered. "You'll find it in the notes."

"Did they ever figure out *where* she was killed?"

"No," Gesch answered. "That remains a mystery."

"Did they have any suspects?"

"Only the most obvious one when a wife is murdered—the husband, Kevin Randall."

"I'll bite," Mac asked. "Other than the obvious, why the husband?"

"His alibi was just a bit on the squishy side, but the investigators didn't have any physical evidence or real motive so they never charged him. From what I can tell in reading the file …"

"They didn't think it was him but they had no other viable options," Wire answered, thumbing the pages of the investigation. "He'd been out of town on a boys' weekend. It should have taken him five to six hours to drive home and it took more like twelve."

"What was his explanation?" Mac asked.

"He said he pulled off to a rest area and slept in his car for six hours since he was so exhausted from the weekend," Dara answered, reading from a page. "Apparently the boys got after the booze pretty good. He said he was tired, weaving on the road and worried he still might blow over the legal limit. So he pulled aside to sleep and get himself right. The rest area he claimed he stopped at is unmanned and there were no cameras to verify him stopping there. It was a rest area, so some guy sleeping in a Toyota 4Runner isn't exactly going to draw suspicion."

"Which means good luck identifying anyone who stopped there and might have seen him during the time he said he was there," Gesch stated.

Mac was flipping through the pages as well. "It doesn't look like he was exactly beloved by his in-laws." The file indicated Rebecca's parents disapproved of the marriage. The two had been together since high school in Auburn, she being a cheerleader and he the football captain. She'd never really dated anyone else from what Mac could tell from the file, and Mom and Dad thought she ought to have played the field. Mom and Dad also thought Kevin might have played the field, *while with their daughter*. It appeared that her parents continued to suspect their son-in-law, even long after the police had moved beyond him as a suspect.

"Yeah, I saw the in-laws' less than loving endorsement," Wire answered. "So that put a target on him as well."

"At least enough that the husband moved away from Ithaca, away from Auburn and away from everything he'd ever known," Gesch replied. "A cloud of suspicion hovered over him and his reputation was totaled, so he left to start over. He wouldn't be the first guy to do that. However, in the end, while the Ithaca PD didn't rule him out completely, they moved in other directions. As of today, they've never found a killer, a motive or even where she was killed, just her car and where she was dumped."

"And no forensic evidence from what I'm seeing," Mac answered. "They really had nothing on the guy. They had nothing on the killer."

"Which is why the investigation moved in different directions after its initial focus on Kevin Randall," Gesch stated. "I suppose he's technically still a person of interest, but in talking to Ithaca, the file is as stone cold as can be. So do you guys want to head up there and see if you can heat it back up?"

"No," Mac answered.

"No?" Wire and Gesch asked in unison.

"Why not Ithaca, Mac?" Gesch asked.

"Because I don't think the answer lies in Ithaca, at least not yet. It lies somewhere in Rebecca Randall's past and who better to answer that than her high school sweetheart and widower husband?"

"Well, in that case, you're going to Philadelphia."

Gesch updated the director on the Reaper investigation. "We're continuing to work Germantown. We have agents picking up every piece of surveillance footage in that town in the two days before he tried to kill Drew. We've found nothing yet, but we're continuing with that."

"What about the Reaper himself?"

"The task force is continuing to go around with the photo array on this man."

"And McRyan?"

"He and Wire are working their angle that we don't have the first victim right, that there's a different victim number one. They are on their way up to Philadelphia to work that." Gesch laid the theory out for the director.

"You buy their theory?"

"You brought them in to take a second look at this case and run a parallel investigation. This is an outside of the box way of looking at the case. I don't know that I fully buy that there's a different victim number one, but I don't dare discount it either. They may be on to something, and by now, I've learned not to question them."

"You've come around on them," the director noted.

Gesch nodded. "They're both arrogant, cocky and overly confident, but the fact is they're also really good. Those two are working this thing when almost anyone else in their conditions, who went through what they did, would be sitting on the sidelines. All they care about is solving it. I'll work with people like that any day."

There was a knock on Gesch's door and Delmonico stuck her head in the door. "There is a call on line three from the police chief in Frederick. You need to take the call."

Gesch ran his hand through his hair, "Chief, what can I do for you?" Gesch listened and then his eyes went wide.

"What?" Director Mitchell asked.

Gesch put his hand over the receiver, "They found McRyan's eleventh bullet in the wall of a tree house."

"And?"

"There's blood on it."

"It goes to the front of the line. I want to know who that blood belongs to fifteen minutes ago," Director Mitchell ordered.

"Ten minutes," the pilot reported.

The FBI helicopter cruised hard north following the Delaware River, a hundred feet in the air, making a speed run. The downtown Philadelphia skyline was growing in size, viewable to their left to the northwest in the early evening light.

"You guys developed this lead," Gesch stated a few hours ago, "you should follow it. Just keep your profile low, at least as long as you can."

Their destination was a parking lot along the river in the Northern Liberties neighborhood just north of the downtown core of Philadelphia.

"I've never been to Philly," Mac said, as he saw Citizens Bank Ballpark, the home of the Phillies, taking shape. The stadium was fully alight, the Phillies game in the early innings. "I always wanted to visit, see the sites, check out the Liberty Bell, say hello to Ben Franklin and maybe catch a Flyers game. Visiting like this is not what I had in mind."

"I see Philly and I think of Hall and Oates," Wire remarked with a smile. "Daryl Hall's voice is just so distinct.

I mean, you hear his voice, that tenor, and you just know that it's Hall and Oates."

"I'm partial to their early stuff myself," Mac added. "For my money, *Rich Girl* and *She's Gone* are their best."

"You like Hall and Oates?" Wire asked, slightly surprised. "I thought you were strictly a Springsteen guy."

"Not strictly," Mac answered, shaking his head. "The Boss is the best, I've seen him too many times to count, but I like all kinds of music. I have three older sisters who grew up in the eighties. The stereo was on all the time upstairs. They loved Hall and Oates, Journey, Def Leppard, they even loved Duran Duran ..."

"Rick Springfield?"

"*Jessie's Girl*, heck yeah. So I love 80s' music even though it's really not *my* decade. But I know all the Hall and Oates songs. I have their greatest hits on my iPod."

"I was always partial to *Kiss on My List* and *Private Eyes* myself," Wire suggested.

"And they did a nice remake of *You've Lost that Loving Feeling*." Mac smiled and started singing, "*Baby, baby, I get down on my knees for you* ..." Mac riffed and Wire was amused and even the pilot smiled. "I love that song, although you can't beat the original from the Righteous Brothers. My dad *loved* that song, sang it to my mom when she was mad at him."

"Really?"

Mac nodded.

"Did it work?"

"Oh hell yeah, she always melted," Mac replied with a big smile. "Ole Simon was a pretty smooth operator when he needed to be."

"Tom Cruise gave a nice rendition in *Top Gun* too," Wire recalled.

"Goose, she's lost that lovin' feelin'," Mac mimicked.

Wire cackled. "I hate it when she does that."

Mac and Wire were in Philadelphia less than two hours after the call with Gesch. As the chopper landed, they were met by a Philadelphia detective named Umland. After a minute of pleasantries, the three deposited themselves into Umland's unmarked black Dodge Charger. "Kevin Randall lives five minutes away, over in the Northern Liberties neighborhood. He knows you're coming."

25

"YIN TO HER YANG?"

Kevin Randall, two plus years a widower, had restarted his life far from Ithaca, New York. He was living anonymously enough as a sales representative for a sports apparel company and quietly residing in a two-story brick townhouse just north of downtown Philadelphia.

With the introductions made in the entryway of the townhouse, Randall led everyone to the right into a small family room. Taking the quick visual measure of the man and his home, Mac could tell he tried to leave his former life completely behind. There were no family pictures displayed around the house, no visible signs of his former life in Ithaca or Auburn, New York. Instead, his home, for all intents and purposes, was a bachelor pad, sparingly decorated and furnished, with his couch and armchairs arranged around the large flat screen resting on a stand to the right of the fireplace in the family room. Mac suspected Randall was doing all he could to keep under wraps the fact that his first wife was murdered and, for at least a time, he was considered the prime suspect. You couldn't blame the man. If your opener with someone was my wife was murdered and I was the prime suspect, things went pretty downhill from there.

There was no preamble. "Why are you here?" Randall asked warily, arms folded, on guard.

"We are here about your wife's death," Mac answered, "but in a different way. We," he pointed to Wire and himself, "think your wife's death might have some tie to the Reaper killings."

"The Reaper killings? The guy who has been on the news nonstop? The killer who leaves bible messages and carves the sign of the cross into women's stomachs, that guy?"

Mac nodded.

"How?" Randall asked in disbelief. "How could that possibly have any tie to Rebecca's death? She wasn't killed in that way."

"Maybe, maybe not," Mac answered. "Does the name Rena Johnson mean anything to you?"

"Rena? Sure, I knew her growing up in Auburn."

"How well?"

"Acquaintances. She and Rebecca were good friends and that's how I knew her. She was killed in a car accident years ago. It was a hit-and-run out in the country outside of Auburn. I don't think they ever found the driver."

"You're right, they never did, and it happened seven years ago to be exact," Mac answered. "But that accident is why we're here."

"And what would that have to do with Rebecca?"

"It's possible that Rebecca was there, part of the accident."

"She was involved in that accident?" Randall asked in disbelief.

"Possibly. Did she ever say anything about that to you?"

"I swear to you, she never said anything about it."

"You're sure?" Wire asked.

"I swear to you," Randall answered, hand on his chest, a shocked look on his face. "Not a word."

Mac's read was that he was telling the truth. "I wouldn't doubt that," Mac replied, explaining some background on the case and the other victims. "None of the family members we talked to ever heard of any such accident. It was as if all of these women never discussed it with anyone. It also appears that the women, for the most part, remained in limited contact with one another. We actually think that all of the victims of the Reaper were at the accident or played some role in it of some kind and this killer is seeking retribution for Rena Johnson's death. So I assume you remember Janelle Wyland?"

"Sure, I knew Janelle, I knew her well," Randall slumped back into a chair, letting his arms fall free and shook his head as a wave a sadness fell over his face. "I try not to think of Becca every day, but it's hard. Janelle's death was a punch to the gut, made me think of Becca a lot, but I never tied the two together, you know?"

"How did they know one another?" Wire asked quietly.

"Janelle and Rebecca were college friends at Syracuse, where we all went to college, Becca, Janelle and I. Janelle lived in Maryland, but we'd see her from time to time. She came out to help when we were searching for Rebecca's body."

"When Janelle came out to help with the search, do you recall anything about her at the time?"

"Like what?"

"Her demeanor? Anything she said, anything like that at all?"

Randall shook his head, "Not that I can recall. Agent

McRyan, please understand I was in a daze at the time. My wife had gone missing and even when the search started, I knew that it wasn't going to end well, that if we found her, we'd find her dead. I wasn't really paying attention to anyone else. If anything I was trying to avoid eye contact with people because I could already tell people suspected me and wondered if I could have done this thing to her. Someone said at the time that the husband is always a prime suspect."

"Having investigated these kinds of cases, I can tell you that's true," Mac answered. "Why would people have had any reason to suspect you at the time? Were there problems in the marriage?"

Randall shrugged, "Kind of. I think at the time we were both a little restless. We were twenty-five, young, married, living in a relatively small town and both wondering if there might have been more to life. Wondering if we'd taken the right path, that we settled down too soon without seeing the world or what else there might have been to offer."

"Bored?"

"I suppose," Randall answered. "We loved each other but, I know for myself at least, that," he hesitated and then answered: "I was a little restless."

"Did you stray?" Wire asked.

Randall shrugged and looked away. He had.

"And she knew, didn't she?"

He nodded in resignation.

Mac changed direction, "Did your wife ever go to any rave type parties?"

Randall snapped back to attention, "Rave parties. Sure, back in the day. I went to a few with her. Now that you mention it, they were a big thing a number of years ago, in the summers. I don't know how people did it, but they'd find these abandoned places, bring a generator and have a party with music, beer, booze."

"And drugs?" Wire asked.

"For sure," Randall answered.

"Do you remember Rebecca ever going to these parties without you?"

"Sure, we weren't attached at the hip."

"Do you ever remember one up near Auburn that she went to without you seven years ago? Maybe in mid-August?"

Randall sat back and thought and then shook his head, "Not that I remember. Not to say that she didn't, it's just that I don't remember it very well. You said seven years ago in August?"

Mac nodded.

Randall shook his head again, "I might not have been around; matter of fact, I'm pretty certain I wasn't. I went on a fishing trip with my dad and uncles for like a month up in Canada and Alaska in August that summer. I remember getting home the day before classes started back up at college, so if she went to a party during that time, I wouldn't have known one way or another. I don't remember her ever mentioning it."

"Do you remember Rebecca being any different when you got back from the trip?"

"Different?"

"Yeah," Mac replied. "Emotionally different? Depressed, sad, a change in her view of life?"

Randall looked away, as if trying to think back and finally lightly shook his head, "I don't. At least not something that ever registered with me. Why do you ask?"

"A couple of the Reaper's victims seemed to change after that summer. One became more serious about life.

Another kind of fell off the rails from the path she looked to be on."

Randall shrugged. "I don't recall anything about Rebecca, or Janelle for that matter. Rebecca was always kind of reserved to begin with. She liked to have a good time and stuff, but she was always a little emotionally ... what's the word ..."

"Distant?" Wire suggested.

"Maybe," Randall answered. "She always kept things close to the chest and was always almost flatlined about things. I think that made her a good elementary school teacher. She never got too riled up about anything."

"How about Janelle Wyland?"

"Mercenary."

"Mercenary?" Wire asked.

"She was perfect for sales. In school she was totally focused, would do whatever it took to get ahead, even cheat on an exam, if that's what it took. She wouldn't let anything stand in her way and would do whatever it took to get ahead."

"Like sleep with her boss?" Mac asked.

"Hell yes," Randall replied with the first smile they'd seen out of him. "She slept with a professor once for an A. She'd do whatever it took to get ahead and had almost no conscience when it came to that. That's why I call her a mercenary. Whatever it took she would do."

Mac and Wire shared an uncertain look. Was Rebecca Randall involved? Was she a Reaper victim? Some of the pieces fit. Others didn't.

"You mentioned changes in Rebecca," Kevin stated, "emotionally or whatever. The only one I really remember was about six weeks before she was killed."

"Why is that?" Wire asked.

"We had a break-in at our house. It was a Friday night and we were at a high school basketball game, I was an assistant coach back then. In any event, we get home and our house was completely ransacked. Our new flat-screen television was gone, along with another older television, our two school issued laptops, our color printer and our tablets were stolen. Our house was a disaster, boxes, clothes, everything was strewn all over our house. The burglars even went through our home desktop computer, looking for identity type information, but for whatever reason, they didn't take it with them. In fact, I still have the computer. The police investigated the case, we had detectives go through the house, the computer, everything, and I remember, she was pretty shocked about the break-in and she was different after that. It affected her."

"How?"

"Scared and a little skittish and I thought that, along with kind of our other problems at the time, she seemed a little off, which again, for someone like her, was a little unusual because she was always the calm one. I was always the more emotional of the two of us."

"Yin to her yang?"

"Exactly, but after the break-in and interviewing with the police detectives, she was pretty rattled for a few weeks."

"Which is understandable," Mac replied.

"In any event, she was like that for like a month and then one day she seemed more normal again. Then …" his voice trailed off.

"She was murdered."

Randall nodded, his eyes welling up, "Yeah, I think it was about two weeks later."

Mac looked over to Wire, who looked at her watch. Given the hour, it was time to go.

"Kevin, it's late. We're going to leave you for now," Mac stated. "We will probably have some more questions tomorrow."

"That's fine," Randall answered. "If her death is connected, I'd like the closure. I could finally show my face in Ithaca again."

An hour later, Mac and Wire sat exhausted at a table in the restaurant of their hotel, a pizza fully devoured. They each had one beer, both of them still on meds and still recovering.

"What do you think?" Wire asked.

"I don't know," Mac answered. "Some parts of what happened to Rebecca Randall fit, others don't. So I just don't know. It feels connected, there's too much here for it to be a coincidence, but there's no way you could really say for sure."

"She never told him about it if she was involved," Wire noted. "I kind of feel like if there was anyone she would have confided in, it would have been him."

Mac shrugged, "Maybe, but then again, from what we can tell, none of the victims ever confided about it to anyone. If they were all involved in Rena Johnson's death, it seems they all took some sort of pact to never talk about it."

"So maybe she's involved," Wire posited with a yawn.

"And maybe she's not," Mac answered, frustrated and tired. "I don't know. It's almost 2:00 A.M. Let's sleep on it."

∼

5:30 A.M.

Gesch rolled over on the uncomfortable, old, short, orange, smelly couch in the employee lounge, trying to get some sleep.

There was a tap on his shoulder; it was Delmonico. She had a cup of coffee and a report, "We have a DNA hit."

"Do we have a name?" Gesch asked as he sat up and yawned.

"Yes." She handed it to him. "The DNA is a familial match."

"To whom?"

"Read the report for yourself."

Gesch scanned the report quickly, looked at the picture of the man matched to the DNA and snorted. "The brother is not dead."

"SOMEDAY IS RIGHT NOW."

At 7:15 A.M., Mac was pounding on Kevin Randall's front door.

Randall opened the door with a yawn, his hair disheveled, wearing a robe. "Back so soon?" And then he read the look on McRyan's face. "What? What is it?"

"We need to talk more about that break-in at your house, *a lot more.*"

Randall let everyone in and they once again convened in the family room. Wire carried in an extra cup of Starbucks coffee and handed it to Randall who gladly accepted.

Mac got right to it, "Last night we talked about Rena Johnson?"

Randall nodded as he sipped from his coffee, "That's right. She was a friend of Rebecca's. You think her death has something to do with Becca's."

"Right," Mac answered as he opened his leather folder. "Turns out Rena had a brother named Drake. Did you know she had a brother?"

Randall shrugged, "I don't recall one way or another.

Like I said, she was a good friend of Rebecca's and I just kind of knew her because of that."

"Well, her brother was named Drake Johnson, Ithaca Police Detective Drake Johnson." Mac handed a picture of Drake Johnson to Randall, "Ring a bell now?"

Randall bolted upright in his chair and scanned the picture closely, "He was one of the two detectives who worked the break-in at our house." Kevin Randall read the leading look on Mac's face. "Did he kill Rebecca?"

"That's what we're trying to figure out. One thing we know for sure is Drake Johnson is the killer known as the Reaper."

An hour ago Mac found out that Drake Johnson's blood was on the missing eleventh bullet. That blood was a familial DNA match to Rena Johnson, whose DNA was in the system due to her death seven years ago.

Supposedly, two years ago Drake Johnson died in a one-car automobile accident on a snowy winter night. However, when Mac got the picture of Drake Johnson on his phone, it was the Reaper staring right back at him. There were some slight differences in appearance and Mac and Wire both suspected Johnson had a little plastic surgery to alter his appearance. "But it's like Dick Lick said, when you see him in context, there's no doubt, he's our guy."

Johnson was a massive 6'3" tall, large round face with a shaved head and small beard around his mouth. He was the man they found on surveillance video, the man he and Wire confronted at Kelly Drew's house, the monster they were after.

He was an extremely dangerous monster. Drake Johnson was a cop. He knew their playbook. They were essentially chasing one of their own.

Johnson's record as a cop in Ithaca was somewhat checkered. He was a package of a lot of brain but also, unfortunately, too much brawn.

As a uniformed officer, he'd been investigated for brutality on three different occasions, one time serving a suspension. However, he also had excellent instincts and it was thought he'd matured enough to be promoted to detective. He served as a detective for three years before he found himself in trouble once again.

Johnson and his partner, due to uniformed cops working a local festival, took a call on a domestic disturbance. The husband drunk, in his bloodied white wifebeater T-shirt, was raging when Johnson and his partner arrived. It was not the first time Johnson responded to a domestic call at the house, having done so more than once when he was a patrol cop. This time was far worse, the beating far more severe and damaging to the man's wife. A week later, the husband, having been released from jail, was found beaten within an inch of his life behind a local bar.

The husband claimed he was beaten by Johnson, who he'd seen at the bar earlier in the evening. The detective's alibi for the time of the beating was not iron clad and distant witnesses described someone fitting the general description of Johnson fleeing from the scene of the beating.

Given his record and history of brutality, Johnson's career as a police officer was hanging in the balance. And not just criminally; he was looking at a potential civil claim as well. This all occurred around the time of his investigating the break-in at the Randall residence.

His parents had died two years earlier. Between life insurance, investments and selling their house and splitting the proceeds with his half-brother, Johnson had in the neighborhood of one million dollars to fall back on if he wanted to disappear. If he didn't, that money may well have been lost to the husband in the civil suit.

The car accident that supposedly took his life was staged two weeks later. He was Drake Johnson no more.

"Aubry, if he wasn't in that car, then who was?"

"Who knows," Gesch answered. "At the time, they identified Johnson with dental records."

"And let me guess, they got the dental records from his older half-brother in Rochester?"

"Bingo. It took less than fifteen minutes for him to crumble under questioning. Drake told him he was looking to get out from under the brutality complaint and potential civil suit. So he flipped the dental records for Drake to match those of the body in the car, probably some homeless cadaver who was similar in height and weight to Johnson. The half-brother claims he had no idea his half-brother's plan was to become a mass murderer."

"Do you believe him?"

"The Rochester PD seems to think he's telling the truth, that he is appropriately freaked out by the whole thing. I've got people on the way up to interview him to get a second opinion on that, but from what I'm gathering, the brother helped stage his disappearance but had no idea what it would lead to."

"Has he been in contact with his half-brother?"

"He claims no."

"And we're going through the half-brother's life?"

"Yes. If he's been in contact with Drake Johnson, or whatever his name is now, we'll find it. So far, we've found nothing to suggest he has, but we're working it hard."

"There isn't much time, Aubry."

"Agreed. He's got the money somewhere offshore. He's going to finish this thing and then he'll be gone."

So the plan was that while Gesch and his team hunted for Drake Johnson, Mac and Wire were to work Randall. It may have all started two years ago with Rebecca Randall. She was the true victim number one.

"So what did Rebecca Randall have that set this all off?" Mac wondered aloud on the call with Gesch.

"That's what you and Wire have to find out and find out fast."

That was an hour ago.

Drake Johnson was the Reaper.

He was avenging the death of his sister Rena.

Rebecca Randall played a role in Rena's death and was victim number one of Drake Johnson. Why?

Mac and Wire's job was to find the answer.

Mac explained all of this to Kevin Randall. "So my question to you, Kevin, is what did Drake Johnson find at your house? He must have found something."

Kevin Randall shook his head and shrugged, "Heck if I know."

"Tell me more about the robbery. I got the cliff notes version last night and now I have the file."

Randall explained the robbery once again. "It was a little odd," Randall noted, "I never would have thought us a target for a home invasion, we didn't really have much at the time, but the detectives told me there was a crew working the area and we were like the fourth or fifth house hit in Ithaca."

"Let's focus on Detective Drake Johnson. What do you remember about him?"

Randall sat back and thought, "He worked the case with another partner whose name escapes me. They interviewed us that night, took an inventory of what was missing and really spent a lot of time going through our house. I remember the crime lab people went through the house with a fine-tooth comb because, like I said, this was part of a string of robberies. They were trying to find any evidence that might point them in the right direction."

"Is there anything else you remember?" Wire asked, jotting down notes.

Mac and Wire walked Randall through the break-in for another hour, picking and prying at Randall's recollections of the break-in.

"One thing I do remember now is the detectives took our home computer for a while because we were concerned some personal information could have been downloaded from it. We were really worried about identity theft. They tried to determine if we needed to be worried about that. In the end, a few days after the break-in, they told us to cancel all of our credit cards, change all of our passwords and monitor our credit score. We did all of that and I don't think we ever had any issues, but it was still all pretty unsettling. I mean, someone goes through your whole life, your belongings, your pictures, records and computer and ..." Randall shook his head. "It puts you off kilter. That's what I really remember about the whole thing is that it put us off kilter, particularly Becca. The whole thing really had an effect on her."

"You've said that before," Wire noted. "What do you mean by that?"

"She had me put in a security system on the house. Rebecca wanted someone with her at all times if she wasn't at work. She didn't want to go out at night for a few weeks, she was really scared, almost paranoid, it seemed."

Mac had a thought, "Was that change in her right after the break-in or did it evolve over time?"

"No ..." Randall started to reply but then stopped and closed his eyes, trying to remember back. "No, it was after the fact, after we got the computer back and the detectives told us to check our credit cards and watch our credit rating. It was after that she seemed to get edgy and that lasted for a few weeks, and those were really bad weeks. But then she seemed to get over it. I remember asking her if I should skip my guy's weekend and she said no. She told me to go ahead and have a good time, so it seemed to me that her period of being rattled had passed."

Mac and Wire shared a look that said they were thinking the same thing. Her paranoia passed because she thought Drake Johnson was dead. Mac looked right at Wire and nodded towards the kitchen. In the kitchen, Mac whispered, "So let's say Drake Johnson stumbles across something while investigating the break-in that ties back to the death of his sister."

"Right, like maybe a picture," Wire suggested.

"That could be, or some notation in a file, an e-mail, a text, something he stumbles across."

"So while he's still a cop, Johnson confronts her about it," Dara suggests. "He does it one-on-one, off the record, no witnesses, no partner, just him and Rebecca Randall."

"Right," Mac nods. "He shows her whatever it was that he found or put him onto her."

"She denies knowing anything about it. She claims to have no idea what he's talking about."

"But he doesn't buy it. He's a cop, a detective no less, he reads her and he knows she's lying," Mac suggests. "And he knows the case is ice cold up in Auburn. He knows that whatever he found isn't enough to move the case forward. But he knows Rebecca knows something about his sister's death but he has no leverage to make her give it up, at least not legitimately."

"Right, he can't move the investigation forward on Rena's

death as a police officer, because as a cop you have to follow rules, procedures, and you have to have sufficient evidence through legal means to pursue a case," Wire answers, pulling on the thread. "But if he's not a police officer ..."

"If people think he's dead," Mac suggested.

"Then the shackles are off of him, he can do whatever he needs or wants to get the answers he needs."

Mac nodded, "Right." He opened the Rebecca Randall murder file and flipped through the report. "She's abducted on Saturday night because the last anyone saw her was when she left the shopping mall. Nobody reports her missing until Sunday morning and she's not found until Wednesday lying in the ditch."

"She was in that ditch by the time she was reported missing."

"But in that window of time, Johnson interrogates her. The autopsy reports revealed ligature marks on her arms and legs, like she was bound to something."

"Like a chair," Wire suggested.

"Like a few of our other victims, because he was interrogating them about the night his sister was killed," Mac answered.

"He gets what he needs from interrogating her and knows that she can't be left alive, otherwise he'll be going to jail."

"So he kills her, dumps her and goes away."

"And now he has some answers. He knows that Melissa Goynes, Janelle Wyland, Hannah Donahue, Sandy Faye and Kelly Drew, along with Rebecca Randall, were involved in his sister's death."

"They were in the vehicle that hit his sister," Mac stated. "He knows this, either from what he found in the wreckage of Randall's house..."

"Or from interrogating her."

"Or both," Mac pushed himself up onto the kitchen counter. "So he spends the next nearly two years researching, investigating and planning to punish those responsible for his sister's death."

"He plans it down to the last detail, Mac," Dara replied, pacing, "including making it look like the work of a crazed serial killer, using biblical verses and cutting their abdomens' open in the shape of the Holy Cross. All of which he uses as a cover so that he can pursue revenge against those responsible for his sister's death."

"Okay," Mac nods. "That all makes sense. But what did he find at Randall's? What was it that triggered all this? *That* is what we have to find? He's not done, remember. There is another victim or victims out there."

Mac walked back into the living room, "Kevin, do you still have all of the things from your house in Ithaca?"

"Yes."

"Good, we need to comb through it. We think Johnson found something at your house that set him off. We need to find what that is."

Randall nodded, "Most of Rebecca's stuff is in a storage garage I have a few blocks away. When I moved away, I packed it all up in boxes, stuffed it in storage. I figured someday I'd get around to going through it all."

"Someday is right now," Mac stated. "Let's go."

"Yes, Director, we'll keep working it," Gesch replied. "I agree holding off until we have this locked down a little better is the way to go." Gesch hung up after finishing his briefing of Director Mitchell on the discovery of Drake Johnson.

"He wants to hold off going to the media?"

"He wants us to be certain he's our guy. I think he is, but after Harrisburg, Frederick and with the White House's skin in the game, he wants to be absolutely one hundred percent certain."

"How much more certain can you be than DNA evidence?"

"Not much," Gesch answered. "Not my call. The director is being careful and wants to be one hundred percent before we go public, which he wants to do later today or even tonight. Let's get the director the certainty he's looking for."

Gesch, Delmonico and four other agents sifted through the reams of records now being unearthed on Drake Johnson and his family. The dental records used to identify Drake Johnson were provided by his half-brother Thomas Johnson, a near retirement dentist in Rochester, New York. The Rochester PD and bureau agents interviewed Thomas and he admitted his knowledge of his brother's plan to disappear and changed his dental records to match those found at the scene. The brother claimed he did it for his brother because of the criminal and civil investigation. He understood that it was Drake's intent to disappear and that it was unlikely Thomas would ever hear from him again. Thomas Johnson claimed he had not been in contact with him since he disappeared and had no idea where he was or how to contact him. "Do you believe him?" Gesch asked the agents on the scene.

"I do," the agent answered. "I think the Rochester PD's take is correct. While we're still going through his phone records, texts, e-mails and all the rest, we haven't found anything yet suggesting he's been in contact with his brother. Right now we're going through his house and office to see if perhaps there is another phone he could be using to stay in touch, but my sense is that on the issue of contact since the disappearance, the half-brother is on the level."

"Has he lawyered up yet?"

"He has, but he knows he's in trouble and he wants no part of what Drake's been up to. We're pushing him to fully cooperate. I think he has and will continue to do so."

"Keep me informed," Gesch answered and went back to the records on Drake Johnson on his desk. Drake Johnson was the son of Warren and Patricia Johnson. Warren was twelve years older than Patricia and the half-brother was from his first marriage. Warren was a successful CPA with a small Auburn accounting firm. Patricia was a longtime manager at a local bank. They provided their son and his sister Rebecca with a comfortable upper middle-class upbringing. The Johnson parents perished within six weeks of one another four years after Rena's death, the mother of breast cancer and then six weeks later the father of a heart attack.

The FBI was digging up records and information on the family by the minute. For five hours a team of agents sifted through record after record on their laptops and on paper, working through the lunch hour, three pizza boxes now stacked on top of the garbage can, coffee cups, ceramic and Styrofoam, strewn across the table, now matched by the empty Diet Coke cans, everyone pumping caffeine into their systems.

Late in the afternoon, Gesch looked up from his computer, yawned and rubbed his eyes. He pushed himself out of his chair and walked down to the restroom and splashed water on his face, hoping the cold water would revive him. As he walked back into his office, he looked to Delmonico, who was nibbling on sea salt and vinegar chips and reading intently. Gesch took the measure of her intensity and realized something on the page was registering with her. He could see it in the intensity in her eyes, the wrinkling of her forehead. "Gracie, what're you reading?"

She held up a sheet of paper, "A property record for a Richard Tanner. It's for a cabin in southern Pennsylvania."

"And who is Richard Tanner?"

"Patricia Johnson's deceased father. Did you know she was an only child?"

Gesch shook his head, sitting back down and swiping the mouse to wake up his computer.

"In any event, while you were looking through Drake Johnson's records, I decided to go through the parents' records. As I was going through the family financials, I saw a record for payment of septic services."

"Septic services?"

"Yeah, it would seem rather odd that the family would have a septic system living in Auburn proper, don't you think?"

"I suppose I would."

"So anyway, I looked further into that payment, and it's for a septic system at a property in south Pennsylvania outside of the town of Wrightsdale in Lancaster County. Turns out it's a cabin along the Octoraro Creek. The cabin is in the name of Richard Tanner."

"Even though Richard Tanner's been dead for five years?" Gesch asked, suddenly interested.

"Yes. I mean, had I not stumbled across this septic system bill, I'm not sure I'd have discovered the cabin, at least maybe not this quickly."

"And there's no record of any sale of the property?"

"No," Delmonico replied, shaking her head. "I'm wondering if it's still somehow in the family."

"And there's no family other than Drake?"

"There's only the half-brother, but he was the son of the father, *not* the mother."

Gesch went to his desk and grabbed his phone, "Find me the name of the Lancaster Pennsylvania County sheriff and then get him on the phone for me." Then to Delmonico he said, "Let's see if anyone's been hanging around that cabin."

In the afternoon, Mac, Wire, Umland and Kevin Randall commandeered two conference rooms at the Philadelphia Police Department and worked through the belongings from Randall's storage closet. There were photos, notebooks, scrapbooks, datebooks and various other documents, all of which were largely unorganized. "After the break-in, everything was messed up and we never really got around to reorganizing it after the break-in and before ..." Kevin Randall caught himself. "Before Becca was killed."

Wire, along with Umland and Randall, sifted through the personal effects while Mac worked with a crime scene tech to get their old desktop computer operating. It took some time. Like anyone the ages of the Randalls, much of their life was on their computer.

Over the next several hours, Mac and the crime scene tech worked through the files on the computer. First, they went through the old e-mail account of Rebecca Randall, searching key terms that included all of the victims' names. Only Janelle Wyland's came up in sporadic e-mails between the two women. There was nothing in any of the e-mail correspondence that seemed even remotely related to the death of Rena Johnson.

After having scanned through the e-mails, Mac clicked

onto the files with photos on the computer. "Holy cow," Mac muttered.

"Must be thousands of photos on her computer," the tech speculated.

Randall overheard them, "Rebecca was a picture hound. She had three cameras and took tons of pictures, not to mention those she uploaded from her cell phone.

For two hours Mac scrolled through photo after photo while Wire and Umland did the same with the personal effects. Wire and Umland took a break around 5:00 P.M. "Mac, you want anything?"

"Diet Coke," Mac answered. "And anything that might pass as edible."

"There's a Jimmy John's across the street," Umland suggested.

"I want a number nine with peppers," Mac answered without hesitation, "and a bag of jalapeno pepper chips. I'm buying." Mac took fifty dollars out of his wallet and handed it to Wire. "Make it so, Number One."

"Aye aye, Captain."

Mac's phone rang and as he reached for the display noted it said Auburn Police Department. "Detective Flynn, I presume."

"I got your message, Agent McRyan," Flynn replied. "You said it was urgent."

"You can't go public with this yet, but the Reaper is Drake Johnson."

There was silence on the other end of the phone. "But McRyan, he's dead. He died in that car accident. They recovered the body, matched the dental records, the whole shebang."

Mac explained the eleventh bullet and the blood. "He

set it up. He set it up to do this because two weeks after he died, I think he killed Rebecca Randall."

Detective Flynn sighed. "Maybe I shouldn't be surprised."

"Why do you say that?"

"He hounded us pretty good in the years after her death to see if we were making progress. He ... I don't know ... I don't think he was ever all that impressed with us. We didn't have any suspects and a few times he was angry, desk pounding angry. I think he was pretty close to his sister."

Flynn snorted, "It figures."

"What figures?"

"You say something callous off the cuff and it always comes back to bite somehow."

"What do you mean?"

"After he died, I made the flip comment one day to Chief Dye that while Drake Johnson's death was tragic, at least I wouldn't have him hounding me anymore."

"So he was an angry guy?"

"Yes. Edgy, and he just had a menacing look to him, like he was on a hair trigger. I suppose I should have said something about all of this when you guys were here, but I didn't think it mattered because he was ..."

"Dead."

"Right."

Mac spoke with Flynn another minute and then hung up. The conversation explained where some of Johnson's motive and anger came from.

While waiting for Wire, Randall and Umland to return with the sandwiches, Mac and the crime scene tech kept scrolling through the photos. He was in a full yawn when he saw it. "Stop," he exclaimed as he grabbed control of the mouse and moved back to the last photo. "Holy shit."

In the photo, standing in front of a silver minivan, all smiles, were left to right, Melissa Goynes and Sandy Faye with arms interlocked, Kelly Drew and Hannah Donahue hugging one another, Janelle Wyland, Rena Johnson and Rebecca Randall had their arms wrapped around each other's shoulders. There was one other woman, leaning back against the van, her hands in her shorts pockets, smiling. Mac had never seen her before. The date in the lower right-hand corner was August 17, seven years ago.

Just then Wire, Umland and Randall walked back into the conference room. "Dara, look."

Wire took in the screen and her eyes went wide, "Is this what Johnson found? This photo?"

"Could be," Mac answered and then turned to Kevin Randall. "Have you ever seen this photo before?"

"No, not that I ever recall."

"Do you recognize these women?"

Randall scanned the photo, "Only Becca, Janelle and Rena."

"How about the blond on the far right that's leaning against the van? Do you recognize her?"

Randall stared at the photo and shook his head, "I don't. She's not familiar. I think I knew all of Becca's friends, and she is not familiar."

"Well, she must have a tie to someone in the picture," Mac speculated. "We need to figure out who she is. Everyone else in this picture is dead."

The Lancaster County sheriff came through a couple of hours later. The cabin was worth a look, a very serious look. "Gear up. The sheriff says a plainclothes deputy went out to the area and showed the photos of Johnson around to a couple of distant neighbors and they recognized our man and they said he's been around."

"Is he around now?" Delmonico asked, grabbing her gun from her desk drawer, along with her FBI windbreaker and vest.

"Deputy says lights are on and there's a white pick-up truck parked in the driveway. So someone looks to be there."

Gesch took out his cell phone, "Director, we may have a location on our man. We can be there in a half hour." He gave the director the quick rundown. "Sir, I would recommend holding off on the press conference you have scheduled in a half hour identifying Drake Johnson as the Reaper until we run this down. I don't want to spook him if he's watching. Right. Wait? You're sure? Yes sir."

"What?" Delmonico asked.

"The director is coming along."

Mac picked up his cell phone to dial Gesch when the man's picture appeared on his screen. "Talk about a smartphone." He answered the call, "Aubry, good timing. I was just going to call you. I think we found something."

"We did too, Mac," Gesch answered and Mac could hear the noise in the background as Gesch spoke. The sound was the whirring of a chopper. "Mac, we may have a line on Drake Johnson." Gesch explained the connection to the cabin. "We're going to be there in thirty minutes."

Mac put the call on speaker for Wire to hear as Gesch explained they were on the way to a cabin in Wrightsdale, Pennsylvania, a cabin that was owned by Johnson's late grandfather. "The sheriff says the lights are on and it looks like someone is there. Neighbors have seen someone fitting the description of Johnson in recent days, picked him right out of a photo array that has the DMV photo and the photos we've developed. We're going to be on the ground within twenty minutes and we should be to the cabin within ten minutes of that. The director is holding off on his press conference until we hit the cabin and see if he's there. So what do you have, Mac?"

"A photo I found on Randall's computer that has all of our victims in it plus one other woman, standing in front of what looks like a silver minivan."

"You think that's what triggered Johnson?"

"I think it's possible. The pieces fit, Aubry. He finds the picture as part of the investigation of the break-in. He fakes his death. He then abducts Rebecca Randall and with her bound to a chair, a knife at her throat, she tells him the whole story of the accident that kills Rena Johnson. Drake gets what he can out of Rebecca, kills her and dumps her and spends the next two years preparing not only his retribution but also ..."

"His way out," Gesch finished.

"Right, so look, we have one more woman to find," Mac started.

"We do, but if we nail this bastard in the next half hour, we don't need to find her."

"Aubry, we do need to find her. She was possibly involved in a vehicular homicide."

"True, Mac, but that can wait."

Mac exhaled, Gesch was probably right. He started thinking about how quickly he could get on a chopper. "What's Wrightdale from here?"

"It's a couple of hours, Mac. If the chopper was still up

there I'd have you jump on that and join us. There's no time."

Mac slumped back in his chair. He'd have to miss it. "Okay, go get him."

"Okay, Mac. You'll be my first call," Gesch signed off excitedly.

"Shit! Shit! Shit!" Mac grumbled, tossing his cell phone disgustedly on the table.

"Dani, how are you holding up?" the woman asked.

"Fine, I guess. I'm scared and tired of watching my back, I can tell you that. I'm not like you. I don't have high-priced security watching me 24/7. I'm totally exposed here and we're the only two left. I think I need to leave town."

"Well, I have good news for you, Dani. The FBI found out who he is."

"Who?"

"Drake Johnson, that girl Rena's brother. He was a cop, staged his own death two years ago and he's been coming after us all. But now the FBI has figured out who he is. There is going to be a press conference tonight identifying him and he's as good as caught. In fact, the FBI knows where he is and it's a long way from here."

"Are you sure?"

"Yes. It won't be long, I promise. I think you're safe and I'm safe and the best news is nobody is the wiser. This thing is as good as over."

27

"YES OR NO?"

"Why didn't she leave the party with you?"

"We lost track of her. She wandered off and someone said the police were coming so we had to leave, we were underage, there were drugs, we had to go and go fast."

The Reaper had watched the interrogation of Rebecca Randall numerous times over the past two years. He always watched before he struck. It was a reminder of why he was doing what he was doing and why in his mind he thought it was just. Whenever he questioned what he was doing, if it was right, if he continued to have the will to finish what he'd started, he watched the videotapes, of Randall, of Goynes, Wyland and Donahue. He watched them all, but when he truly needed motivation, the one video he always came back to was Rebecca Randall.

Rebecca Randall was his sister's friend, the one who took her to the rave party when she knew Rena was inexperienced in such things. The friend who didn't look out for Rena, didn't go see if she was alive in the ditch when the van hit her, the friend who buried the truth about the accident for five years until he found it by accident when investigating the break-in at Randall's home. Just happening to flip by the picture on the computer, seeing the August 17 date in the lower right-hand corner, seeing all of the women in the picture, the silver minivan in the background and knowing the picture was taken the night his sister was murdered.

"Why didn't you protect her, Rebecca? You were her friend."

"I tried, but we couldn't find her anywhere," Rebecca pleaded. "I looked and looked but I couldn't find her. I didn't know where she went. I searched. I tried. *I tried!*"

He'd confronted Rebecca about it one-on-one, no partner and no husband around. He just went to Rebecca's house one day and asked if he could come in. In the kitchen of her home, with a cup of coffee in their hands, he sprung the photo on her and watched for her reaction. It was all he needed to see. The look in her eyes, the expressional change on her face, the way she gasped before catching herself, she knew what she was looking at and she knew that he knew.

Rebecca Randall knew what happened to Rena.

He demanded an explanation but she didn't give in. She composed herself and claimed to know nothing about it; that she was shocked to see a picture of Rena and that she had no idea how it got on her computer. That morning, in the kitchen light, when it was just the two of them, she wouldn't admit to anything.

His life was a shambles at that point. He was going to lose his job and certainly was going to lose the brutality case and since he beat the husband on his own time and not while he was working, he was looking at his own civil liability and there wasn't any insurance policy that was coming to bail him out. He would pay for it for the rest of his life. And here was Rebecca Randall denying she knew anything about his sister's death.

The photo in and of itself meant nothing without more evidence. He knew what was in the case file up in Auburn. The photo wouldn't move the case forward without more, and there was no way to get more—at least not legally.

The only answer was using some other means.

"So tell me how it happened after you left."

"We drove away and turned right, away from where we wanted to go back towards Auburn because we saw police lights approaching." Rebecca sniffled and more tears rolled down her cheek from that night over two years ago in the basement of the abandoned building in Ithaca. "It was foggy and the road was winding and we were all over the road. We came around a corner fast and there she was."

"And you hit her. The van hit Rena. You hit Rena," It wasn't a question.

Rebecca nodded.

"You hit her, didn't you? Say it!"

"Yes," she answered quietly.

"And when you hit her what happened?"

Rebecca just shook her head, whimpering, "No... no..."

"Tell me! Tell me what happened!" he thundered.

"She went flying in the air and down into the ditch."

"So you stopped?"

Rebecca didn't respond, she just cried and shook her head.

"Answer yes or no!"

"No."

"Why not?"

She kept shaking her head and mumbling "No, no, no ..."

"Look at the camera! WHY NOT!"

"We were so afraid and we hit her going so fast that everyone thought she was dead, that she had to be dead. Nobody could have survived that."

"Nobody said to stop?"

"I did, but I wasn't driving and I couldn't make them stop. *I couldn't!*"

"You knew it was Rena, right?"

Rebecca weakly nodded her head.

"Yes or no?"

She nodded, "I knew it was her. Even in the flash of an instant, I knew it, I knew it was her."

"Your friend. Your *best* friend right?"

Rebecca nodded, tears streaming down her face.

"Yes or no, she was your best friend?"

"Yes."

"And you didn't stop."

"I wanted to stop. I wanted to but I wasn't driving. I couldn't make them stop. They wouldn't stop. I begged them to stop and they wouldn't."

An alarm went off on another program open on his computer.

He closed the video of Rebecca Randall and opened the other window and a little smile creased his face. "And let the fun begin."

9:32 P.M.

It was nearly dark, the sun now down behind the hill to the west of the river. The FBI had a heat signature of a large body in the cabin, lying on the couch in what looked to be a family room area.

Gesch carefully approached the front of the cabin.

Lights were on inside and as reported, to the right of the cabin, a pickup truck, a Dodge Ram, was parked in front of the garage with the garage door closed. He had an agent flanking him on his left and a Lancaster County sheriff's deputy to his right, carrying a battering ram. Agents were approaching from the south to the left and two more from the north. Deputies were down river in speedboats, awaiting the signal to approach. Everyone held one hundred feet out, deadly quiet. There was light flickering inside the cabin, the unmistakable light from a television.

"Go," Gesch ordered.

The deputy sprinted ahead, battering ram in hand.

Delmonico was on the line on Wire's cell, which she had put on speaker for Mac to hear. Delmonico was providing the play-by-play. "Gesch just gave them the go," Grace reported.

Mac's cell phone rang. He looked at the display: Dara Wire. "It's him," Mac said ominously. "Hello, Drake."

"Ahh, you know, I won't ask how, but you know. So nice we can finally be on a first name basis now, Mac," the Reaper replied lightly, but then turned sinister. "But Mac, you, you of all people should understand me by now. I mean, don't you think I'd be prepared for this? Didn't you think I'd know it was possible that someone like you would find me eventually and that when you did, I'd be prepared, that I would have taken action to be ready?"

Mac was ready to respond with a taunt of his own, but

hesitated. The Reaper wasn't just calling to taunt him. There was more to the call. He could hear it in the killer's voice. "What kind of action, Drake?" he asked warily. "What are you ready for?"

"Well, right now, I'm watching Senior Special Agent Aubry Gesch and, well, there went the front door, oh and the back door as well. Oh my goodness, we have cops and agents coming from every direction. My only disappointment is that you and Dara don't appear to be there as well."

Wire was watching Mac and she saw the look of horror slowly overtake his face. This was all wrong. "Drake, what are you up to?"

"I think you know, Mac," the Reaper replied darkly and Mac knew.

It was a trap.

He grabbed Wire's phone, "Grace, pull them out of there! *PULL them out of there now!*"

It was too late.

The explosion blasted over the phone.

Delmonico screamed in horror.

"Oh my God, Mac," Dara croaked in horror, taking the phone. "Grace, are you there! Grace! GRACE!"

Mac sat down in a chair in shock, not believing what had happened, only to hear someone laughing uncontrollably in a sick and sadistic laugh. Mac looked down at his hand. The laughter was coming from his cell phone. Drake Johnson was still there.

"You son of a bitch," Mac said darkly, the anger raging inside him.

"I win again. Your losses are piling up, Mac."

"You know your bible verses, right, Drake?"

"I do."

"Then let me remind you of Romans: 'Vengeance is mine; I will repay, says the Lord.'"

"That's Romans 12:19, to be exact, Mac. But first things first," the Reaper replied sickly. "The night ... is only beginning."

28
"WE'RE TOO LATE."

Mac and Wire pulled up in front of the FBI's Washington, DC, Field Office and were immediately greeted by a security detail that kept the media swarm at bay. The security didn't prevent many questions from being asked, all of which Mac and Wire ignored as they briskly strode into the building to find Director Mitchell awaiting their arrival.

FBI Director Thomas Mitchell, sensing as everyone else that the Reaper was at the cabin, was present monitoring from the perimeter when the cabin exploded. He witnessed it firsthand and the impact of it was evident on his face, a mixture of anguish, sadness and anger. He lost men tonight and witnessed their loss firsthand, a rare occurrence for an FBI director.

The night's events cast an equally dark pallor over the field office, people somber, quiet and sad with their heads down. Yet there was also a quiet determination in the air to press on and keep working. That determination would be needed if there was any truth to Drake Johnson's last words to Mac.

Mac and Wire fell in behind the director, loosely surrounded by the security detail, automatic weapons visible, as they entered the field office. The three of them were led into a private conference room.

"How many dead, sir?" Mac asked quietly.

"Six men dead, many others injured," the director answered sadly, hands in his suit pant pockets, looking out the window, "Gesch, three other bureau agents and two deputies from the Lancaster Sheriff's Department died. If there was any saving grace, their deaths were instant. The devastation is complete, there is nothing left of the cabin and the garage but debris and rubble. The pickup truck is a melted wreckage. The fire department was still working the site when I left, everything was still smoldering."

"Director, he detonated this thing remotely. I was on the phone with him when he did it," Mac reported. "And the last thing he said to me was, 'The night is just beginning.' That means ..."

"He's got his next victim lined up," Wire finished. "He could attack any minute."

"And we think we know who that victim is, sir," Mac added, and took out the picture they'd found on the Randall's computer. "In this photo are all of our victims except one, sir, this woman." He pointed to the blond woman. "The picture is seven years old, but nevertheless, we need to figure out who she is. We need people on Gesch's team, anyone here in the field offices, other jurisdictions on the task force, contacting the families and friends of all of the victims. Most of all, sir, we must now go public with Drake Johnson's picture. We need people on alert. Johnson knows we've identified him. We can do the full press conference in the morning but we need to give the media the picture *now*."

Mitchell gave it a moment's thought. "Do we have media out front?"

Wire flipped her fingers between the vertical blinds. "They were there aplenty a few minutes ago and the swarm is growing by the minute."

"Let's go. You two come with."

The director walked out the front door of the field office at 11:25 P.M., Mac and Wire in tow, and said to the assembled media, "I'll give you one minute. You need to go live."

The director gave them two minutes, then he started with little prologue. "We will have a press conference in the morning to answer questions regarding the bombing in Pennsylvania this evening. Right now, everyone needs to be on the lookout for the Reaper. Today we have identified the Reaper as Drake Johnson formerly of Ithaca, New York. We are making available, as we speak, additional information and pictures of Johnson. He is responsible for the deaths of six law enforcement officers this evening. He has murdered four women, we think we've identified another he may have killed, attempted to murder another in Frederick and we believe is looking to strike again tonight. In fact, we believe he has identified his next target. It is this woman," the director showed a cropped picture of the woman leaning against the van. "We have only just within the last few hours identified her as the next potential victim. We do not know who she is. If anyone recognizes this woman in the picture, contact the FBI immediately. Her life is in danger."

The reporters attempted to ask questions, but the director stuck to his guns. "We aren't taking questions now. The information on Johnson is being made available. We'll answer questions in the morning. Thank you."

The director turned around and walked back inside, Mac and Wire right behind him. Once inside, the director said to the agents surrounding him, "Get the information on Johnson and the picture of this woman out now, to everyone, to every television station, radio station, network, newspaper, news website, anyone and everyone who can help us reach the public. Do it and do it now."

The director looked at his watch. It was just after 11:30 P.M. "I hope we can get to her before it's too late." Then he turned to Mac and Wire, "Listen, unless we catch a break tonight, we will have the press conference in the morning and we'll have to answer some questions. I am going back to the Hoover Building and will monitor things from there until we get to the press conference in the morning. I want you both there. In fact, Mac, there is something I should discuss with you before the press conference. I need you to do something for me."

"Yes sir. What do you need?"

"We'll talk early in the morning," Director Mitchell answered. "Be at the Hoover Building at 7:00 A.M. In the meantime, see if you can figure out who our next victim is."

Just then four members of Gesch's team approached. "What do we know about the possible victim?" a short and stocky agent named Kurt Keller asked. He had three other agents with him.

"We just have this picture. We haven't had a chance to figure out who she is yet. In addition to getting this out to every imaginable media outlet, everyone needs to start calling family and friends of our victims right now to see if they know who she is. He's going to act tonight."

Keller and the agents ran off and suddenly Mac and Wire stood and looked at one another. "What do we do now, Mac?"

"Wait," Mac said, exhaling a breath and rubbing his temples, his headache returning. His energy reserves were running low and the concussion effects were returning. But there was no stopping. He made his way towards the cafeteria. "We hydrate and wait."

The wait took fifteen minutes.

"Mac," Keller yelled as he ran into the cafeteria. "Danica Brunner. She lives in Arlington. Here's the address."

"Do you have a phone number?"

"Just a cell."

With the owner out of town, Danica wasn't able to leave the gallery until 11:15 P.M., having finished the books for the day, a very good day for the gallery. She loved the work, a manager at age twenty-seven. Nevertheless, it had been an agonizing couple of weeks with the dual responsibilities of running the gallery dawn to dusk and also constantly looking over her shoulder, paranoia sweeping over her. There were only two of them left from that horrible night. The call earlier in the night put her mind at ease finally. The killer would be caught. He might be in custody already. It was over.

That night seemed so long ago yet often still felt like it had just happened. It was a nightmare that never seemed to end and she just wanted it to end, to go away. It took her a long time, but now, for once, after all these years, she was allowing herself to be happy. She'd decided, right or wrong, that she wasn't the driver of the van, just a passenger. The Rena girl wandered away from them at that party and she was walking along a dangerous dark road. It was part her fault too.

Ultimately, that's how she brought herself to be able to rationalize it. Did she call 911 that night? No.

Did she make the van stop?

No, but she wasn't driving.

Should she have done something?

It would have been the humane thing to do, the right thing to do.

She wrestled with those questions every day for years. There were days, heck, there were years, she literally willed herself out of bed every day, to keep going despite what happened that night.

It wasn't her fault, despite the massive guilt she felt. To make amends, she no longer drank alcohol, didn't do drugs and regularly donated money to Mothers Against Drunk Driving (MADD). She tried to live a clean life, having learned something from the night.

Now, she just wanted to get to Sam's place, take a shower and climb into bed with him, let him rub her shoulders and wrap his arms around her. They'd been together for nearly a year now and she could feel he was the one, the one to settle down with and start a life together, to move on from her past, to just leave it all behind.

She was finally ready for it and she could sense he was as well. Having just turned thirty-two, his business taking off, he'd started talking about commitment, marriage and even hinted at kids. The kind of hints someone drops when they're thinking about the final step, and the thought of it made her so happy. They were going on vacation next month to San Francisco. She couldn't think of a more romantic city for him to propose in. It was all so exciting and exhilarating to her.

The call earlier was comforting. The last month had completely worn her out. Now, she wanted to live her life.

Exhausted, her mind was shutting down and she just wanted to relax. "I need music," she said to her empty car, flipping to The Blend on satellite radio for some light rock. It was time for some easy listening.

He saw the illumination begin to the south, the powerful engine of the Audi A3 approaching, the lights getting brighter and then turning hard left into the alley. The engine purred as the car pulled into the driveway, the Sara Bareilles song *Brave* quietly audible. She killed the engine and turned off the lights. A few seconds later he heard the car door open and then close, followed by quick footsteps, high heels echoing on the cement driveway. The cedar fence door swung open and she strolled carefree down the dark sidewalk.

She walked just past him, reaching in her purse, her cell phone ringing.

She never saw him, and with the phone ringing, she never heard him.

He jumped her, the rag over her mouth before she could scream or even react.

Instantly, he wrapped his left arm around her and lifted her petite five-foot frame off the ground. He went down on his right knee, pushed her down to the ground and laid on top of her, smothering her, pinning her underneath him leaving no room for her to fight or wriggle free, the rag never leaving her mouth, jamming it up to her nose, making her suck in the fumes, her efforts to break free simply futile.

It took a minute of breathing in the toxic fumes of the chloroform before he could tell that she went completely still and was subdued.

He rolled her over, Danica Brunner lying flat on her back, and ripped open her blouse, the buttons flying, the fabric ripping. He slid her skirt down and then her panties well below her navel to where he could see her pubic hair.

He took out the Ka-Bar and without any hesitation, plunged it into her just below her belly button, then twisted the blade violently and then ripped angrily upwards, grunting to get the jagged edge of the knife to slice up through her, the blood pouring out, her body convulsing. He quickly lengthened the vertical cut up and down. Next, he made the horizontal cut for the cross, the well-honed knife slicing deeply through the soft skin of her upper abdomen, taking the cut four to five inches left and then right of the long vertical gash.

Satisfied, he pulled the knife out of her and wiped the blood off on her blouse and put it back in the knife case. Next, he rolled her onto her right side, pulled her legs up to her stomach and folded her arms around her chest, putting her into the fetal position. Finally, he pulled out the plastic bag holding the verse and placed it in her right hand.

"That's for Rena, you bitch!" he said under his breath.

The whole process took less than five minutes from when he'd put the rag over her mouth.

The Reaper pushed himself up, took off his rubber gloves and stuffed them into a plastic bag and put it into his backpack for later disposal. He slipped on black leather gloves and noticed her cell phone ringing again. He reached inside her purse for the phone. The display had a familiar number and then he heard them in the distance, the sirens.

"She's not answering," Mac stated, putting his cell phone back in his pocket. "How do we know the picture is Danica Brunner?"

"Woman called in from California, said she went to college with her at Washington and Lee here in Virginia," Keller reported from the backseat. "The woman said she was certain that was Danica Brunner."

The FBI motorcade sirens and flashing lights moved what little traffic there was at midnight out of the way as they made their speed run down to Springfield.

"Have the locals in Springfield been notified?" Mac asked.

"They're on their way," Keller reported. Just then Keller's phone rang. "I suspect they are there," he added and answered his cell, "Special Agent Keller." His head immediately went down. He looked back to Mac and shook his head.

Springfield, Virginia, was a bedroom community located southwest of Washington, DC, just outside of the I-495 beltway. Mac and Wire arrived to find flashing lights and crime scene tape already up at the end of an alley. The FBI motorcade pulled up and parked. Mac and Wire put their FBI shields around their necks and showed their identification to a uniformed officer who, upon seeing the names, gave them an extra look of recognition, then a respectful nod before letting them under the crime scene tape.

They jogged a hundred feet down the alley to a small driveway where a black Audi A3 was parked. The door in the dark red cedar fence was open to the right of the garage. While pulling on rubber gloves, Mac and Wire walked through the opening in the fence which led to a winding paver path that weaved its way around the left side of the garage. Halfway down the path, lying partially in the bushes under the canopy of a low hanging branch from a tree, was the victim, twenty-seven-year-old Danica Brunner. She was posed in a pool of blood. Brunner's lower abdomen was cut like all the others. However, this time even more viciously. Her belly was cut wide open, the slices longer and more jagged, as if she was cut in a frenzy and a hurry.

The Springfield police chief, a woman named Trudy Miles, greeted them both. "I'm sorry; this is an absolutely brutal night for you guys. Can't tell you how sorry I am about Aubry Gesch. He was a good man."

"You knew him?" Wire asked.

"I worked a case with him a couple of years ago. He was a pro's pro."

"That he was, Chief," Mac answered but stayed on task. "What do we have here?"

"Just the person you were looking for, Danica Brunner," the chief answered. "My men arrived ten minutes ago and knocked on the front door, which was answered by her boyfriend who was asleep on the couch. He led my men around the back and they found the body lying in the bushes. Other than checking for a pulse, she hasn't been moved." Miles nodded to the two-story house behind them. "The boyfriend was expecting her around midnight, which is usually when she shows up here. She's been working nights lately, usually until 11:00 or a little later managing an art gallery."

"That had to be ... awful," Wire said sadly, crouching down, looking at the wound. "To find her like ... this ..." Shock overtook Dara's face as she inspected the cuts on Brunner. Even in the dark Mac could tell she was going pale.

"That's something you'll never forget," Mac added, hands on hips, taking in the murder scene. "This is just ... vicious," he remarked, shining his light on the wound. "I wouldn't say the other times he sliced women open were surgical, especially Sandy Faye, but this is more ... I don't know, brutal."

"Escalated," Dara added, her hand to her mouth. "He's escalating."

"Or he was just excited by what happened at the cabin perhaps, euphoric even, so much so he was in a exhilarated frenzy when he killed her," Mac answered, nonplussed, evaluating the scene as if he had no pulse.

"Agent McRyan," Chief Miles asked, "how can you look at this ... I mean, it looks like she was attacked by a wild animal, for Christ's sake. How can you look and talk about it so ... calmly?"

Mac kept looking over Brunner while he answered, "That's the sad part, really, Chief. This stuff doesn't faze me anymore. It hasn't for a while." Which was one of the reasons he didn't miss regular cop work as much as he thought he would; being away from the dead bodies had allowed him to get back in touch with his humanity. Still, even he was surprised at how unaffected he was by the state of the Brunner's body; it was horrifying but it just didn't affect him in that way. He was looking at it unemotionally, clinically. On the other hand, Wire wasn't desensitized like he was. "You okay, partner?" he asked.

"Fine," she answered, although she was anything but that. She turned her back to the body and tried to suck in some fresh air. "Let's keep working."

"Okay," Mac turned back and leaned down to the body again. "Man, the wound is fresh. She hasn't been dead long," Mac stated as he walked back towards the alley and to the Audi parked in the driveway. He felt the hood, it was still warm, and shook his head. "I bet we missed by five minutes, maybe less." Mac walked back and found her purse.

"Chief, I'm reaching inside her purse."

"What are you looking for?" Miles asked.

"Cell phone." The screen revealed four missed calls, all his, the first one made twenty-one minutes ago. "Damn it. We were so close."

Mac looked back from the body to the path, leading to the driveway. The path followed the contours of the outside of the garage, turning left for five feet and then right as the path made its way to the back door of the house. The path was concealed under a canopy of mature trees and by a row of tall bushes. With his flashlight, Mac pointed towards a notch in the garage's exterior where the path turned left. "He waited right there," Mac suggested, pointing, angling the flashlight down. "Those footprints look fresh. I bet they're size thirteen. Let's do things by the book and get a mold, Chief."

"Will do."

"So he got inside the fence, there's no lock, and waited here, knowing she was coming because he'd been stalking her for days," Wire suggested, now steadied, walking towards the house, stopping halfway. "In the dark, no way you could see him hiding there from the house. It's too dark and the spot is hidden."

"Did she come over regularly around midnight?" Mac asked the chief.

"Boyfriend says she did. She managed an art gallery that would close at 10:00 P.M. She would usually work another hour and then come over and spend the night. They've been together for a year. The poor guy, he was getting ready to pop the question."

"Do we have a Bible verse?" Mac muttered, looking at Brunner's hand. It was there, in a plastic bag. Mac carefully pulled it out of her fingers and held it up to his flashlight and read aloud: "Then said Jesus unto him, Put up again thy sword into his place: for all they that take the sword shall perish with the sword." Mac studied the words, "I think that's Matthew."

"Very good, McRyan. Matthew 26:52 to be exact," Chief Miles answered. "I teach Sunday school. With a name like McRyan, you must be Catholic."

"As Irish Catholic as they come," Mac replied.

"Chief, are your people canvassing?" Wire asked, getting back on task.

"As we speak, Agent Wire, every door is being knocked on," the chief answered. "My people know what this murder is. They'll be on their game."

Mac handed Miles a copy of the photo array of Drake Johnson. "Chief, show everyone this photo. It's the same one the FBI director talked about less than an hour ago. The Reaper is a man named Drake Johnson. He's a former cop. If anyone gets a bead on him, they should immediately call for backup. The man is a beast and taking him alone is extremely dangerous."

Miles looked over the photo. "I heard that statement by the director. Just how long have you had his name?" the Springfield police chief asked, curious.

"We've known for less than twenty-four hours, really since yesterday morning. The bureau thought they had a bead on him at a cabin up in Pennsylvania. Instead it was a trap."

"The explosion?" the detective asked.

"Yes," Wire answered. "So now there will be no holding back. The whole nation will know who the Reaper is, who Drake Johnson is. In this day and age, there will be no place for him to hide."

"Where's the boyfriend?" Mac asked. There was only one thing he really needed to know from the boyfriend.

"Inside the house," the Springfield chief answered.

Mac and Wire walked inside the small two-story red brick house and found the boyfriend sitting at the kitchen table, elbows on his knees looking at the floor. Mac and Wire team interviewed him, walking through the last two days, getting the answers they largely expected. "Did you see this man hanging around?" Wire asked, showing him the photo spread of Johnson.

"No," he answered. It appeared he'd not yet seen the news. "Is he this Reaper?"

"Yes," Mac answered. "Look, I know you're still in shock, but I have to ask some questions."

"Okay."

Mac pulled out the photo they'd taken from Randall's computer. "You can see Danica in this picture. Do you know any of these other women in the photo?"

The boyfriend took the photo in his hands and studied it. "No, I don't."

"You're sure?" Mac pressed. "None of them look even vaguely familiar?"

Sam shook his head.

"Did she ever mention the name Rena Johnson?"

"No."

"How long have you known Danica?"

"We met a little over a year ago at a party. Up until then I'd never met or seen her before. How old is that picture?"

"Seven years," Mac answered.

"Man, you'd have to ask her family," he answered. "I can't begin to tell you how reluctant Dani was to talk about her past, about college, about the years after college. She just never talked about it, like there were bad memories she was trying to forget. If the topic ever came up, she just kind of shut down and wanted to talk about something else. For whatever reason, she wanted to act as if those years of her life never existed."

Mac and Wire shared a knowing look. The past she never wanted to talk about finally came back to get her.

29

"I THINK HE SYMBOLIZES A COLD-BLOODED SOCIOPATHIC KILLER."

4 A.M., THE HOOVER BUILDING

While Wire sacked out on the beat-up couch in the employee lounge, Mac sipped at a large coffee and read through the file the FBI had developed on Drake Johnson during the past twenty-four hours. Despite the fact that he'd read the FBI profile on the Reaper, confronted him once and spoke on the phone with him twice, this was really the first time he was actually getting some in-depth information on the man he'd spent weeks hunting for.

He was the son of Warren and Patricia Johnson of Auburn, New York. Nine years after his birth, he gained a baby sister named Rena. The FBI file revealed that while there was a nine-year gap between Drake and Rena Johnson, the two siblings were very close. In a short time, the FBI had obtained a number of family pictures and it was clear from the photos, the genuine smiles and affection that Drake Johnson loved and doted over his little baby sister. This was probably one of the reasons Drake Johnson stayed close to home, going to State University of New York (SUNY) at Cortland, a mere half hour away, and living at home for much of his college years. At SUNY Cortland, he majored in criminology and subsequently joined the police force in Ithaca just a half hour from Auburn.

Once with the police force in Ithaca, his record for his first eleven years was solid. His evaluations revealed excellent performance, several commendations and as a result, he was promoted to detective by the time he was twenty-nine years old. The only blemishes were the three brutality complaints, one for which he served a suspension, but otherwise he looked like a pretty solid cop.

The first real sign of trouble appeared nearly four years ago, a brutality complaint arising out of the investigation of a hit-and-run automobile accident. Johnson was alleged to have used excessive force in the arrest of the driver of the vehicle. Johnson served a short suspension but in reading the file and some analysis provided, the fact the incident involved a hit-and-run accident, not unlike the one that resulted in his sister's death, seemed to serve as a trigger that started a downward emotional spiral for Johnson.

A second brutality complaint followed a year later arising out of a domestic dispute and investigation. The husband was found at a local bar and took a swing at Johnson when he and his partner attempted to arrest him. Johnson responded with a full onslaught, punching the man three times in the face, breaking his nose, knocking out two teeth and giving him two black eyes. Johnson attributed his reaction to the heat of the moment and fear for his own safety. Johnson's partner backed his version and the witness accounts for others at the bar varied greatly as to the aggression of the suspect as well as the appropriateness of Johnson's reaction. Mac had been through similar situations numerous times where his own survival instinct kicks in. However, as much as he was prone to side with any officer who defended himself from an assault by a suspect, even to him the response seemed exceedingly excessive.

His record then remained officially clean for two years, although in reading between the lines on the performance evaluations, it appeared Johnson continued to teeter on the edge. The FBI file indicated that two current Ithaca officers were interviewed and off the record stated that Johnson had developed an anger management problem and always seemed to be on a hair trigger, always ready to blow. "I think his sister's death devastated him, the way she died, a hit-and-run and the driver was never found. It just ate him up inside." Those same officers also said Johnson was an exceedingly good investigator, dogged and tenacious. Another officer stated: "I think given what happened to his sister, he always identified with the victim. That made him a good investigator, he closed cases and that's why I think they tolerated his temper and brutality issues. When he was on his game he was good for the statistics."

Then his parents died. The same officers indicated that Johnson became depressed, started drinking excessively and was, at times, scary. Three months after his father's passing, new trouble arose out of an interrogation of a rape suspect where Johnson was accused of "tuning" up the suspect to obtain a confession.

This time Johnson was suspended for thirty days, ordered to seek counseling and basically told that if it happened again, he would be done.

Upon his reinstatement, things seemed to calm down for Johnson. His performance as an investigator remained solid and the message seemingly received. As one of his former colleagues stated, "He seemed to turn the corner although you could tell he was fighting to keep things together."

Then the break-in at the residence of Kevin and Rebecca Randall happened and the bottom dropped out of Johnson's life. Mac figured, as did FBI analysts putting together the file, that somewhere in the investigation of the burglary, Johnson stumbled on the picture of his sister with Goynes, Wyland, Donahue, Faye, Drew, Rebecca Randall and Danica Brunner. Shortly thereafter, Johnson was involved in another investigation involving a domestic incident where a wife was brutally beaten but ultimately refused to make a complaint against her husband. Apparently, the incident set Johnson off. The husband came into a bar where Johnson was drinking. The report indicated that Johnson left the bar. He may have waited in the back for the husband. When he came out the back of the bar, Drake Johnson beat the man to within an inch of his life. While it was off duty, his job with Ithaca was nevertheless in the balance and the civil lawsuit would be forthcoming and he would almost certainly lose.

Two weeks later, while on suspension, Johnson staged his death. A couple of weeks later, Rebecca Randall was murdered. Two years later the Reaper killings began.

Mac closed the file and looked at the picture of all of the victims standing in front of the minivan again, thinking what impact that must have had on Johnson when he saw it, the date in the lower right-hand corner, knowing that within hours of that photo, his sister died. As he scanned the picture, he ran his hand through his short blond hair. He'd looked at the photo a hundred times now and still, after that many looks, he couldn't help but think he was missing something.

An hour later, now at the Hoover Building, Mac, Wire and Director Mitchell and another FBI senior agent named Dan Galloway sat at the large conference table in his spacious office, quietly sipping on coffee while the two of them briefed the director on Danica Brunner.

"How close were we to getting him or saving her?"

Mac held his thumb and index finger an inch apart, "A matter of minutes."

"I shouldn't have been up in Pennsylvania with Gesch," Mitchell muttered, shaking his head. "I was so anxious to catch him, to be a part of it, to see it, that I lost perspective on what the director's job is. No one case should consume all of my time."

"Big case," Wire stated. "Close by, political consequences, White House pressure. It was only natural to want to be there."

"I'm not allowed that emotion," Mitchell answered with a dismissive wave. "If I'm here, we react quicker in getting Johnson's picture out, Danica Brunner's picture out. If I am here, at a minimum, she is still alive."

"Maybe," Mac replied, studying the picture from Randall for what seemed like the thousandth time. "Who knows how things turn out if you'd have done this or that."

"And Danica Brunner isn't without some political consequences," the director stated.

"How so?"

"I've just learned," the director added, "that our victim has some political ties. She's the niece of a big K Street lobbyist by the name of Hubert Brunner. Brunner has a great many friends in this town, the best of which apparently is Jesse Richardson."

"The Senate minority leader? Good grief," Wire muttered.

"The one and only," the director answered. "Brunner is a close friend. I'm sure we'll hear from ole Jesse today. He's a bit of a bomb thrower for a leader."

"Be nice if all he said was catch this bastard, and left the politics out of it," Mac offered bitterly.

"True," the director answered. "But he won't. That's not his style. Not with Danica Brunner dying. Speaking of dying, is he done? Is the killing over?"

"Everyone in the picture is dead," Wire stated.

Mac snapped a look at Wire, "Say that again."

Wire looked at him quizzically, "Everyone ... in the picture ... is dead."

"I wonder."

"What? You wonder what?" Wire and the director asked in unison.

"Not everyone in the picture is dead," Mac stated, pulling the picture close again and a small smile crept across his face. "I've been looking at this picture for hours now, thinking I've been missing something."

"And what are you missing?" Mitchell asked.

"Who took it?" Mac answered. "Who took this picture?"

"What makes you think whoever took it had anything to do with this?" Wire asked.

"A couple of things," Mac answered. "First, see how Goynes and Faye have arms locked behind the other, Donahue and Drew have their arms around each other's shoulders, and Rena Johnson, Rebecca Randall and Janelle Wyland have their arms all locked together?"

"Yeah, so?"

"Yet Brunner is off by herself, why?"

"She doesn't know the other girls as well, I suppose," Mitchell offered.

"Or, it's *her* buddy who is taking the picture."

"Rebecca Randall had the photo on her computer, though, so doesn't it stand to reason that whoever took it was a friend of hers?"

"Possibly, or she's a friend of both Randall and Brunner. Look, all of these women are connected through each other, but they were not all friends together. Donahue, Goynes and Sandy Faye, who was then Helen Williams, went to the AAHC Camp together. Kelly Drew was a long time friend of Hannah Donahue's who had a summer place up near Auburn. Wyland is connected to Rebecca Randall from Syracuse University. Rebecca Randall is connected to Rena Johnson from growing up together in Auburn. What's the connection of Danica Brunner? How did she fit into this group?"

Mac opened the file that Galloway brought in on Brunner. "Danica went to college at Washington and Lee. None of our group did. She was born and raised here in Virginia. None of our other victims were. She doesn't fit, unless she fits ..."

"With whoever took the picture," Wire finished. "So there's possibly ..."

"One more victim out there," Mac looked to the director. "Look, we need to get people all over this picture. We need to go through Randall's computer again and see if we can determine how she received this picture. Wire and I need to go through Brunner's life with a fine-tooth comb and figure out the connection. We may even need to simply go public with the picture to see if our person comes forward."

"Okay, Mac," the director replied. "We'll do that. Agent Galloway, see to it."

"Yes sir."

"Wait a minute ..." Mac began to protest.

Director Mitchell held up his hand. "Dara, do you mind if I have a word with Mac alone?"

"No sir," Wire answered, looking at Mac, asking with her eyes, 'what's up?'

Mac shrugged his shoulders in response; he had no idea.

Once Wire closed the door to the director's office, Mitchell got up out of his chair and walked around to Mac's side of the table, bringing the coffee pot with him. He poured Mac a new cup. "Mac, I need a favor."

"What is it, sir?" Mac asked, taking a sip of coffee.

"There is a press conference at 9:00 A.M.," the director replied, and then dropped one on Mac. "I need you to handle it with me."

Mac looked up from his coffee cup, surprised. "Me?"

"Yeah, you."

"Why?" The thought of addressing the media was not one he relished. Dead bodies didn't bother him, the media did.

"Because Aubry Gesch's scorched body is lying in the morgue. Grace Delmonico is too junior for the assignment and too traumatized from last night, she's just not up to it. Nobody in the bureau, including your extremely capable partner out in the hall, knows the case better than you do. On top of that, you have a better understanding of the Reaper, of Drake Johnson, than anyone else. We're as close as we are to catching this asshole because of you."

"But sir, with all due respect, I've spent my whole career trying to avoid the media. I *hate* the media and, frankly, they hate me."

"I know," Mitchell replied. "And you're probably nervous about facing them."

"Well *yeah*," Mac answered. "You saw how swimmingly my last brush with them went."

Mitchell laughed, trying to lighten the mood, "That was a cluster no doubt, but trust me on this, she wasn't a legitimate reporter. No legitimate reporter goes where she went. She'll end up on some two-bit cable channel doing D-List celebrity news soon enough. And between you, me and these four walls, I kind of loved how you went off on her. But listen," the FBI director said, turning serious, "I'm really quite certain that you *are* the man I want up there with me."

"Why?"

"A couple of reasons. First, after last night I need to project confidence and determination. Your blunt manner, your direct approach, your intensity and even arrogance is what I need up there with me," Mitchell stated. "We were hit hard last night. I want to present someone who is a fighter and someone who knows the case inside and out. You check both of those boxes. Mac, you're *exactly* what I need right now."

"Who's running the investigation now?" Mac asked. "Shouldn't they be up there as well?"

"He will be, because it's you," Mitchell answered, stunning him for the second time.

"Sir, I'm temporary FBI, an out-of-work homicide cop from St. Paul."

"Who's out of work by choice."

"Yes, that's true, I suppose. You offered me a job, sir," Mac answered exasperated, "but you can't put me in charge. People will have your head, *not to mention mine.*"

"Look," the director answered nonplussed, "Senior Special Agent Galloway will, by title, run the investigation and do all the bureaucratic bullshit for you. He's efficient and can get and arrange for you anything you need. He excels at that kind of work. But when it comes to the actual running the investigation, that will be you, and until this thing is done, until we have this bastard, you report directly to me on it. He killed four of my men last night and two sheriff's deputies. Whether he is done killing or not, we are never going to stop looking for this asshole."

Mac leaned back in his chair, looking at the ceiling, contemplating this turn of events. His quick assessment was he really didn't have a choice. If the director of the FBI asks you for your help, you give it. "Okay, sir, but I can't promise you won't regret this. I tend to ... speak my mind."

"Good, do that, within reason of course," Director Mitchell cautioned.

"You said a couple of reasons you wanted me to do this. What's the other?"

"He's calling you."

In that moment, Mac understood another of the director's motivations and immediately liked it, "And this is my chance to speak to him."

"Correct."

With that an idea started forming in Mac's head based on his review of the FBI file on Drake Johnson, how close he was to his sister, how her death obviously haunted him, the impact seeing the photo he found at Randall's had on him and what he must have learned from interrogating Rebecca Randall. There were buttons that could be pushed. However, before he got too far with that idea in his mind, he looked at his appearance, rumpled clothes, two days of razor stubble and his short hair sticking in various directions. "Director, I'm not exactly presentable at the moment."

"That's why that beautiful girlfriend of yours dropped some things off for you. You'll find them in my personal washroom. She brought fresh clothing options and your toiletries so you can clean up."

"Sir, if Sally knows about this, the White House does as well then," Mac warned. "I know you make your own decisions, but how do you think they'll feel about this?"

"Well, they do know Mac, so if I might quote the president: Tell Mac to give them hell," Director Mitchell answered with a smile. "Listen, reporters are like any other group of people you run into. Some are straight shooters, asking straight questions, looking for straight answers."

"And others?"

"Others are pricks who will have a different agenda."

"Well, funny thing is, Director, I have an agenda too, and if what I have planned works, we'll need to set a couple of things up."

Sally sipped nervously from her coffee. Sitting on the couch in the Judge's office, aware of what Mac was trying to accomplish, she was nevertheless terrified, both for Mac and for political reasons. William Donahue would undoubtedly be watching and the Judge forewarned the man he wouldn't like everything he heard and that Hannah may have been caught up in a vehicular homicide seven years ago. It wasn't a pleasant conversation. "It is what it is, he asked for our involvement. I put two of the best there are on his daughter's murder. He'll have to live with the results."

"The law of unintended consequences, I guess," Sally suggested.

"Exactly," the Judge answered as he twirled a cigar in his fingers, his own nervous tick. The press conference was moments from beginning. Few people knew just how much Mac hated the television media. Newspaper reporters he was okay with, and he wasn't afraid to occasionally speak to them off the record. Television news media he avoided. He hated and had little time or regard for most of them, save a few, and even them he wouldn't talk to. "I don't speak in sound bites," Mac would often say.

"That's the only way they talk in this town," was Sally's teasing reply. "You better learn."

"That's not going to happen, I'm not changing. I'm here because I love you, but I'm not going to love what you do and have to do."

She never wanted him to, but then again she never figured he'd be handling a press conference on an investigation that suddenly was gripping the nation. "I don't think he's ever done this, Judge," Sally warned for the tenth time. "I've never seen him do a press conference. He thinks of most of the news media as fools and he won't suffer them gladly."

"He'll be fine."

"How can you know? I know him better than anyone and I don't know that he'll be fine."

"Sally, some people are born to rise to the moment. Mac's one of those guys, he's done it his whole life. Plus he has a strategy here and that will keep him focused. It'll cause him to shelve just enough of his attitude and disdain to get the job done. Just take the measure of him when he walks on the podium with Thomas. You'll know if he's up to it. You'll know if his frame of mind is good."

"I hope you're right."

"I hope I'm right too," the Judge replied ruefully. "By the way, how did your off-the-record call with Ms. Foxx go?"

This is when Sally knew Mac was at his operating and manipulative best. How else would she explain him calling forty-five minutes ago asking her, of all people, to call Heather Foxx on his behalf. Mac knew that Sally recognized that Foxx had the hots for him, always had, and Sally's existence, and his clear devotion to her, hadn't stopped her from pursuing him. It was a mildly uncomfortable conversation and Sally could have sworn she could hear Heather Foxx smiling on the other end of the phone. When she called to tell Mac she'd delivered his request, she said, "You need to find a new reporter you can trust. I don't trust her, I don't like her, and if you ever *ever* ask me to do that again, I'll break both your legs."

The director approached the podium with Mac standing behind him to his right. The director started with a statement about the case and the events in Pennsylvania. Sally didn't even really listen to Director Mitchell. She knew all of that anyway.

Instead, she focused in on Mac. He picked the black suit with the light pinstripe, white dress shirt and sharp sky blue tie. He looked really good, she thought, handsome, sharp, smart and serious. Then she looked at his face, his icy blue eyes in particular, taking stock of his demeanor. He was stoic but his eyes reflected a cool intensity and a purpose. Mac was operating. When he was doing that, he was dangerous —in a good way. A wave of relief washed over Sally before Mac ever spoke. She could tell Mac was plenty ready.

"Mac looks like he's loaded for bear," the Judge mused, having been sizing up Mac just as she was.

"I know the look, Judge," Sally answered, looking to the Judge with a devilish look, the confidence back in her face. "This should be interesting."

෴

"Director Mitchell, when did you determine that the Reaper was Drake Johnson?"

"Yesterday, and we put forward every effort to determine his whereabouts before going public with his name."

The CBS reporter followed up: "And how were you able to identify the Reaper?"

"Through DNA from blood found on a bullet we recovered in Frederick. Agent McRyan, who will speak shortly, wounded him in the chase from the home of Kelly Drew."

"Was the DNA a match to Drake Johnson?"

"It was a familial match to a woman named Rena Johnson, his younger sister who was killed seven years ago in a hit-and-run car accident in upstate New York."

"Does her death have something to do with the present case?"

"I think the best person to answer that question and the others you may have is Special Agent Michael McRyan. So at this point, I'm going to turn the press conference over to him. Agent McRyan joined our investigation a number of weeks ago and has been integral to the progress that we have made. I think he's the best man to answer many of the questions you have."

Mac stepped to the podium, cupping the edge of the podium with his right hand. He pointed to a woman from FOX News with his casted left hand.

"Agent McRyan, was it you who shot the Reaper, or should I say Drake Johnson, in Frederick?"

"Yes."

"Do you have anything additional to add about shooting the Reaper?"

"Such as?"

"A description of how he was shot?"

"No, just that I shot him." Mac pointed to the reporter from ABC News.

"Was the explosion in Wrightsdale, Pennsylvania, last evening in which Senior Special Agent Gesch and five others were killed, related to the hunt for Drake Johnson?"

"Yes. The cabin belonged to Drake Johnson. It was passed down through his family."

"Just a follow-up," the ABC reporter asked. "A property search by ABC News revealed the property belonged to a Richard Tanner, is that an alias?"

"No," Mac answered easily. "That is Drake Johnson's grandfather on his mother's side. Mr. Tanner died five years ago but the property title was never changed over to the Johnson family." Mac pointed to a reporter from CNN.

"Agent McRyan. Do you know what caused the explosion last night?"

"Beyond the fact that the explosion was detonated remotely, the answer is no. That is being investigated as we speak. There is an FBI forensic team, as well as a crime scene unit from Lancaster County on site, sifting through the wreckage, trying to determine exactly how the explosion occurred."

"Were explosives involved?"

"Like I said, that is being investigated, although I think it is safe to say an explosive of some kind was used."

"What can you tell us about the victim last night in Springfield, Virginia?"

"A twenty-seven-year-old woman named Danica Brunner," Mac answered crisply, moving along, getting some questions out of the way. However, it was time to get to what he wanted to talk about. He pointed to a friendly face.

"Agent McRyan, Heather Foxx, NBC News. Director Mitchell mentioned a Rena Johnson and being a DNA match to Drake Johnson who the FBI is saying is the killer known as the Reaper. Two questions for you: who is Drake Johnson and what does the death of Rena Johnson have to do with the current investigation?"

"The answer requires a rather long explanation, so please bear with me. By way of background, Drake Johnson is thirty-six years old. He was a police officer, a detective in

Ithaca, New York, up until a little over two years ago when he was thought to have died in a one-car automobile accident on a wintery March night. His vehicle veered off the road, down a steep bank and crashed into a large tree, setting off an explosion of the car. By the time the fire was extinguished and the body was removed from the wreckage, it was only identifiable by dental records. The vehicle belonged to Drake Johnson. The dental records for Johnson were supplied by his half-brother, a dentist in Rochester, New York. Johnson's half-brother has confirmed that he falsified the dental records for his brother. I'll get to the reason Drake Johnson requested his half-brother falsify the records in a minute."

Mac took a sip of water and then continued, "As for his investigative record, let's just say Drake Johnson was a less than stellar officer. Specifically, in his relatively short police career in a town of just over 30,000 residents, several police brutality complaints were made against him, two of which led to formal disciplinary action. Following the last brutality complaint, he was warned he would lose his job were there another.

"Then two weeks before his disappearance, he investigated a domestic assault case. The wife would not press charges. Rather than letting the case go, Johnson engaged the husband at a local bar, and unprovoked, beat him senseless in the back alley. This off-the-job act led to a civil lawsuit against Mr. Johnson, a lawsuit he was almost certain to lose. As a result, not only would he likely lose his job, but also his money, which included nearly a million dollars that he inherited upon the passing of his parents. This was the reason he gave his half-brother for falsifying the dental records. He was seeking to stage his own death, escape with his money and avoid paying the damages that almost certainly would have been awarded in the civil lawsuit. However, as we've now learned, his scheme to disappear was clearly about more than asset preservation.

"Shortly before staging the accident and before the altercation and beating at a bar in Ithaca, Johnson, still employed as a detective for the city of Ithaca, investigated a burglary at the home of Rebecca Randall. It was a standard home invasion case. As part of the investigation, we think Drake Johnson stumbled across this photo." Mac looked back to an assistant, "Can we get the enlargement placed on the easel? Thank you."

The assistant placed the photo on the easel.

Mac reached for a laser pointer and moved left to right across the photo.

"The first two people embracing each other are Melissa Goynes, the first victim and the fourth victim, Sandy Faye, who was then known as Helen Williams before she changed her name. The next two are Hannah Donahue, the third victim and Kelly Drew, the woman who has survived but remains in a coma. Next, standing by herself is last night's victim Danica Brunner. Finally, the last three with their arms around each other are Rena Johnson, the sister of Drake Johnson, Rebecca Randall and Janelle Wyland, the second victim."

"This picture was taken on August 17th seven years ago, the night Rena Johnson was killed."

"Agent McRyan," Heather Foxx interrupted, "how was it that Rena Johnson was killed?"

"On the night of August 17th, she attended a rave party south of Auburn, New York. She drank a lot of alcohol, did some weed and Ecstasy and wandered off from the party at an abandoned farmhouse. She found herself walking just past a tight turn on the narrow shoulder of County Highway

5 when a silver vehicle, likely a Dodge or Chrysler minivan or SUV, struck her and projected her some thirty or forty feet until she landed at the bottom of a deep ditch where she was found hours later, dead."

"Agent McRyan, were the victims of the Reaper involved in Rena Johnson's death?"

"I think it's safe to assume Drake Johnson thinks so. However, as best we can tell, all he has is the picture which in and of itself means absolutely nothing."

"Agent McRyan," a reporter from FOX News blurted, "did any of the victims have a vehicle matching the description or at least paint of the vehicle that struck Rena Johnson?"

Mac had a theory on this, but not one he was going to share with the media. "No, the FBI has gone deep on the vehicle records for not only the victims but their families as well, and nobody owned that particular kind of vehicle in that window of time, nor did anyone rent one."

"Were there any witnesses to the accident?" FOX News asked on follow-up.

"No," Mac replied. "No witnesses that the Auburn police ever found in the investigation. In fact, none of the victims of Drake Johnson were ever questioned as part of the investigation. Their names never came up."

"So why is Drake Johnson killing them?"

"If I knew I'd tell you," Mac answered. "If anything the man has done was understandable, I'd explain it. There's no evidence in any investigative files I've seen on the death of Rena Johnson that ties the women Drake Johnson has murdered to that accident in any way, shape or form. Not one shred of evidence."

"Do you have any theories as to what his motive would be then?"

"Theories? Sure, tons," Mac answered and realized he was being just a bit flippant. He quickly sobered. His whole view of the case had been a theory all along, confirmed in the last twenty-four hours, but he had less proof of the victims' involvement in the death of Rena Johnson than Drake Johnson probably had, given what he may have resorted to in interrogating and torturing some of the women. But then again, that was speculation too. Mac answered the question, somberly. "We have some ideas, but I don't think it is yet time to engage in open speculation, not without more evidence to go on."

"Agent McRyan," a *Washington Times* reporter asked, "what do you think this Reaper symbolizes?"

This was not a question Mac had expected, but it was helpful nonetheless. "He's a disgrace to good police everywhere. He's a coward who ran from the consequences of his own actions. I think he symbolizes nothing more than a cold-blooded sociopathic killer with little regard for human life. I think the whole use of biblical verses and the symbolism of the Holy Cross are indicative of a desire for attention, for fifteen minutes of fame. Yet in the end, when this is all over, Drake Johnson will be nothing more than some nut bar the Investigation Discovery Channel dedicates an hour to some day on one of their investigation shows. He'll be programming filler."

"Yet," a reporter from the *Washington Sentinel* suggested, "you're on this investigation thanks to White House intervention. Doesn't that provide a political element to this investigation?"

"I don't see how," Mac answered with a bite. "We're after a killer, nothing more and nothing less. I see nothing political about that." Mac answered, boring in on the reporter who had a political angle of some kind. "The president and

Judge Dixon asked Dara Wire and I to help with the investigation and that's what we've done."

"Is the White House directing this investigation?" the reporter pressed, "in an effort to protect the reputation of the daughter of William Donahue?"

"No."

"Seriously, you expect us to believe that, Agent McRyan? You live with the White House deputy director of communications." Now Mac truly understood the reporter's political angle, which was *partisan* politics.

"Now I'm a little concerned," Sally said, sitting up on the couch.

"Me too," the Judge added.

Come on, Mac, Sally thought, don't take the bait and blow it.

"First, I wasn't aware I'd been appointed as FBI director, giving me all this power over the investigation," Mac replied. "Second, this is all I'll say about my relationship with Sally Kennedy. It's like one of hundreds, perhaps thousands, in this town where both people work for the federal government. Under your line of questioning, that makes all of those relationships questionable as well. Is that what you're suggesting?" Mac didn't give the reporter a chance to respond. "I am a *temporary* special agent of the FBI, a consultant if you will, and I report to Director Mitchell." Mac pointed with his left hand, the cast visible to all. "I have had one mission and one mission only since I became part of this investigation and that is to help the FBI find the killer, nothing more and nothing less. I don't give a rip about politics, about any of that stuff. All of that may be relevant to Sally Kennedy and the White House, but I don't give a damn about it. What I care about is finding Drake Johnson and ending this."

"That was a good answer, Mac," Sally exclaimed, clapping.

"That was the answer of a pro. You're sure he's never done this before?" the Judge asked.

Mac was knocking it out of the park.

"There are some who don't think these women are innocent," another reporter blurted. Mac had seen this woman on a cable channel somewhere. "They have to be guilty of something."

"Maybe they are," Mac answered, "but I have to operate on the basis of evidence, not supposition. At this point in time, I have no evidence that supports that view. No evidence, beyond a picture, that these victims were involved in Drake Johnson's sister's death. Instead, what I have is a man who has killed every woman in this picture and I've yet to find a single evidentiary reason for him to have done so." Now he was poking Drake Johnson. He didn't believe what he was saying or was about to say; he wondered whether people in the room would believe it, but they were not his target.

"The only theory that seems to have any credence, the only thing I see them being guilty of, is that they all went to a party with Rena Johnson. They all had a good time, had too much to drink and maybe got into some drugs. As a result, things got a little out of hand and Rena Johnson wandered away, or her friends lost track of her, whatever it was, and a tragedy occurred. Is one person negligently wandering off at a party a reason to kill the other seven people she might have gone to the party with? Is that worth killing six law enforcement officers last night? Let there be no doubt, he murdered six men last night. Whatever he once might have been, Drake Johnson is now an animal, a monster, an unbalanced, irrational murderer of innocent people and we will never rest until he is caught."

The room went silent for a moment and Mac took an opportunity to take a sip of water.

"Agent McRyan, what else can you tell us about the killer?" another reporter asked.

"Drake Johnson, in addition to being a sociopath and cold-blooded killer, is a large man and is extremely strong physically. You can't appreciate the degree to which that is true unless you are confronting him; which I have," Mac held up his cast again. "He is a monster in every sense of the word, an absolute animal who has the added advantage of police training. He's as dangerous a person, a killer, as you can imagine."

"Agent McRyan," the ABC reporter asked, "do you have any leads on Mr. Johnson's whereabouts?"

"We do," Mac answered, lying just a bit. "We are pursuing them as we speak. As Director Mitchell noted, the picture of Drake Johnson is everywhere now. We know who he is. If anyone sees him, I am encouraging them to immediately call the FBI at the number people can see on their television screen. Do not, under any circumstances, engage this man on your own." Mac held up his left hand, "He is far too dangerous."

Mac had been answering questions for nearly thirty minutes. Director Mitchell stepped forward and whispered, "One more question."

Mac pointed to a reporter from the Associated Press, "Last question."

"Last night's victim lived in Springfield, Virginia. Do you believe the killer is still in the Washington, DC, area?" the Associated Press reporter asked.

"That is possible, yes."

"Do you believe he has identified his next potential victim?"

"I don't know."

"Do you think he has another target?" Mac thought he did, but couldn't be sure.

"We don't know."

"Does that concern you?"

"Yes, because he's killed six women and tried to kill another. He killed six men last night. I want to find him, arrest him and put him on trial for his crimes. We don't have a moment to waste in finding this killer. The clock is ticking and we need the public's help. Thank you."

Director Mitchell walked off the dais and Mac followed and once through the doors, the director turned around, "Not bad for a guy who claims to never have done a press conference. So do you think he'll bite?"

"We'll see."

30

"WE NEED TO LOCK EVERYONE ON THE INTERSTATE!"

Drake Johnson was just north of Washington, DC, on I-270, approaching the I-495 Capitol Beltway, gripping the steering wheel tight, incensed, as he weaved through traffic. He couldn't get the press conference out of his mind.

Sociopathic killer.

Unbalanced.

Irrational murderer of innocent people.

"Unbalanced!" he growled, pounding the steering wheel.

Nut bar.

Coward.

He didn't expect McRyan to be at the press conference, let alone be the centerpiece of it. Yet there he was and he spoke about him, belittled him, diminishing him to the entire country. He trashed Rena!

The Reaper merged his panel van into the traffic, traveling east on I-495, falling in with the thick flow of the midday traffic.

Killer of innocent women.

Monster.

Animal.

He'll simply end up in the dust bin of history having made no impact whatsoever.

McRyan was wrong.

Rena was innocent. Rebecca Randall, Melissa Goynes, Janelle Wyland, Hannah Donahue, Helen Williams, Kelly Drew and Danica Brunner, they were the cowards, the murderers, the killers of an innocent woman.

He grabbed a new burner phone out of the bag in the passenger seat and dialed the number he now knew from memory.

Galloway nodded, grabbed his radio from his hip, "He's calling. Start the trace." Then he looked to Mac, "We're good."

Mac took a look at his watch, 1:09 P.M., took a breath and answered the phone, "Hello, Drake. How are you today?"

"Nut bar!"

"Don't forget sociopath and coward," Mac added, walking away from Galloway and Wire, pacing. Mac's singular goal at the press conference was to draw Johnson out.

Drake took the bait.

"You should be careful, very careful with what you say," Johnson growled in a low sinister voice.

Mac could hear the anger in the killer's voice. It was time to filibuster. "Or what, Drake? I mean, what could you possibly do that's worse than what you've already done? You've killed six women and the seventh is hanging on by a thread unlikely to ever regain consciousness. You killed six innocent men last night, police officers; you killed six of your own last night. So what could you do that's worse than what you've already done?"

"There's a lot, McRyan. You have people you care about, that care for you, love you, that are not out of reach. I've proven I can get to people."

"Making this a bit personal, are we?" Mac replied, instantly thinking of Sally.

"You made it that way with the press conference this morning, talking about Rena like that, making all these women out to be innocent when they're not. So you're damn right it's fucking personal."

Wire signaled string the call out with her hands —and mouthed: we need a couple of minutes. Mac nodded, looked at his watch, 1:10 pm., and responded: "What? That I told the entire country that your sister went to a party, got drunk and high? That she was irresponsible? That she was stupid and immature? That she contributed to her own death?"

"Killer of innocent women! You called me a killer of innocent women. They're the killers, McRyan. They're the ones who took an innocent life. They're murderers, not me. I'm administering justice. Justice you wouldn't dare dispense, that you wouldn't deign to mete out. Justice those six men last night would never dare administer."

Mac laughed on purpose and strung it out before turning serious, "Drake, you call this justice? You call this reaping what you sow? Listen, Drake, and I am being completely serious with you here. You can look it up, I'm Irish Catholic. I went to Catholic school. I was an altar boy. I go to mass. I believe in what we don't answer for in this life, we answer for at the Gates of St. Peter. I believe there is a hell."

"So?"

"If these women committed a crime, prove it. If you can't prove it, then they won't answer in this life, they'll answer in the next."

~

"They committed a crime in God's eyes, McRyan. They did in God's eyes," the Reaper raged. "They sinned! They murdered."

"And so have you!!!" McRyan barked at him. "Eye for an eye doesn't make it right. You've committed the ultimate sin, premeditated murder of twelve people. *Twelve!* There can be no greater sin."

"People like you failed, McRyan. The cops in Auburn, they failed. Me? I failed. I failed when I tried it the so-called right and honorable way. It didn't work, it wouldn't work. These women could hide behind the law, it would not punish them. There would be no justice, not *your* way. But *my* way, justice has been nearly and fully achieved. Those responsible have answered, *in this life*. I'm not waiting for the next."

~

"People sin every day, Drake, should they *all* be killed?' Mac asked, checking his watch, Wire hovering nearby on her cell. "What about the bible verses about forgiveness? What about atoning for your sins? What about redemption?"

"Not for this!" he growled. "This is a life for a life, McRyan, a life for a fucking life!"

"What did they do, Drake? Tell me what they did,

because from where I'm sitting I don't see it. They maybe went to a party with your sister. For that they should die?"

"They killed my sister."

"How? How did they kill your sister, Drake?"

"They were in the van. They hit Rena with that van and sent her flying into that ditch. Rebecca, Melissa, Janelle and Hannah all confirmed it. You know it's true, McRyan. And do you think one of them went to check on her? That one of them would have called 911 when she was down in that ditch?"

"You're saying she could have been saved?" Mac asked, checking his watch.

"She could have been saved, that's right. She could have been saved."

"But they left her there?"

"They left her there to die."

"Is that what Rebecca Randall told you? Is that what she told you when you tortured her?"

"Torture, hah," Johnson mocked.

"Are you an expert at administering it?"

"What I did to her was nothing. Like you've never used some enhanced interrogation techniques? Give me break."

"I play by the rules," Mac lied. He'd used Riley and Rockford to issue a tune-up on occasion, particularly to save the chief a few years ago. "I don't need to cheat."

"You're so full of yourself, McRyan," Drake raged, grabbing the steering wheel. "I don't need to cheat, give me a fucking break."

"I don't," McRyan answered. "Drake, there is no evidence

that these women were involved in your sister's death. Did you ever stop to wonder if Rebecca Randall just told you what you wanted to hear so that you wouldn't kill her? So that you'd stop beating and torturing her? Did that ever occur to you as you've gone on this killing spree?"

"I got the truth."

"If you did, you cheated," McRyan answered arrogantly.

"So what?"

∼

"Cheating is for the weak," Mac pushed, looking at his watch. He was digging under Johnson's skin, under the Reaper's skin. "You're weak, Drake. Rena was weak."

"No, no she wasn't. She was murdered!"

"She got drunk, she got high, she did X, she wandered off and stumbled along impaired on the narrow shoulder of a county road on a dark, humid, foggy night. What do you expect?"

"She made a mistake. She didn't deserve to die."

"Nor did the victims, Drake, they didn't deserve to die either. Maybe they made a mistake too."

Mac heard Galloway mutter, "He's north of DC somewhere. Get the Maryland State Police in the loop."

∼

The anger returned. "Rena paid for her mistake with her life, McRyan. What price did those women pay? Those incompetent fools in Auburn didn't even have Randall, Donahue, Wyland, Williams or any of those women in their file anywhere. They weren't going to be found. I found them by accident."

"Accident, exactly," McRyan replied. "We keep coming back to that term, Drake. It was an accident. The whole thing was an accident."

"Where was the accountability, McRyan? Where was the one person in that group with the courage to step up and be accountable? Not one did. *NOT ONE!*" he screamed.

"So you snapped, didn't you? You couldn't live with the fact that they got away with it."

"No, so I got justice," Johnson answered darkly. "I got justice on them all," and Mac thought he'd made the case against Johnson on all six murders.

"You know what this call tells me, Drake?"

"What?"

"You're ill. You're mentally ill."

"No, I'm not."

"You are. You need help. There's something wrong, your brain chemistry is off, it happens to people all the time. There's no other explanation for this, Drake. It's mental illness. It is no sin. It's not your fault, it just happens. There was a trigger that set your illness off, that made you go crazy, Drake. It was finding that picture with your sister and those women. It made you go crazy. It made you do things you'd never otherwise do. You're a danger to yourself and others, Drake."

"Only to those who were responsible for Rena's death, McRyan," Johnson answered, "and to those who would stand in my way for justice for her."

"Drake, you have to stop. You need to turn yourself in and let us help. Let me help. Let me help you with your pain, the pain that is eating at you. Drake, it's why I spoke to you at the press conference this morning. I wanted to talk to you, to tell you there is help available, that there's something wrong and we can help you. I want to help you but this has to stop and you have to turn yourself in. Otherwise the killing will never stop, Drake. Now that you've started killing, you'll never be able to stop. These women will not be enough. You have a taste for it now. You'll find others, you'll find some reason justifiable to you and you'll kill others. You may not think you will, but you will. We need to make this stop."

"Fifteen seconds," Wire whispered.

He looked straight ahead in silence. McRyan was right. He knew his brain chemistry was wrong, that he'd changed, but he shook his head, "No, you can't help me, McRyan. You can't."

"You're murdering people, Drake."

"They're the murderers, McRyan."

"No, Drake. You're the only murderer here."

"No! No! No!"

"Drake, all you'll be remembered as is a crazy killer. Is that what you want? Nobody will ever remember Rena. Her negligence, her carelessness, will simply be part of the story."

"We got him," Galloway exclaimed quietly. "He's on I-495, Capitol Beltway, north side somewhere between Georgia Avenue and New Hampshire." Then into the radio he said, "Flood the area. Everything we got and shut down the Interstate." To Mac, he said, "Longer the better, we can zero in."

"No, McRyan, you're wrong. Rena ..."

He slowed down, the traffic slowing down dramatically in front of him. He had to quick move a lane to the right to avoid hitting the car in front of him. He looked in his rearview mirror to make sure he wasn't going to get hit and in the distance he saw flashing lights. The Reaper looked straight ahead and saw more flashing lights in the distance on the eastbound side. The dashboard clock read 1:13 P.M. He'd been on the phone four minutes, maybe more.

"You son of a bitch," the Reaper railed and then threw the burner phone out the window.

He needed to get off the interstate but he was stopped in traffic, two lanes from the right shoulder. The lights were approaching from both directions.

"Screw it," he muttered, hitting the gas, turning the wheel hard right, caving in the front driver's side of the compact car to his right. As he crossed the first lane, he took out the rear quarter panel and pushed the Ford Explorer into the far right lane and then turned hard left around the Explorer and accelerated down the shoulder, the exit five hundred yards ahead.

"Drake! Johnson!" Johnson was gone. "Shit, I lost him," Mac said, putting his phone into his pocket and going to Wire, who had a laptop up with a map of the Capitol Beltway.

"He's in this area," Dara pointed on a map she was holding, "between Georgia Avenue and New Hampshire Avenue."

"Still in DC," Mac stated with a pensive look as he examined the map, thinking one thing but seeing another. "There are two exits, Colesville Road and University Avenue. We need a chopper!"

"On the way, almost over the area," Galloway reported. "Maryland State Police chopper."

"We need to get cars on those off-ramps, shut them down. We need to lock everyone on the interstate!"

The Reaper accelerated down the shoulder, pushing the needle on the panel van past sixty miles per hour. The exit lane was a hundred yards ahead. A car started sticking its nose out and he clipped the front right quarter panel, shoving the car back into the rest of the cars. The collision pushed the van into the concrete barrier on the right of the shoulder but he powered through the impact. He hit the accelerator again and kept going, speeding to the exit ramp to southbound University Avenue.

He could see two squad cars were coming up northbound University Avenue from the south as he floored it down the exit ramp.

There wasn't much time. He had to ditch the van.

"Exit ramps are shut down," Galloway reported as they rushed down the hall to the communications center. "We've got troopers and the local cops closing in, Mac. The chopper is over the area. If he's on the interstate, we'll get him."

"Traffic cameras, get us hooked into the traffic cameras for that area," Mac ordered as they burst into the communications center.

"On it," an agent said, hitting a number of key strokes and pulling the cameras up on his computer screen. "This is Colesville Road on the left and University Avenue on the right."

"Traffic is stopped cold on Colesville," Wire noted.

"On University as well, but ... what is that?" There was smoke billowing from a car and a jumble of cars in the two left lanes. "Where is that camera pointing?" Mac asked.

"That one looks north of the University Avenue exit," the agent replied.

"Roll the tape back on that camera, can you do that?"

"Yes, give me a second," the tech hit some key strokes and maneuvered his mouse. "I'm going back five minutes."

"Run it fast-forward."

The tech fast forwarded the tape. Mac, Wire and Galloway hovered over his shoulder. "There, what's that?" Mac shouted, pointing at the screen.

The tech stopped the video, ran it back and pushed play at normal speed. A white panel van was driving fast down the shoulder as a car stuck its nose out a hundred yards short of the exit ramp. There was a collision and the van powered through, not stopping and kept going.

"That *has* to be him," Mac exclaimed. "Is that the exit to southbound University Avenue?"

"Uhh ..." the tech started, "yes. Yes, south on University." The tech checked the map for that exit. "He can only go south."

"Get us traffic cameras for that. Do they exist?"

The tech hit some more key strokes, "No cameras in that specific area. Let me see what's closest."

"Galloway, tell everyone, white panel van, right front caved in, traveling south on University. That's where we need the presence. Get that chopper going south on University."

～

The Reaper reduced his speed, traveling through the residential area on south University Avenue. He couldn't drop the van around here, it was too conspicuous and there was no place to blend in.

He stayed south but he needed to get out quick.

A shopping area was visible in the distance. In fact, several shopping areas were on both the left and right side of the street. He didn't want to drop the van in the middle of a parking lot, but he wanted the crowds of the shopping centers to blend into.

The Takoma Crossroads Shopping Center was on his right.

He turned right into the mall lot and took the lane on the far north edge of the parking lot to the driveway to the backside of the large strip mall.

～

Mac and Wire pored over the map of the area south of I-495 along University Avenue. The phone call had been over for four minutes now.

"Mac, he's going to ditch the van. He's got to be thinking we'll catch him on camera somewhere."

"I agree, but he needs a good place to ... drop ..." Mac traced University Avenue south on the map with his finger to where it crossed with New Hampshire. "This is the best closest spot. This shopping area, there's the Takoma Shopping Center and Langley Park Shopping Center."

"Lots of people and traffic," Wire added, nodding. "He could blend."

Mac looked to the tech, "Traffic cameras in that shopping area, search now!"

"On it."

To Galloway, he said, "Flood that area with cops. Get the chopper there."

He was out of the van. Slipping in an open rear door, he walked inside, through a maintenance area and into the mall proper and towards the main front entrance. At the front doors, he peered outside. Hanging around was not an option. The blending helped but he needed to keep moving. He pushed through the front door and turned right, walking along the sidewalk, under the canopy, a Washington Nationals baseball cap on his head, sunglasses, everything he needed from the van stuffed into his backpack.

He could hear the whoosh of a chopper in the distance as well as sirens. The walls were closing in. There wasn't much time. He saw a cab waiting in the distance.

Then he saw another option.

"Agent McRyan, look at this," the tech suggested. "The camera looks north on University from where it intersects with New Hampshire. Look up here," the tech pointed to the upper left corner of the screen.

"White panel van with a front bumper very askew,

turning right into that parking lot. What's that a parking lot for?"

"Takoma Shopping Center."

"How many minutes ago?"

The tech grimaced. "Three minutes."

"Galloway."

"On it, Mac," the senior agent answered, barking orders into his radio. "Takoma Shopping Center. Everyone converge now. Lock it down, lock down a five-block radius."

The FBI Suburban turned hard left onto Jackson Street and pulled up just short of the driveway behind the mall. Mac and Wire filed out even before the truck fully stopped, jogging towards the van, already being worked by an FBI forensic team.

It had been less than fifteen minutes.

"This is the van," Wire observed. "The bumper is barely hanging on, a kaleidoscope of paint from other vehicles and enough body work to keep a repair shop busy for an entire day."

Mac walked away from the van. "So where does he go? Where did he run off to?"

"Is he inside the perimeter still?" Wire wondered.

There was a five-block perimeter, squad cars everywhere. The doors to the mall were locked while each store was searched. Officers were searching other vehicles and interviewing bystanders, showing the picture of Drake Johnson.

The Langley Park police chief approached. "Agent McRyan, we've got a perimeter set. We have police from all nearby jurisdictions and the Maryland State Police. It's tight as can be. We're letting nothing move. People have been ordered to stay in their houses. Everyone is frozen in stores here at the mall."

"Thanks, Chief. My only question is, how quickly did you set that perimeter?"

The chief grimaced as they walked around to the front of the mall, "From the time we knew this was the place, it took a few minutes to get it tight, to get everyone in here."

Mac nodded and understood, already thinking they might have missed their shot. They were a few minutes behind the whole way. If only they could have kept him on the interstate. "What do you think?" he asked Wire, who was looking past him.

"I think he got out. How about you?"

"He could be hunkered down in one of these houses around here," Mac replied in a more hopeful tone. "It's the middle of the day, people off at work, he gets inside and hides until we clear."

"Maybe," she replied as she walked past him. He turned to see her approaching a police officer fifty feet away talking to a young boy, perhaps thirteen or fourteen years old.

Mac turned to look for the Langley Park police chief, "Chief, it's possible he's one, hunkered down in a house around here, or two, he slipped through or out before the perimeter was set. So if he were to get away from here, what? Taxi? Bus? Steal a car or truck?"

"Those would be the likely options."

"Let's start checking those."

"Mac!" Wire yelled. He turned to see her still talking to the police officer and a kid in front of a video game store. "You need to hear this."

Mac jogged over.

Wire said to the kid, "Tell Agent McRyan what you told me."

"Sir, I was inside the store, looking at games. When I came out, my new black mountain bike was gone."

The Reaper pedaled fast but calmly along the wooded path, having beaten the road blocks by maybe thirty seconds to a minute before they encircled the neighborhood around the mall. Even in the distance now he could hear more and more sirens and media choppers hovering overhead. If they looked down, they would not have seen him, the path running underneath the canopy of large trees blowing lightly in the breeze. The sound of the sirens started to fade behind him the farther he pedaled.

He breathed a little easier.

6:48 P.M.

Mac leaned against the Suburban, his aviator sunglasses softening the glare of the bright July sun as it slowly meandered towards the western horizon. The five-block perimeter remained tight and the house-to-house search continued, though at this point nearly complete. Two police helicopters continued to hover overhead, with more television helicopters hovering farther in the distance. Thankfully, with such a large perimeter, the media was held back. Mac said he'd handle the news conference; he didn't agree to media updates. To the extent there would be any further updates, they would be handled by Galloway.

They couldn't find Johnson.

Wire approached with two bottles of water, handing one to Mac. He opened it and took a long sip, downing half the contents along with four Ibuprofen gel capsules.

"I'd say he got through," Dara said matter of factly as she took a position to Mac's right, leaning against the truck.

Mac nodded, kicking at some tar with his left shoe, "Man, do you think he really pedaled his way out of here?"

"It's the only conveyance missing."

"Conveyance?"

"I'm trying to use one word to describe all modes of transportation with which he could have escaped."

"Well, now you used more words than if you'd have just said cars, trucks, motorcycles, taxis, buses and apparently, mountain bikes."

The kid's bike had not been found and nobody fitting the description had been seen by a witness or appeared on surveillance video riding away. It was as if the guy disappeared into the ether.

"We just needed another thirty seconds on that phone, maybe a minute and we'd have had him. We just couldn't tighten the circle quickly enough."

"I can't believe you kept him on as long as you did. You had him on over four minutes. You played him as well as you possibly could have."

"Maybe," Mac answered but then looked up at one of the helicopters, drifting to the west. "One of the by-products of having played him like that is he's pissed, really pissed. So pissed, in fact, that he ..."

Dara shook her head, "If he has another target, Mac, he's not going to hit tonight. He's going to run and hide."

"We don't know that, Dara."

"The heat is too much tonight. Self-preservation says he runs and hides."

"Fine, even if he does hide tonight, he's not going to hide long. He's going to hit soon. He has to."

"Because we're closing in."

"Right. He can't hold on but a few more days, if that, at least around here," Mac answered, waving to the area. "His picture is everywhere, so unless he goes to hide in a cave, someone eventually is going to see him. So if he's going to hit one more time, if he has one last target, he won't wait long." Then his look brightened just a bit, "Although, one thing does occur to me."

"What's that?"

"His target must be in the DC area. Otherwise ..."

"Why still be around here?" Wire finished his thought. "Who, though?"

"We gotta figure out where that picture came from. We should head back."

"Assuming your theory is correct that the picture taker is the last one left."

"It's all we have to go on."

As Mac and Wire were getting into the Suburban, the Langley Park police chief approached. "Agent McRyan, we've got a house break-in and car missing over in Takoma Park, the next city over to the west. There is a mountain bike sitting where the car used to be. It's the kind missing from here."

It took five minutes for the police convoy to make it over to Takoma Park and a two-story white house with a two-car garage. The Takoma Park police chief, a barrel-chested mid-fifties man chewing a toothpick, named Bird, greeted them at the end of the driveway. Quick introductions were made and Chief Bird led them up the driveway.

"As best we can tell, he got into the house around back," Bird suggested, walking them to the back door. "You see the scraping around the latch bolt and door plate, he used something to jimmie it open. We have some metal shavings."

Mac kneeled down and looked at the doorplate. "Like he broke it open with a knife perhaps?"

"Like our knife," Dara suggested. "So what happened next, Chief?"

"Homeowner says there are car keys that hang on the wall, just underneath the cabinet here in the kitchen," Bird reported, pointing to five small plastic hooks mounted on a rust-stained board. "One set was for an older black Toyota Camry, that as you look out to the left stall of the garage, you'll see is no longer there."

"And in its place is a shiny brand-new black mountain bike," Dara said.

"Any idea how long the car has been gone?" Mac asked.

"Homeowner was gone all day working so there is no way of knowing. The car could have been gone an hour or four hours. We've done a quick canvas and nobody remembers seeing the car leave or any activity around the house."

"The owners didn't miss the car?" Dara asked.

Chief Bird shook his head, "The Camry belongs to their college-age daughter who is on a summer trip to Europe. It hasn't been started or driven in weeks."

"It would take what, fifteen, maybe twenty minutes to bike to here from Langley Park?" Mac asked Bird.

"Bout that if he's moving at a good clip. Maybe a little quicker if he comes direct. My guess is that your boy went riding around a bit to find a place. This house has good cover, lots of mature trees, tall shrubs and a garage hidden around the back of the house. He could break in, even in broad daylight, and slink away if he knew what he was doing."

"When it comes to slinking around, he knows," Wire retorted bitterly.

"Let's go, Dara," Mac decided. "He's gone."

31

"KEEP THE FAITH."

At 9:48 P.M., Sally opened the back door, turned off the security system and let the Secret Service agents into the townhouse. While two agents searched the house, a third agent waited with Sally while she dropped her purse and briefcase on the center island and started looking at her options in the wine fridge. She was in the mood for a red tonight, maybe a Merlot or a Cabernet. A bottle of Markham was drawing her particular attention.

"All clear, Ms. Kennedy," the tall and lanky lead agent reported. "Please set your alarm. We'll be in our cars watching in the front and back and we'll take you into the White House tomorrow."

"Is this really all necessary?" Sally asked for what must have been the sixth time. After his chat with the Reaper, Mac's first call was to Judge Dixon, and ten minutes later, two Secret Service agents were at her office door and they'd been with her since. Two more were added to the detail once she left the White House. Mac later explained why but she still thought it overkill.

"We're here by orders of the president and Judge Dixon,

ma'am, so until they tell us otherwise, we'll be on the job. There's a dangerous man out there killing women. We are not going to let one of them be you."

If nothing else, Sally felt very safe as she locked the door, poured herself a glass of the Markham and went upstairs to the bedroom. As she hung up her suit in the spacious walk-in closet Mac built for her, she heard her phone beep the sound of a slap shot, which meant she had a text from Mac. She picked up the phone and the text said: Home in one.

Mac had a long and eventful day and had slept perhaps two hours in the last forty-eight hours, and he was still hurting from the confrontation with the Reaper. She checked the Ibuprofen bottle in the kitchen in the morning and it was nearly empty. While popping Ibuprofen was far better than getting hooked on painkillers, that much anti-inflammatory medication in that short a period of time wasn't good for you. Mac didn't know she was texting back and forth with Dara, who was keeping watch. Wire said he was holding up throughout the day but that the wall couldn't be far away.

Sally shook her head.

She knew how fruitless it would be to ask him to dial it back. He wouldn't listen; stubborn might as well have been his middle name. Easing up was something the man simply wouldn't, and in many ways couldn't, do. His wiring wouldn't allow it, especially at this point in the case. She was surprised he was actually coming home.

Well, if he was, she didn't want the night to go to waste. He needed a little therapy and she had the perfect thing in mind.

She opened one of her built-in drawers and starting pulling out the candles.

Mac nodded to the two Secret Service agents parked in the alley behind the townhouse, appreciating their presence along with the two in front. While he was home, Sally would be plenty safe. However, after the call with the Reaper and the less than veiled threat about people he loved, he told the Judge he didn't want her going anywhere without protection. "Judge, you got me into this case. If something happens to Sally ..."

"She'll have protection in five minutes," the Judge answered and the man was as good as his word.

Mac pushed inside the back door into the kitchen, locked it and reset the alarm system. He turned to see a single red candle burning on the center island, a glass of wine and a note sitting next to it. While sipping the wine, he read the note and smiled. It was a handwritten spa pass.

He walked up to the second floor and pushed open the door to the bedroom to find Sally lying facing him in a little red teddy that covered barely anything, a glass of wine in her hand, candles lit all over the bedroom. As he walked in, she slipped off the bed, walked over and kissed him, at first lightly, then softly and deeply.

"Hi," he said, wrapping his right arm around her, feeling the silk of the teddy in his hands.

"Hi back," she answered, pecking his lips one more time, breathing in the smell of the wine on his breath. "I have it on good authority you've had a very long day."

Mac exhaled, a tired exhale, "I have."

"Then let me take care of you. For three years, when I've had a long or bad day, you've pampered me, rubbed my back, my feet, my temples, whatever I've needed. For once, it's your turn. Get undressed, lay down on the bed and let me give you a massage," she said in a whisper, kissing him lightly again. "You can tell me about your day."

Mac did as ordered and for the next half hour, Sally worked his shoulders, arms, back and legs with her hands, working out the knots and the tenseness in his muscles.

They talked about the case and how they just missed Johnson. "I swear, Sally, we missed him by a minute at most, probably less. We were literally that close." Mac described how Johnson eluded them on a mountain bike while she rubbed his legs.

"So what's your next move?"

Mac sighed, "Figuring out who took that picture."

"You know, that could have just as easily been someone at the party who has nothing to do with this."

"Yeah, that's possible, but I just don't think so. He'd be gone otherwise, not cruising around the Washington, DC, area, calling me because I got under his skin. If he was done, I think he'd be long gone. He's not. Drake Johnson is still hanging around for a reason. We have to find that reason."

"I assume until you do, I'm going to have the Secret Service tailing my every move."

"Yes. And babe, that is nonnegotiable."

"Okay," Sally answered quietly. She knew the tone and there would be no point arguing with him about it. She changed back to the photo, "Any luck on that picture?"

"Not yet. Galloway has people all over that problem, going through the computers, cameras, pictures, everything back at Randall's and at Danica Brunner's. If it's there, we'll find it eventually."

"If you find her? Then what?"

"We will sit and wait for him to come."

"You think he's coming for whoever took the photo?"

"I don't know if I think so or I hope so, or both. He's

come this far. If there is one person left to punish, he's going to do it, he's going to go for it. For once, I'm hoping I get the call in the middle of the night."

"Perish the thought," Sally replied, working the area around his shoulder blades.

"I'm serious, though. He can't hold out long. He'll be looking to move quick, any minute. In some ways, I feel guilty lying here in your hands. I should be up doing something."

"No," Sally stopped rubbing and rolled him over. "You can't keep going nonstop, day after day, without rest. You're less than a week from a concussion, you have a broken wrist and you barely sleep as it is. You're exhausted, beat-up and ..." she caught herself, her eyes welling up.

"What? I'm what?"

"Vulnerable. Weak."

"I'm not weak and I'm not vulnerable."

"You are ..."

"No I'm not. I'm maybe not at my best," he answered with a smile, holding up his casted left arm, "but I'm good enough to do what I'm doing, babe. Keep the faith. I'm fine."

Sally laughed, but was still worried, "You better be."

"Now you sound like my mom."

"Ew, don't kill the mood."

"Sorry," Mac answered laughing, back to relaxing, a light laugh.

"Roll back over," Sally instructed. "I'll keep rubbing your back."

After another ten minutes, Sally eased up, and started scratching his back lightly, "My hands are starting to wear out."

Mac rolled onto his back and smiled up at Sally, "Best I've felt in a long time," he said, looking up at Sally's worried face. "Keep the faith, babe. This will be over soon." He drew her down to him and kissed her, a long day about to come to a good end.

He even got nearly six hours of sleep, the phone ringing at 6:06 A.M. It was Galloway. "We think we know who took the picture."

"And?"

"Well, things could be a little tricky."

Mac sighed, "Well why wouldn't they."

32

"CHRYSLER TOWN AND COUNTRY MINIVAN, VIRGINIA PLATES."

WASHINGTON, DC - 7:00 A.M.

"Today could be interesting," Wire suggested as Mac maneuvered his way through early Wednesday morning rush hour in DC, making his way to the Hoover Building. The news radio station was reporting nonstop on the approaching hurricane. "Tonight as well."

"Do you mean the storm or Richardson?"

Wire cackled, "In the end, what's the difference. Either one has the potential to create a huge mess."

To the southeast, the heavy clouds of Hurricane Francesca were rolling in. By noon the heavy rain would start, with the full thrust of the storm to arrive in the evening. While the eye of the storm would make landfall two hundred miles to the south in southern Virginia, it would nevertheless be a rough night in DC, the category two storm sure to pack a good wallop.

"Have you ever been through one?" Wire asked.

"A hurricane?"

"Yeah."

"No," Mac answered. "In Minnesota, we have severe

thunderstorms and, on occasion, tornados, although those rarely hit in the inner city. The damage can be pretty severe, although usually in much smaller areas and the storms only last for a few hours."

"Is your townhouse ready for the storm?"

"As ready as can be, I guess," Mac answered. "If I'm not around tonight, Sally's going to ride it out at the White House, which I don't mind with Johnson still floating around out there."

Five minutes later, Mac pulled the X5 in under the Hoover Building and in another five they were admitted to Director Mitchell's office to find the director along with Galloway, Agents Keller, Reilly and Grace Delmonico. Mac and Wire had been on the phone with Grace when Johnson triggered the explosion. She'd taken the whole thing in.

"Grace," Mac said quietly, going right to Delmonico, putting his hands on her shoulders, "I'm so sorry about Aubry."

"Thanks."

"Are you up for getting back in the game?" he asked, looking her in the eyes, getting a quick assessment. The eyes were sad but determined.

"I need to do something. Otherwise I just sit around thinking about it and Gesch would be pissed at me for that, so I'm in."

"Good. We need you," Mac answered, pulling away and letting Wire go in for a quick hug of her own.

Mac looked to Keller who was holding up the photo. "So tell me, how did you connect the photo to Richardson?"

"Our picture of death is a cell phone picture."

Mac never gave it much thought, but when they'd found the photo on Randall's computer, it struck him that the picture was just a bit grainy, more so than the other photos on the computer. Not enough that he said anything about it, but enough that he'd briefly noticed it. Since they'd been able to immediately identify all of the victims, Mac never gave it another thought, never said a word about it to anyone. The thought simply drifted from his mind.

However, the grainy nature of the picture registered with Keller.

"It's been about seven or eight years that we've had the ability to take pictures with cell phones," Special Agent Keller stated. "And as Galloway stated when he called, the taker of the picture was Mychal Richardson."

When the hunt for the taker of the photo started, it was thought the picture was most likely from a woman, so when the name Mychal Richardson showed up in a couple of e-mails and correspondence for Rebecca Randall, it was initially ignored, as it was assumed Mychal was a unique way to spell the name Michael. It was only later in the night when a member of Keller's crew, noticing another unrelated picture in Randall's e-mail from Mychal Richardson, said: "I know we think it's a woman. I knew a woman named Mychal in college."

"We still didn't find the picture or reference to it anywhere in Randall's e-mail, so we took a look at her cell phone records. This picture was sent from Richardson's cell phone to Randall's on that August 17th, almost immediately after the photo was taken. We found it going through Randall's old cell phone records. Again, we didn't necessarily give those a deep look because …"

"We found the picture and had the connection," Mac answered nodding, looking at the cell phone records, shaking his head. It was always the little things that tripped you up. "We didn't need to go back further."

"Right," Keller answered. "In any event, Richardson sent

Rebecca Randall this picture, it's right there in the cell phone record. Later, Randall uploaded the picture onto her computer."

"And we're sure it's Mychal Richardson, this Mychal Richardson?" Wire asked, looking at a picture of an attractive blond, an attractive blond that was on television frequently.

"Unfortunately, yes," Director Mitchell replied.

Mychal Richardson was the daughter of United States Senator Jesse Richardson. Senator Richardson was the Senate minority leader. Now, Mac and Wire, involved in the investigation at the behest of the White House, were about to implicate the daughter of the minority leader in a seven-year-old vehicular homicide.

"What is the connection of Richardson and Randall?"

"Richardson and Randall went to college together. Danica Brunner, who is the daughter of a DC lobbyist, was a childhood friend of Richardson, although from what we can tell those two haven't been in significant contact for a number of years. However, guess what?"

"They have been recently," Mac suggested.

"Quite a bit, in fact, and as recently as yesterday, in fact, in the early evening," Keller replied, holding up a list of cell phone calls.

"You don't say," Wire mused.

Keller provided a knowing smile, "After what appears to have been at best sporadic contact the last seven years, there have been no less than ten calls in the last month."

"Ten?" Wire asked, surprised.

"Ten."

"Where do we find Richardson?" Mac asked.

"Big law firm, K Street," the director answered.

"Did Mychal Richardson or her family own a silver Dodge or Chrysler minivan at the time that Rena Johnson was killed?" Mac asked and cringed in anticipation of the response.

Keller held up another record with a wicked smile, "Chrysler Town and Country minivan, Virginia plates. Oh, and did I mention this little body repair bill three days later for it?"

"Oh boy," Mac exhaled as he stood up and walked to the window. The heavy clouds of the hurricane were rolling in and the heavy rain and winds of the storm wouldn't be far behind. It served as a good metaphor of what was to come.

Baltimore, Maryland. 9:30 A.M.

Drake Johnson wore an Afro-like wig and was dressed in cargo shorts, a navy blue golf shirt along with sandals and a Yankees baseball cap with wraparound sunglasses, perfect for the humid and sunny day now at hand.

After dark, he took the plates off the black Camry he'd stolen and replaced them with a set he lifted from another vehicle parked in a lot behind a bar south of DC. That maneuver got him back to his camping area safely. He monitored the computer and television in his camper overnight as well as the police band and there was nothing, no reported sightings, simply a Be-On-The-Lookout (BOLO) for a black Toyota Camry with the plates he'd dumped. But even with the switched plates he couldn't keep the Camry, too risky in the long run. At this point, the FBI and other law enforcement officers would be looking for any reason, or maybe no reason, to pull over a black Camry in the vicinity of Washington, DC. So at the crack of dawn, he drove into Baltimore and dumped the Camry in a tough part of West Baltimore. Now, he simply needed a cab ride to pick up the vehicle he would finish things off with.

He still had his plan, but he had no choice, he had to finish it now.

McRyan played him and now he could feel the noose tightening.

Tonight was the final act.

She would be the last act of his little play.

When it was over, it would be talked about for a long time.

He'd prepared for this last step long ago. She was actually the first he followed to get a feel for the hunt and she was making it easy for him, putting herself in such a vulnerable position. He was close to taking her when he realized she couldn't be the first. If she went first the storm would have been massive from the start. He'd have never had the room to maneuver to do all that was to be done. So he decided she would be the last.

From time to time over the last several months he'd checked back in on her to make sure that the pattern remained the same, that she was continuing to engage in her reckless behavior and that she was continuing it with the same prominent man, on the same night of the week and in the same place.

She didn't fail him.

It would be just him and her.

Her lover's young, beautiful wife had no idea what he was up to.

Soon the wife and everyone else would know.

There may be a hurricane coming, but that would be nothing compared to the firestorm that was coming.

Dust bin of history?
Zero impact?
Unbalanced?
Nut bar?
We'll see, Mac McRyan, he thought.
We'll see.

33

"DON'T PISS ON MY LEG AND TELL ME IT'S RAINING."

The legendary O'Bannon Gardiner law firm with its 1,500 attorneys strong in ten offices in the United States and twenty worldwide was located on K Street. Their building was the standard five-story law firm like building along that famous avenue of power legal and lobbying firms. However, when Mychal Richardson was called to meet with Special Agents McRyan and Wire, it was in a private windowless meeting room in the basement, away from any other human. If she was guilty of what Mac thought she was, he'd have loved nothing more than to go after her upstairs in a windowed conference room for everyone and their brother to see. Word of that encounter would quickly make its way outside of the walls of the firm and undoubtedly into the media where Drake Johnson would learn they were onto his next, and most likely last, target.

Mychal Richardson, daughter of the great senator of Georgia, Jesse Richardson, was thirty years old, two to three years the senior of the other victims, was a fifth-year lawyer at the firm, a senior associate dedicating her legal talents to issues of particular importance to the Richardson Political

Brand. She was a frequent guest and talking head on the cable networks discussing political issues important to her generation, particularly how people her age were not engaging in the greed and carelessness of older generations. She talked often of the importance of taking responsibility for your actions, being a good citizen and not engaging in reckless behavior.

The irony was not lost on Mac.

The door opened, and the statuesque blond southern belle strolled into the room in her perfect black power business suit and white V-neck button-up blouse leaving just a hint of cleavage. Richardson was followed by two other men in dark business suits and earbuds, high-priced security.

Mac and Wire shared a quick look while the men did a very quick sweep of the room before departing, leaving Richardson alone with Mac, Wire and Grace Delmonico.

Wire made the quick introductions and finished with: "Thanks for coming down."

"Thanks for letting me come down," Richardson answered casually, unbothered. "It's never a good thing when the FBI comes to visit you at work. No offense, but that's especially the case if it's you two right now." She was unfazed by being in the room. Foreigner's *Cold as Ice* flashed through Mac's mind.

"So I presume you know why we're here?" Wire asked pleasantly, playing the role of good cop.

"I have no idea," Richardson answered.

"Really?" Mac answered with an acerbic snort and bad cop tone. Her face betrayed no knowledge but Mac bored in on her eyes. He could read her eyes. She knew exactly why she was in the room. "That's how you want to play this?"

"Play what?"

"Your role in the vehicular homicide of Rena Johnson

nearly seven years ago," Mac answered sternly, while leaning back in his chair, trying to convey the same level of confidence as Richardson. "You know, you might want to have your lawyer present to hear this."

"Am I under arrest?"

"Not yet," Delmonico answered flatly, taking notes, not looking up.

Richardson laughed. "One, I'm a lawyer, and two, I haven't seen anything yet that I need to be the least bit worried about."

"What?" Mac asked. "You haven't heard the old bromide the lawyer who represents himself has an idiot for a client?"

"Sure," Richardson answered. "But I'm not an average lawyer. I was a prosecutor for two years before I moved to O'Bannon. This isn't my first rodeo."

"Fine," Wire said evenly and then slid the picture from Randall in front of Mychal Richardson, "You took this picture."

Richardson casually took the picture into her hands and scanned it for a moment and shrugged. "It doesn't look familiar."

"As you can see from the date, it was taken nearly seven years ago, matter of fact, tomorrow it would be exactly seven years ago. *And you took it,*" Mac stated, taking the cell phone record from Delmonico and sliding it in front of Richardson. "You took the picture and then e-mailed it from your phone to Danica Brunner and Rebecca Randall on that same night."

Richardson took another look at the picture, acting calm, "Okay. It looks vaguely familiar. I think we were all at a party."

"So you remember taking the picture then?" Mac asked.

"Possibly," Richardson answered. "But look, rather than

go through some long question and answer session here, why don't you just get to it, Agent McRyan. You think I was responsible for something, show me."

Mac didn't hesitate, reaching inside his backpack, "On the night of August 17th, seven years ago, you took this picture," he stated. "Later that night, Rena Johnson," Mac pointed to Johnson in the picture, "was killed. She wandered away from a rave party at an abandoned farm outside of Auburn, New York, and was walking along the shoulder of a nearby county road. She was hit by a vehicle traveling at a rapid speed, sent flying and landed at the bottom of a deep ditch. Rena was found the next morning, dead from massive internal injuries and bleeding. She'd taken the brunt of the impact from the vehicle in the area of her abdomen, although she had two badly broken legs among other assorted injuries. Sadly, despite the exceedingly violent impact from the vehicle, she didn't die right away. In fact, it appears she lived for some time after the accident. She could have perhaps been saved with immediate medical attention. Yet sadly, nobody stopped, nobody checked on her and nobody called 911."

"The police investigating the case found paint from the vehicle on Rena Johnson's body," Wire noted, sliding a page of the forensic report in front of Richardson. "The paint was silver and was matched to paint used on Dodge and Chrysler minivans and SUVs."

Mac sipped from his coffee, "Interestingly enough, at the time of the accident, your family owned a silver Dodge Town and Country minivan. In fact, I believe it to be the van in this picture that all of these women are standing in front of."

Wire jumped back in, sliding a set of papers in front of Richardson like exhibits at a trial, "These are bills for the repair of your family's silver minivan dated August 20th, three days later, at a body shop in McLean, Virginia."

"Drake Johnson, the killer people know as the Reaper? His sister ... was Rena Johnson. He's killed, or tried to kill, all of the other women in this picture. The only woman he hasn't tried to kill yet—*is you*," Mac stated, looking Richardson in the eye. Her face twitched slightly but remained otherwise placid. Too placid, he thought; a poker player placid. She was treating it like a game.

Mac continued.

"So here's what I think happened. I think all of you girls went to that party that night. Rena wandered off, her body full of booze and drugs. The cops were coming and there was underage drinking and drugs at the party. The daughters of Jesse Richardson, William Donahue and Amherst Brunner couldn't be caught at such a party, so you guys do the natural thing, you bail. You, or maybe Rebecca Randall, her friend from Auburn, might have even quick looked for Rena. But after all, she was from Auburn, she'd find her way home, so you guys get in the van and bolt. As you're leaving, maybe you see the approaching lights of the police cars from Auburn. So you turn away from the approaching police and go south on Country 5 in the opposite direction of Auburn. Mychal, you're driving the van, it's your van. You came flying around that corner on the county road and there she was."

"No time to react," Wire suggested quietly.

"And bam, before you could veer away, you hit Rena, who was walking along the shoulder of the road. Now, at that point, you certainly were in some trouble, but a woman's life was hanging in the balance. You all had cell phones, after all, you took this picture with it. You could have dialed 911, yet ... nobody ... called."

"You could have called. Rena Johnson was certainly at fault," Delmonico suggested.

"Contributory fault," Mac added. "I mean, in a civil suit, she'd have never recovered a dime."

"But you didn't stop, you kept right on going," Wire added.

"And in doing that, that makes it a vehicular homicide," Mac finished.

Richardson smiled, "That's it?"

In that moment, looking in her eyes, her cold calculating lifeless eyes, he realized he was dealing with another sociopath.

"That's all you have."

"For now," Mac replied and in his heart knew where this was heading. She wasn't going to back down. "It's an interesting story, but as for the van, I hit a deer."

"A deer?" Wire asked.

"Oh yes. I remember this now."

"Oh do you?" Mac asked derisively. "Shocking how it all comes back to you now."

"Mock me all you want, Special Agent McRyan. I was driving home from New York and hit a deer on the way home, somewhere in Pennsylvania. So I took it to Sorenson's because they were good friends of our family and did the work on all of our cars. Bobby Sorenson worked on the van. I'm sure he'll remember that I hit a deer."

"Did you ever report hitting the deer to the police?"

"No. Wasn't aware something like that had to be reported."

"How about reporting it to your insurance?" Wire asked. "Lots of people do that."

"I don't know if we did," Richardson answered. "I don't know if I did, or my dad did or Wallace did."

"Wallace?" Delmonico asked.

"Wallace Llewellyn," Richardson replied. "He's our family lawyer."

Mac snorted. He'd heard Llewellyn's name before in passing from Sally. Wallace Llewellyn was a classic Washington fixer, a consigliere for the Richardson family.

"Where did that happen? Hitting the deer," Mac asked.

"I don't recall exactly, but I was somewhere in the middle of Pennsylvania. It was at night, it was dark. The deer jumped out of the woods and I hit it in the hind end. If I remember correctly, the deer hobbled into the woods. I jumped out, checked the front end of the van, assessed the damage and remember thinking it was good enough to drive home. So I did."

"Convenient story," Wire suggested.

"More plausible than yours," Richardson answered easily, as if batting away a mosquito. "So here's what you have," she suggested coolly, going into defense lawyer mode. "You have no physical evidence of me at the scene. The van you allege me to have had? We got rid of it long ago. As for the repair, as I told my dad and our people who fixed it, I hit a deer. Any witness you might have had to this accident if what you say happened, happened? They're all dead. You have as weak a circumstantial case as possible and my actual lawyers, the best defense lawyers money can buy, against some well-meaning county prosecutor in upstate New York? Give me a break."

"And you're not the least bit concerned about Drake Johnson, the Reaper, coming after you?"

"I'd suggest to you, Special Agent Wire, that if he's coming after me, well, you better do your best to stop him. You wouldn't want him to kill someone who's innocent now, would you? You have enough blood on your hands already."

Mac knew coming in she'd either roll over and confess or tell them to fuck off. She'd selected door number two. Ice ran through Mychal Richardson's veins. She'd driven the van, of this Mac was now completely certain, and she knew he knew. But she was unbothered because she felt untouchable. Mychal had thoroughly analyzed the case, understood the law and had a complete understanding of the facts and circumstances, including the fact that everyone who could have fingered her for the crime, for even being at the scene, was now dead.

Mac knew he was beat, at least for now.

But he was unbowed. He leaned forward and stared Richardson down.

It was time to try to take her down a peg.

"Whether I can prove it right now or not, Ms. Richardson, here's what *I know*. You killed Rena Johnson. You know it and I know it. Those two security mopes standing outside the door watching you are proof enough of that."

"I'm the daughter of a senator who is regularly on television and has some controversial views. I'm always concerned about my safety."

"Don't piss on my leg and tell me it's raining," Mac mocked. "You are the daughter of one of the nation's most prominent senators, and seven years ago you used that. You used that status to bully these other girls into covering this up when most of them at age twenty or twenty-one didn't know better. They were scared, vulnerable and suddenly found themselves in a situation where their life could be ruined. They probably all reached for their cell phones thinking we have to do the right thing, but not you. Just like you have about the current circumstances, you quickly and coldly evaluated that situation and decided you could escape without any damage to your name. Maybe Hannah

Donahue and Danica Brunner helped you, given their political backgrounds, but you threatened to bury anyone if they came forward. You are a privileged, spoiled manipulator, a hypocrite to all your bromides about personal accountability. You are nothing more than a murderer, and whether I can prove it right now or not, you and I both know, *that's, what, you, are.*"

Richardson smiled and laughed, "Special Agent McRyan, I'm not under arrest am I." It was a statement.

"No," Mac answered. "You are free to go."

Mychal Richardson pushed herself up from the table and strolled to the door.

"I would be careful if I were you, though. Drake Johnson's looking to kill you. I'd be happy to protect you, but I only protect people who play ball, who tell the truth."

Richardson smiled and shook her head, "You're wasting your time. I have nothing to be afraid of."

"Is that what you said to Danica Brunner last night when you talked to her? What, you think your little rent-a-cops with nine millimeters on their belts can protect you from an extremely motivated killer? You think they can protect you from a man who has killed six other women? A man who killed six men, six law enforcement officers the other night?" It was Mac's turn to laugh. "Good luck."

"I appreciate your *overwhelming* concern for my well-being," Richardson needled.

"Oh, and there's one more thing," Mac stated, leaning back in his chair, casually twirling his pen.

"What's that?" Richardson asked back, one hand on the doorknob, ready to leave.

"You should ask around about us. Ask Donald Wellesley Jr., you know him, don't you?"

"I know he's in jail."

"And we're the ones who put him there."

"What's your point?"

"What Donald Jr. would tell you is that I'm not someone you want digging around in your shit, because if there is dirt to find, I will find it and when I do, you'll have *really* wished you played ball with us today."

Richardson maintained her poker face although her cocky smile dissipated ever so slightly. "Are you finished?"

"For now."

"Well, I'll take your little cautionary tale under advisement, Special Agent McRyan," Richardson retorted, the cockiness back. If she was going to flinch, she wasn't going to let him see it. She turned and left the room, one security man walking in front of her and another one tailing her.

Wire shook her head. "She was the driver, wasn't she?"

"No doubt in my mind, and the sad thing is ..."

"She isn't the least bit bothered by it because everyone who could have testified to that ..."

"Is dead," Mac finished, tossing his empty Starbucks off the wall and into the garbage can. "Nobody can place her at the scene."

"So what are we going to do?" Dara asked.

"As much as it galls me, we're going to do our job, and watch her. Drake Johnson is going to go for her and we need to be there when he does. And we're going to do one other thing."

"What?"

"We're going to take a crack, *a real crack*, at the Rena Johnson case. We know Mychal Richardson owned the van. We know she was there. We know she did it. We just have to find a way to prove it."

Drake Johnson watched through the sheets of rain as the black Suburban pulled out of the parking garage beneath O'Bannon Gardiner, recognizing the FBI agent behind the wheel, one of Gesch's men. No doubt McRyan and Wire were in the backseats behind the dark tinted windows.

The FBI figured out the missing part of the picture—Mychal Richardson.

He wasn't surprised.

It was only a matter of time before McRyan and Wire realized there was one person missing.

And Richardson knew he was after her. She knew he was out here and coming for her. The security detail on her every minute of the day told him that. It was good security, ex-military certainly, but they were not perfect.

There was a hole in her protection.

What her security detail didn't know, what McRyan didn't know, was that tonight, regardless of the protection she had, she was her most vulnerable.

The high-priced, high-end security would not stop him.

The fact that the FBI would be watching in great force would not stop him.

Mychal Richardson was the final piece, the last one that needed to be punished, the one who needed to be punished the most.

Given his plan, the conditions for his strike, weather or otherwise, couldn't be more perfect.

34

"BOOTY CALL."

"Keller, what's your status?" Mac asked, peering at the laptop. Wire, Delmonico, Galloway and Director Mitchell hovered nearby. He had three units in panel vans and another black SUV in the area.

"Agent McRyan, I'm now a block and a half south of the townhouse but have a good view of the front, even with this hurricane. Richardson is still inside and has been for a good hour now, since she got home a little after 7:00 P.M. Our units are now set in every direction and we have at least eight sets of eyes on the townhouse." Not to mention the tracking device on her Audi A6, a little maneuver Mac pulled while in the parking garage at O'Bannon Gardiner.

"And the rent-a-cops?"

"They are parked in front and behind and their strength has increased. There are now three two-man teams. They clear everywhere she goes. They took ten minutes to clear her townhouse and it has a high-end security system to boot. She's secure."

They'd since learned the private security was from Grogan Systems. "Grogan guys are former military, Mac.

They do a lot of government contracting," Wire stated knowingly. "I've run into them from time to time. They have a very good reputation. They're serious guys. Richardson isn't messing around and they won't either."

"Any sign of Johnson?" Mac asked back into the radio.

"No sign of our guy anywhere," Keller answered. "I have two other teams driving the immediate area, working a grid, nothing so far but. However, if he were going to move, he'd be waiting for dark."

"Copy that, Agent Keller."

"Mac, if she moves or we get a whiff of Johnson in the area, you'll be the first to know."

Mac, Wire and Delmonico manned the conference room at the DC Field Office, monitoring the radio and video feed of the evening surveillance. He absolutely hated being so far away from the action. However, their faces were too known to Drake Johnson to be in close proximity to anywhere Mychal Richardson was. "At this point, he's in my head as much as I'm in his. He can probably see me coming from a mile away," Mac sighed hours ago, particularly after having drawn him out the day before.

They would have to monitor from afar. If Johnson was spotted, then Mac and Wire would move. Richardson's townhouse wasn't but five minutes away.

"We should eat," Delmonico suggested.

"I got this," the director answered. A half hour later boxes of Chinese food arrived from down the street. "If there's better Chinese than Wong Zee's in DC, I don't know where," Director Mitchell stated, taking some Egg Foo Young and plopping it down onto a paper plate. This was a meal for a stakeout and Mitchell, deep down, was still a cop, an agent.

While digging into a box of sweet and sour chicken with

his chopsticks, Mac opened the copy of the file on the Rena Johnson case.

Giving the file a quick once–over, he immediately admonished himself for not having done this sooner. The case started moving so quickly and her case, seven years old, while viewed as a potential catalyst for the Reaper, was not viewed as integral to solving the case. It should have. Had he given the file a closer look, he couldn't help think he might have taken a closer look at Drake Johnson to begin with, instead of hearing he was dead and never giving it a second thought. Drake Johnson read this file. How could a brother, especially a brother who was a police detective, not want vengeance? If something like this happened to one of his three sisters, Mac could imagine he'd want to do something.

Rena Johnson was, from the looks of things, a kind, caring and *spiritual* person. The rosary beads in her hands were always with her. Even at the age of twenty-one she was very involved in her local church and in ministry at college and was scheduled to take a mission the following summer. According to her brother, as well as her parents, all interviewed the day after her death, they were very surprised she would have been at such a party, because she rarely drank and never took drugs. Yet she'd had a blood alcohol of .23 in her system, along with Ecstasy and marijuana. A mixture of chemicals that was likely very foreign to her. According to the notes of Detective Flynn up in Auburn, New York, Rena Johnson's parents said their daughter was not someone who partied or engaged in that kind of behavior. She typically frowned on people who did.

Mac thought back to the first time at a high school party he got so drunk on beer and shots that he couldn't think straight. He stumbled into his friend's backyard and passed out in the garden, lying between the cucumber plants and the raspberry bushes. There was compromising photographic evidence of his predicament that made its appearance every five years at high school reunion time.

The combination of drugs and alcohol had to have left Rena Johnson significantly impaired and she probably had no idea what she was doing. The investigators thought she made her way down a winding path through the woods that came out along County Road 5. It would have taken her, given her impaired condition, a good fifteen, maybe twenty minutes to walk or stumble from the farm down to the county road.

The file included an aerial photo of the area, photos of the path and where it emerged from the woods to County Road 5. Once she reached the end of the path, she should have turned left to walk back towards Auburn. Instead, she turned right and moved along on the narrow shoulder and walked around the sharp bend in the road, and just after she made it around the corner she was struck, propelled through the air and down into the deep ditch. The speed limit for the turn was thirty miles-per-hour but a crash investigator calculated the van took the corner speeding at least fifty miles-per-hour. The driver saw Rena, braked hard leaving skid marks, but it was after impact.

"You were the driver, Mychal," Mac mumbled, "I'd wager a big bet in Vegas on it."

"What?" Wire asked, looking up at him from her spicy chicken box.

"Nothing."

Rena Johnson being hit was an accident.

The coroner said Rena survived the impact for a while and may have been able to be saved with immediate medical attention, which was a 911 call away.

Instead, she was left behind. The coroner indicated that

she likely pulled herself into the fetal position and somehow managed to get her rosary beads into her hands.

"Why not call?" he moaned quietly, reading from the report.

There were two reasons not to call.

One reason was because the driver was impaired and couldn't afford or wouldn't afford to be caught in that situation.

So why not simply call it in anonymously?

Because of the second reason they couldn't call. Mac snorted, "You couldn't call because if she lived, she would have recognized who hit her. You couldn't afford that, could you, Mychal? It would be too big a hit to the family name. Better her life in total than inconveniencing yours," Mac bitched.

"Okay, enough, what are you mumbling about?" Dara stated, coming to sit down next to him.

"The investigative report on the night Rena Johnson was killed."

"And?"

"It makes me sick to my stomach," Mac answered. "She didn't need to die. She survived the impact. With quick medical attention, she could have survived. She could have been saved. All that was required was for someone, anyone, to do the right thing."

"Are you sympathizing with Drake Johnson?" Wire asked skeptically.

"We've been calling him a sociopath or a psychopath. I don't think he's those things. He's off the rails, he's snapped, but I don't know that he's those things."

"What is he then?"

"He's a vigilante, a junior Bruce Wayne out to avenge his sister's death."

"Except," Wire reminded, "Batman refused to kill the criminals. He was incorruptible."

"True."

"Would you do what he's doing?" Wire asked more seriously.

"Were this one of my sisters, or Sally, or you, and the police were unable to solve it and I thought I knew who was responsible, would I take action into my own hands?" Mac asked. "Yes, although not to *this* degree. I would hope I would not become a murderer, but I'm not walking in his shoes." He looked over to Wire. "I think I know what you'd do," he suggested, thinking to her beating the son of the vice president years ago when he revealed the name of her confidential source with the Giordano crime family in New Jersey. She beat him within an inch of his life. It cost her career in the bureau, at least at the time. "Do you ever regret it?"

"No," Wire answered, shaking her head. "I lose no sleep over it. He got what he deserved. My guy died a vicious death. Donald Jr. had to have plastic surgery to fix his face after I turned it into hamburger. He got off easy."

"It cost you," Mac suggested.

"Small price to pay," Wire answered dismissively. "I do probably owe the Judge into perpetuity, however."

"Did all these women get what they deserved?" Mac asked, holding up the now familiar picture of the women standing in front of the van. "Did this night mean they were fatally bound together?"

"I don't know," Dara answered, taking the picture from him. Quietly she murmured, shaking her head, "Did all of them really deserve this?"

"I'd love to know that answer," Mac replied. "And right now, there's only one person who can answer that question."

"Speaking of which," Delmonico yelled, "Richardson is on the move."

∼

"The house is clear, and secure, Ms. Richardson. We will wait inside with you?" the short security man asked.

"The house is clear?"

"It is."

"The dead bolts are solid?"

"They are, and all windows are secure."

"Then that will be all. You can wait on the street and you will be discreet and keep back from the townhouse," she directed.

"Ma'am, with the hurricane outside, visibility is a real issue. We need to stay close and, again, we should have someone inside. We'll stay out of the way, but we should be inside," the tall security man suggested.

"No!" Richardson barked her response. "You watch from the outside and you keep your distance. If I need anything I will call. Otherwise, I'll summon you in the morning. If I'm not up by 7:00 A.M., call."

"Yes, ma'am," they both sighed reluctantly, and left down the back steps and through the garage.

Richardson took out her phone and called, "The coast is clear. I'll be waiting for you upstairs. I have a little something *special* for you."

∼

"What's the address again?" Mac asked Keller, as he looked over a street map of Georgetown.

"So the townhouse is right here on Thirty-Third

between N and O Streets," Wire pointed, "not that far from your place, Mac, for what that's worth."

"Agent Keller, was anyone there to greet her?" Mac asked.

"Not as far as we can tell. It's tough to get too close in this area. Tight streets and alleys make it hard for us to get close without being spotted and it is hard to see in these conditions. The rain is coming down in sheets and the wind is blowing the branches of trees violently so visibility is extremely poor."

"What about her security detail?"

"They swept the place, exited and now they've moved back a good block with two units watching the front of the townhouse and the other is a street over on Thirty-Fourth watching the narrow rear alley, which are the only two ways to access the townhouse."

Mac looked to Wire and Director Mitchell, "So nobody is there to greet her. Security clears the place and leaves." Mac grabbed the radio again, "Keller, are there any lights on in the townhouse?"

"Negative."

"Any lighting at all?"

"Hold on."

"What the heck is going on?" Delmonico asked. "This makes no sense. Who goes out on a night like this?"

Keller came back, "Mac, Agent Reilly reports from his position that he can only see some dim, almost faint lighting flickering on the second floor in the back of the townhouse."

Mac looked to Wire and smiled. "You know what this has the feel of, don't you?"

"Oh yeah," Wire answered with broad grin and a laugh. "Booty call."

"For sure," Mac answered laughing and dropping himself into a chair.

After five minutes of laughter and joking, Director Mitchell asked: "Who owns the townhouse? Richardson?"

"Negative," Delmonico answered looking up from her laptop. "It's owned by Weiss Family Real Estate Holdings, Inc."

"Weiss Family Real Estate Holdings? Seriously?" Mac asked. "You know which family that is, don't you?"

"No, who?" Wire asked, but the director knew.

"The Weiss family, and in this town, that would be Ulysses Weiss."

"Ulysses Weiss? Ulysses Weiss the congressman?" Wire asked, shocked.

"The one and only," Mac answered.

"Mychal Richardson's booty call is with Congressman Weiss? No way," Wire couldn't believe it. "He wouldn't dare."

Fifteen minutes later they had their confirmation. Keller called in a plate number for a black Cadillac CTS sedan.

"Car belongs to the congressman, black Cadillac CTS sedan," Delmonico reported.

"You just can't make this shit up," Mac laughed, using one of his favorite phrases. The case took another unexpected twist. "*Un-be-lieve-a-ble*. She's got a murderer after her, private security all over the place, not to mention the FBI at a respectful perimeter, yet she's scheduling a booty call with a married congressman. Talk about chutzpah."

"He's married," Dara complained, disgusted by the whole affair. "I saw the *People* spread last month. His wife is gorgeous, *gorgeous*, the kids are adorable. I don't understand it."

"Oh, I do," Mac replied nonplussed.

"How? How can you, someone who was cheated on by

his ex-wife, someone who is as loyal a person as I've ever seen, possibly understand this?"

"Let me clarify. It's more like I understand the type."

"Which is what?"

"He's a hound, Dara, and once a hound, always a hound. I know men like the congressman. They love the institution of marriage, love their wives and kids, but they hate the day-to-day and they can't stay monogamous. If a hound has the option, he takes it. Congressman Weiss? Good looking, rich and powerful. He appears to be a hound. Mychal Richardson, despite the fact I find her to be an ice-cold bitch, is smokin' hot. These two are made for each other."

"I'd agree he's a dog, a dog whose head I'd like to bash in. That's what *I'd* like to do," Wire answered, arms crossed, defending Mrs. Weiss, a member of the sisterhood.

Mac looked over to his partner, who was clearly peeved at the shocking discovery of yet *another* unfaithful husband in the world. He grabbed the radio, "Keller, I assume the lights have remained dimmed?"

"Affirmative."

Mac looked at his watch, 9:48 P.M. "Settle in then, I suspect this could take a while."

"Copy that."

It took over four hours. "Mac, Cadillac is on the move," Keller reported.

"And Richardson?"

"She must still be inside. There is only one person in the Caddy."

"Stay on her, she may stay and ride out the storm," Mac directed and then yawned, a big yawn. It was after 2:00 A.M.

Wire sat curled up in a leather chair, nodding off, exhausted.

"You two go home," Delmonico suggested. "The night is

over. All they're doing at this point is sitting on her, waiting for her to awake from her sex-induced slumber. If anything happens we'll call."

Mac looked to Wire, "You want the spare bedroom?"

"Yes."

Fifteen minutes later, Mac's head hit the pillow.

He slept deeply, sinking into the soft, comfortable bed, loving the coolness of the house, the strong hum of the air conditioner keeping out the outside noise. He didn't react at the first ring, or even the second, but the ringtone eventually lifted him out of his slumber.

The alarm clock showed it was 7:30 A.M. The display on his phone told him the call was from Delmonico, "Gracie, what's up?"

"Mac, we've got a problem, a great big problem."

"What?"

"Mychal Richardson is missing."

35

"HOW THE HELL DO YOU THINK IT IS WE FOUND YOU?"

At 7:45 A.M., Mac and Wire, gumball flashing, rapidly approached the townhouse on Thirty-Third to find multiple Washington PD patrol units, three crews of bureau agents and the three from Grogan Security. A patrol officer let the X5 through and Mac pulled up behind Keller's black surveillance van. As Mac stepped out of the SUV, he looked back to see media trucks approaching.

Keller saw Mac and Wire arrive and stepped down off the front steps and jogged over.

"What the hell happened?" Mac asked as he took in the chaos surrounding the scene.

"Well," Keller scratched his head, and grimaced, "what can I say, she's gone."

"How?"

"Honestly, we haven't figured that out yet."

"What have we figured out?"

"Reilly and I are sitting down the street to the south, across N Street but right on the corner, we have a decent view of the front door, especially once the storm started easing around 3:00 A.M. Anyway, a few minutes after 7:00

A.M., two of the guys from Grogan went to the front door. One agent is knocking on the door and the other is on the phone. As we watched, the pounding got more frantic and the other guy on the phone is clearly agitated, gesticulating with his arms. Then they kicked in the front door and we knew there was a serious problem. So we pulled across N Street and got a little closer. Two minutes later all the Grogan guys are out on the steps, panicked, frantically running around and it became pretty clear something bad happened."

"Then what?"

"Well, we were thinking she was dead inside, but that wasn't it. Richardson wasn't there, she was gone, but we could tell from the looks on the Grogan guys' faces that she didn't leave willingly."

"What are the security guys saying?"

"At first they weren't terribly communicative, but eventually they told us that she wouldn't let them in the house with her and that she would call if she needed anything. Unless she contacted them, they were to give her a wake-up call at 7:00 A.M. if she wasn't up," Keller reported. "They followed orders and she didn't answer her cell phone despite repeated attempts. There was no response to their door knocking. Then they kicked it in and a few seconds later, it was apparent she was gone. At that point we approached, got them to talk, and now you know what we know."

Mac quickly walked up the steps and into the front of the townhouse and immediately upstairs to the bedroom and stopped at the doorway. The bedroom was definitely set up for a booty call, candles and satin sheets and in her night bag on the chair, other unmentionables from Victoria's Secret. Then he saw it to the left of the bed; lying on the floor was the champagne bucket with the hardwood floor still damp, the water having run under the molding. As he kneeled down, Mac saw it lying on the floor under the bed, a needle cover. Mac was betting it was for the sodium pentothal.

"We need to get a photo of this," Mac pointed and Wire walked around to see the syringe cover on the floor.

Mac leaned over the side of the bed and smelled the sheets and the pillow on the right side and he got a light whiff of it at first and then more as he leaned down close to the pillow.

"What do you smell?" Wire asked from the doorway.

"Chloroform, Johnson was here," Mac stated and then looked to Keller, "We need an evidence team to go through this place."

"On it," Keller answered, his phone already to his ear.

"How? How did he get in?" Dara asked.

"She drives here," Mac replied. "The place is cleared by the security. A half hour later the ..." Mac and Wire shared a knowing look and together exclaimed: "The congressman."

Mac and Wire sprinted down the steps and grabbed Keller and Reilly along the way. Mac called Delmonico. "Gracie, I need the address for Ulysses Weiss, text it to me. Second, we need people at Richardson's place. Third, someone better inform the senator his daughter is missing. Fourth, I need traffic camera footage from this area, we need to see if we can see the congressman's Cadillac, no matter the fact it was storming like mad outside. Fifth, Richardson is his last possible victim, we need a search made of every basement, empty or vacant building or warehouse in the area. Get Galloway to coordinate with the District PD on that. I think Johnson is going to take his time with her, so that maybe gives us a chance, a window to find her."

The congressman lived out in McLean, Virginia, west of DC. With flashing lights, they made it in less than fifteen minutes. Congressman Weiss's home rested on a sprawling five-acre lot with a beautiful expansive two-story red-brick colonial sitting at the end of a long winding driveway. Two McLean PD squad cars were waiting for them at the end of the driveway.

Mac powered down his window and asked the officers, "Have you approached?"

"No," the senior officer answered. "We got here a minute ahead of you and heard your sirens. We thought we should wait."

Mac nodded, "Follow us," and hit his accelerator, driving up the long, winding driveway to the circular turn in front of the expansive house, stopping at the front door. Mac quickly jumped out, his Sig Sauer in his right hand, as he approached the front door. He rang the doorbell but there was no response. Mac looked in the side window and couldn't see anything. They fanned out around the house, Mac and Wire going left, Reilly and Keller right and McLean PD remaining in front.

Around the back, Mac and Wire scaled a six-foot-tall black wrought iron fence surrounding the pool and patio area. They approached the back of the house with their right hands on the butt of their guns, looking in the windows. Mac stepped up onto a stone patio and went to the sliding glass door and stopped and looked inside through a narrow slit in the shade. Wire walked past Mac and to a door that led to the garage and tried the knob when they both heard it.

Thump. Thump. Thump.

"From the garage?" Mac asked quietly.

Thump. Thump. Thump.

"Yes," Wire whispered.

Keller and Reilly came around the other side of the garage. Mac opened the gate to let them in and whispered, "Noise in the garage." Both men nodded and stacked up behind Mac, weapons drawn, while Wire positioned herself. Mac nodded and Wire stepped back and kicked the door and Mac, Keller and Reilly burst into the garage. To the left, on the floor, bound tightly with rope around his torso and legs and with duct tape over his mouth, kicking a wood cabinet, was Congressman Weiss.

Ten minutes later, Congressman Weiss was sitting wearily at a kitchen table, sipping a bottle of water, ice packs applied to his head and the left side of his neck. Mac hung up his cell phone, after updating the director. Mac and Wire introduced themselves. Mac grabbed a chair, turned it backwards and sat down in front of the congressman. "So what happened?"

"I was getting ready to leave the house. I walked into the garage and I was hit from behind, and when I woke, my mouth was duct taped and my arms and feet were tied."

"What time were you attacked?"

"It was just after 9:00 P.M."

"You said you were leaving; where were you off to on such a stormy night?" Mac asked with a knowing tone.

"I was just going out to get a little something."

"Hah," Wire mocked. "I bet you were."

"Excuse me, Agent Wire?" the Congressman Weiss snapped.

"You were off to see Mychal Richardson at a townhouse between N and O Streets on Thirty-Third in Georgetown."

"Mychal who?"

"Please," Dara replied tersely. "Please don't insult our intelligence. Not if you don't want to walk out of here without a limp to go along with that little itty bitty bump on your head."

Mac stifled a laugh. Dara was still fired up and wanted to get her shots in. Someone had to defend Mrs. Weiss. "Ms. Richardson is the next intended target of the Reaper. She is now missing."

"Look, Agent McRyan, I don't have any idea of what you're talking …"

"Really? Are you going to keep trying this?" Mac replied smirking, "How in the hell do you think it is that we found you?"

"I don't like your tone."

"I don't give a rip, Congressman. You were set to meet Mychal Richardson last night at a townhouse on Thirty-Third between N and O Streets in Georgetown that is owned by your family, so can we dispense with the bullshit. My guess is that this was hardly the first time you and Ms. Richardson were getting together," Mac stated.

"Listen, Agent McRyan, you might think that since the president is your buddy, you don't have to respect me …"

"Let's be very clear, Congressman Weiss, I don't respect you, but that has nothing to do with who I work for. You see, the Reaper, Drake Johnson, attacked you here in this garage, took your car, and during a hurricane drove to that townhouse and took Mychal Richardson. Now, how would he know that's where she would be, unless the two of you made this a regular thing, if not a regular Wednesday thing?"

"I have no idea …"

"You see," Mac continued, not letting Weiss finish, "the Reaper, he follows his victims for days, maybe even weeks, to find them at their most vulnerable point and apparently, in watching Richardson, he found the weakness to get to her."

"Which was what?" Weiss asked.

Mac shook his head in disbelief. The congressman's head must really hurt or maybe, just maybe, he was that dumb. Having now spent five minutes with Weiss, Mac was pretty sure it was dumb.

So was Wire, who jumped in to bitterly complete the thought, "You're the weakness, you lying, cheating, bastard. I hope your wife takes you for a ton when she finds out about this."

"My wife doesn't need to know anything ..."

"Whatever," Wire replied. "Given what's happened this morning, the cat is out of the bag, Congressman. She's going to know. You better start working on your story."

Mac looked to Weiss and shook his head, "Look, frankly, I don't care about your marital situation. I really don't. Maybe you have an open marriage, maybe you don't, whatever, not my concern. Right now, my only question is whether you know anything that could help us find Mychal Richardson?"

"Like what?"

"Oh, so you finally admit you were having an affair," Wire stated mockingly.

Mac turned around and gave her a look that said that was enough, at least for now.

"Yeah, yeah," Wire muttered with a dismissive way and strolled away.

"Congressman, is there anything you know that could help me? Did Mychal ever say anything about the Reaper?"

"No," the congressman replied, shaking his head.

"Did you know she had personal security following her?"

"Yes, for about a month or so now."

"She ever you tell you why?"

"Said she was getting threats about some of the things she was saying on television. Her father put the security on her, she said. It seemed a little over the top to me. If you're in politics or talk politics, you're always getting threats. She's been getting them for a couple of years. I'm not sure why now, all of a sudden, she needed security."

"But she never said anything about the Reaper?"

"No," Weiss answered quietly. "We never really talked about our professional lives. I didn't really care about her career, nor did she care about mine. It was really just about sex."

"Of course it was."

36

"MCRYAN BELIEVES IN THE SYSTEM. I DON'T, NOT ANYMORE."

The Reaper took a long sip from the bottle of water and casually wiped the dirt from his hands. The isolation of the basement of the farmhouse, miles from any other soul, would allow him the privacy to do as he pleased.

About now it was being discovered that Mychal Richardson was missing. He drove right into the garage for the townhouse, just like he watched the congressman do six times before. The stormy weather, the constant sheets of rain, the thunder, the lightning, the wind gusts and violently swaying branches of the trees, made it that much easier. The anticipation walking up the steps to the upstairs bedroom was two years in the making. When he reached the door and peeked in the crack, she made it easy for him, lying with her back to him. He took out the rag, burst through the door and was on top of her before she knew what was happening, the rag to her mouth. She was subdued within a minute and drugged.

After subduing her, shooting her up with the sodium pentothal, he took his time to bind and gag her tightly. Once secured, he carefully made his way down the steps of the house and into the garage and deposited her into the trunk of the congressman's Cadillac. He waited the requisite four hours the tryst typically took and then simply backed out of the garage with his baseball cap pulled down low. In the rainstorm there was no way to tell it was him and not the congressman. The FBI, which was also watching, wasn't interested in Ulysses Weiss, only Mychal Richardson. He took her out right from underneath their noses. It was sweet.

Now it was 10:00 A.M. and he had evaded McRyan and his crew, was hundreds of miles away, and had her in his possession and control. Sitting twenty feet away was the person *most* responsible for taking away his little sister and for starting the downward spiral of his life.

She would now be punished.

She would now learn why.

He took one last sip of water and tossed the empty bottle into the garbage bag. Next, he walked over to Richardson. She was now awake. Her long thin arms were tied tightly behind the back of the chair with rope and her legs duct taped to the front legs of the chair. Sitting two feet to her left was a small TV tray. On the tray sat a laptop.

The killer took a metal folding chair and placed it opposite of Richardson who was still dressed only in her little slinky black teddy she'd been wearing, waiting for her night with Weiss. The teddy was now dirty, sweaty and torn. The Reaper leaned down and looked into Mychal's terrified eyes. Eyes that feared her life was about to end. He reached up with his right hand and viciously ripped away the piece of duct tape covering her mouth and slapped her hard, knocking her over to the floor.

Richardson whimpered and shook as he lifted the chair off the floor and set it back down on its four legs.

He then slowly took a seat opposite her on the other side of the TV tray. He reached around and pushed the play button for the video on the laptop.

"Do you recognize her, Mychal?"

Richardson nodded weakly.

Rebecca Randall appeared on the screen, bound to the chair, sitting under a single solitary bright light, tears streaming down her face, her mascara caked on her face, her white blouse ripped open and soiled. She wore no pants, socks or shoes and she shivered. "She looks a lot like you do right now," he pointed out grimly.

Richardson looked away and closed her eyes.

He stopped the video and then reached across and slapped her crisply. "Look at the monitor. Look at it!"

Mychal slowly turned her head back to the laptop.

He pushed play again.

"State your name?" the Reaper's deep voice asked forcefully from off-screen.

"Re... Re ... Rebecca. Rebecca Ra.. Ra... Randall."

"What is your age?"

"Twenty-five years old."

"Were you a good friend of Rena Johnson?"

"Yes."

"Were you her best friend?"

"Y ... y ... yes."

"What happened to Rena on August 17th five years ago?"

"She was killed."

"No!" the Reaper's voice barked. "She was murdered!"

"It was an ...an ... accident," Rebecca answered weakly through her tears. "It was ... an accident. I'm so sorry," she pleaded. "I'm so ... sorry," Rebecca's voice trailed away.

There was a thirty-second pause, where the questions stopped and Randall cried.

"What happened?" the voice stated calmly. "I need all of the details. Start from the beginning."

The interrogation played for twenty minutes. Every so often he would have to bark at Richardson to get her to watch. Twice more he slapped her with his right hand, the second time so viciously, her chair tipped over again and she crashed to the floor. "*You will Watch!*" he barked as he stood over her.

The video continued.

"When you went to leave the party, why didn't you take Rena with you?"

"We couldn't find her," Randall sobbed. "We couldn't."

"You were her friend, one of her best friends. She trusted you, what do you mean you couldn't find her?"

"I tried," she pleaded. "We all tried, but we couldn't find her anywhere. She'd wandered off somewhere and we had no idea where and the police were coming and we were underage, we'd been drinking, we'd done drugs."

"And you had Rena do these things?"

Randall nodded, "She did them."

"Did you force her to?"

Randall hesitated and the Reaper noticed how Richardson's head bowed.

"This girl named Mychal Richardson, the one who drove us to the party, she ..." Randall said.

"She what?"

"She embarrassed Rena because Rena would barely drink and wouldn't take Ecstasy. She mocked and bullied her into it. She was so unmerciful on Rena."

The Reaper pushed stop on the video. He turned in rage and smacked Mychal with the back of his right hand, sending her chair careening violently to the floor again. He leaned down, grabbed her by her long blond hair and pulled her back up. She was bleeding from her nose and mouth, the blood dripping down her chin. Richardson's body was shaking violently as the woman was feeling real palpable fear and pain for the first time in her life. "Watch!"

The Reaper pushed play again.

"Why didn't you stop her from bullying her; you were Rena's friend."

"I tried but ... this girl, Mychal, was ...manipulative. She was older. She pushed and pushed and pushed. Rena was ... she ... was ..."

"She was what?"

"Weaker. This Mychal, she smelled blood. We'd tell her to ease up but she smelled blood and she just kept hammering away at her like it was sport."

"And Rena gave in."

Randall nodded.

The rage took over again. He raised his left hand.

"No, please no ..." Richardson pleaded.

"Did you show any mercy to Rena?" the Reaper growled as he smacked her with the back of his left hand, knocking her to the floor again. He stopped the video and let her lay on the hard dirt floor for a few minutes before he picked her up again. Now there was a gash above her left eye, blood dripping down the left side of her face.

The video continued.

"So you left without her?"

"Yes."

"But you had everyone else, right? You had Melissa, Hannah, Janelle, Sandy, Kelly, and Danica, right?"

"Yes."

"Who drove?"

"Mychal. It was her van. She was driving."

"When you left the party, you turned right onto County Road 5, didn't you?"

"Yes."

"And then what happened?"

"No ... No ..."

"*TELL ME!*"

"She was driving the van super fast and we came around that corner and there she was just on the right shoulder."

"And you hit her?"

"I didn't hit her, Mychal did. She was the one driving, not me. I didn't hit Rena."

"And when you hit her?"

Randall sobbed some more and didn't respond. She just shook her head.

"Answer the question."

"She went flying so far. We didn't even realize it was Rena until we ..."

"Until you what?"

Randall shook head, "I looked down into the ditch and I could tell it was her."

"Was she alive?"

Rebecca began to sob and shook her head.

"WAS SHE ALIVE!" Johnson growled.

Randall nodded her head and whispered, "I don't know, I didn't go down to check."

"Why not?"

"Mychal, Janelle and Helen pressed us to go. That we had to leave because we were in such trouble."

"You didn't even call 911, did you? You couldn't even do that for your friend, could you, for your best friend?"

She shook her head. "No," she answered meekly.

"In fact, nobody did."

Rebecca shook her head again.

"Did you have a cell phone?"

She nodded.

"One of your best friends was lying in the ditch, badly hurt but alive, and you didn't call 911. Why?! Why didn't you?!"

"I was so scared, we all were. You have to believe me, we were all so scared. We were in huge trouble and Mychal said she couldn't have this on her record and that if we didn't flee the scene, if anyone of us called 911, she said her dad, a senator and this lawyer who worked for him, Wallace something, would bury us, ruin our lives."

"And you believed her?"

Randall nodded, "I know it was wrong, but you weren't there. You don't understand what this girl was like. She was scary when we were dealing with this. And two of her friends, Danica and this Hannah, they had powerful families too and they wanted to get away from the scene, to just get away from it. I ... I ... I should have stayed. I should have stayed ..."

He turned off the videotape and stared at Mychal Richardson, tears and blood streaming down her face, terror in her eyes, her body shaking. The chickens finally came home to roost.

The Reaper pulled his chair close to her so that his knees were touching hers. From the sheath on his hip he pulled out the long knife and held it in his hands. He waved the knife slowly in front of her face, her eyes bulging from their sockets.

"I used this knife on Rebecca Randall after we finished that recording, when I learned of everyone involved. When I learned *you* were the driver, the one *most* responsible," he said in a low voice as he followed the contours of her nose and mouth with the sharp long tip of the knife.

"Then of course there was Melissa and Janelle," he said calmly as he ran the tip of the Ka-Bar vertically down her throat, lightly applying pressure as Mychal's body shook. "I did them just like Rebecca. I videotaped them to confirm that what Rebecca told me was true. It was, wasn't it?"

Richardson didn't reply, she just whimpered.

He put the blade of the knife to her throat, "Rebecca told the truth, didn't she?"

Mychal nodded, "Y... y...yes."

"Hannah Donahue was next and I took a good long while with her in her basement, a rich little bitch in need of punishment," the Reaper said as he moved the blade down to her cleavage, slowly rolling the tip around the contours of her large breasts, watching her body tremble as he applied just enough pressure with the tip of the blade to make a small puncture wound over her right breast and let the blood slowly drip down and soak into the satin fabric of the slinky nightgown.

"Helen, or I guess Sandy now, this knife ripped through her," he said casually as he ran the tip down the front of the teddy, pricking little holes in the black satin as he made his way down to her navel. "When I cut them, I started right here," he declared, pushing the tip against her abdomen, not cutting, just holding it, applying just enough pressure so she could feel it, feel how close it all was to coming to a grisly end. "I would start right here and then rip upwards until the sternum stopped me," he said, making the motion, stopping the tip at the bottom of her sternum.

"Your friend Danica experienced that the other night. I didn't use the sodium pentothal with her either. Her body convulsed like you wouldn't believe when I plunged the knife in and began ripping up."

He moved the blade back down to her navel. "Then,

after I reach the sternum, I then push down with the blade and slice until I reach the pubic bone, so I end up with this long vertical incision."

Richardson's body was shaking as she tried to pull away from the knife, but she was tightly bound to the chair and her movements simply caused her body to brush against the knife. As she moved and he held the knife steady, she caused little cuts to be made which caused little drips of bleeding from her chest and stomach.

"You see, after I make that long vertical cut, I then make the horizontal incision. I make the Holy Cross in honor of Rena. After you left her in that ditch, she held God close to her, her rosary beads, those beads, that faith you so callously mocked," Drake said as he ran the tip across her stomach a few inches below her breasts. "I did that on almost all of them, Melissa, Janelle, Hannah, Sandy and Danica. I'd have done it to Kelly Drew as well but I was interrupted by FBI Agents Mac McRyan and Dara Wire. They came to see you yesterday, didn't they?"

Mychal nodded.

"I was watching. Have they figured out the whole story? Do they think you drove the van?"

Mychal nodded weakly.

"Yet they were powerless to do anything about it, weren't they? They let you walk your manipulative perfect little ass right out of there, didn't they?"

She nodded meekly again.

"I bet you arrogantly sat there and told him to go pound sand, didn't you? McRyan knows what happened but he has no proof, no evidence, and the only people who witnessed what happened were all dead, am I right?"

Richardson looked down and away.

He reached for her face and turned it to him, "Am I right?"

"Yes."

The Reaper shook his head and snorted, "Mac McRyan and Dara Wire think you can play by the rules, but you can't. Not in this world, not anymore. He would probably like nothing more than to arrest you and put you away for what you've done. McRyan believes in the system. I don't, not anymore. The system didn't protect Rena, didn't bring justice for her, and now, it won't for you."

The Reaper stood up and pushed his chair away and left her in the chair and walked to the cellar steps, stopped and turned to Mychal Richardson, "I believe in my own form of poetic justice, and tonight I'm going to bring it to you."

37

"I DON'T LIKE THE TONE, MCRYAN."

Mac and Wire left Congressman Weiss with a crew of agents and the McLean, Virginia, police. As they departed Weiss's house, they had to slowly drive through a sea of reporters at the end of the winding driveway. The media had learned Mychal Richardson was missing and here was Mac and Wire at Congressman Weiss's house. For all of their shortcomings, the media could add up that there was a connection between the two and it wouldn't take them long to put it all together.

If there was one thing he learned in his brief stint working a high-profile FBI case, he wasn't in the Twin Cities anymore when it came to the media. A case like this back home and he would have a few televisions stations hovering around, maybe a newspaper reporter from the *Star Tribune* on the case, but that was it. Here, there was media everywhere, seemingly able to get to any location instantly, and when they arrived, they arrived in force and with a relentless intensity.

He kept his windows up as he slowly and carefully drove his SUV through the crowd of reporters, cameras and microphones. The fact his window was up didn't stop the questions from being shouted, the cameramen from rolling film and the photographers from snapping pictures. He may have conducted a press conference the day before, but Mac had no intention of answering questions again. There was work to do. The congressman's car had been found.

Twenty minutes from the congressman's home, the dashboard flasher parting the early afternoon traffic of the beltway for him, he finally let out a breath and relaxed just a little, twenty minutes away from his next destination.

"So will you wait for Congressman Weiss's wife to find out in the media about her husband's affair, or are you going to access FBI resources to contact her directly," Mac inquired whimsically, his eyes raised, a smile spread across his face. "You may not have long. The reporters will figure it out soon enough."

"Now that's a thought," Dara suggested. "But I'll probably let Mrs. Weiss figure it out all on her own. Now, if she stays with the bastard, I might have a little chat with her."

Mac laughed.

"You're awfully lighthearted, given our last victim is likely to be sliced and diced here any minute."

Mac nodded, "Is she a victim? I mean, is she *really* a victim?"

"No, she's the Ice Queen, but ..."

"We have a job to do. I'm not quitting, but if we fail ..."

"You won't be that disappointed."

"I don't know, no, yes, maybe," Mac replied, shaking his head. "We solved it. We know who the killer is and why he's doing it. To be honest, I don't really care about the victims anymore. They were responsible for Rena Johnson's death and didn't do a damn thing about it. Not one of them stood up and did the right thing. So they made their bed and now they're lying in it. Now Gesch and those agents he killed? That's a different story and I want to put that fucker down for that. If in the process, we could find a way to get real justice for Rena Johnson? *Now that would be satisfying.* In my mind, Gesch, those agents and deputies and Rena are the true victims here."

Keller and Reilly were waiting for them, standing by a black Cadillac parked in an alley behind a restaurant in Columbia, Maryland, northeast of Washington, DC. The trunk was open and a forensic team was already taking pictures.

"Looks like she was in the trunk," Keller stated.

"We have some blood," Reilly added, using his flashlight to illuminate the small specks of blood in the dark charcoal fibers of the trunk.

"This was his exchange point," Mac answered. "Anyone know what was parked here?"

"We're on it," Keller said as he waved Reilly to follow him inside the restaurant.

"So if he rolls out of DC around 2:00 A.M., it's still storming, being careful, following the posted, he's here around 3:00 A.M. and it's around 2:00 P.M. right now," Wire speculated. "He's got eleven hours on us. That's an awful big radius we have to potentially be looking. He could be anywhere in eight or nine states."

Mac's phone rang. "Yes, Director. When?" He looked at his watch. "Yes sir, on our way."

"What?" Wire asked.

"Senator Richardson."

"Mac, please, please, please behave yourself," Sally pleaded as Mac parked at the Hoover Building. He and Wire had an audience with Senator Richardson and Director Mitchell.

"No promises," Mac answered.

The Senate minority leader was not someone known for understanding and patience. What Sally knew was that Mac was not someone who suffered such treatment without biting back.

The mix could be combustible.

"Mac, he's going to provoke you, he's going to blame you, he's going to come after you and he's very *very* good at that."

"Let him," Mac replied, not worried. "I've got plenty to fight back with."

"Look, just let him blow up and then go back to doing your job," Sally suggested. "If you engage, he'll make it ugly."

"For who?" Mac asked. "Me or the White House?"

"Hey, now wait a minute!" Sally exclaimed, annoyed.

"Mac!" Wire warned.

"Whose partner are you anyway?" he asked Wire, a smirk on his face.

"Yours," Dara answered. "Sally's protecting *you*, you dumbass."

"Thank you, Dara," Sally added sweetly.

"I don't need protection," Mac answered, but then veered to safer territory, "Sally, it'll be fine. I'll be on my best behavior," he said with as much sincerity as he could muster as they walked into the elevator.

Two minutes later they were admitted to the director's office.

"Where's my daughter?" Senator Richardson demanded. No introductions, no handshake, no time to explain, no time for a briefing of the status of the case, no chance for a breath. As Sally warned, the senator had a reputation as a bully and he came right out of the box being one.

"Right now I don't know," Mac answered calmly and honestly. "I can explain where the investigation is at ..."

"Right now, you don't know?" the senator replied bitterly, moving into Mac's personal space. "That's all you have for me?" The senator then looked to the director, "This is who is running the investigation looking for my daughter?"

"Yup, I'm that guy," Mac retorted before the director could rise to his defense.

The director gave Mac a stern look and Wire lightly grabbed the back of his arm to get him to step back, but Mac knew there was only one way to deal with a bully. Be an asshole back, regardless of who they were. "But you have one part wrong. I'm not hunting for your daughter. I'm hunting for the Reaper. I'm hunting for Drake Johnson."

"And what about my daughter? She's the victim here."

"If I find him, I'll find her."

"I don't think you understand, McRyan, my daughter is missing."

"I'm quite aware of that," Mac answered flatly, his hands on his hips, not shriveling from the confrontation.

"Where are you in finding this sociopath?"

"I'm working on it."

"You're working on it."

"Yes, I am. Of course, this meeting only delays from me doing so."

"Excuse me?"

Director Mitchell jumped in, "I think what Special Agent McRyan is trying to say is ..."

"Special Agent? That's a hoot. There's nothing special about him," Senator Richardson blustered and then stuck his finger inches from Mac's face. "You let my daughter slip through your fingers," he pointed at Mac and Wire. "Yeah, I know you two met with her yesterday, told her she was a target of this maniac. Where the fuck were the two of you last night?"

"We were watching your daughter. Of course, we were fighting for space with your battalion of private security from Grogan monitoring her movements," Mac answered. "So let me ask you a question, Senator. Why was it that your daughter had that security detail on her anyway? Because I checked, she's had that detail on her for at least a month now. Why?"

"She's on television quite a bit, says some provocative things and receives threats from time to time."

"I've heard that bullshit party line already. She's said provocative things for at least a couple of years, so why all of a sudden the security in the last month?" Mac pressed.

"I don't like the tone, McRyan."

"I didn't think you would, but answer the question, Senator."

"Answer mine first you, insubordinate shit. I want to know what happened. I want to know how *you* failed to protect my daughter."

"Okay," Mac answered, "But I'll warn you, you may not like what you hear. First, your daughter was abducted from a townhouse belonging to Congressman Ulysses Weiss. Did you know that?" Mac asked, looking the senator in the eye.

"What of it?"

"Well, she was having an affair with a married man, a married congressman, and it has been going on for months."

"Does that mean she should suffer at the hands of this madman?"

"If that were all she was guilty of, no."

"What do you mean if that were all she were guilty of? What the hell are you talking about?"

"Seven years ago, did you own a silver Chrysler Town and Country minivan?" Mac asked, boring in on the senator's eyes. His face betrayed little but the mention of the minivan caused his eyes to widen. The eyes, the window to the soul, they always give people away.

"Why is that relevant?"

"It's a simple question, did you or didn't you?"

"I don't know if we owned one at one time."

"Fact of the matter is," Mac replied, reaching in his backpack, "you did own such a van," He slid the vehicle registration across the table.

"So? What's your point?"

"I think the van is why your daughter is in the position she is." Mac took out the picture of the victims, "Unless you've been living in a cave, you've seen this picture." It was what they now called the Picture of Death. "Melissa Goynes, Janelle Wyland, Hannah Donahue, Sandy Faye, who back then was named Helen Williams, Kelly Drew, now a vegetable in hospital, Danica Brunner, Rebecca Randall and a woman named Rena Johnson, the sister of our killer. But you know what the really interesting part about the picture is, Senator?"

"No, what?"

"Who isn't in it—your daughter."

"Right, she's not in that picture. Again, what's your point?"

"She took it."

This, Mac could tell, the senator did not know.

"She took the picture in front of this minivan, your minivan. I think this van was the van that struck and killed Rena

Johnson seven years ago, on August ... 17th ..." Mac went slack jawed and strode away from the senator over to the conference table, putting his hands on the table and shaking his head. "Seven years ago ... today. No way, is that what he's doing?"

"McRyan?" the senator pressed.

"Mac?" Wire asked, seeing the look on his face.

"Mac, what is it?" Director Mitchell asked.

Mac turned around, "Director, I need a plane."

38

"YES. YES. YES. NOW GET ME OUT OF HERE, PLEASE!"

11:41 P.M.

It was still a balmy seventy-nine degrees in the countryside outside of Auburn, New York. The humidity was thick in the air, creating a dense pocket of radiation fog on the isolated road.

The Reaper carefully drove along County Road 5, keeping the silver Chrysler Town and Country minivan a good foot or two inside the white line marking the right edge of the road. On his right he passed the long driveway to the long abandoned farmhouse where all of this started seven years ago. The driveway was now blocked with a swinging gate and padlock as well as a large No Trespassing sign.

He'd taken the back two rows of seats out of the van. Lying on the floor, tied up, gagged, yet squirming was Mychal Richardson.

She wouldn't have long now.

He passed the yellow diamond sign signaling a tight turn ahead, warning to reduce speed to thirty miles-per-hour.

The Reaper carefully, expertly negotiated the tight turn,

a turn he'd made several times over the afternoon and early evening, knowing that fog was potentially, and helpfully, moving in. It also provided him the opportunity to dig the small post hole earlier in the day, the hole that would seal Mychal Richardson's fate.

Around the tight corner, he pulled ahead another one hundred feet and stopped along the narrow shoulder of the road, just past a small orange flag he'd placed on the shoulder. Stopped, he hit the button to open the rear tailgate of the van.

Lying on the floor in the back, barely clothed in her ripped teddy, arms and feet tightly tied to an eight-foot-long 4x4 wood beam, was Mychal Richardson. The Reaper looked down at Richardson's face, the resignation in her eyes, tears again running down her dirty, blood-soaked face, small cuts and gashes on her body, her face bruised and battered. She was almost unrecognizable.

Grabbing the top of the wood post she was tied to with both hands, he slid it out of the back of the van. He dragged Richardson ten feet until he reached the post hole. He turned her around so she would face the corner and slid the bottom of the post into the hole until she was upright. Her hands and feet were tied tightly to the post. In addition, rope was tied around her upper torso, waist and thighs, her feet dangling two inches above the ground. She couldn't even squirm, the bindings were so tight. He removed the gag.

"Somebody help me?! Please somebody help me?!" she wailed, crying.

"Nobody can hear you out here, Mychal," the Reaper stated coolly. "Nobody. There isn't a house for three miles. The only house is the abandoned one where the rave took place. It was abandoned then, what do you think it is now?

Mychal, out here there is nothing but woods. On a night like tonight, with this fog and the danger of driving, there is nobody out on the roads, *nobody*."

"I'm sorry. I'm so sorry," Richardson pleaded.

"It's far too late for that. Seven years ago, right at this very spot, that was the time to say you were sorry. That was the time to do the right thing and accept the consequences of your negligent act. Instead, you hit my sister with that van of yours and left her for dead. Consider this poetic justice."

The Reaper left her to scream. He slid into the minivan and pulled forward and did a U-turn in the road and drove past and around the corner.

Richardson screamed, "*Help! Help!* SOMEBODY HELP ME!"

∼

Mac watched the van disappear around the corner.

"Go, Mac," Wire exclaimed into his earbud from her perch across the road.

From the edge of the tree line, he sprinted down the short hill and into the ditch.

"*Help! Help! SOMEBODY HELP ME!*" Richardson wailed.

"Enough already," Mac answered dismissively as he climbed the other side of the ditch. "We heard you."

Mychal turned her head left to see him, "Get me out of here!" she wailed.

"We have a few questions first," Wire added, coming from the other side of the road, gun drawn, looking back down the road in the direction Johnson drove.

"Seriously?" Mychal wailed. "Cut me loose."

∼

Johnson drove a mile west, slowed and did a U-turn in an area where the shoulder widened. As he turned around, he could see flashing police lights ahead in each lane.

The lights stopped and blocked the road.

"Nooooooo!" Drake raged, shaking the steering wheel violently. "No! No! No! You mother fucker, McRyan! Nooooooo!"

He put his foot to the accelerator.

Mac stood in front of her, "Were you driving the van that killed Rena Johnson?"

"What? You're asking that now. Get me out of here."

"Mac, he's coming!" Wire exclaimed, pressing her hand to her right ear.

"Mychal, I'm not going to help you unless you answer my question. Were you driving the van that killed Rena Johnson seven years ago?"

"Are you crazy, get me out of here!"

"I asked a question. Were you driving the van that killed Rena Johnson? I'm not saving you until you answer the question."

Richardson nodded.

"Yes or no, please."

"*YES!* Yes, I was driving that van when we hit Rena. Now get me out of here!"

"Why didn't you stop? She could have lived."

"Cut me loose!"

"Answer the question, why didn't you stop?"

"Mac!" Wire wailed. "He's coming. He busted through the roadblock, he's coming. Get her cut loose now!"

"Not yet," Mac replied quickly, flipping open his knife

and then looking to Richardson, "Let me ask this another way. Did you leave Rena in this ditch because you were afraid what would happen to you, your father, what would happen to your other friends with political fathers, if it were found you were drunk, on drugs and hit someone along the road? Were you afraid of going to jail for that?"

"Yes! Yes! Yes! Now get me out of here!"

The bright lights flew around the corner, the engine roaring as McRyan and Wire dove down into the ditch.

"Oh my God! No! No! No! No!" Richardson wailed.

The lights came to a screeching halt, ten feet short of her. The vehicle was a silver Chevy Suburban. A heavyset man jumped out and walked up, a smile on his face.

"Are we good?" Mac asked, pushing himself up and brushing off his clothes.

"We're awesome," Auburn Detective Flynn answered with a smile. "He rammed our roadblock, but there were two patrol cars and two Suburbans and all he had was the soccer mom minivan. One could say it was a very poor choice of a ramming vehicle. In any event, he is very banged up but cuffed, stuffed and in custody. Ambulance on the way." He looked up at Richardson still tied to the post, a shocked look on her face. "So how are we doing here?"

"Excellent," Mac answered, having hatched the plan two hours ago. He walked up next to Detective Flynn and held up his T-shirt so Richardson could see the microphone taped to his chest. "In the immortal words of Colonel Hannibal Smith, I love it when a plan comes together," he said as he went to work on the rope around her chest.

"You were recording this?" Richardson exclaimed incredulously as Mac was cutting the ropes tying her to the post.

Mac looked up from cutting the ropes and snorted, "Duh."

"You set me up!" Richardson wailed. "You set me up!"

"I can't think of someone who deserved it more," Wire stated with her arms folded and a smile. "You got off easy. You're alive, you should be thanking us. I, of course, won't hold my breath waiting for that to happen."

Mac finished cutting Richardson free from the post and eased her down to her feet. "Detective Flynn, this is Mychal Richardson," Mac stated. "Ms. Richardson, this is Auburn Police Detective Flynn. I believe the detective has something he's wanted to say for a very *very* long time."

"Indeed I do," Flynn replied as he took out his handcuffs and walked behind Richardson. "Mychal Richardson, you're under arrest for the vehicular homicide of Rena Johnson."

7:12 A.M. August 18.

Wire pushed the door into the hospital room open. Mac stepped through, followed by Detective Flynn. Drake Johnson lay in the hospital bed, his bruised and battered body tethered to the bed, his hands cuffed to the railing on each side and both legs shackled to the bed posts. Two officers stood post over the end of the bed. Johnson wasn't going anywhere.

Mac and Wire stood at the end of the bed for a moment and stared down at Johnson. "Officers, if you'll excuse us for a minute," Mac suggested. "We have fresh coffee and donuts in the hallway."

The two officers pushed themselves out of their chairs and left them to it.

"So we meet," Johnson said with a raspy voice, making

no effort to move. He was beaten and battered from the collision of his minivan with the roadblock. The doctors had diagnosed him with a broken arm, four broken ribs not to mention a concussion to go with the cuts and scrapes on his face, all now patched with varying amounts of bandages, butterflies, stitches and staples.

Mac pulled a chair up to the left side of the bed, Wire and Flynn standing at the end of the bed.

"Detective Flynn," Johnson greeted.

"Drake," Flynn answered.

"I bet you're all asking why?"

"I think we all are," Wire answered.

"They killed Rena. Someone had to get justice for Rena."

"Justice?" Mac asked, shaking his head. "You call this justice? Is that what Aubrey Gesch was in Pennsylvania? Is that what the lives of six peace officers were the other night? Is that what Wire's and my lives were in Frederick? You didn't get justice. What you got was revenge."

Mac played the tape of Richardson confessing to him.

"I can prove Mychal Richardson was the driver that killed your sister. Now *that's* justice. You? You're a murderer of women and you're a murderer of six law enforcement officers, four of whom were federal agents. Detective Flynn, what's the sentence for killing an agent of the FBI?"

"I believe it's death by lethal injection."

"You killed six women and six peace officers. The only way the death penalty ends up off the table is your confession to all of the murders, every single one. You admit what you did, every single despicable act."

Drake Johnson closed his eyes, defiant. "I'll take the needle."

"Good," Mac answered. "I'll be there when you get it."

The FBI plane would arrive in ninety minutes. In the meantime, the case over, Mac and Wire sat in a quiet booth at the Lucky Seven Pub in Auburn. A pitcher of beer, two beer glasses and towering cheeseburgers and a bushel of french fries had their full attention.

"What did Sally say?" Dara asked, pouring more ketchup into her burger basket.

"Are you okay?"

"And once she knew that."

"That was all she really cared about."

"No politics, no wondering about what Hannah Donahue or Mychal Richardson are guilty of?"

"Oh, there was more than a little of that," Mac answered. "I think it's now official that she's been corrupted by DC. She said each side got hit."

They sat in silence, watching some of the news reports as well as clips from Director Mitchell's brief morning press conference. The director wanted Mac to give a press conference either later today or tomorrow. Mac said he'd think about it. With the case over, his duties to the bureau were over and, looking at the cast still on his left wrist, the exhaustion he was feeling and the lingering headache pounding in his head, he was inclined to fade away from public view. He was flat wrung out. There was nothing left in his tank. He wanted to simply go home and sleep.

With the burger baskets cleared away, Mac sunk back into the booth and slowly sipped his beer. For the first time in weeks, the angst and stress was gone. His mind was calm and he felt some level of peace.

"Did we win here?" Wire asked.

"The case?" Mac asked.

"Yeah, did we win?"

"Oh, I don't know," Mac answered, giving it some thought. "In a case like this, I'm not sure victory was possible. I mean, I came into the case thinking we were after a sociopathic killer, a sadistic whack job who was slicing up women. In the end, the mass killer was a grieving brother incensed that eight women could ruthlessly and coldly leave his sister to die in a ditch rather than do the right thing."

"Drake Johnson wasn't a sociopath?"

"No. A sociopath doesn't care about others. They have charm and charisma, but they think only of themselves and blame others for the things that they do. They have a complete disregard for rules and lie. A sociopath never feels guilt. In this case, who fits that bill?"

"Mychal Richardson," Wire answered with a nod. "Drake Johnson, on the other hand, had feelings, feelings of love for his sister."

"He couldn't handle her death, particularly once he figured out what happened. He went off the rails," Mac replied. "It's one thing to be distraught about a loved one's death and want vengeance. It's quite another to turn into a mass murderer. He killed twelve people, six women, six law officers, left another woman a possible vegetable and tried to kill yet another. He's no saint to mourn. He is worthy of very little if any sympathy in my mind."

"Mental illness maybe?" Wire suggested. "He might get off from the needle because of that?"

"I don't know," Mac answered sipping his beer, "Maybe. Or maybe at this point, I just don't care. The great state of New York, as well as all of the other jurisdictions, will have plenty of time to figure that out. Until they do, he'll be in a maximum security prison cell. His brain chemistry got screwed up, but he also knew what he was doing. He hunted these women down one by one. He became a brutal cop and then a remorseless human."

"For that reason, do you think his videotape of Randall will be admissible into evidence?"

"I don't know," Mac answered. "I don't know that they'll need it for Richardson, although you and I watched it. It matches what she told us, so who knows. I'll let a higher pay grade figure it out."

"I worry that Richardson will come in with some big guns for defense counsel against the locals out here."

"Me too," Mac answered. "But Director Mitchell has an interest in seeing the case properly prosecuted, so the Justice Department will be involved and the Judge ..."

"The Judge?" Wire asked.

"The Judge is going to discreetly reach out to some lawyer friends of his and encourage them to offer some assistance to the folks up in Cayuga County. But you know what I think?"

"What?"

"In the end, this thing will never go to trial."

"You don't think so?"

"No," Mac shook his head. "A deal will be cut and as a result Mychal Richardson's public career, not to mention legal career, will be over. From what I've observed over the last couple of days, that's a very good thing. She just needs to do her time and then go away."

"Without Johnson doing what he did, could we have solved his sister's homicide? Would we have found that Richardson drove that van? Would we have been able to put the case together?"

Mac nodded, "I think any case can be solved. With the right resources, with intellect, with dedication and determination, any case, any homicide, any robbery, any terrorist event, any crime can be solved. There is no such thing as the perfect crime, the unsolvable crime."

"You believe that, don't you?"

"I do. It requires resources. We had the resources here. But if you have them and you keep at it long enough, I think you can figure anything out."

"Is this your last foray as a special agent of the FBI?"

"You never know," Mac answered, filling Wire's glass and his with more beer. "I did like having all the federal toys at my disposal, and I can feel the director wanting to take another run at us."

"Me too, but I don't want to go back full time."

"Me neither," Mac answered, shaking his head. "I've come to like my freedom and I don't miss the daily grind, but every once in a while I don't mind coming out of the bullpen when an interesting case comes along. It's good to get back in the trenches and solve a tough case every so often. I know one thing, though."

"What's that?"

"I won't do it without my federal partner," Mac said, raising a toast.

"Federal partner?"

"Yeah, if I go back to St. Paul, I work with the boys, and if I'm working a federal case ..."

"You want to work with me?" Wire asked, smiling.

"Exactly, Dara Wire."

"To partners then," Dara answered, returning the toast. "It was indeed good to work together again."

"It was. I'm glad we survived it."

"True that," and they toasted again and then Wire's phone beeped. She looked down at it and smiled and giggled.

"Dara, is that a certain gentleman from Miami who is

texting you?" Mac asked with a knowing smile. "Or should I say sexting you?"

Wire nodded, "I'd like to get down there for a few days, but geez, I've really neglected my business for a while here..."

Mac shook his head, "Can I offer a word of unsolicited advice?"

"Do you offer any other kind?" Wire needled.

"Funny. But in all seriousness, your work can wait another few days. Go down to Miami and let the guy pamper you, take care of you and spoil you. He clearly wants to and, most importantly, you need it and you deserve it."

Wire nodded. "You're right," and she proceeded to text Gonzalez back, reading it out as she wrote: "Be there tomorrow."

"Excellent. Now, when you do get back from your little sojourn down to Miami, I need your help with something that needs a woman's perspective."

39

"I HAVE JUST ONE SMALL MINOR AMENDMENT TO THAT PLAN."

FOUR WEEKS LATER. ST. PAUL

It was a beautiful mid-September night with just a whiff of fall in the air. The president was on a trip to South America for a conference and Sally didn't have to go along, so they'd managed to slip away from Washington. Mac was only too happy to get back home and relax and spend some quiet time at their St. Paul home, visiting with family and friends, the pressures of Washington a thousand miles away.

Mac was finally feeling better physically, the cast off his left wrist and the bruising around his eyes finally gone. He looked like himself again. He'd even been able to go for a run earlier in the day, a short three miler, his first run in nearly two months. His conditioning needed serious work. Good news was that he had plenty of time now available to devote to it.

After dinner was finished, they sat on their back porch, sipping the remainder of the bottle of red from dinner and enjoying a quiet bonfire. Sally stared off into the distance. Despite the relaxing environment of being at home, he could tell she'd been distracted, deep in thought for the last two days, something bothering her and making her nervous.

"What's on your mind, Sally?" Mac asked casually, looking straight ahead, sipping from his wine.

"Our plan."

"Our plan?" Mac asked, turning to look at her.

"Yeah, you asked me what our plan was a while ago and I've been giving it a lot of thought." She turned to him, sitting on the edge of her chaise lounge, looking down. "It scares me to death."

"Why?"

"I'm worried you will want certain things, a certain thing that I can't give you."

"What can't you possibly give me?" Mac asked, confused.

"Children."

"Children?" Mac looked at her quizzically, having sat up. "Are you telling me you can't have kids?"

Sally teared up and sniffled, looking down, nodding her head. "David and I wanted to have a child. We tried to have a child but I couldn't get pregnant. So I went to the doctor and that's when I found out."

"Found what out?"

"I have a lazy ovary. Having a child is extremely unlikely for me. This is *really* why David and I ended up getting divorced. When I couldn't get pregnant ... " her voice trailed off.

Mac smiled, sat up and faced Sally, "How long have you been worried about telling me *that*?"

"For three years I've been wondering how to tell you about this, because I know how much you love kids, want kids, want to have a family and what if I can't give that to you?"

"Do you like kids?"

"I love them."

"Do you want kids some day?"

"I'd love lots of kids."

"Sally, David was a fool and I thank God every single day that he was. But babe, there are lots of ways for us to have kids. There's adoption, there's surrogacy, there's ways. If we want a family, there is a way for us to have a family, even if we can't get there the old-fashioned way."

"Yeah?"

"Hell yeah."

"You're sure?"

"Absolutely. This is not an issue, not for me."

Sally gave him a long, tight hug. He could feel three years of worry simply wash off her body in that embrace. After a minute, she pulled back and kissed him softly and said, "I thank God Meredith was so stupid. She has *no idea* what she's missing."

"Things have worked out well for us, I think."

Sally stood up and walked around the patio, getting some space, bouncing around, suddenly relaxed and visibly happy. She stopped and turned to him. "Mac, can I have four years? I want one term with the president and let me help him get reelected if he runs. Then I'm done. Then I want us to have our life together with a family wherever you want that to be, here, Washington, wherever you want. I just want a term with the president and I'll walk away and we can have the rest of our lives and have a family, everything." She had a hopeful smile on her face, relieved to have everything out in the open. "What do you think?"

Mac smiled. "I think that sounds really good. I have just one small minor amendment to that plan."

"What's that?"

He slowly stood up, took a breath, a nervous breath, reached in his pocket and walked to Sally and then dropped down to one knee down in front of her, taking her left hand in his right, "Sally Loughlin Kennedy, will you marry me?"

In his left hand he was holding a stunning ring, silver band, five-carat diamond sparkling gloriously in the night. It was spectacular. Wire had helped him pick it out two weeks ago. He'd been walking around with it looking for the right time.

Now they both knew what they wanted.

Now there was a plan.

Now was the right time.

Sally was shocked, her hands to her mouth. There had been no discussion about this, no preparation or subtle hints that Mac usually dropped when leading up to something. She could almost always read him and sense what he was thinking, yet this? This she had not seen coming. This was something that she thought would come down the road.

She may not have been completely ready. This wasn't part of what she thought was the immediate plan, but that didn't matter.

There could only be one answer.

She took a deep breath, composed herself and smiled.

"Yes, I say yes!"

∼

A note to my readers...

Thank you for reading and I sincerely hope you enjoyed **Fatally Bound**. As an independently published author, I rely on each and every reader to help spread the word. If you enjoyed the book please tell your friends and family and if it isn't too much trouble I would sincerely appreciate a brief rating or a review.

The next standalone thriller in the McRyan Mystery Series is *Blood Silence*. I've also started a second series called the FBI Agent Tori Hunter Series and the first book is *Silenced Girls*.

Thanks again and I'm always writing a new book so look for Mac in the next mystery! To stay on top of the new releases and new series please join the list at www.RogerStelljes.com and I'll let you know when the next one comes out.

ALSO BY ROGER STELLJES

MCRYAN MYSTERY SERIES

First Case - Murder Alley

The St. Paul Conspiracy

Deadly Stillwater

Electing To Murder

Fatally Bound

Blood Silence

Next Girl On The List

Fireball

The Tangled Web We Weave

Short Stories

Stakeout - A Case From The Dick Files

Box Sets

First Deadly Conspiracy - Books 1-3

Mysteries Thrillers and Killers - Books 4-6

FBI AGENT TORI HUNTER

Silenced Girls

To receive new release alerts join the list at
www.RogerStelljes.com

ABOUT THE AUTHOR

Roger Stelljes is the New York Times and USA Today bestselling author of the McRyan Mystery Series and the FBI Agent Tori Hunter Mystery Series. He has been the recipient of several awards including: the Midwest Book Awards–Genre Fiction, a Merit Award Winner for Commercial Fiction (MIPA), as well as a Minnesota Book Awards Nominee.

Never miss a new release again, join the new release list at www.RogerStelljes.com

Made in the USA
Las Vegas, NV
19 August 2024

94068072R00266